JANES IN LOVE

Published by DC Comics,
1700 Broadway, New York, NY 10019.

Printed in Canada.
DC Comics, a Warner Bros.
Entertainment Company.

ISBN: 978-1-4012-1387-9

COVER BY JIM RUGG

Karen Berger, Sr. VP-Executive Editor Shelly Bond, Editor Angela Rufino, Assistant Editor
Robbin Brosterman, Sr. Art Director Paul Levitz, President & Publisher
Georg Brewer, VP-Design & DC Direct Creative Richard Bruning, Sr. VP-Creative Director
Patrick Caldon, Exec. VP-Finance & Operations Chris Caramalis, VP-Finance
John Cunningham, VP-Marketing Terri Cunningham, VP-Managing Editor Alison Gill, VP-Manufacturing
David Hyde, VP-Pubicity Hank Kanalz, VP-General Manager, WildStorm
Jim Lee, Editorial Director-WildStorm Paula Lowitt, Sr. VP-Business & Legal Affairs
MaryEllen McLaughlin, VP-Advertising & Custom Publishing John Nee,Sr. VP-Business Development
Gregory Noveck, Sr. VP-Creative Affairs Sue Pohja, VP-Book Trade Sales
Steve Rotterdam Sr. VP-Sales & Marketing Cheryl Rubin, Sr. VP-Brand Management
Jeff Trojan, VP-Business Development, DC Direct Bob Wayne, VP-Sales

JANES i

by CECIL C

and JI

with lettering b

and gray tone

m

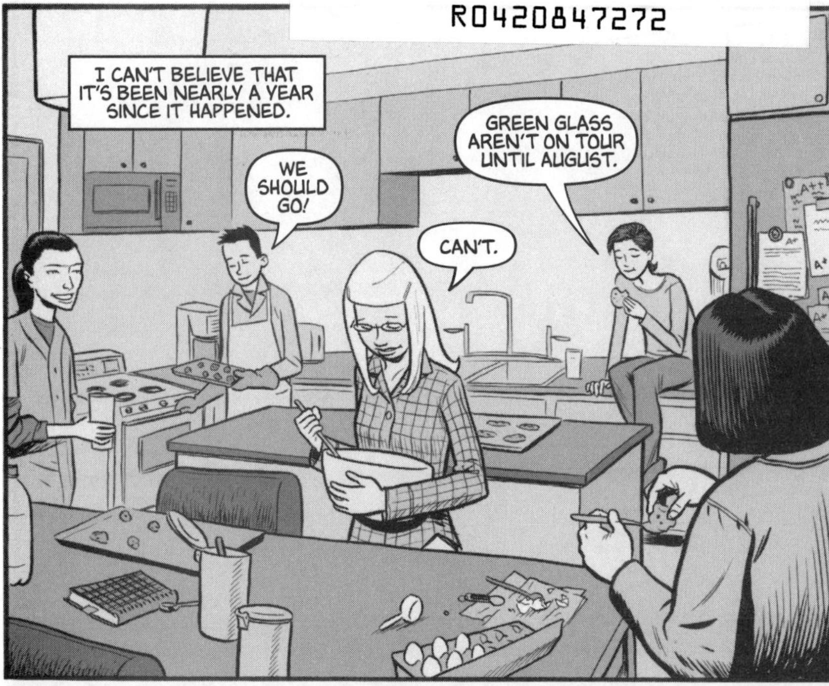
I CAN'T BELIEVE THAT IT'S BEEN NEARLY A YEAR SINCE IT HAPPENED.
WE SHOULD GO!
GREEN GLASS AREN'T ON TOUR UNTIL AUGUST.
CAN'T.

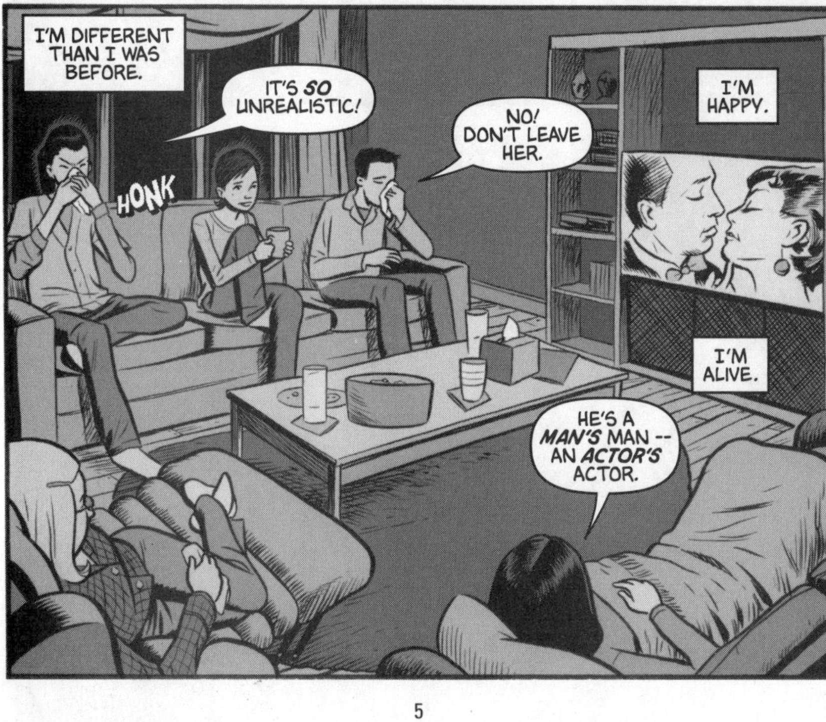
I'M DIFFERENT THAN I WAS BEFORE.
IT'S *SO* UNREALISTIC!
HONK
NO! DON'T LEAVE HER.
I'M HAPPY.
I'M ALIVE.
HE'S A *MAN'S* MAN -- AN *ACTOR'S* ACTOR.

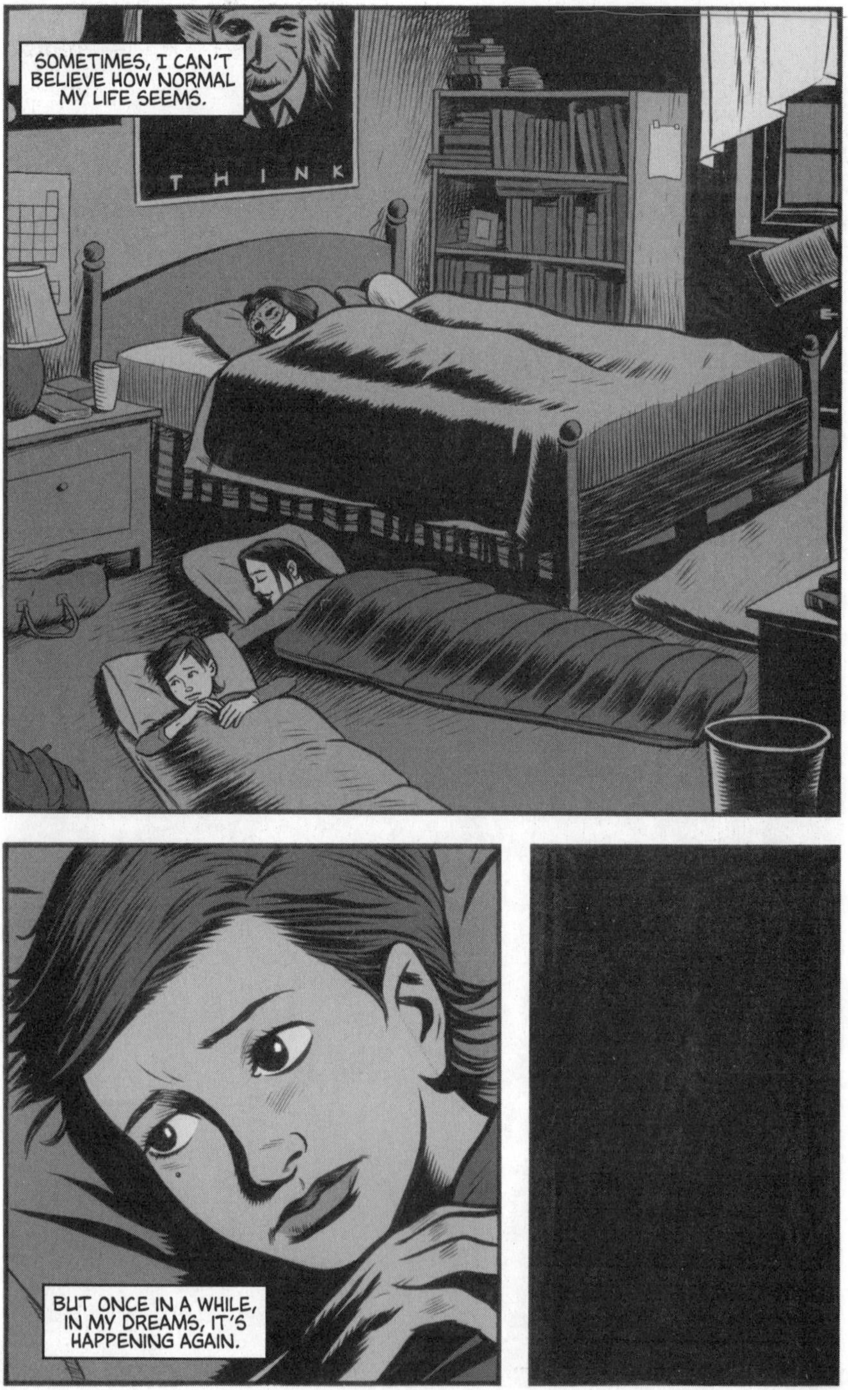
SOMETIMES, I CAN'T BELIEVE HOW NORMAL MY LIFE SEEMS.
THINK
BUT ONCE IN A WHILE, IN MY DREAMS, IT'S HAPPENING AGAIN.

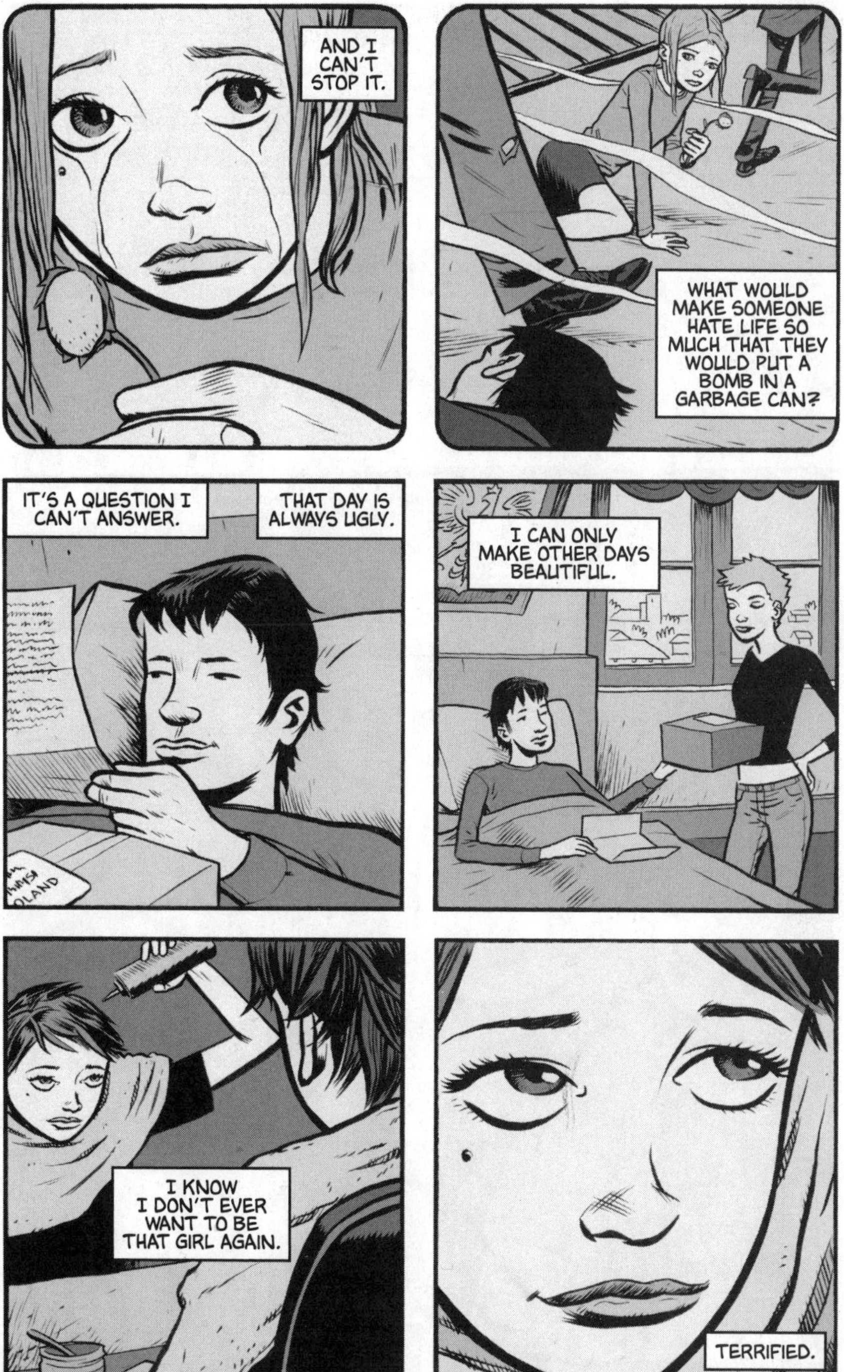
AND I CAN'T STOP IT.
WHAT WOULD MAKE SOMEONE HATE LIFE SO MUCH THAT THEY WOULD PUT A BOMB IN A GARBAGE CAN?
IT'S A QUESTION I CAN'T ANSWER.
THAT DAY IS ALWAYS UGLY.
I CAN ONLY MAKE OTHER DAYS BEAUTIFUL.
I KNOW I DON'T EVER WANT TO BE THAT GIRL AGAIN.
TERRIFIED.

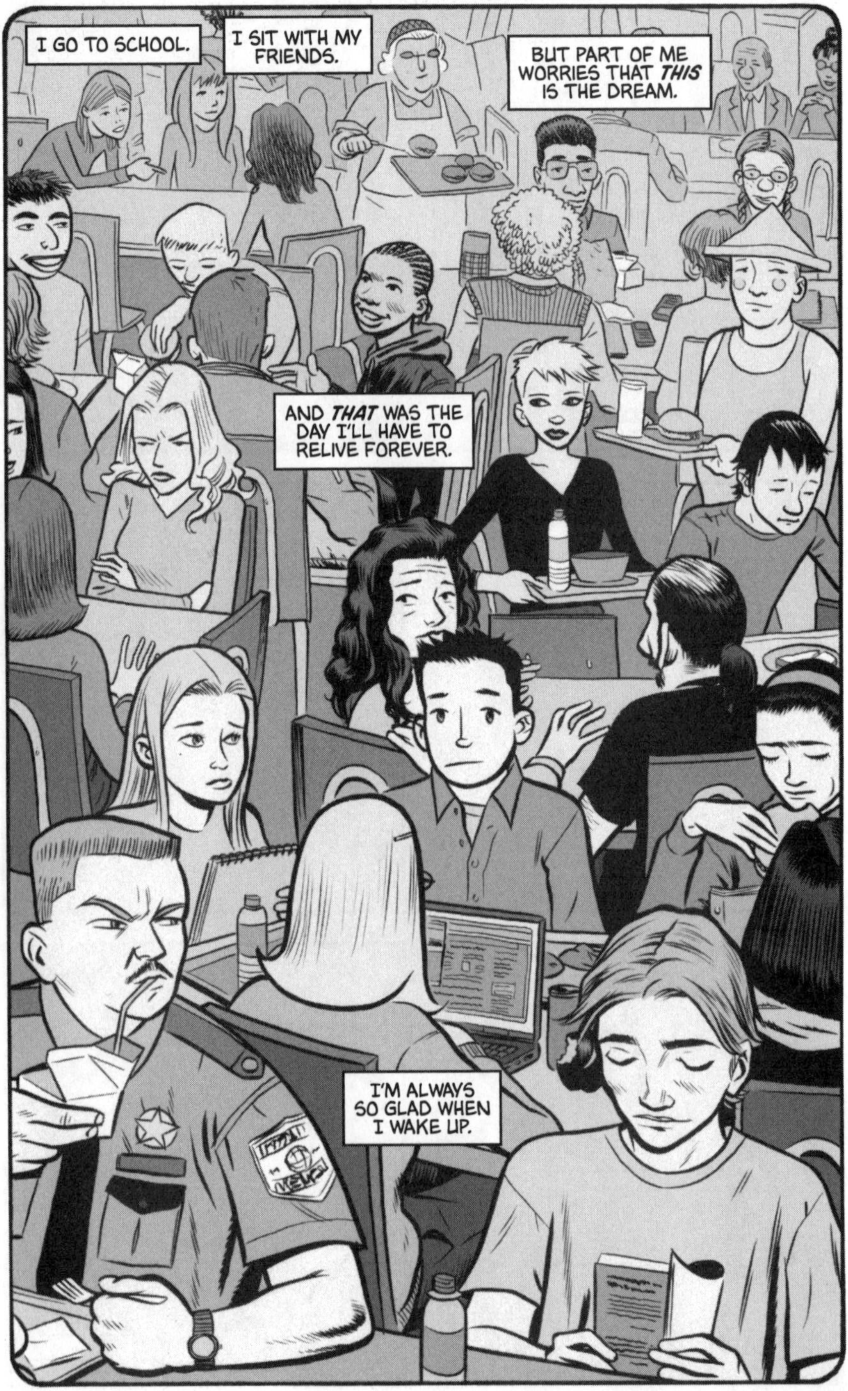
I GO TO SCHOOL.
I SIT WITH MY FRIENDS.
BUT PART OF ME WORRIES THAT *THIS* IS THE DREAM.
AND *THAT* WAS THE DAY I'LL HAVE TO RELIVE FOREVER.
I'M ALWAYS SO GLAD WHEN I WAKE UP.

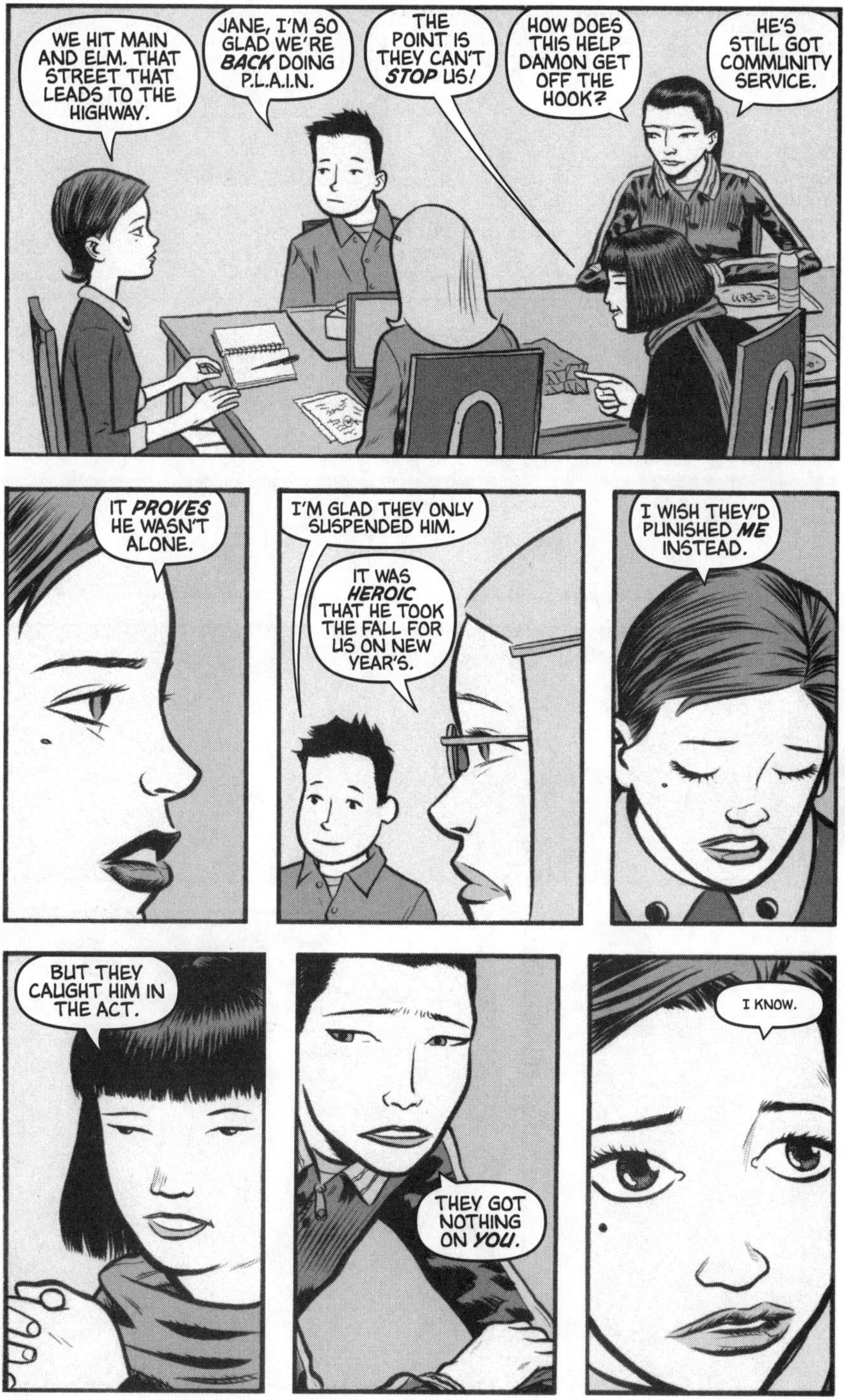
WE HIT MAIN AND ELM. THAT STREET THAT LEADS TO THE HIGHWAY.
JANE, I'M SO GLAD WE'RE BACK DOING P.L.A.I.N.
THE POINT IS THEY CAN'T STOP US!
HOW DOES THIS HELP DAMON GET OFF THE HOOK?
HE'S STILL GOT COMMUNITY SERVICE.
IT PROVES HE WASN'T ALONE.
I'M GLAD THEY ONLY SUSPENDED HIM.
IT WAS HEROIC THAT HE TOOK THE FALL FOR US ON NEW YEAR'S.
I WISH THEY'D PUNISHED ME INSTEAD.
BUT THEY CAUGHT HIM IN THE ACT.
THEY GOT NOTHING ON YOU.
I KNOW.

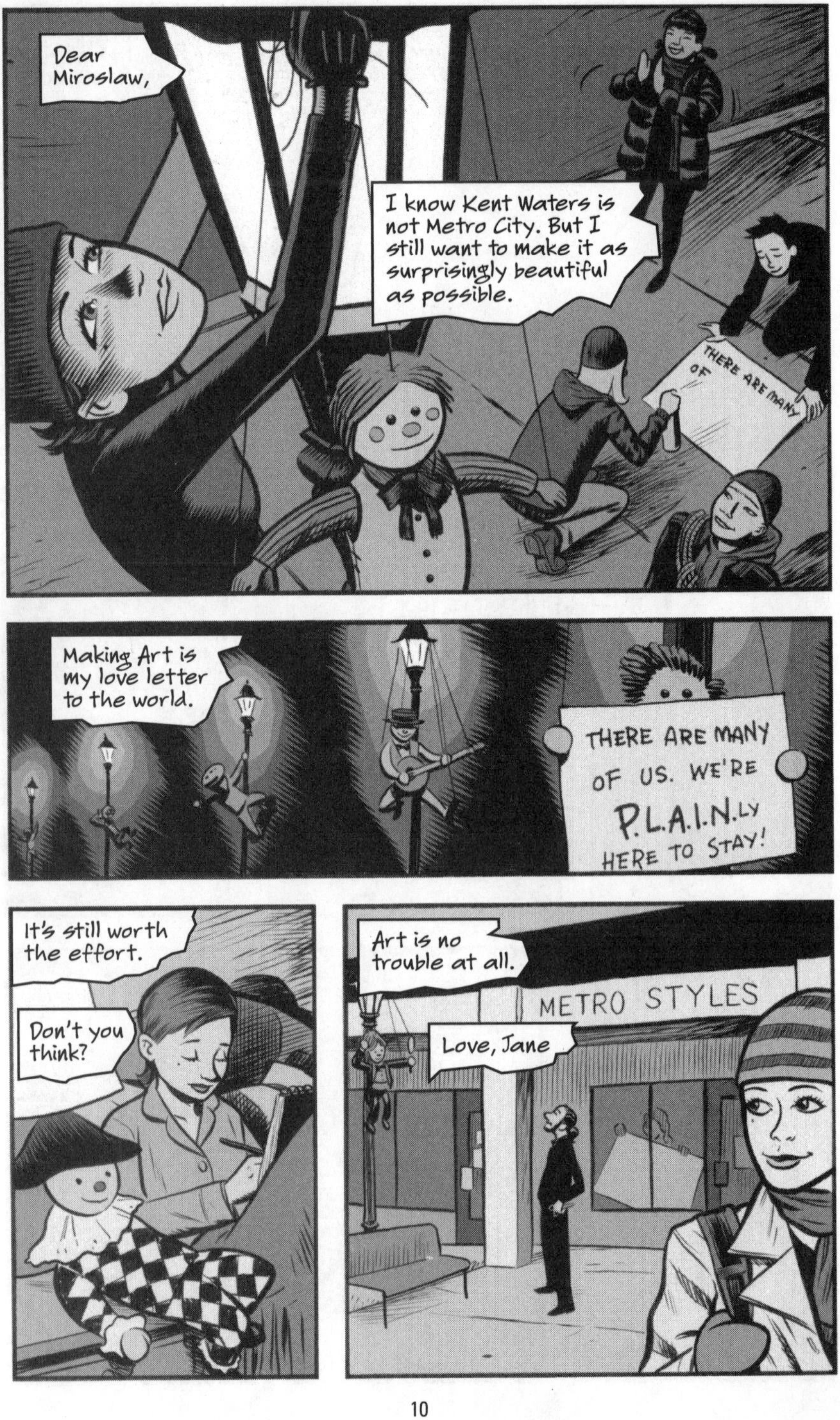
Dear Miroslaw,
I know Kent Waters is not Metro City. But I still want to make it as surprisingly beautiful as possible.
THERE ARE MANY OF
Making Art is my love letter to the world.
THERE ARE MANY OF US. WE'RE P.L.A.I.N.LY HERE TO STAY!
It's still worth the effort.
Don't you think?
Art is no trouble at all.
METRO STYLES
Love, Jane

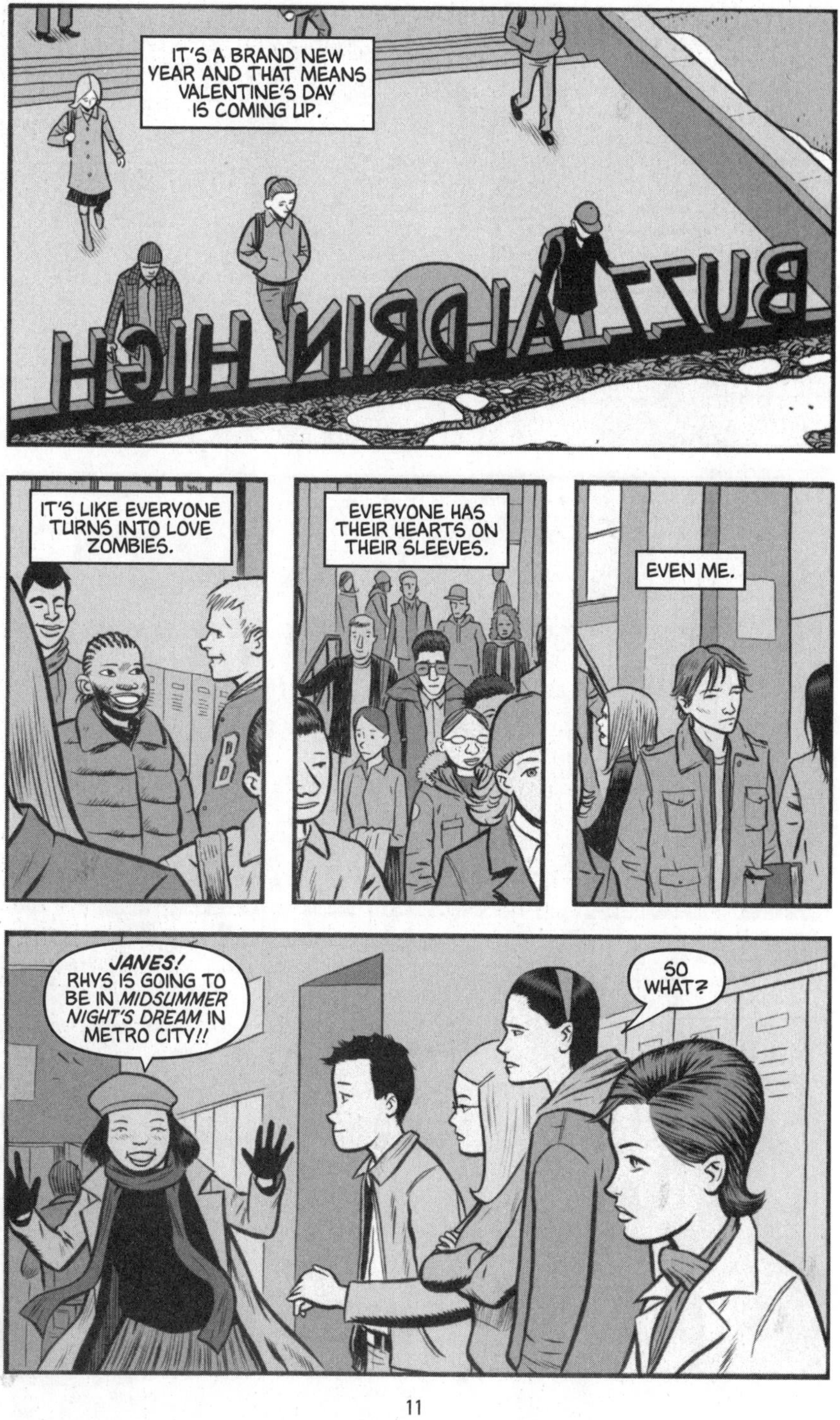
IT'S A BRAND NEW YEAR AND THAT MEANS VALENTINE'S DAY IS COMING UP.
IT'S LIKE EVERYONE TURNS INTO LOVE ZOMBIES.
EVERYONE HAS THEIR HEARTS ON THEIR SLEEVES.
EVEN ME.
JANES! RHYS IS GOING TO BE IN *MIDSUMMER NIGHT'S DREAM* IN METRO CITY!!
SO WHAT?

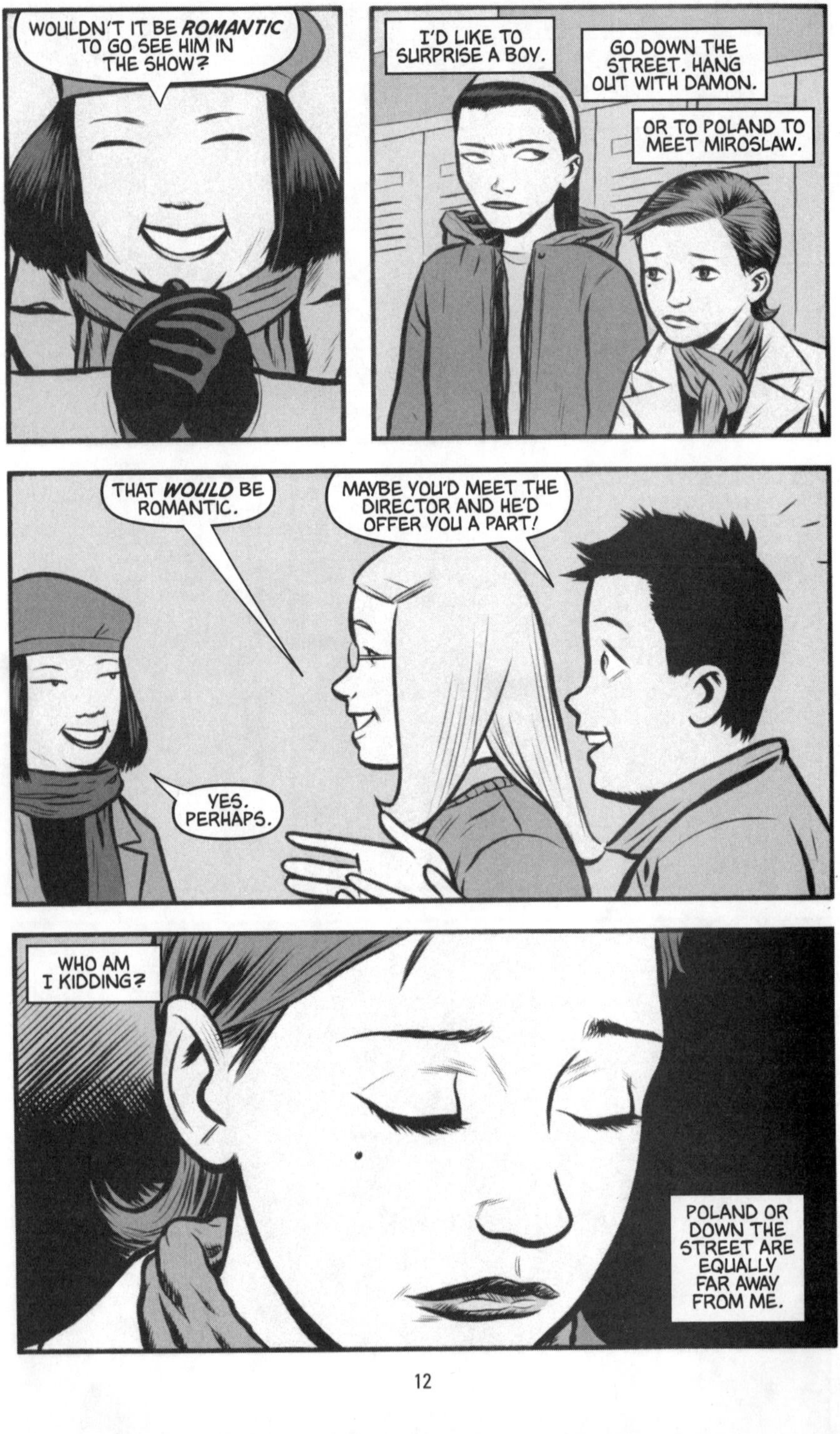
WOULDN'T IT BE *ROMANTIC* TO GO SEE HIM IN THE SHOW?
I'D LIKE TO SURPRISE A BOY.
GO DOWN THE STREET. HANG OUT WITH DAMON.
OR TO POLAND TO MEET MIROSLAW.
THAT *WOULD* BE ROMANTIC.
MAYBE YOU'D MEET THE DIRECTOR AND HE'D OFFER YOU A PART!
YES. PERHAPS.
WHO AM I KIDDING?
POLAND OR DOWN THE STREET ARE EQUALLY FAR AWAY FROM ME.

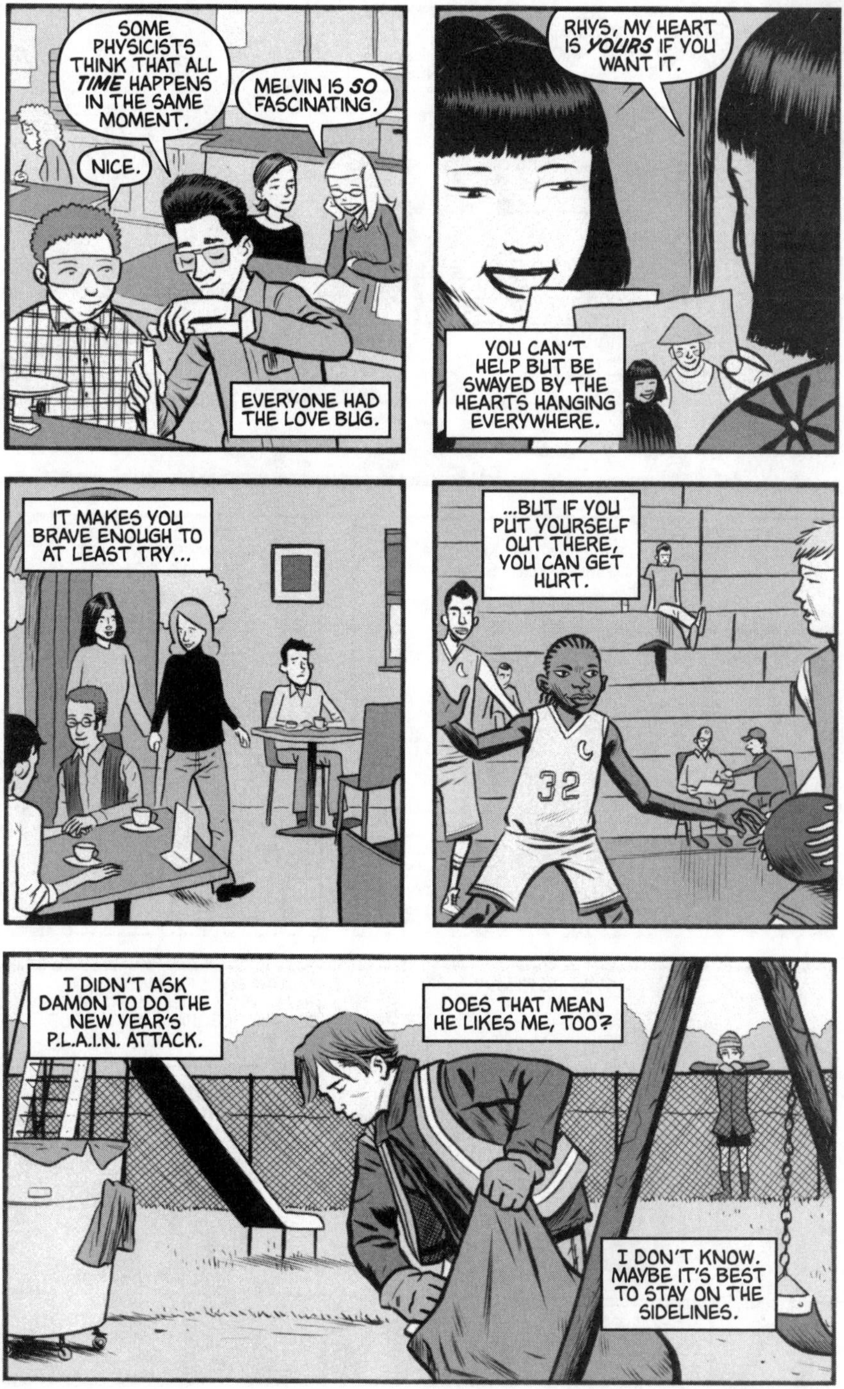

SOME PHYSICISTS THINK THAT ALL *TIME* HAPPENS IN THE SAME MOMENT.
NICE.
MELVIN IS *SO* FASCINATING.
EVERYONE HAD THE LOVE BUG.
RHYS, MY HEART IS *YOURS* IF YOU WANT IT.
YOU CAN'T HELP BUT BE SWAYED BY THE HEARTS HANGING EVERYWHERE.
IT MAKES YOU BRAVE ENOUGH TO AT LEAST TRY...
...BUT IF YOU PUT YOURSELF OUT THERE, YOU CAN GET HURT.
32
I DIDN'T ASK DAMON TO DO THE NEW YEAR'S P.L.A.I.N. ATTACK.
DOES THAT MEAN HE LIKES ME, TOO?
I DON'T KNOW. MAYBE IT'S BEST TO STAY ON THE SIDELINES.

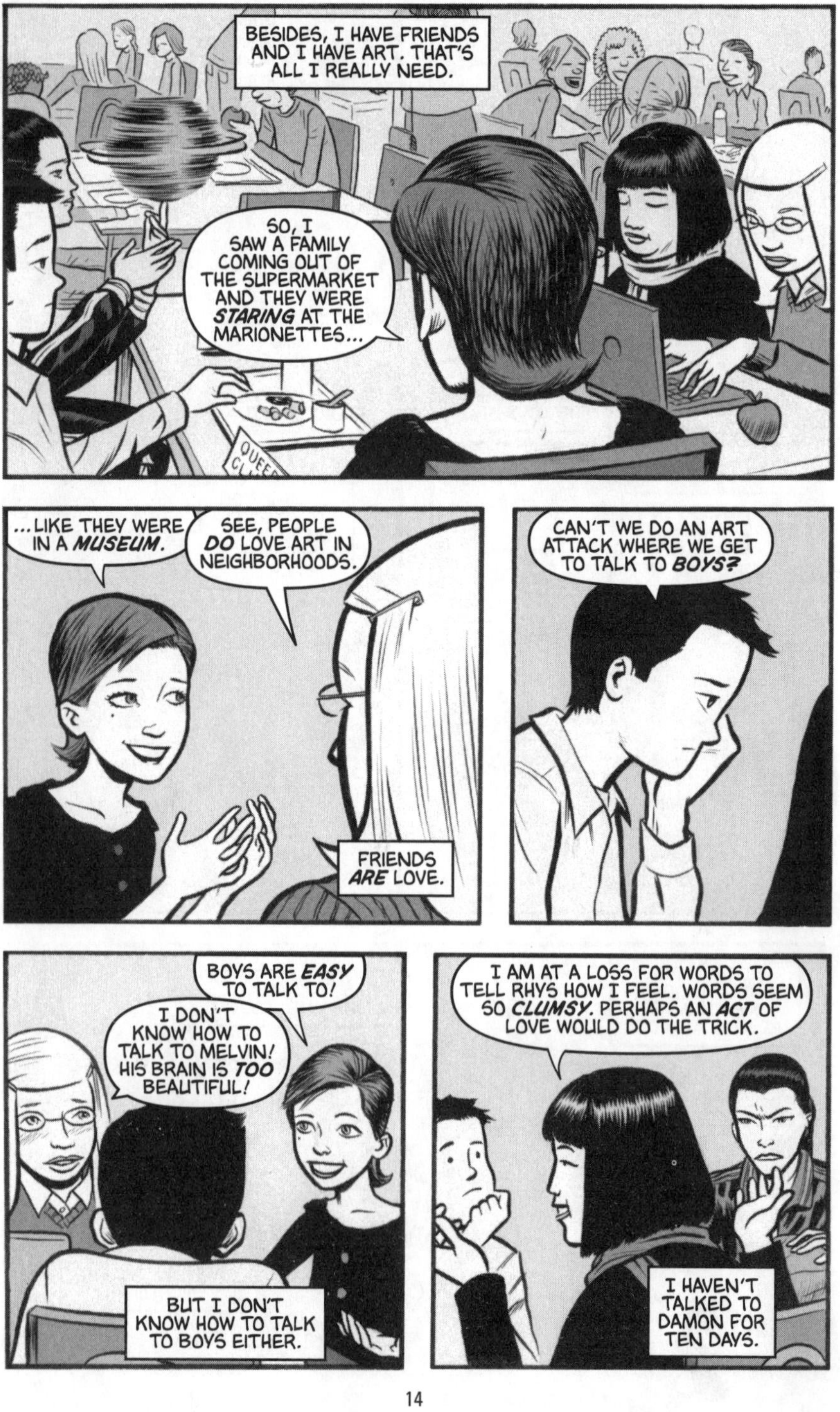
BESIDES, I HAVE FRIENDS AND I HAVE ART. THAT'S ALL I REALLY NEED.
SO, I SAW A FAMILY COMING OUT OF THE SUPERMARKET AND THEY WERE STARING AT THE MARIONETTES...
...LIKE THEY WERE IN A MUSEUM.
SEE, PEOPLE DO LOVE ART IN NEIGHBORHOODS.
FRIENDS ARE LOVE.
CAN'T WE DO AN ART ATTACK WHERE WE GET TO TALK TO BOYS?
BOYS ARE EASY TO TALK TO!
I DON'T KNOW HOW TO TALK TO MELVIN! HIS BRAIN IS TOO BEAUTIFUL!
BUT I DON'T KNOW HOW TO TALK TO BOYS EITHER.
I AM AT A LOSS FOR WORDS TO TELL RHYS HOW I FEEL. WORDS SEEM SO CLUMSY. PERHAPS AN ACT OF LOVE WOULD DO THE TRICK.
I HAVEN'T TALKED TO DAMON FOR TEN DAYS.

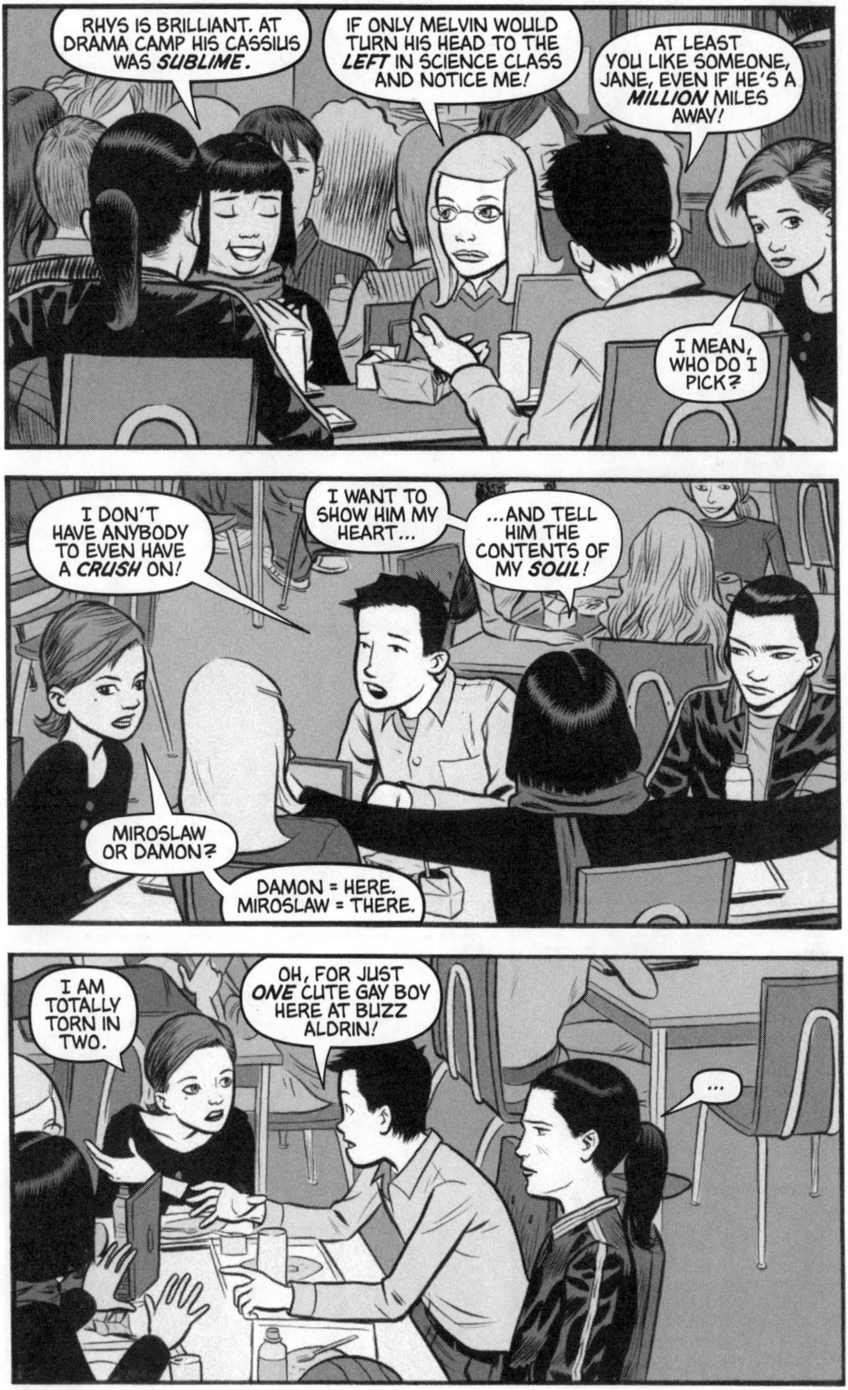

RHYS IS BRILLIANT. AT DRAMA CAMP HIS CASSIUS WAS *SUBLIME*.
IF ONLY MELVIN WOULD TURN HIS HEAD TO THE *LEFT* IN SCIENCE CLASS AND NOTICE ME!
AT LEAST YOU LIKE SOMEONE, JANE, EVEN IF HE'S A *MILLION* MILES AWAY!
I MEAN, WHO DO I PICK?
I DON'T HAVE ANYBODY TO EVEN HAVE A *CRUSH* ON!
I WANT TO SHOW HIM MY HEART...
...AND TELL HIM THE CONTENTS OF MY *SOUL*!
MIROSLAW OR DAMON?
DAMON = HERE. MIROSLAW = THERE.
I AM TOTALLY TORN IN TWO.
OH, FOR JUST *ONE* CUTE GAY BOY HERE AT BUZZ ALDRIN!
...

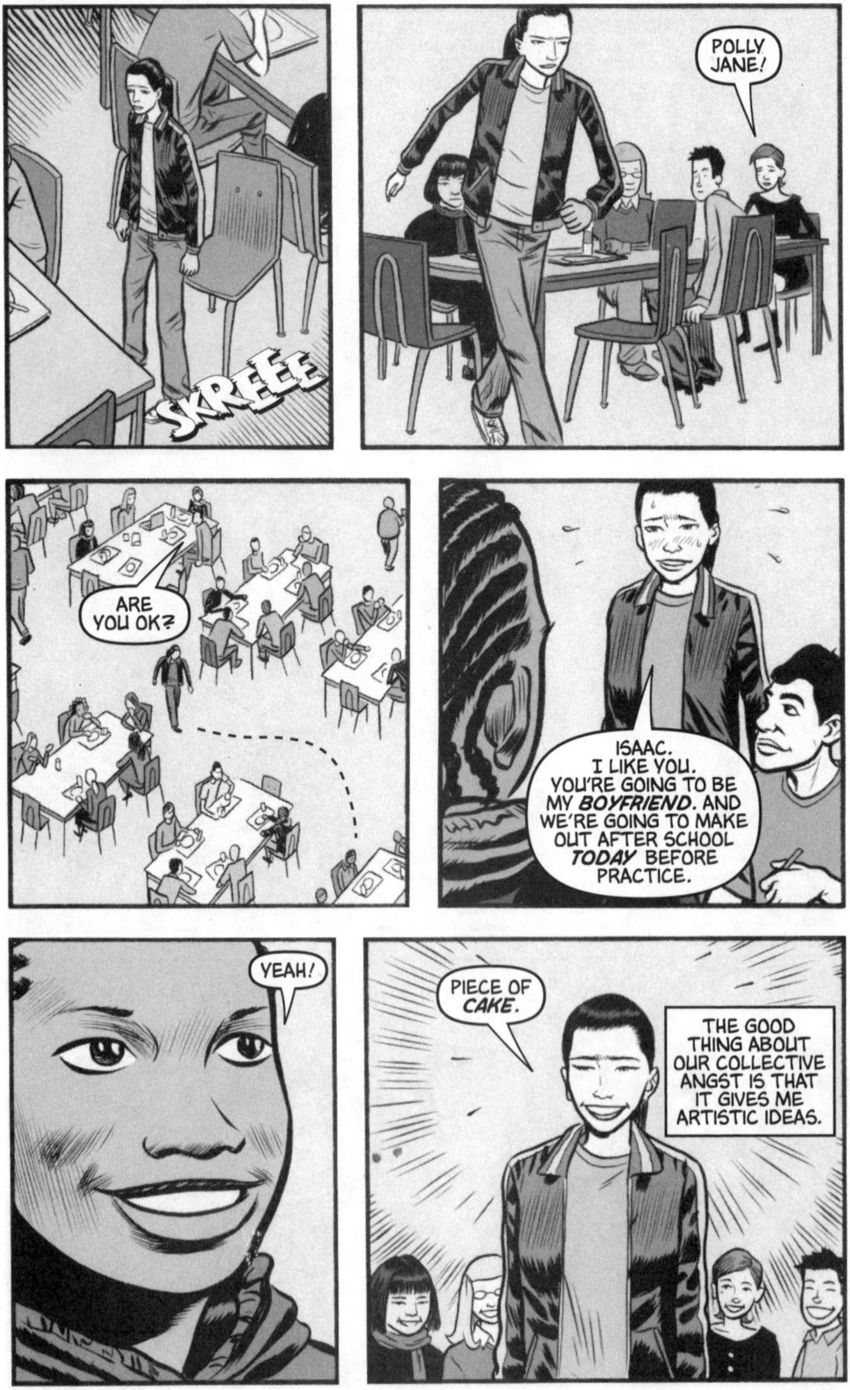
SKREEE
POLLY JANE!
ARE YOU OK?
ISAAC. I LIKE YOU. YOU'RE GOING TO BE MY *BOYFRIEND*. AND WE'RE GOING TO MAKE OUT AFTER SCHOOL *TODAY* BEFORE PRACTICE.
YEAH!
PIECE OF *CAKE*.
THE GOOD THING ABOUT OUR COLLECTIVE ANGST IS THAT IT GIVES ME ARTISTIC IDEAS.

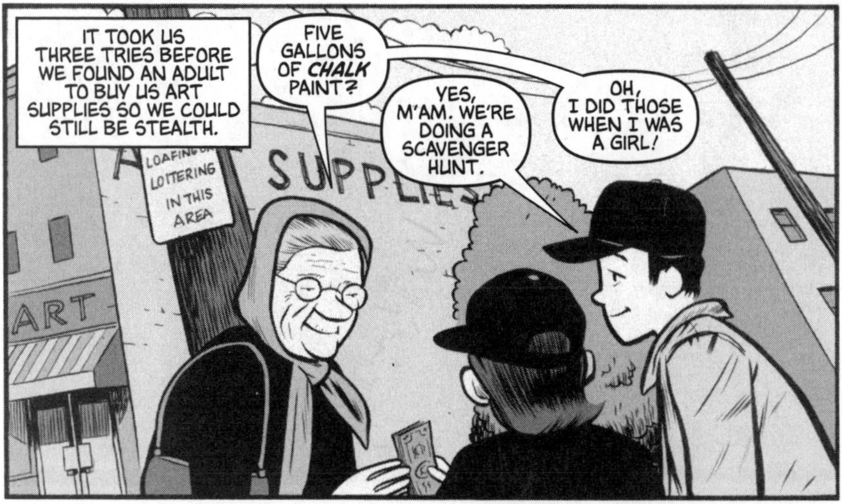
IT TOOK US THREE TRIES BEFORE WE FOUND AN ADULT TO BUY US ART SUPPLIES SO WE COULD STILL BE STEALTH.
FIVE GALLONS OF *CHALK* PAINT?
YES, M'AM. WE'RE DOING A SCAVENGER HUNT.
OH, I DID THOSE WHEN I WAS A GIRL!
LOAFING OR LOITERING IN THIS AREA
SUPPLIES
ART

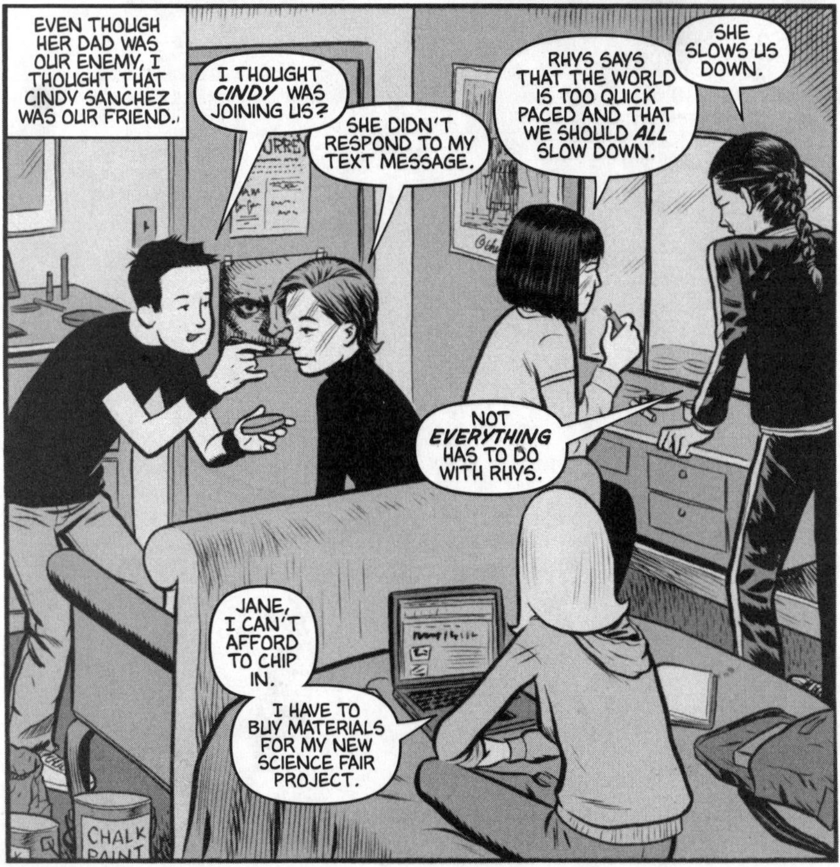
EVEN THOUGH HER DAD WAS OUR ENEMY, I THOUGHT THAT CINDY SANCHEZ WAS OUR FRIEND.
I THOUGHT *CINDY* WAS JOINING US?
SHE DIDN'T RESPOND TO MY TEXT MESSAGE.
RHYS SAYS THAT THE WORLD IS TOO QUICK PACED AND THAT WE SHOULD *ALL* SLOW DOWN.
SHE SLOWS US DOWN.
NOT *EVERYTHING* HAS TO DO WITH RHYS.
JANE, I CAN'T AFFORD TO CHIP IN.
I HAVE TO BUY MATERIALS FOR MY NEW SCIENCE FAIR PROJECT.
CHALK PAINT

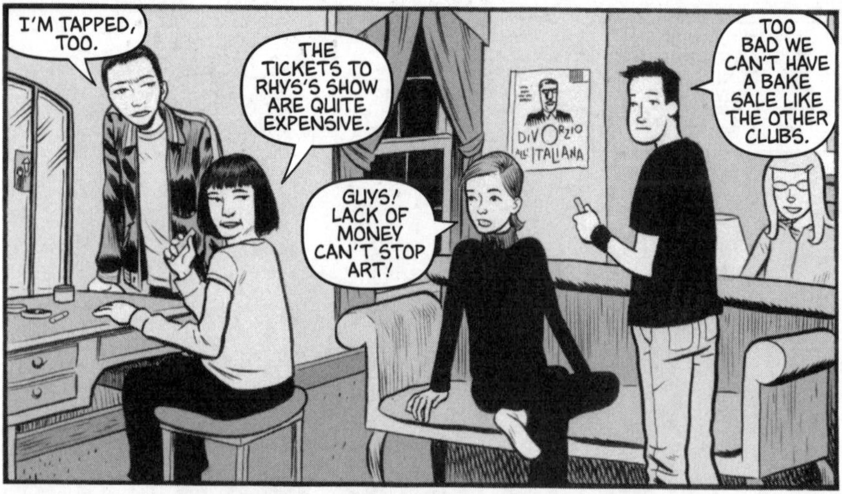
I'M TAPPED, TOO.
THE TICKETS TO RHYS'S SHOW ARE QUITE EXPENSIVE.
GUYS! LACK OF MONEY CAN'T STOP ART!
DIVORZIO ALL'ITALIANA
TOO BAD WE CAN'T HAVE A BAKE SALE LIKE THE OTHER CLUBS.

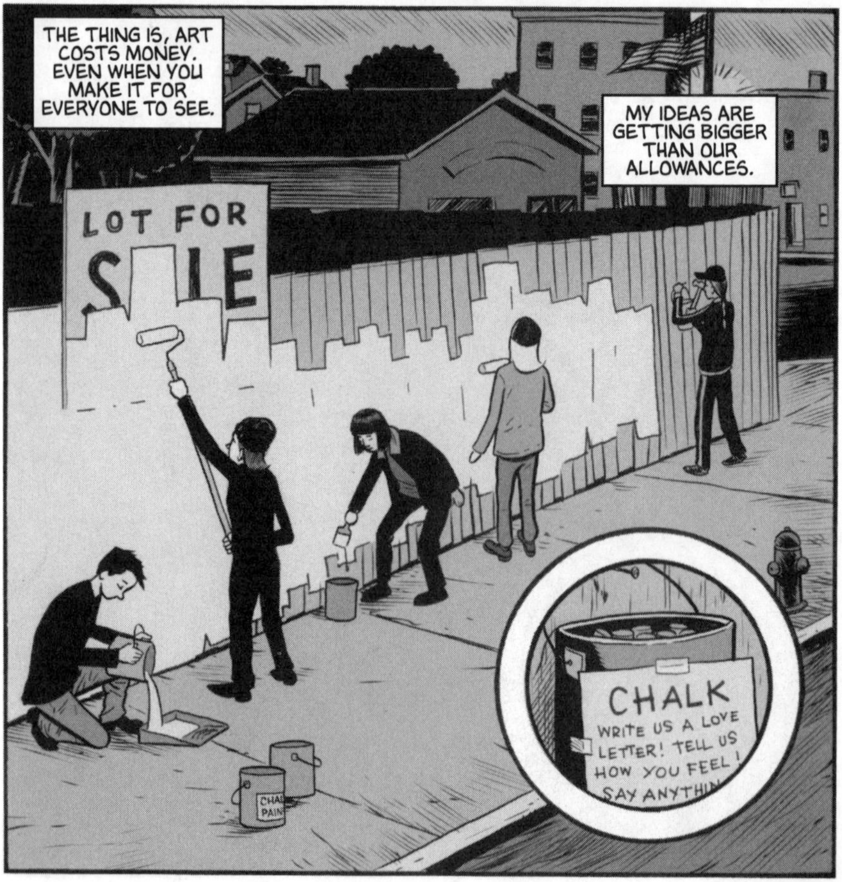
THE THING IS, ART COSTS MONEY. EVEN WHEN YOU MAKE IT FOR EVERYONE TO SEE.
MY IDEAS ARE GETTING BIGGER THAN OUR ALLOWANCES.
LOT FOR
S IE
CHALK
WRITE US A LOVE LETTER! TELL US HOW YOU FEEL!
SAY ANYTHIN

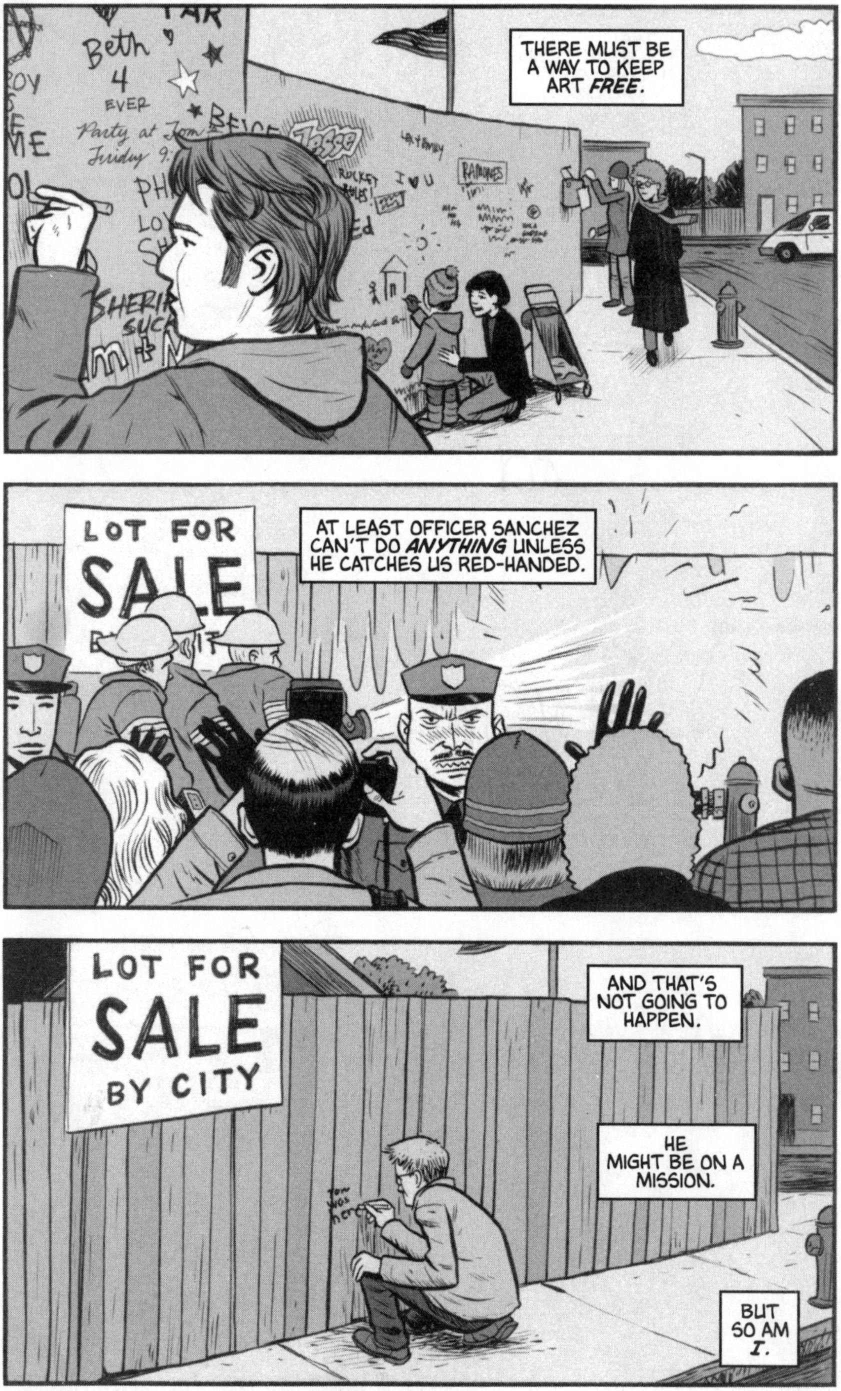
THERE MUST BE A WAY TO KEEP ART FREE.
Beth 4 EVER
RAMONES
LOT FOR SALE
AT LEAST OFFICER SANCHEZ CAN'T DO ANYTHING UNLESS HE CATCHES US RED-HANDED.
LOT FOR SALE BY CITY
AND THAT'S NOT GOING TO HAPPEN.
HE MIGHT BE ON A MISSION.
BUT SO AM I.

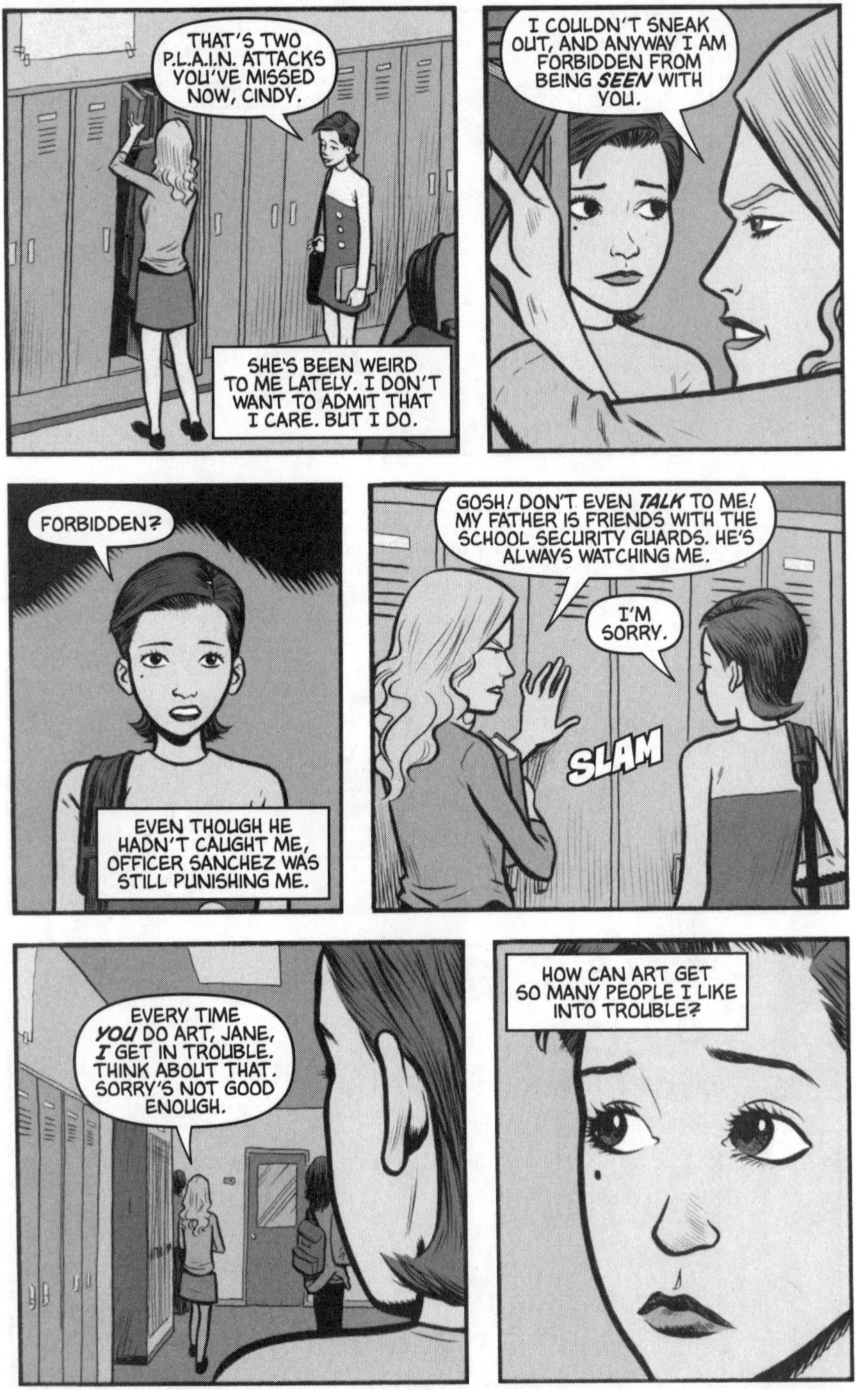
THAT'S TWO P.L.A.I.N. ATTACKS YOU'VE MISSED NOW, CINDY.
SHE'S BEEN WEIRD TO ME LATELY. I DON'T WANT TO ADMIT THAT I CARE. BUT I DO.
I COULDN'T SNEAK OUT, AND ANYWAY I AM FORBIDDEN FROM BEING SEEN WITH YOU.
FORBIDDEN?
EVEN THOUGH HE HADN'T CAUGHT ME, OFFICER SANCHEZ WAS STILL PUNISHING ME.
GOSH! DON'T EVEN TALK TO ME! MY FATHER IS FRIENDS WITH THE SCHOOL SECURITY GUARDS. HE'S ALWAYS WATCHING ME.
I'M SORRY.
SLAM
EVERY TIME YOU DO ART, JANE, I GET IN TROUBLE. THINK ABOUT THAT. SORRY'S NOT GOOD ENOUGH.
HOW CAN ART GET SO MANY PEOPLE I LIKE INTO TROUBLE?

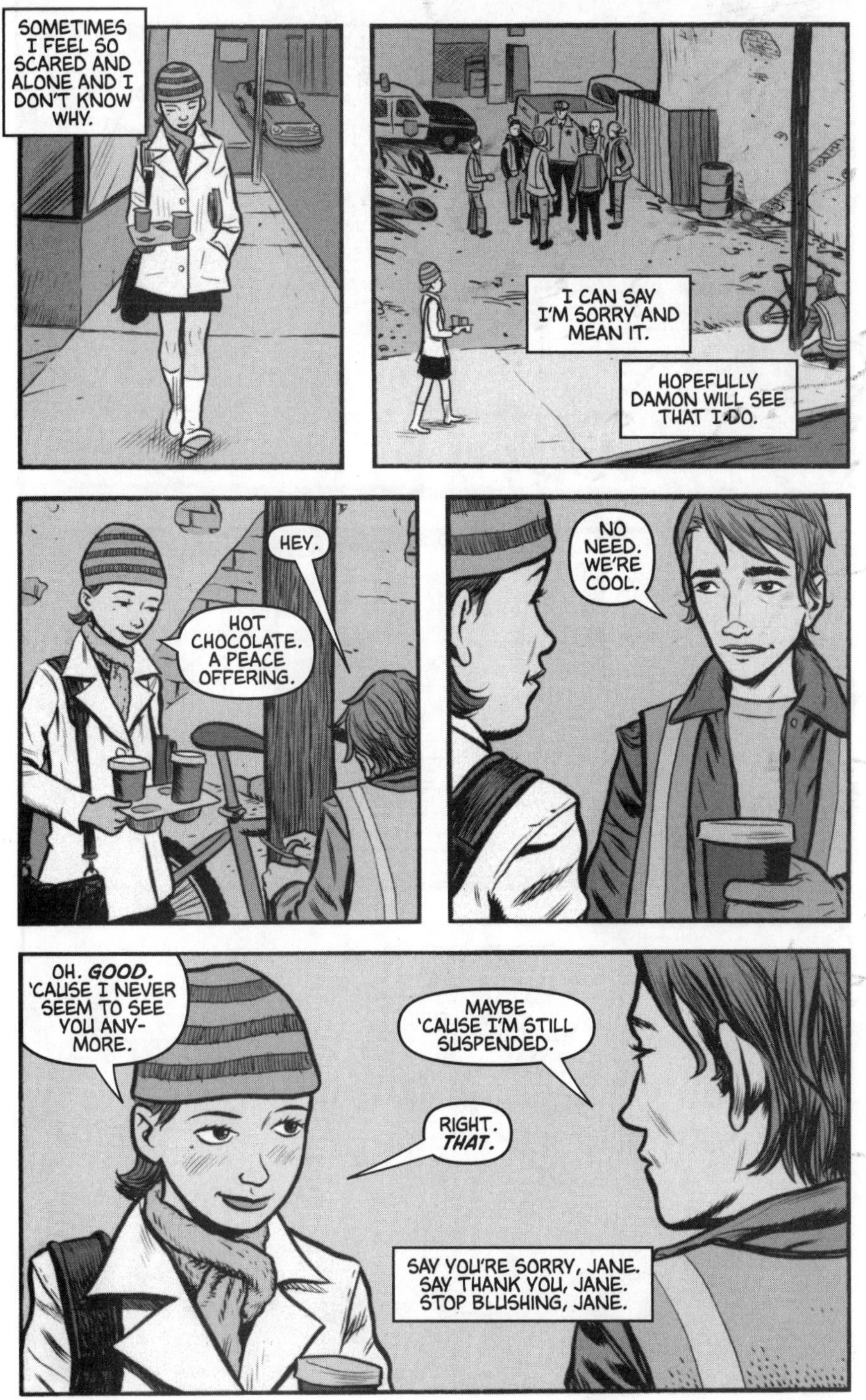
SOMETIMES I FEEL SO SCARED AND ALONE AND I DON'T KNOW WHY.
I CAN SAY I'M SORRY AND MEAN IT.
HOPEFULLY DAMON WILL SEE THAT I DO.
HEY.
HOT CHOCOLATE. A PEACE OFFERING.
NO NEED. WE'RE COOL.
OH. GOOD. 'CAUSE I NEVER SEEM TO SEE YOU ANY-MORE.
MAYBE 'CAUSE I'M STILL SUSPENDED.
RIGHT. THAT.
SAY YOU'RE SORRY, JANE. SAY THANK YOU, JANE. STOP BLUSHING, JANE.

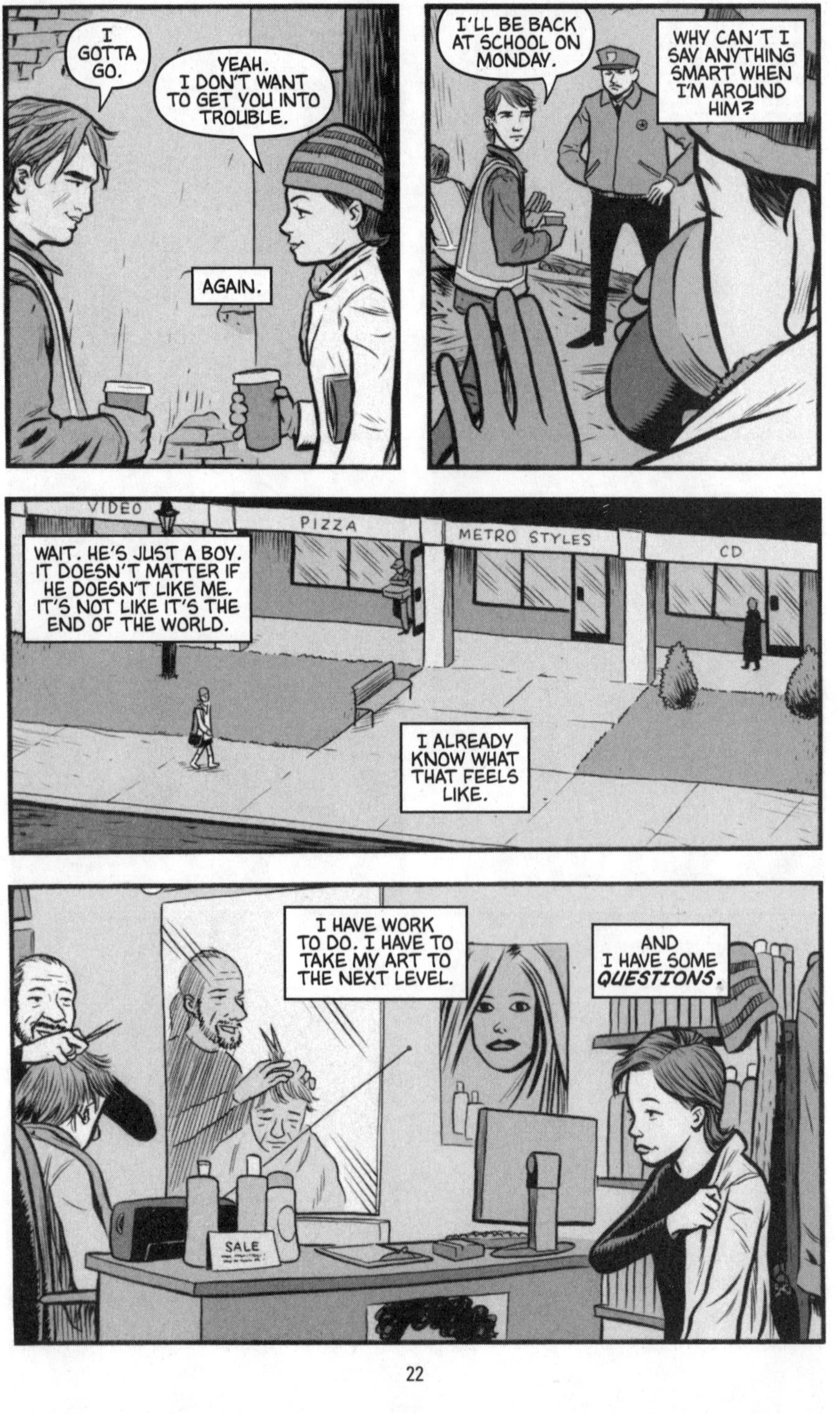
I GOTTA GO.
YEAH. I DON'T WANT TO GET YOU INTO TROUBLE.
AGAIN.
I'LL BE BACK AT SCHOOL ON MONDAY.
WHY CAN'T I SAY ANYTHING SMART WHEN I'M AROUND HIM?
VIDEO
PIZZA
METRO STYLES
CD
WAIT. HE'S JUST A BOY. IT DOESN'T MATTER IF HE DOESN'T LIKE ME. IT'S NOT LIKE IT'S THE END OF THE WORLD.
I ALREADY KNOW WHAT THAT FEELS LIKE.
I HAVE WORK TO DO. I HAVE TO TAKE MY ART TO THE NEXT LEVEL.
AND I HAVE SOME ***QUESTIONS***.
SALE

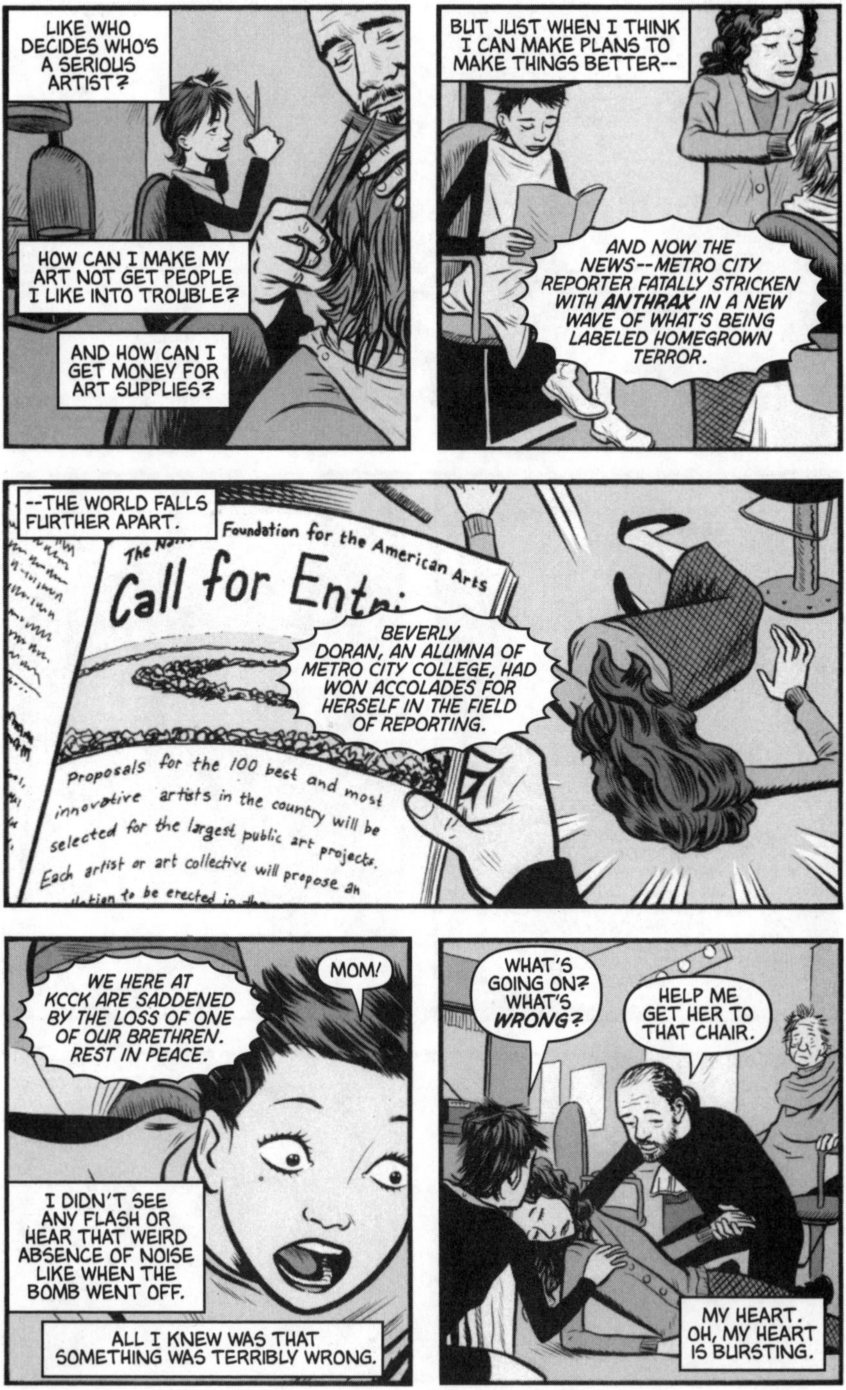
LIKE WHO DECIDES WHO'S A SERIOUS ARTIST?
HOW CAN I MAKE MY ART NOT GET PEOPLE I LIKE INTO TROUBLE?
AND HOW CAN I GET MONEY FOR ART SUPPLIES?
BUT JUST WHEN I THINK I CAN MAKE PLANS TO MAKE THINGS BETTER--
AND NOW THE NEWS--METRO CITY REPORTER FATALLY STRICKEN WITH ANTHRAX IN A NEW WAVE OF WHAT'S BEING LABELED HOMEGROWN TERROR.
--THE WORLD FALLS FURTHER APART.
Foundation for the American Arts
Call for Entr
BEVERLY DORAN, AN ALUMNA OF METRO CITY COLLEGE, HAD WON ACCOLADES FOR HERSELF IN THE FIELD OF REPORTING.
Proposals for the 100 best and most innovative artists in the country will be selected for the largest public art projects. Each artist or art collective will propose an
WE HERE AT KCCK ARE SADDENED BY THE LOSS OF ONE OF OUR BRETHREN. REST IN PEACE.
MOM!
I DIDN'T SEE ANY FLASH OR HEAR THAT WEIRD ABSENCE OF NOISE LIKE WHEN THE BOMB WENT OFF.
ALL I KNEW WAS THAT SOMETHING WAS TERRIBLY WRONG.
WHAT'S GOING ON? WHAT'S WRONG?
HELP ME GET HER TO THAT CHAIR.
MY HEART. OH, MY HEART IS BURSTING.

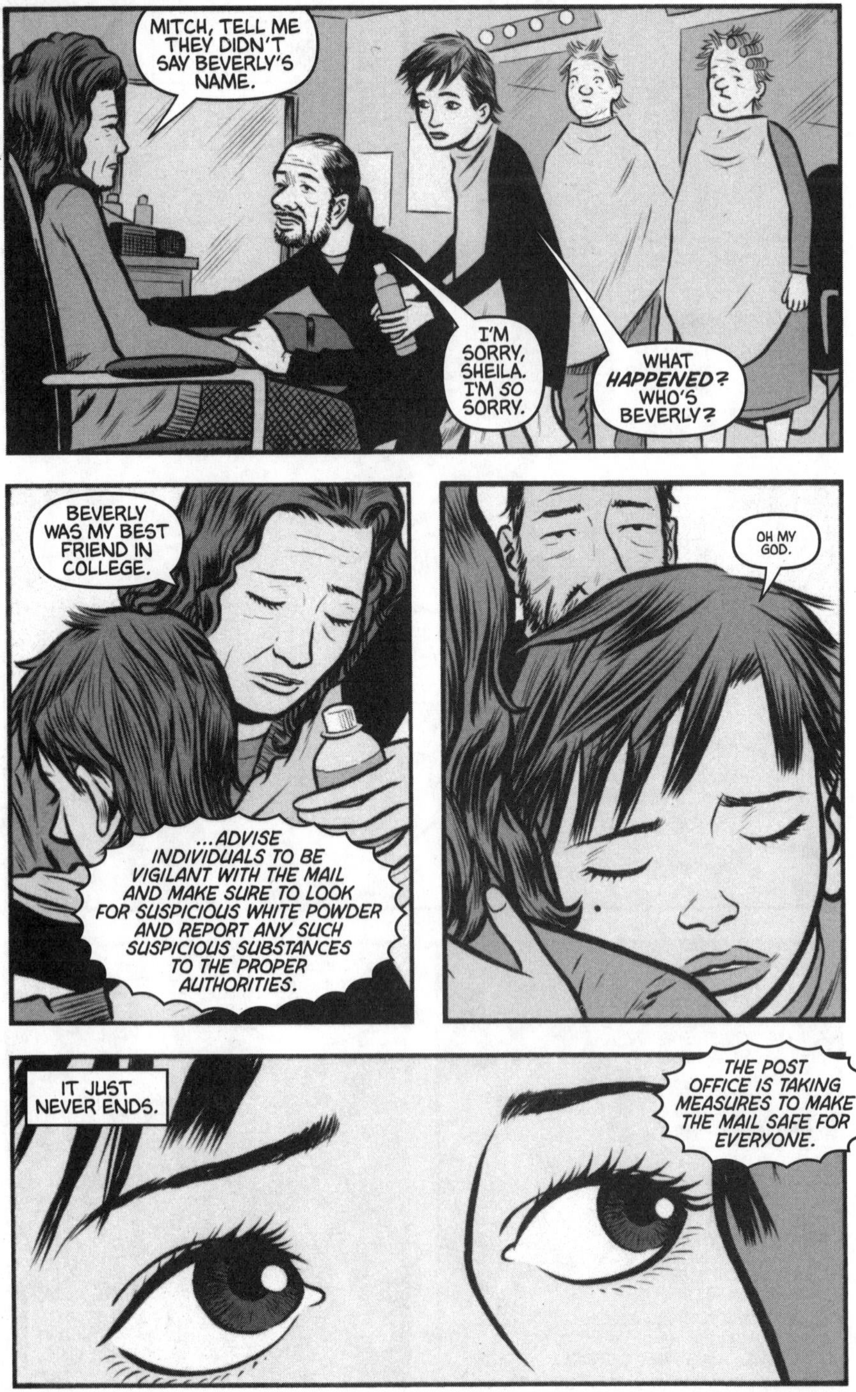
MITCH, TELL ME THEY DIDN'T SAY BEVERLY'S NAME.
I'M SORRY, SHEILA. I'M *SO* SORRY.
WHAT *HAPPENED*? WHO'S BEVERLY?
BEVERLY WAS MY BEST FRIEND IN COLLEGE.
...ADVISE INDIVIDUALS TO BE VIGILANT WITH THE MAIL AND MAKE SURE TO LOOK FOR SUSPICIOUS WHITE POWDER AND REPORT ANY SUCH SUSPICIOUS SUBSTANCES TO THE PROPER AUTHORITIES.
OH MY GOD.
IT JUST NEVER ENDS.
THE POST OFFICE IS TAKING MEASURES TO MAKE THE MAIL SAFE FOR EVERYONE.

I'M FEELING SO SMALL.

DAMON IS BACK BUT KIND OF COLD. AND CINDY IS STILL MAD AT ME.

I JUST WANT HER TO SAY SOMETHING.

DON'T *EVEN* LOOK AT ME, JANE.

DID YOU EVER HAVE AN ARGUMENT THAT NEVER ENDED? MY MOM AND DAD DO.

MY MOM HATES MY DAD'S PONYTAIL. SHE WANTS TO CUT IT OFF. MY DAD LIKES THE PONYTAIL. THINKS IT MAKES HIM LOOK BOHO IN SOME WAY.

NO TALKING KEEP YOUR EY ON YOUR OW

DAD SAID MOM COULD CUT HIS PONYTAIL OFF LAST NIGHT. SHE WENT TO GET THE SCISSORS. TOLD HIM TO SIT.

DAD SAID MOM COULD HAVE HER WAY WITH HIS HAIR IF SHE LEFT THE HOUSE AND DID IT AT THE SALON.

BLAH, BLAH, BLAH...

IT'S BEEN A WEEK SINCE THE ATTACK KILLED HER FRIEND.

MOM WON'T LEAVE THE HOUSE.

I hate the silent treatment I miss you guys. Please talk to me again

ELA ES EVER

EVEN THOUGH SHE WANTS TO CUT THAT PONYTAIL OFF LIKE CRAZY.

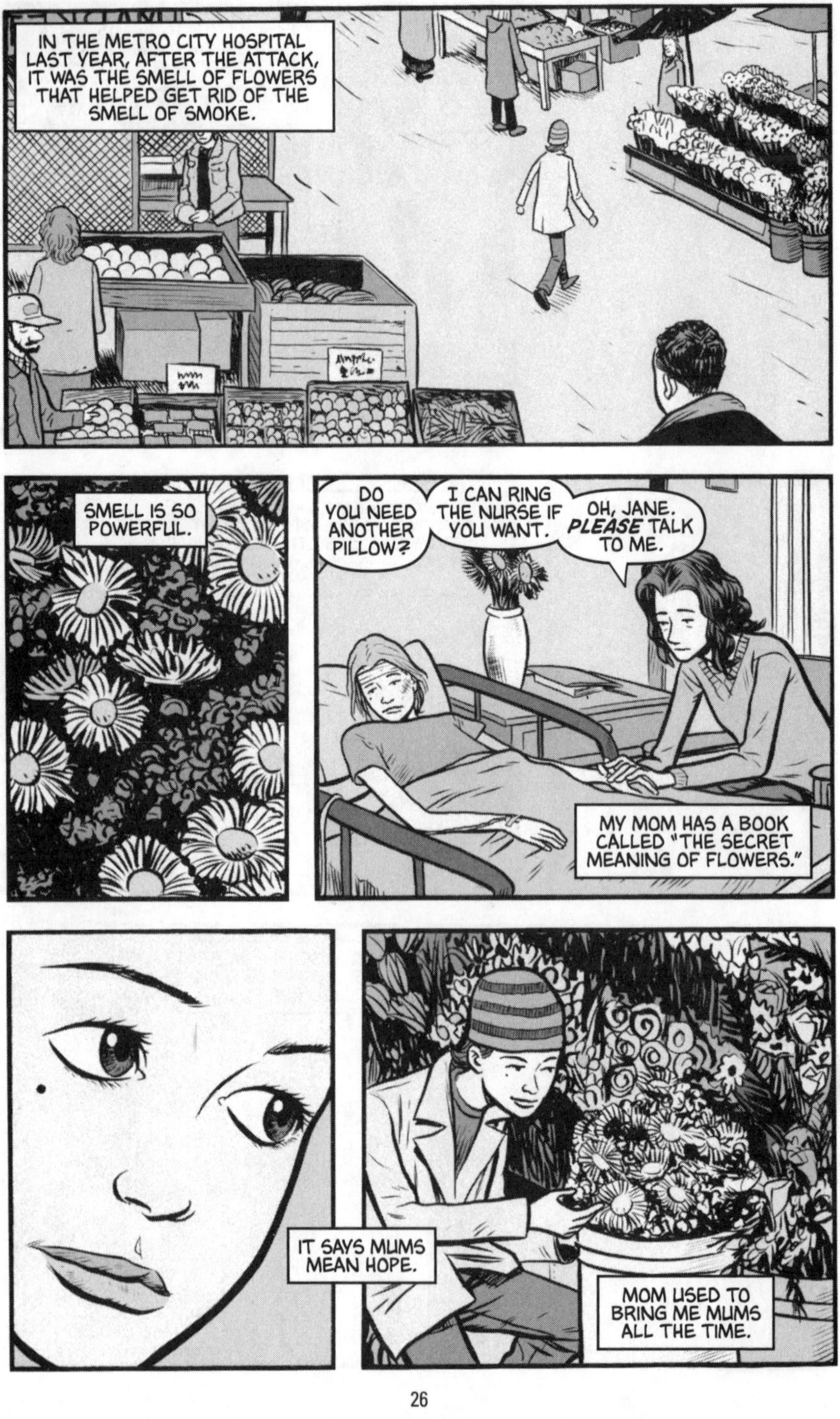
IN THE METRO CITY HOSPITAL LAST YEAR, AFTER THE ATTACK, IT WAS THE SMELL OF FLOWERS THAT HELPED GET RID OF THE SMELL OF SMOKE.
SMELL IS SO POWERFUL.
DO YOU NEED ANOTHER PILLOW?
I CAN RING THE NURSE IF YOU WANT.
OH, JANE. *PLEASE* TALK TO ME.
MY MOM HAS A BOOK CALLED "THE SECRET MEANING OF FLOWERS."
IT SAYS MUMS MEAN HOPE.
MOM USED TO BRING ME MUMS ALL THE TIME.

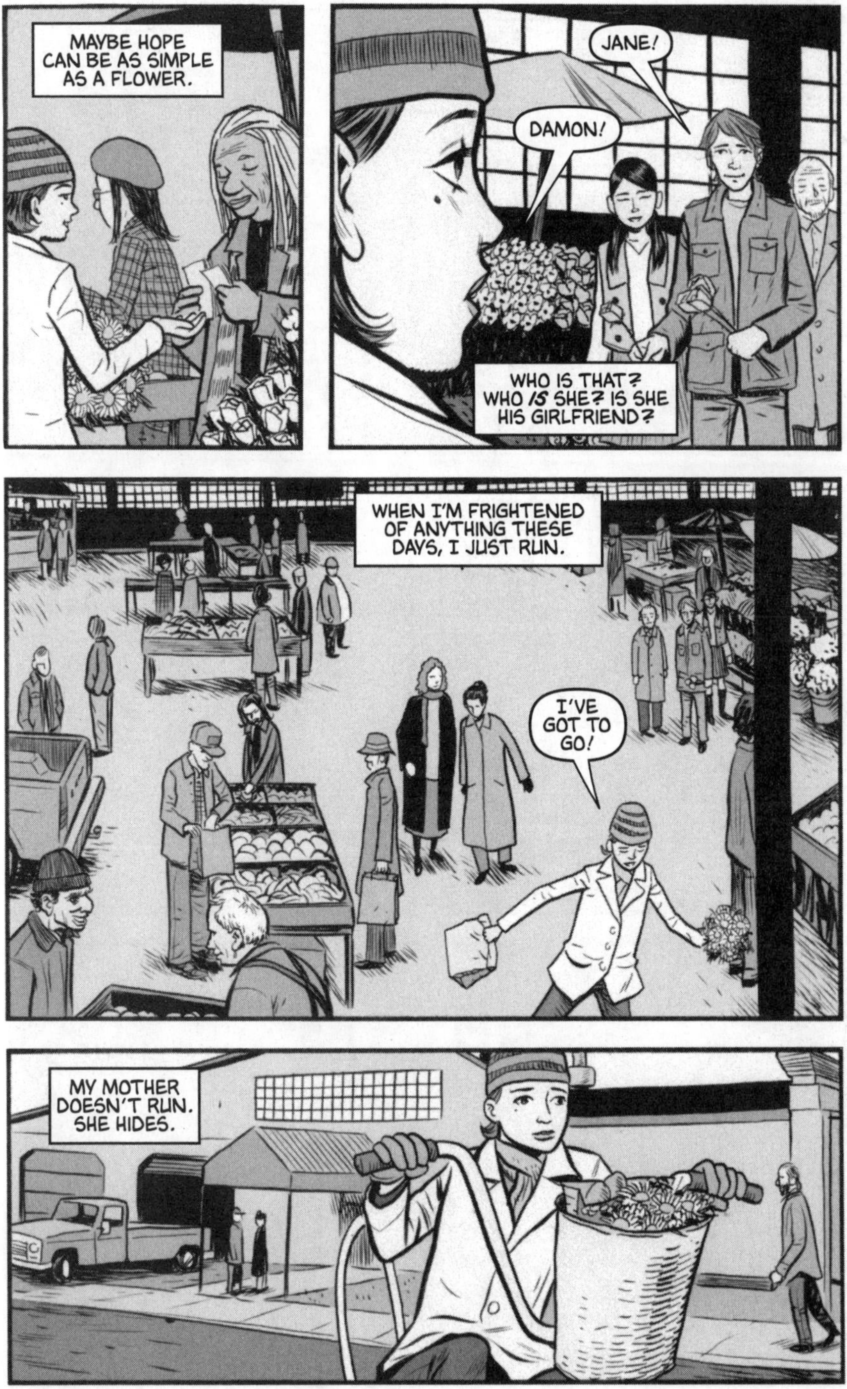
MAYBE HOPE CAN BE AS SIMPLE AS A FLOWER.
JANE!
DAMON!
WHO IS THAT? WHO *IS* SHE? IS SHE HIS GIRLFRIEND?
WHEN I'M FRIGHTENED OF ANYTHING THESE DAYS, I JUST RUN.
I'VE GOT TO GO!
MY MOTHER DOESN'T RUN. SHE HIDES.

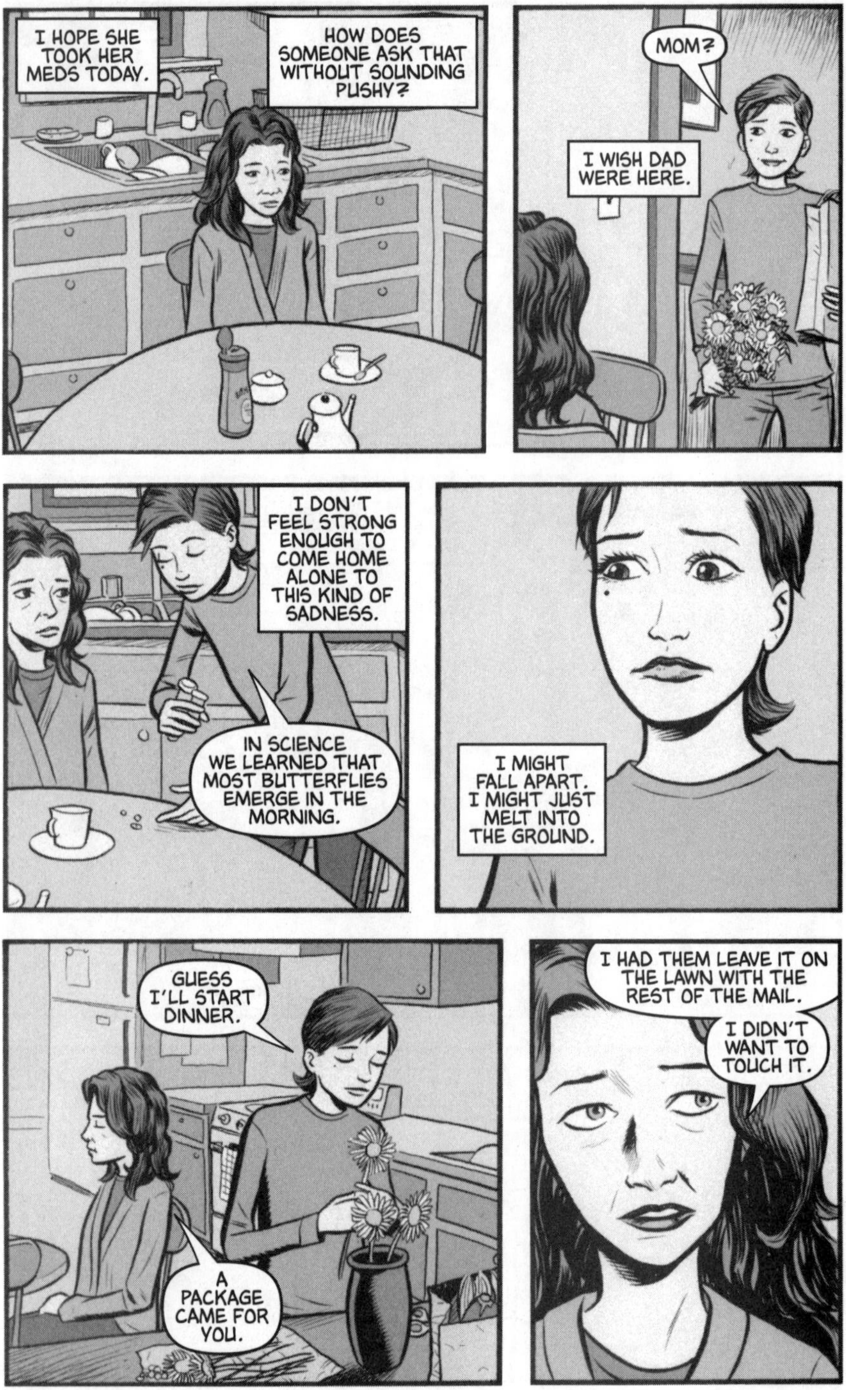
I HOPE SHE TOOK HER MEDS TODAY.
HOW DOES SOMEONE ASK THAT WITHOUT SOUNDING PUSHY?
MOM?
I WISH DAD WERE HERE.
I DON'T FEEL STRONG ENOUGH TO COME HOME ALONE TO THIS KIND OF SADNESS.
IN SCIENCE WE LEARNED THAT MOST BUTTERFLIES EMERGE IN THE MORNING.
I MIGHT FALL APART. I MIGHT JUST MELT INTO THE GROUND.
GUESS I'LL START DINNER.
A PACKAGE CAME FOR YOU.
I HAD THEM LEAVE IT ON THE LAWN WITH THE REST OF THE MAIL.
I DIDN'T WANT TO TOUCH IT.

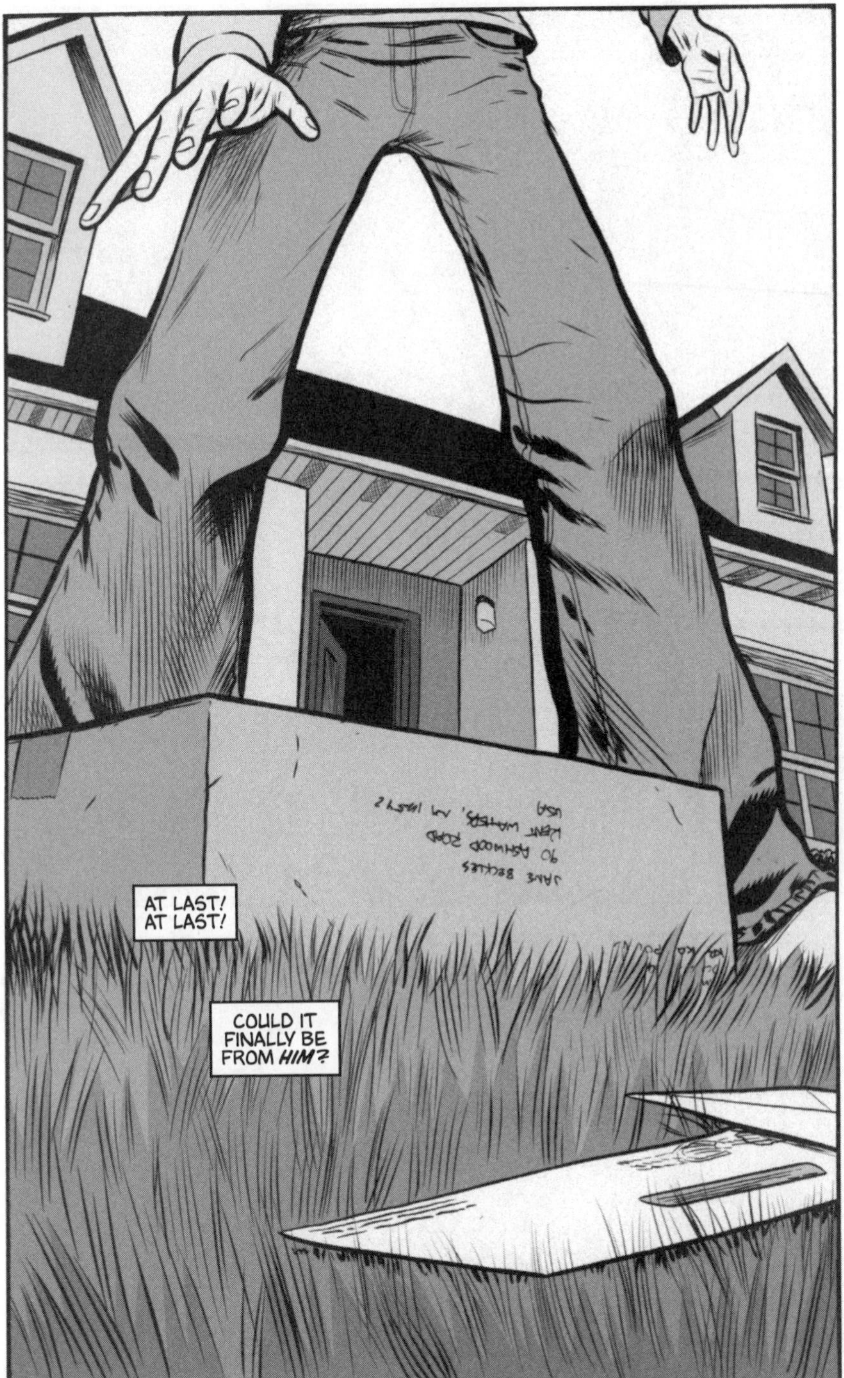
AT LAST!
AT LAST!
COULD IT FINALLY BE FROM *HIM*?

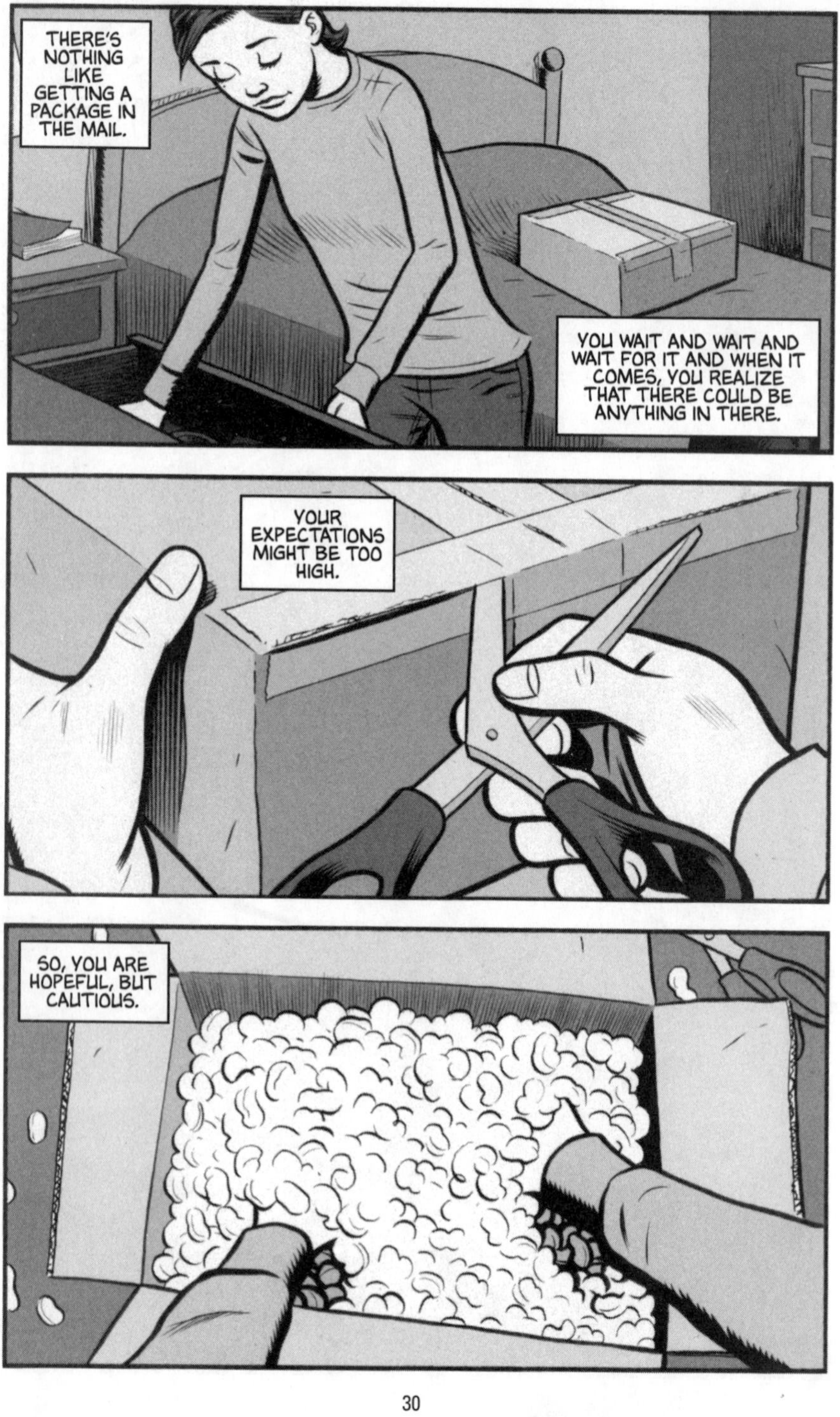

THERE'S NOTHING LIKE GETTING A PACKAGE IN THE MAIL.
YOU WAIT AND WAIT AND WAIT FOR IT AND WHEN IT COMES, YOU REALIZE THAT THERE COULD BE ANYTHING IN THERE.
YOUR EXPECTATIONS MIGHT BE TOO HIGH.
SO, YOU ARE HOPEFUL, BUT CAUTIOUS.

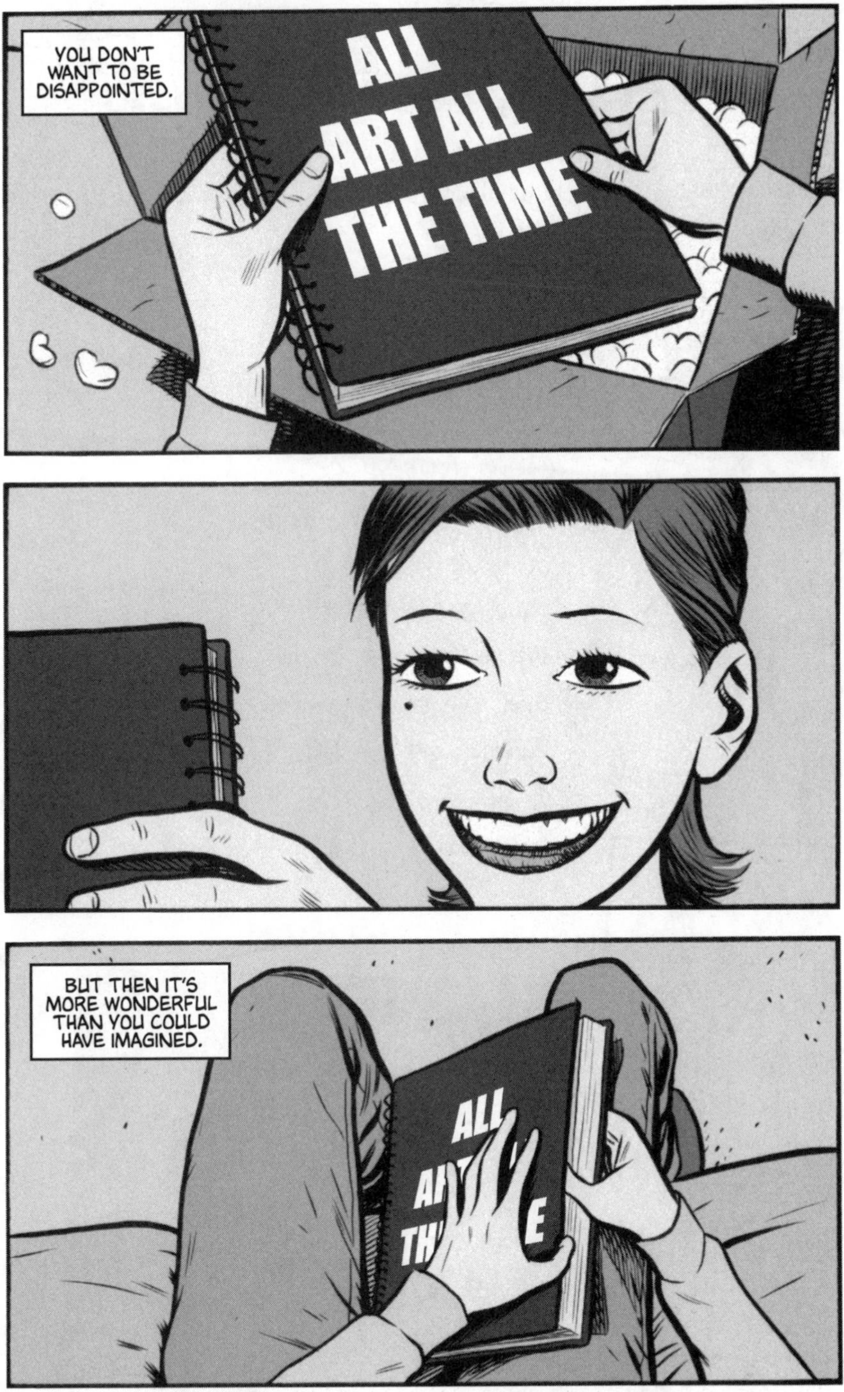
YOU DON'T WANT TO BE DISAPPOINTED.
ALL ART ALL THE TIME
BUT THEN IT'S MORE WONDERFUL THAN YOU COULD HAVE IMAGINED.

DEAR JANE

Hello. How wonderful to be able to say these words to you.
Hello, dear Jane. Light of my life.

Slow is the world
I have to take things
At a slower pace
Thoughts like molasses
Careful steps
Cautious
When I speak I slur
And the soup my mother feeds me
Dribbles out the left corner of my mouth.
I am safe now
Back again in the world of light

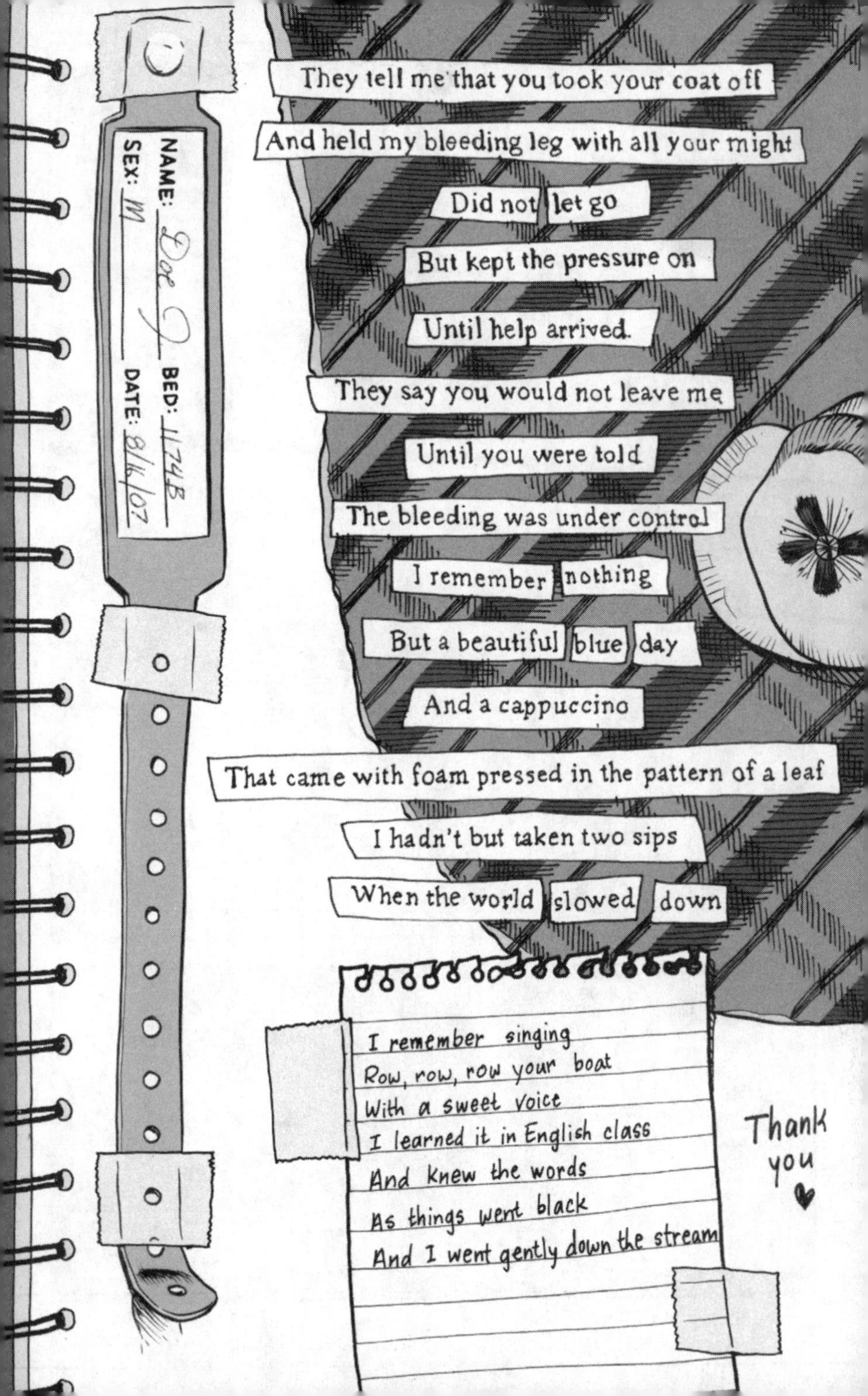
NAME: Doe J
SEX: M
BED: 1174B
DATE: 8/16/07
They tell me that you took your coat off
And held my bleeding leg with all your might
Did not let go
But kept the pressure on
Until help arrived.
They say you would not leave me
Until you were told
The bleeding was under control
I remember nothing
But a beautiful blue day
And a cappuccino
That came with foam pressed in the pattern of a leaf
I hadn't but taken two sips
When the world slowed down
I remember singing
Row, row, row your boat
With a sweet voice
I learned it in English class
And knew the words
As things went black
And I went gently down the stream
Thank you

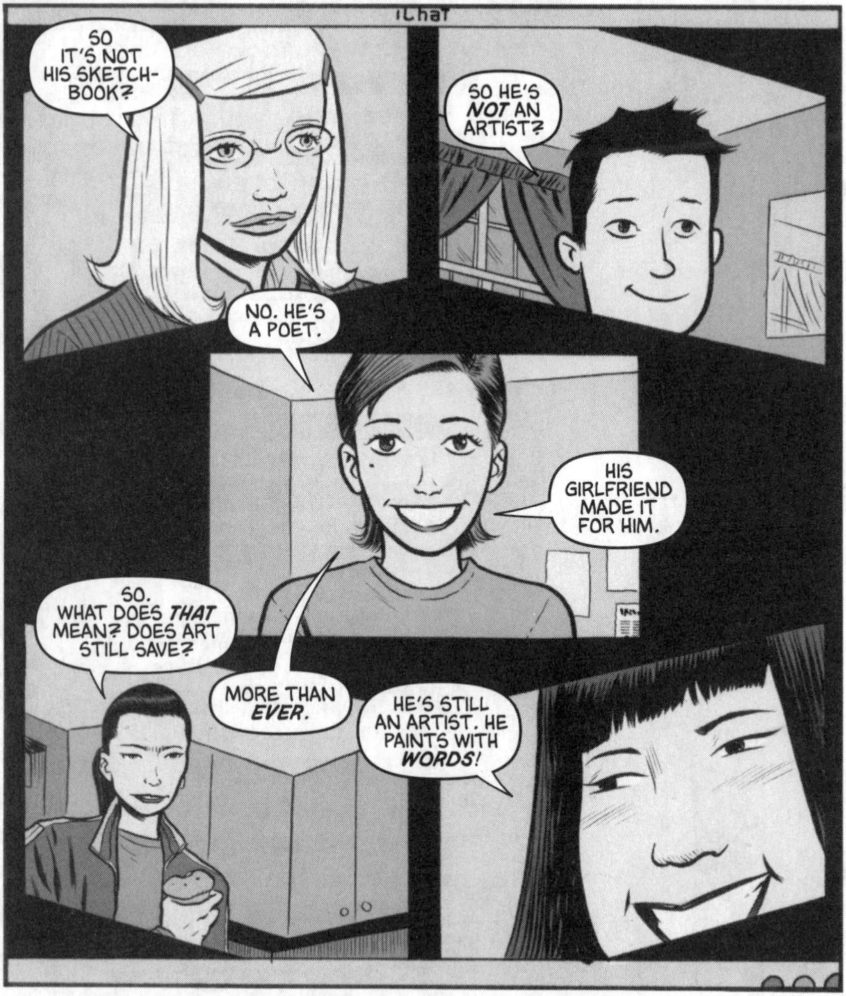
iChat
SO IT'S NOT HIS SKETCH-BOOK?
SO HE'S *NOT* AN ARTIST?
NO. HE'S A POET.
HIS GIRLFRIEND MADE IT FOR HIM.
SO. WHAT DOES *THAT* MEAN? DOES ART STILL SAVE?
MORE THAN *EVER*.
HE'S STILL AN ARTIST. HE PAINTS WITH *WORDS*!

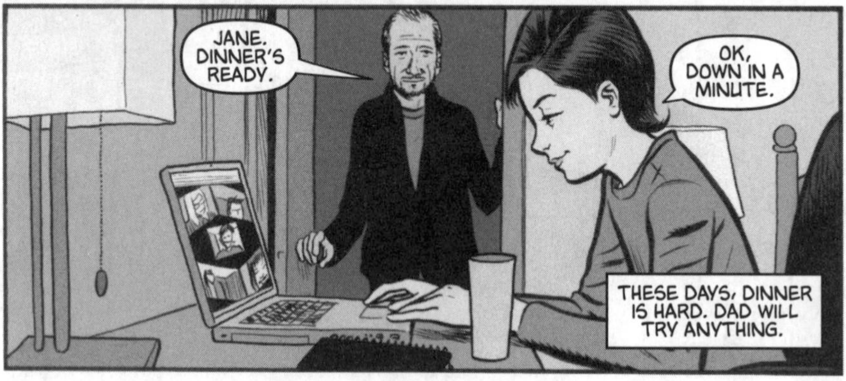
JANE. DINNER'S READY.
OK, DOWN IN A MINUTE.
THESE DAYS, DINNER IS HARD. DAD WILL TRY ANYTHING.

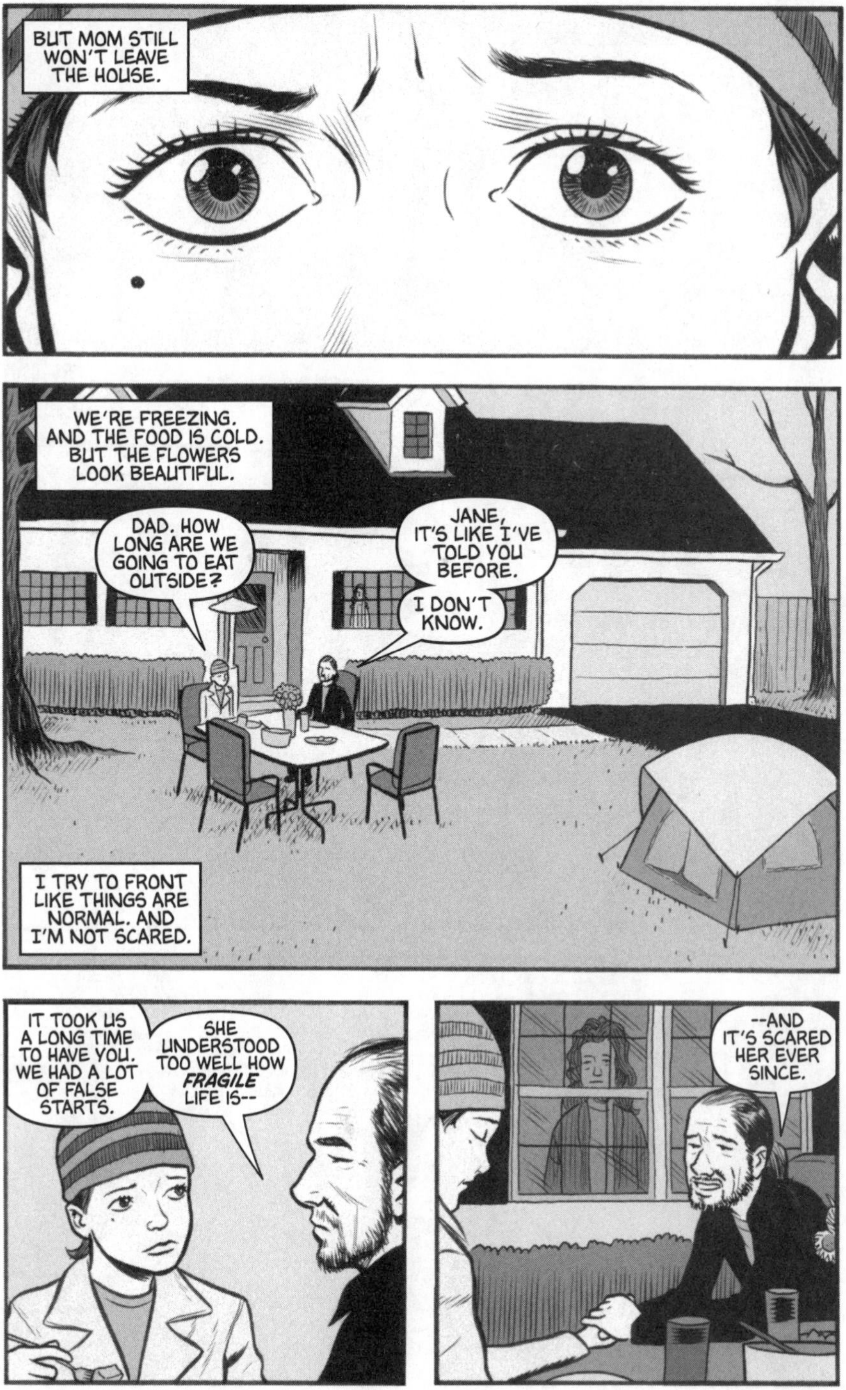
BUT MOM STILL WON'T LEAVE THE HOUSE.
WE'RE FREEZING. AND THE FOOD IS COLD. BUT THE FLOWERS LOOK BEAUTIFUL.
DAD. HOW LONG ARE WE GOING TO EAT OUTSIDE?
JANE, IT'S LIKE I'VE TOLD YOU BEFORE.
I DON'T KNOW.
I TRY TO FRONT LIKE THINGS ARE NORMAL. AND I'M NOT SCARED.
IT TOOK US A LONG TIME TO HAVE YOU. WE HAD A LOT OF FALSE STARTS.
SHE UNDERSTOOD TOO WELL HOW *FRAGILE* LIFE IS--
--AND IT'S SCARED HER EVER SINCE.

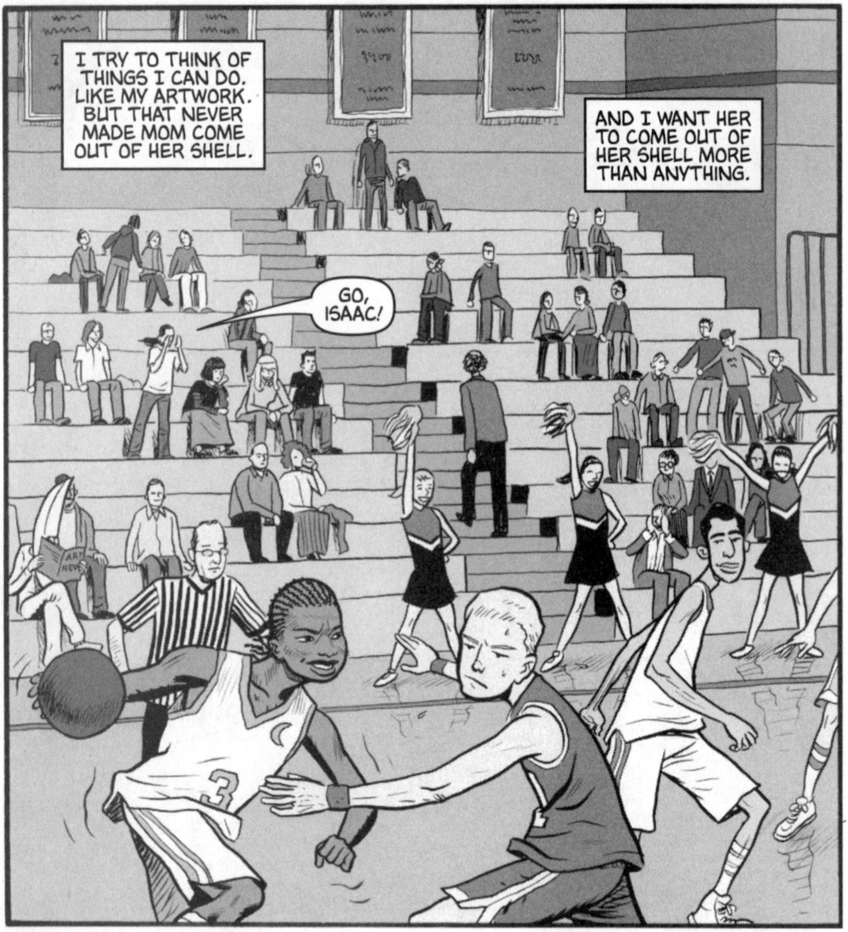
I TRY TO THINK OF THINGS I CAN DO. LIKE MY ARTWORK. BUT THAT NEVER MADE MOM COME OUT OF HER SHELL.
AND I WANT HER TO COME OUT OF HER SHELL MORE THAN ANYTHING.
GO, ISAAC!

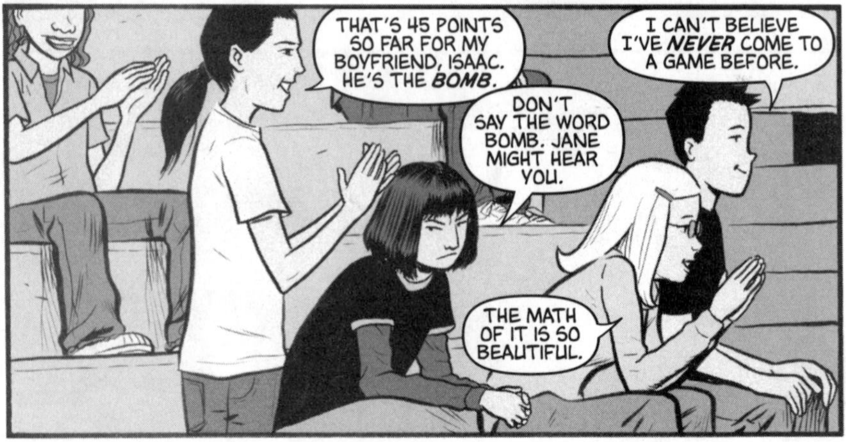
THAT'S 45 POINTS SO FAR FOR MY BOYFRIEND, ISAAC. HE'S THE ***BOMB***.
I CAN'T BELIEVE I'VE ***NEVER*** COME TO A GAME BEFORE.
DON'T SAY THE WORD BOMB. JANE MIGHT HEAR YOU.
THE MATH OF IT IS SO BEAUTIFUL.

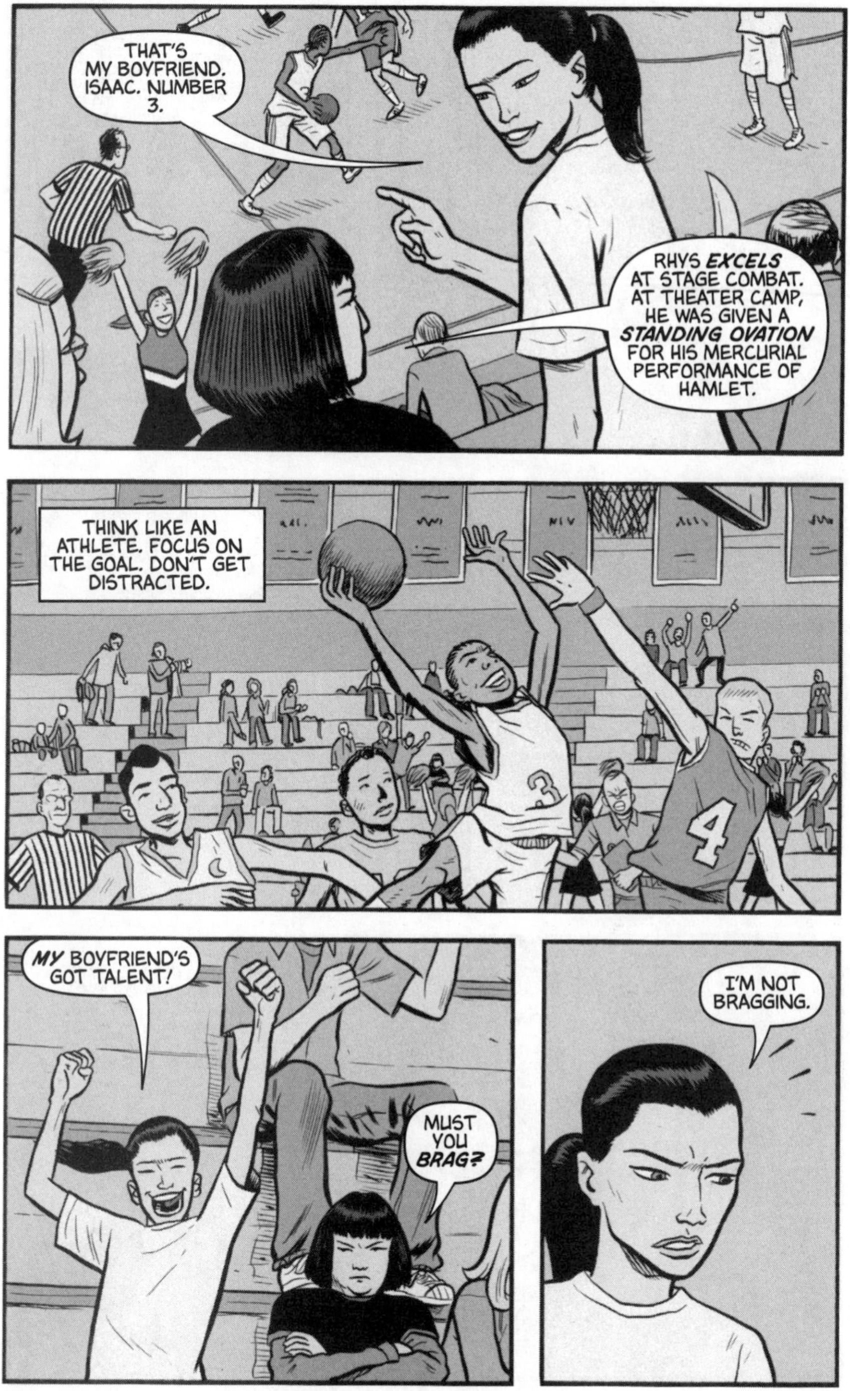
THAT'S MY BOYFRIEND. ISAAC. NUMBER 3.
RHYS **EXCELS** AT STAGE COMBAT. AT THEATER CAMP, HE WAS GIVEN A **STANDING OVATION** FOR HIS MERCURIAL PERFORMANCE OF HAMLET.
THINK LIKE AN ATHLETE. FOCUS ON THE GOAL. DON'T GET DISTRACTED.
3
4
MY BOYFRIEND'S GOT TALENT!
MUST YOU **BRAG?**
I'M NOT BRAGGING.

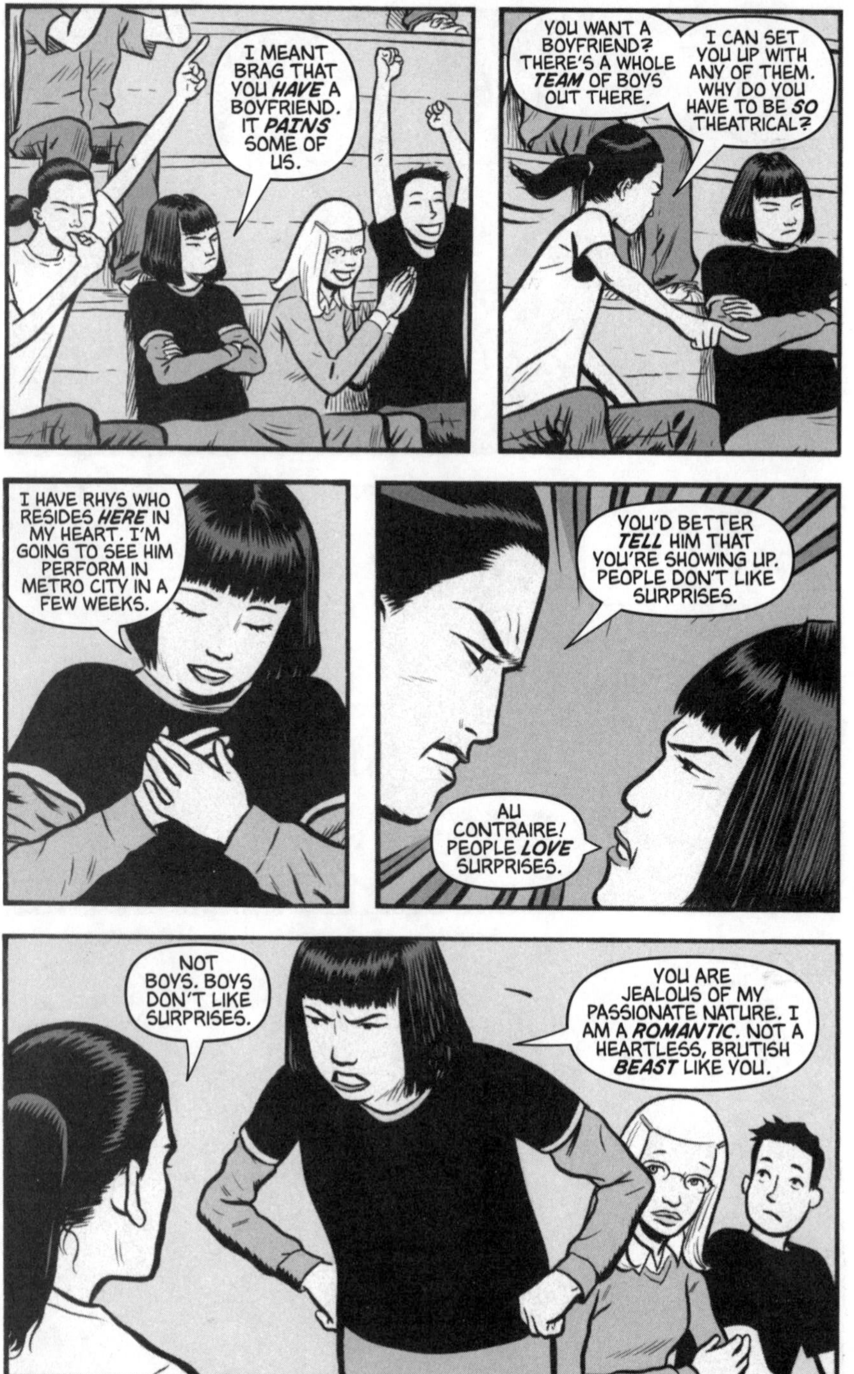
I MEANT BRAG THAT YOU HAVE A BOYFRIEND. IT PAINS SOME OF US.
YOU WANT A BOYFRIEND? THERE'S A WHOLE TEAM OF BOYS OUT THERE.
I CAN SET YOU UP WITH ANY OF THEM. WHY DO YOU HAVE TO BE SO THEATRICAL?
I HAVE RHYS WHO RESIDES HERE IN MY HEART. I'M GOING TO SEE HIM PERFORM IN METRO CITY IN A FEW WEEKS.
YOU'D BETTER TELL HIM THAT YOU'RE SHOWING UP. PEOPLE DON'T LIKE SURPRISES.
AU CONTRAIRE! PEOPLE LOVE SURPRISES.
NOT BOYS. BOYS DON'T LIKE SURPRISES.
YOU ARE JEALOUS OF MY PASSIONATE NATURE. I AM A ROMANTIC. NOT A HEARTLESS, BRUTISH BEAST LIKE YOU.

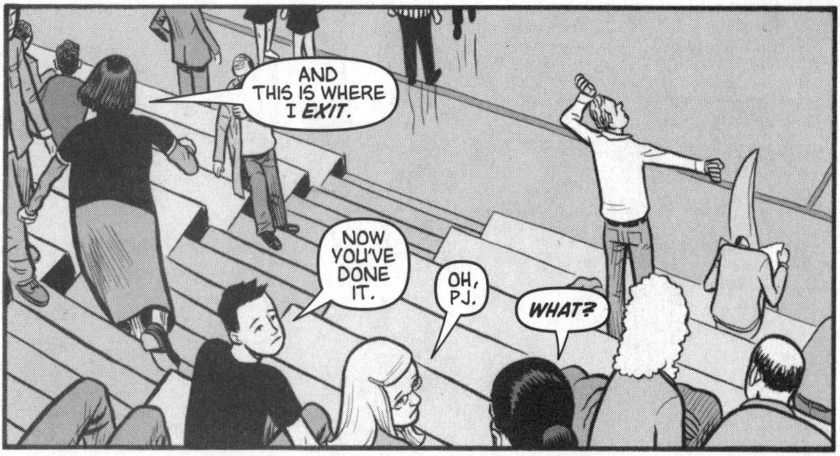
AND THIS IS WHERE I EXIT.
NOW YOU'VE DONE IT.
OH, PJ.
WHAT?

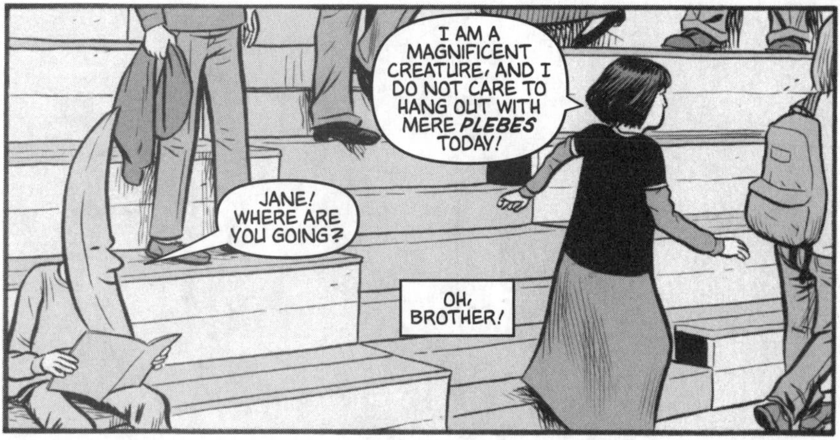
I AM A MAGNIFICENT CREATURE, AND I DO NOT CARE TO HANG OUT WITH MERE PLEBES TODAY!
JANE! WHERE ARE YOU GOING?
OH, BROTHER!

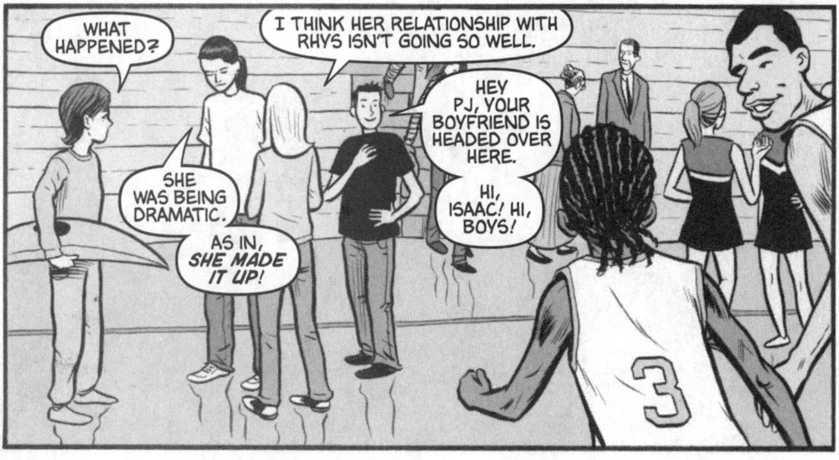
WHAT HAPPENED?
I THINK HER RELATIONSHIP WITH RHYS ISN'T GOING SO WELL.
SHE WAS BEING DRAMATIC.
AS IN, SHE MADE IT UP!
HEY PJ, YOUR BOYFRIEND IS HEADED OVER HERE.
HI, ISAAC! HI, BOYS!
3

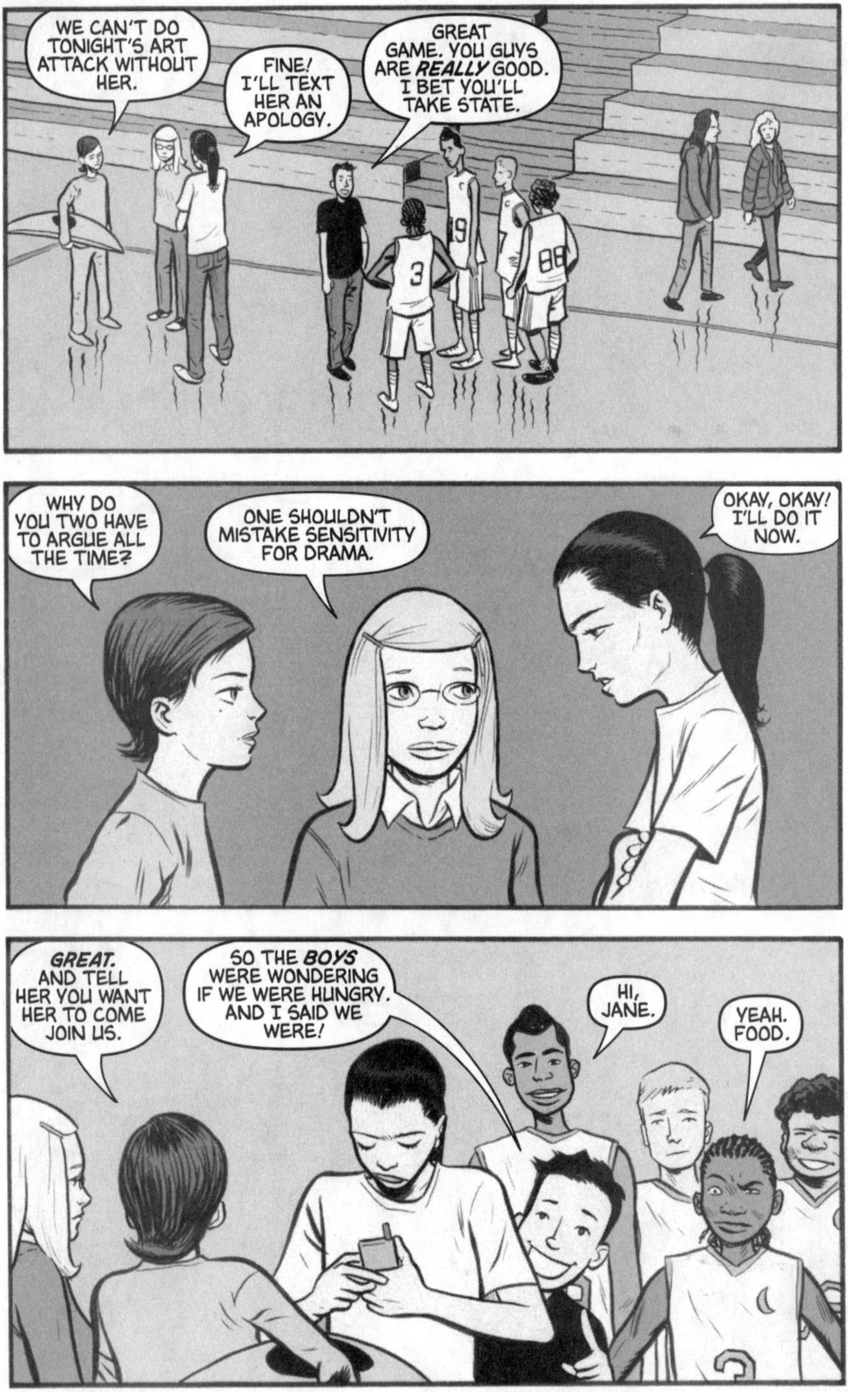
WE CAN'T DO TONIGHT'S ART ATTACK WITHOUT HER.
FINE! I'LL TEXT HER AN APOLOGY.
GREAT GAME. YOU GUYS ARE *REALLY* GOOD. I BET YOU'LL TAKE STATE.
WHY DO YOU TWO HAVE TO ARGUE ALL THE TIME?
ONE SHOULDN'T MISTAKE SENSITIVITY FOR DRAMA.
OKAY, OKAY! I'LL DO IT NOW.
GREAT. AND TELL HER YOU WANT HER TO COME JOIN US.
SO THE *BOYS* WERE WONDERING IF WE WERE HUNGRY. AND I SAID WE WERE!
HI, JANE.
YEAH. FOOD.

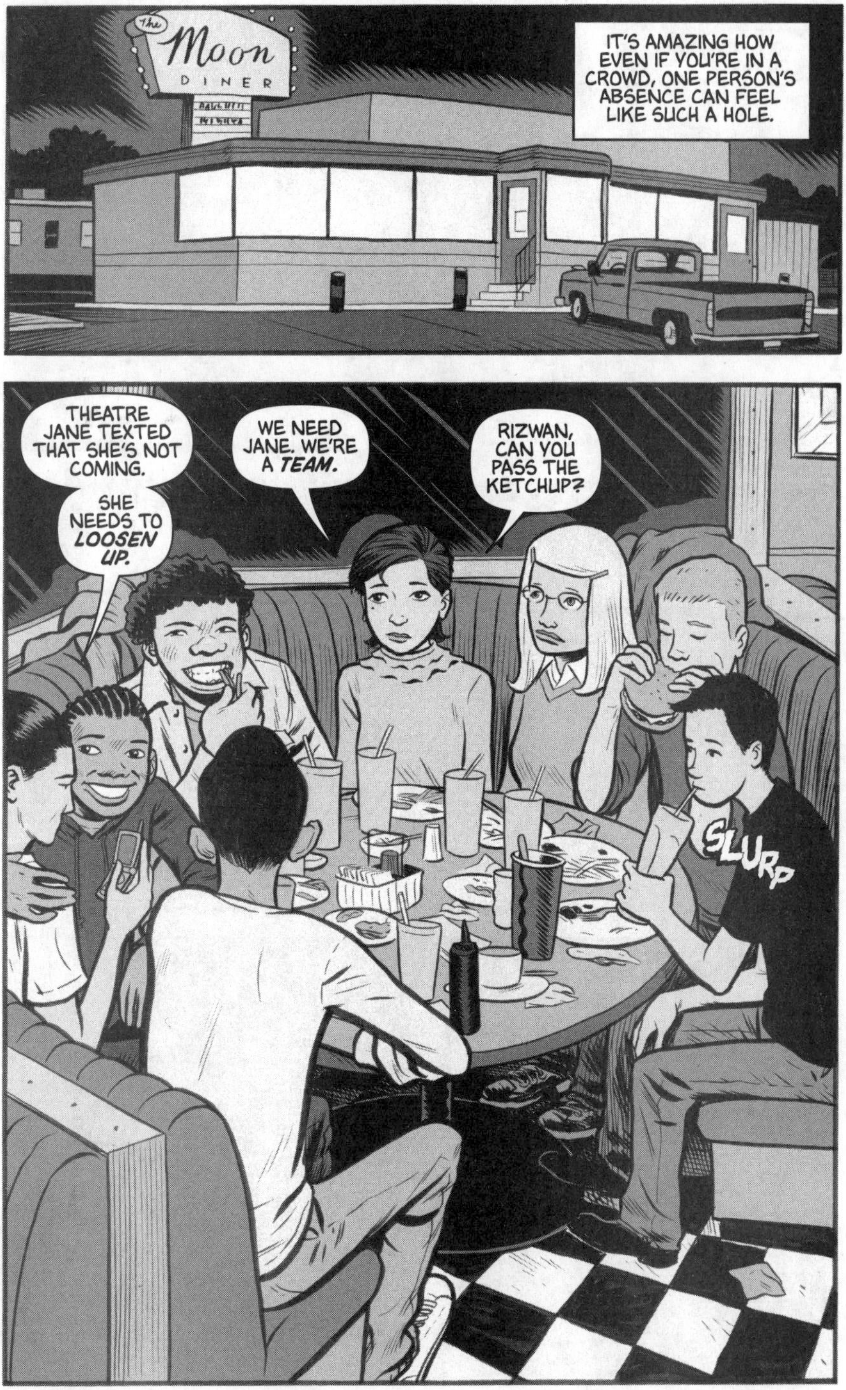
The Moon DINER
IT'S AMAZING HOW EVEN IF YOU'RE IN A CROWD, ONE PERSON'S ABSENCE CAN FEEL LIKE SUCH A HOLE.
THEATRE JANE TEXTED THAT SHE'S NOT COMING.
SHE NEEDS TO LOOSEN UP.
WE NEED JANE. WE'RE A TEAM.
RIZWAN, CAN YOU PASS THE KETCHUP?
SLURP

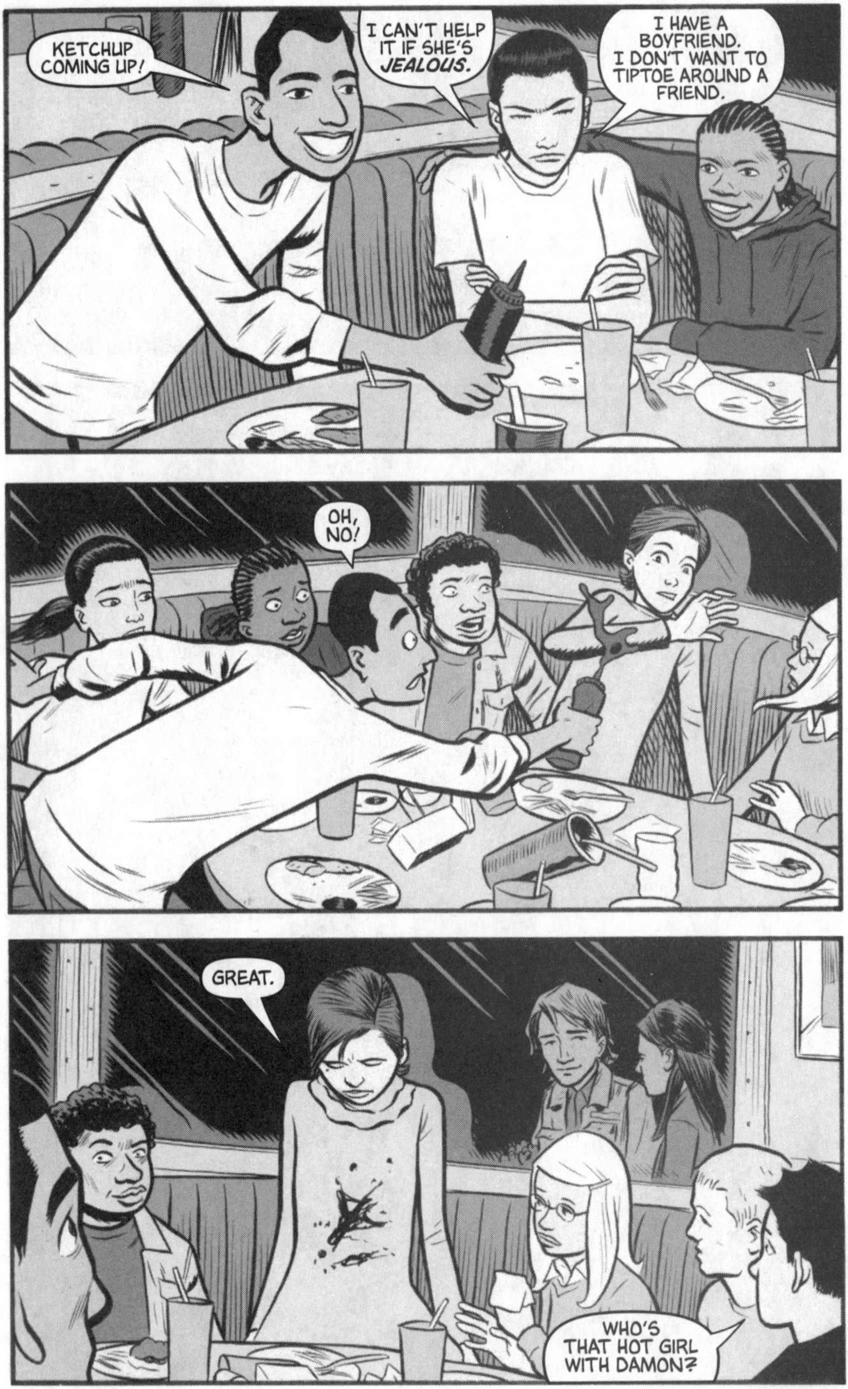
KETCHUP COMING UP!
I CAN'T HELP IT IF SHE'S *JEALOUS.*
I HAVE A BOYFRIEND. I DON'T WANT TO TIPTOE AROUND A FRIEND.
OH, NO!
GREAT.
WHO'S THAT HOT GIRL WITH DAMON?

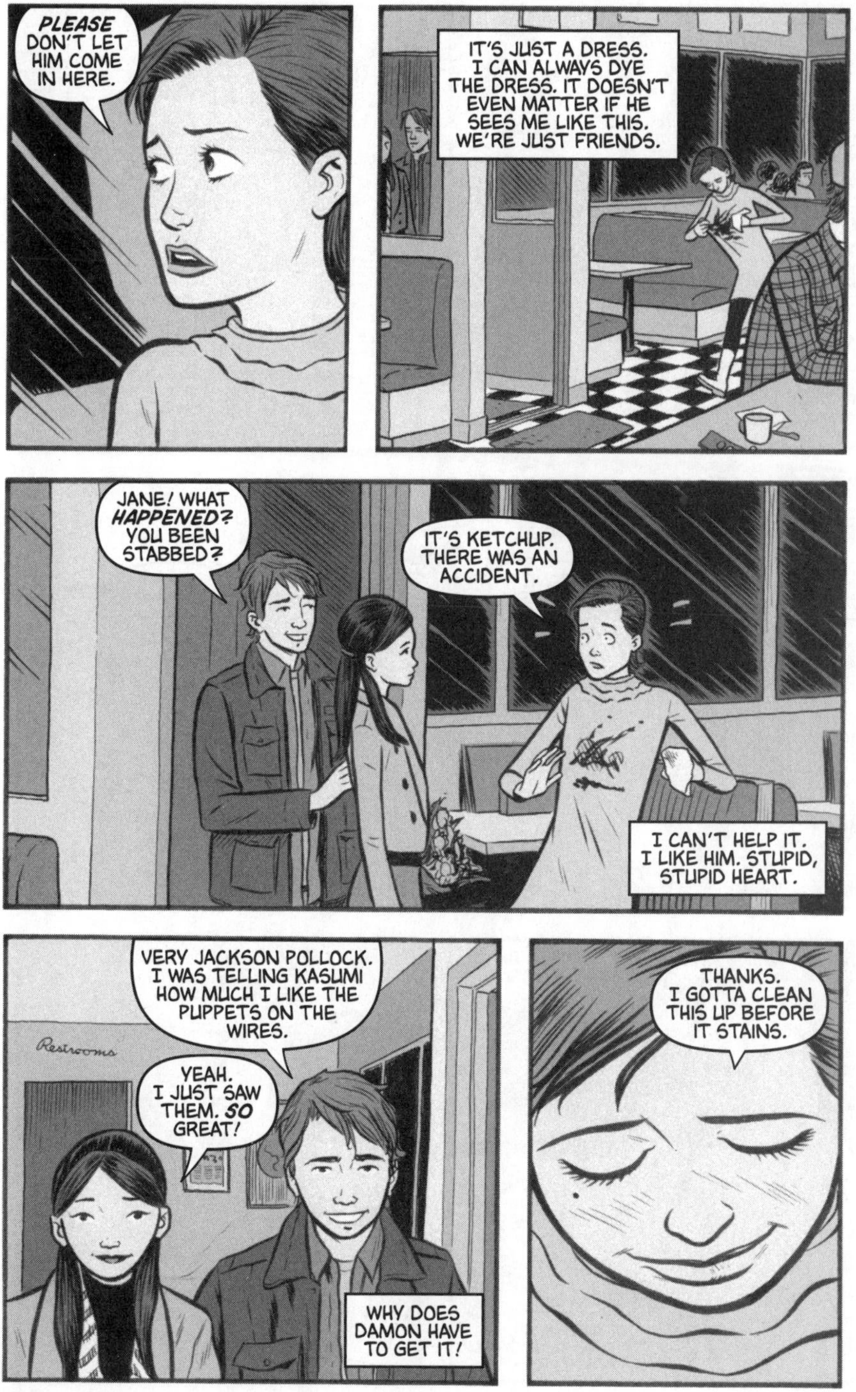
PLEASE DON'T LET HIM COME IN HERE.
IT'S JUST A DRESS. I CAN ALWAYS DYE THE DRESS. IT DOESN'T EVEN MATTER IF HE SEES ME LIKE THIS. WE'RE JUST FRIENDS.
JANE! WHAT HAPPENED? YOU BEEN STABBED?
IT'S KETCHUP. THERE WAS AN ACCIDENT.
I CAN'T HELP IT. I LIKE HIM. STUPID, STUPID HEART.
VERY JACKSON POLLOCK. I WAS TELLING KASUMI HOW MUCH I LIKE THE PUPPETS ON THE WIRES.
Restrooms
YEAH. I JUST SAW THEM. SO GREAT!
WHY DOES DAMON HAVE TO GET IT!
THANKS. I GOTTA CLEAN THIS UP BEFORE IT STAINS.

SMOOTH, JANE. REAL *SMOOTH*.

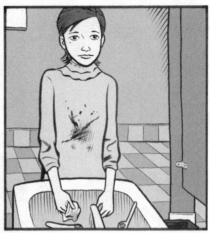

RIZWAN SAYS YOU MAKE HIM NERVOUS.

FOR SOMEONE WHO IS SO GRACEFUL ON THE BASKETBALL COURT, HE SURE IS A *KLUTZ* IN REAL LIFE.

YOU WANT ME TO SET YOU UP? HE'S *REALLY* NICE.

NO, THANKS.

STILL STUCK ON DAMON? I DON'T BLAME YOU.

IT DOESN'T MATTER. HE *OBVIOUSLY* HAS A GIRLFRIEND.

I'M SORRY ABOUT THEATER JANE. IT'LL BE OK TONIGHT. WE COOL?

YEAH. WE'RE GOOD.

44

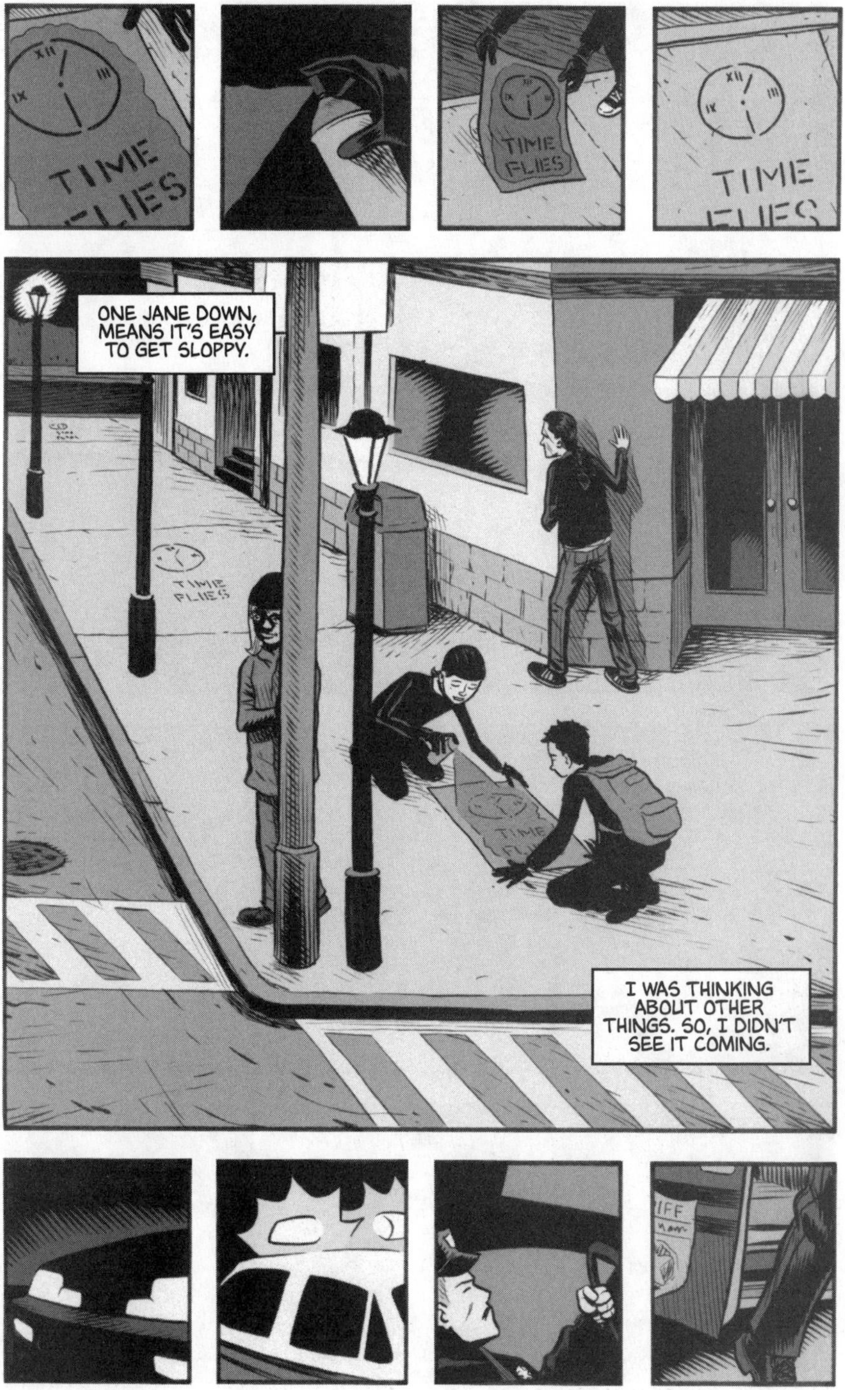
TIME FLIES
TIME FLIES
TIME FLIES
ONE JANE DOWN, MEANS IT'S EASY TO GET SLOPPY.
TIME FLIES
I WAS THINKING ABOUT OTHER THINGS. SO, I DIDN'T SEE IT COMING.

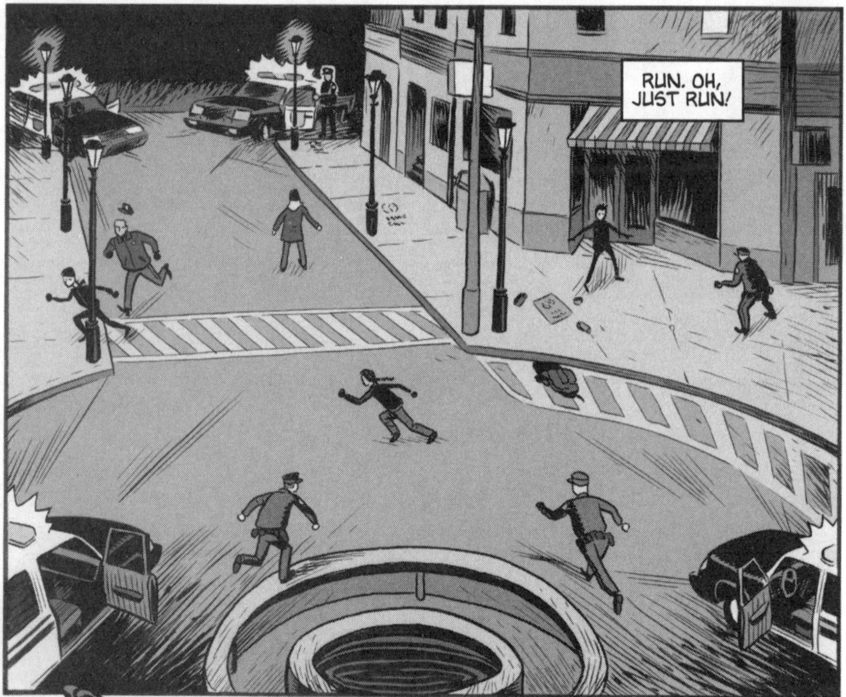
RUN. OH, JUST RUN!

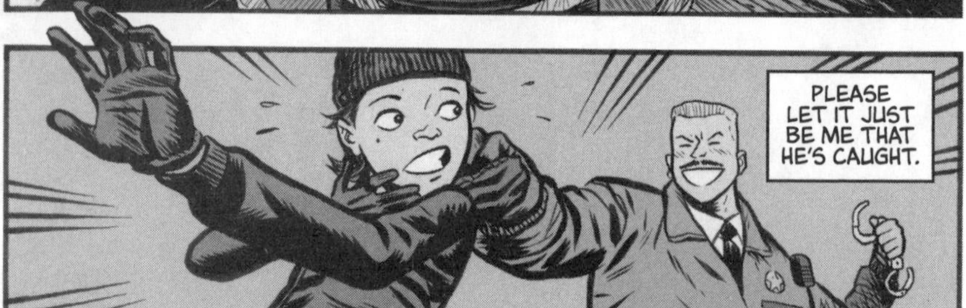
PLEASE LET IT JUST BE ME THAT HE'S CAUGHT.

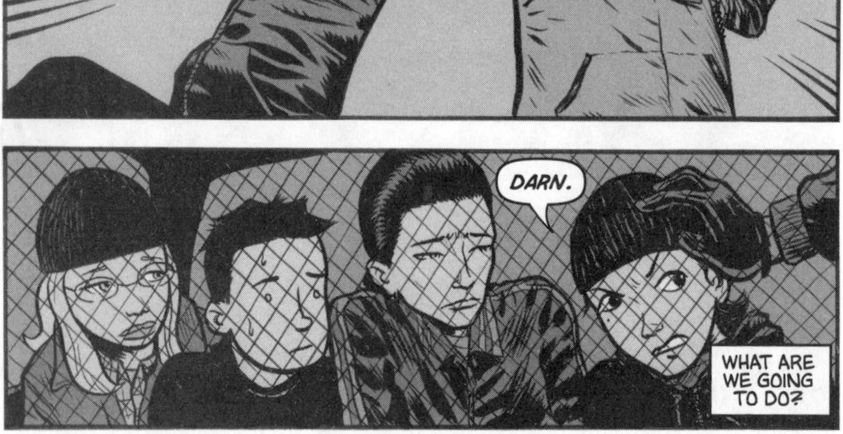
DARN.
WHAT ARE WE GOING TO DO?

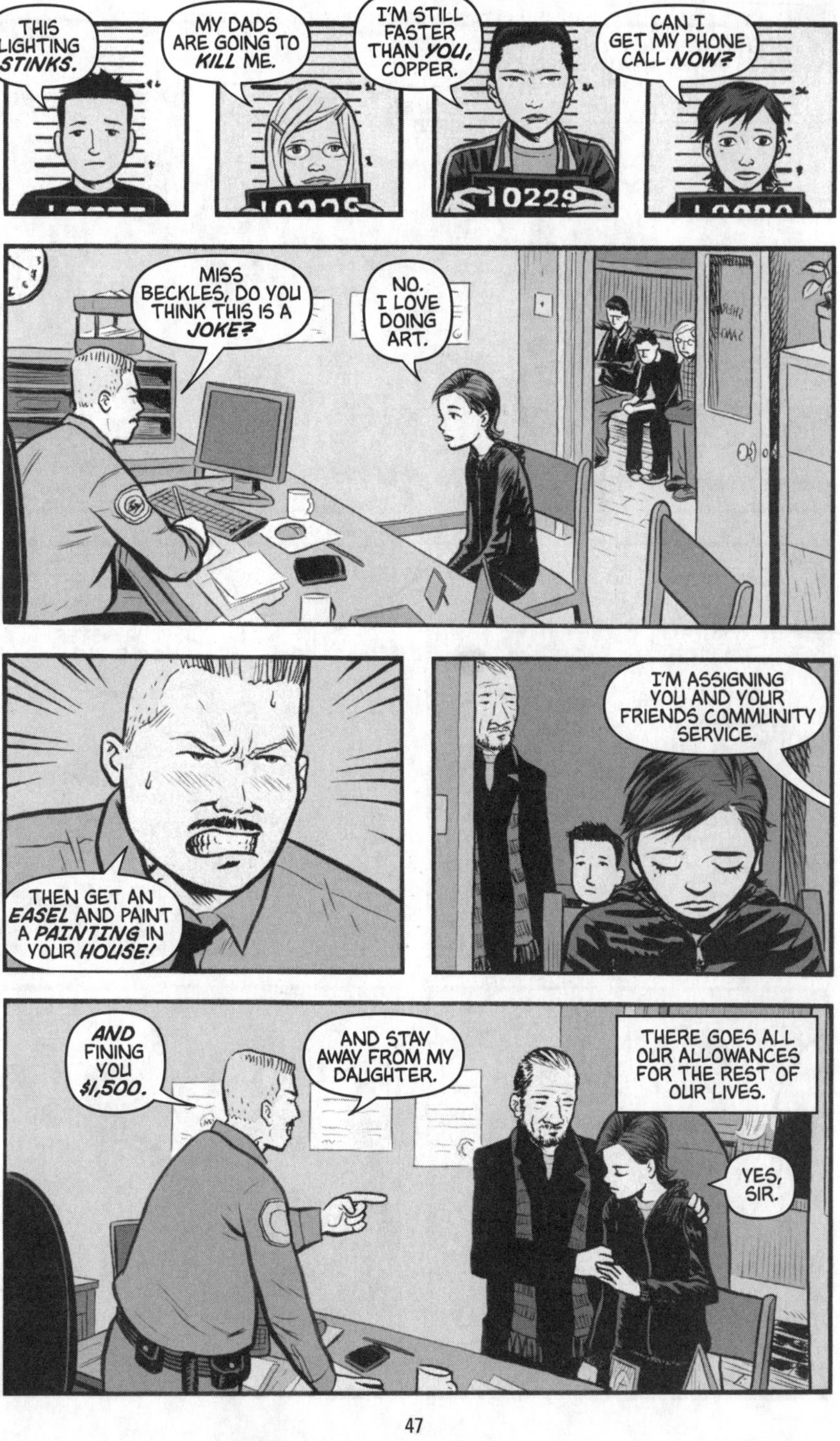

THIS LIGHTING STINKS.
MY DADS ARE GOING TO KILL ME.
I'M STILL FASTER THAN YOU, COPPER.
10229
CAN I GET MY PHONE CALL NOW?
MISS BECKLES, DO YOU THINK THIS IS A JOKE?
NO. I LOVE DOING ART.
THEN GET AN EASEL AND PAINT A PAINTING IN YOUR HOUSE!
I'M ASSIGNING YOU AND YOUR FRIENDS COMMUNITY SERVICE.
AND FINING YOU $1,500.
AND STAY AWAY FROM MY DAUGHTER.
THERE GOES ALL OUR ALLOWANCES FOR THE REST OF OUR LIVES.
YES, SIR.

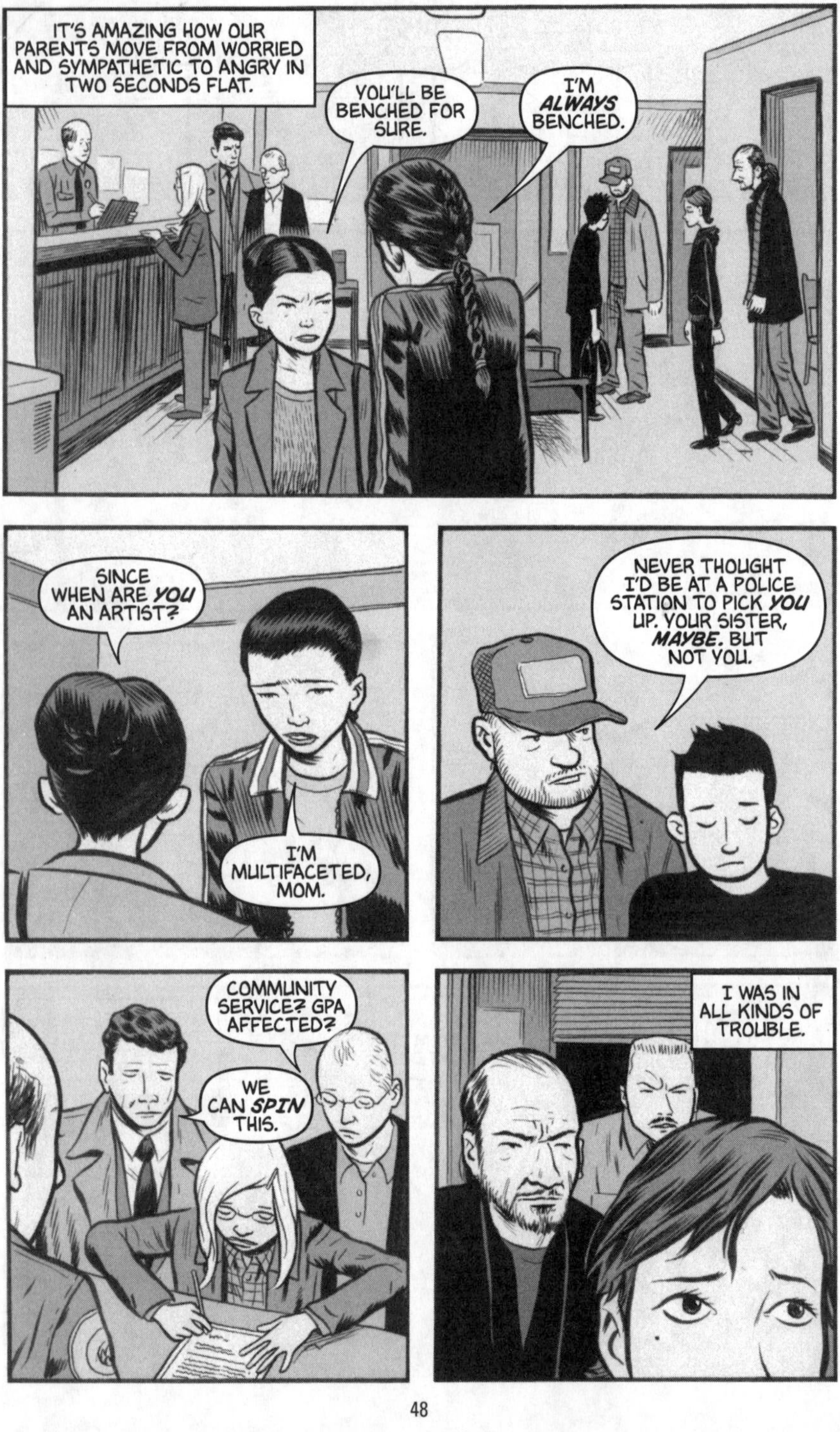
IT'S AMAZING HOW OUR PARENTS MOVE FROM WORRIED AND SYMPATHETIC TO ANGRY IN TWO SECONDS FLAT.
YOU'LL BE BENCHED FOR SURE.
I'M *ALWAYS* BENCHED.
SINCE WHEN ARE *YOU* AN ARTIST?
I'M MULTIFACETED, MOM.
NEVER THOUGHT I'D BE AT A POLICE STATION TO PICK *YOU* UP. YOUR SISTER, *MAYBE*. BUT NOT YOU.
COMMUNITY SERVICE? GPA AFFECTED?
WE CAN *SPIN* THIS.
I WAS IN ALL KINDS OF TROUBLE.

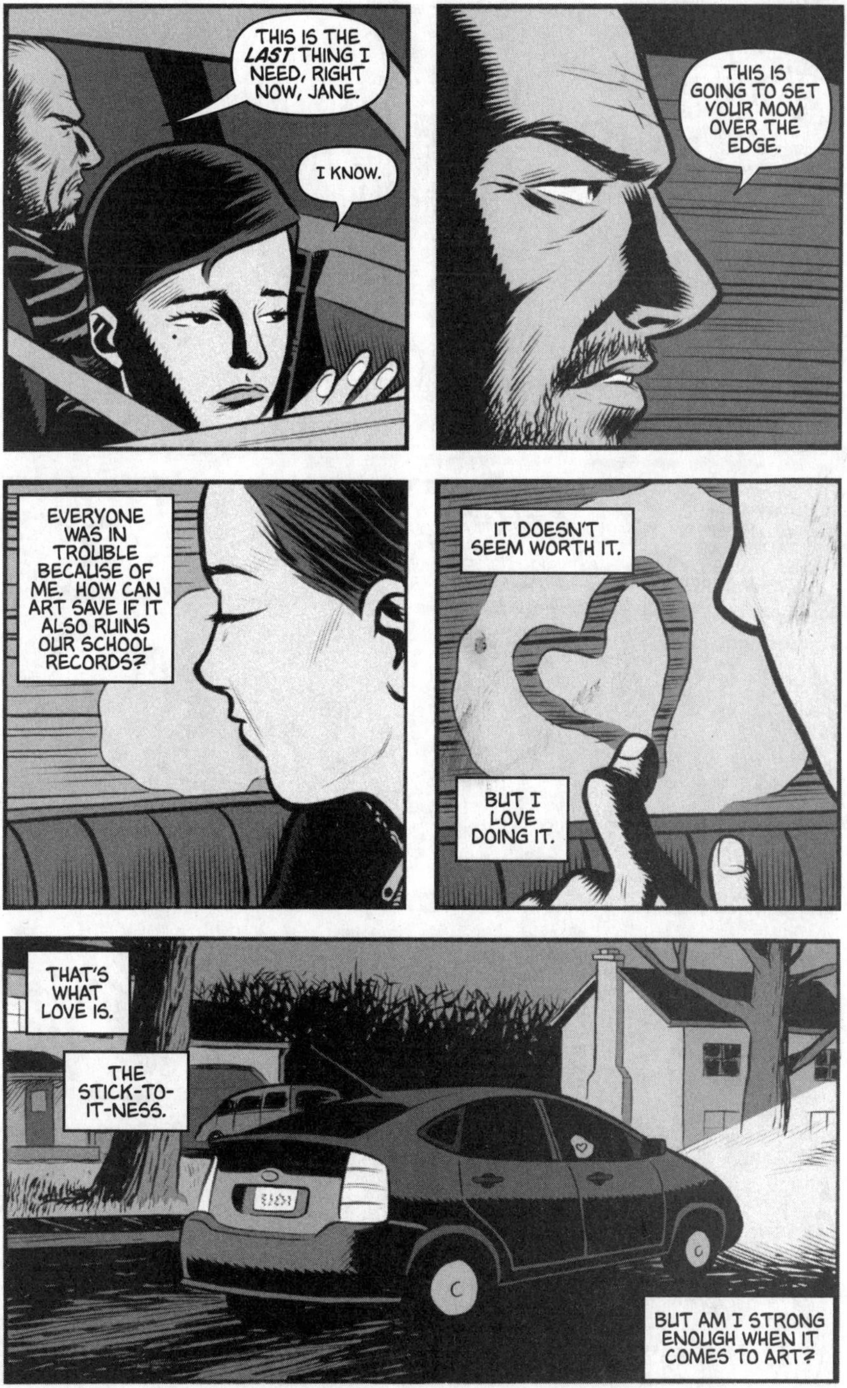
THIS IS THE *LAST* THING I NEED, RIGHT NOW, JANE.
I KNOW.
THIS IS GOING TO SET YOUR MOM OVER THE EDGE.
EVERYONE WAS IN TROUBLE BECAUSE OF ME. HOW CAN ART SAVE IF IT ALSO RUINS OUR SCHOOL RECORDS?
IT DOESN'T SEEM WORTH IT.
BUT I LOVE DOING IT.
THAT'S WHAT LOVE IS.
THE STICK-TO-IT-NESS.
BUT AM I STRONG ENOUGH WHEN IT COMES TO ART?

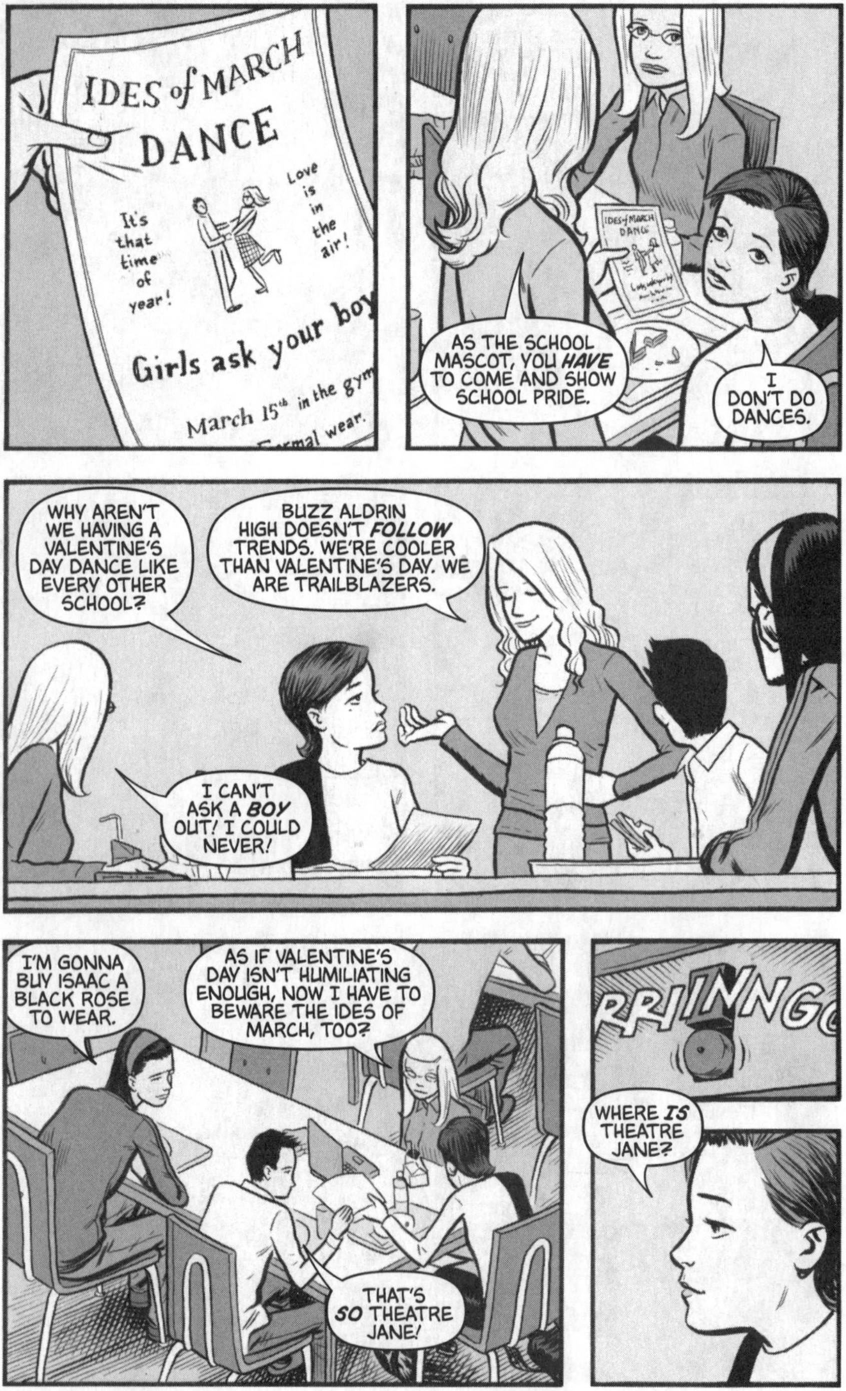
IDES of MARCH
DANCE
It's that time of year!
Love is in the air!
Girls ask your boy
March 15th in the gym
Formal wear.
AS THE SCHOOL MASCOT, YOU HAVE TO COME AND SHOW SCHOOL PRIDE.
I DON'T DO DANCES.
WHY AREN'T WE HAVING A VALENTINE'S DAY DANCE LIKE EVERY OTHER SCHOOL?
BUZZ ALDRIN HIGH DOESN'T FOLLOW TRENDS. WE'RE COOLER THAN VALENTINE'S DAY. WE ARE TRAILBLAZERS.
I CAN'T ASK A BOY OUT! I COULD NEVER!
I'M GONNA BUY ISAAC A BLACK ROSE TO WEAR.
AS IF VALENTINE'S DAY ISN'T HUMILIATING ENOUGH, NOW I HAVE TO BEWARE THE IDES OF MARCH, TOO?
THAT'S SO THEATRE JANE!
RRIINNG
WHERE IS THEATRE JANE?

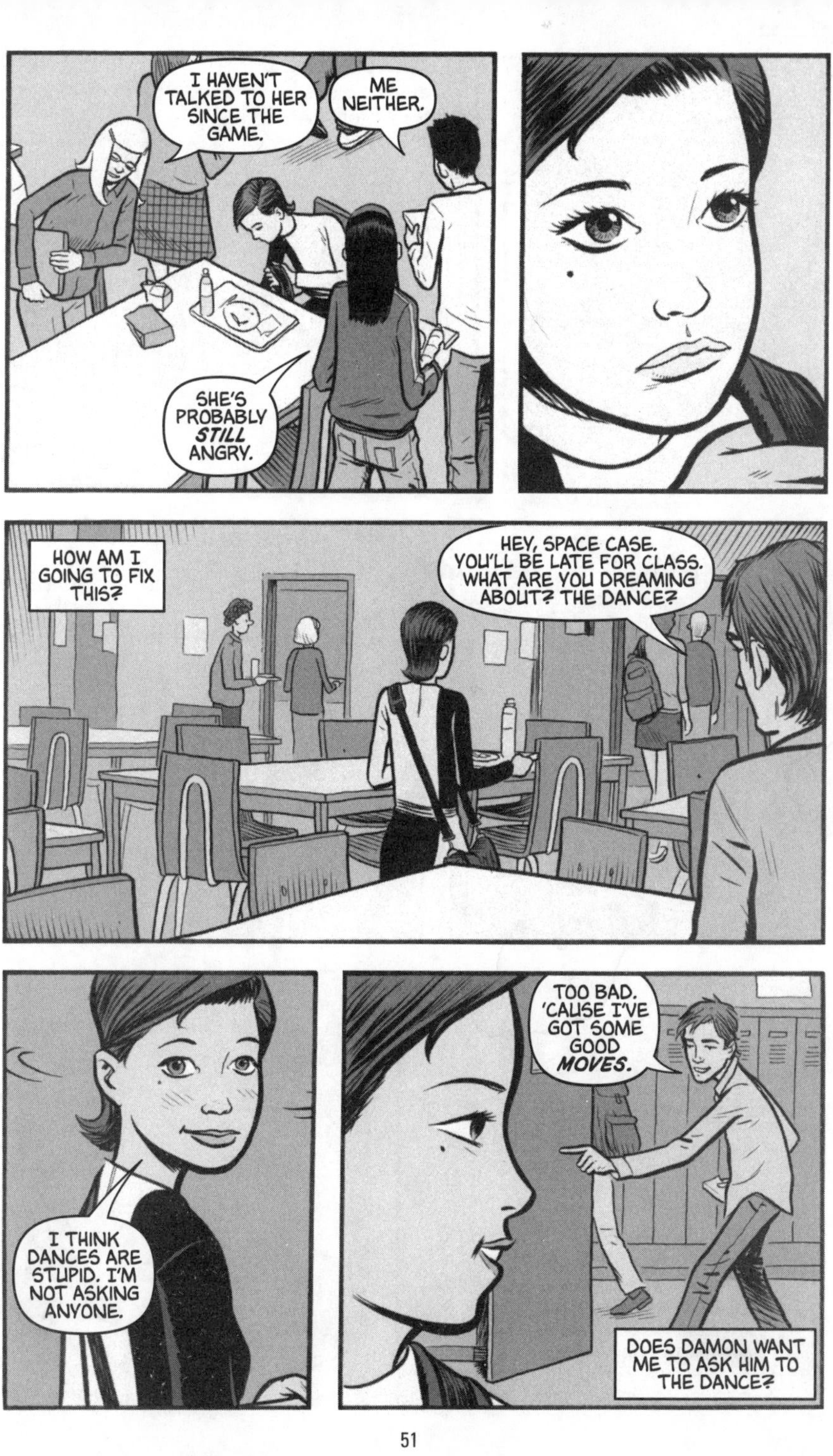
I HAVEN'T TALKED TO HER SINCE THE GAME.
ME NEITHER.
SHE'S PROBABLY *STILL* ANGRY.
HOW AM I GOING TO FIX THIS?
HEY, SPACE CASE. YOU'LL BE LATE FOR CLASS. WHAT ARE YOU DREAMING ABOUT? THE DANCE?
I THINK DANCES ARE STUPID. I'M NOT ASKING ANYONE.
TOO BAD. 'CAUSE I'VE GOT SOME GOOD *MOVES.*
DOES DAMON WANT ME TO ASK HIM TO THE DANCE?

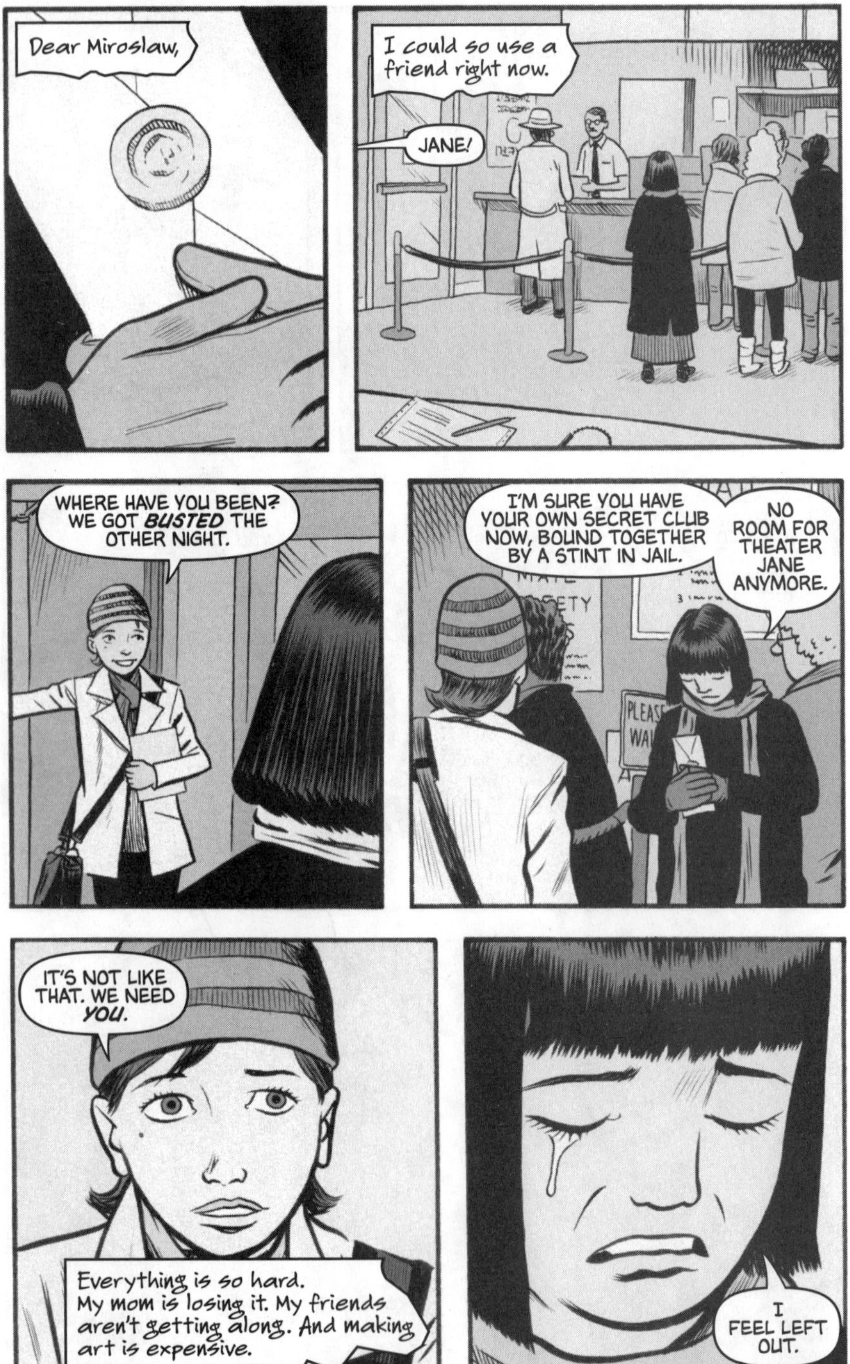
Dear Miroslaw,
I could so use a friend right now.
JANE!
WHERE HAVE YOU BEEN? WE GOT BUSTED THE OTHER NIGHT.
I'M SURE YOU HAVE YOUR OWN SECRET CLUB NOW, BOUND TOGETHER BY A STINT IN JAIL.
NO ROOM FOR THEATER JANE ANYMORE.
IT'S NOT LIKE THAT. WE NEED YOU.
Everything is so hard. My mom is losing it. My friends aren't getting along. And making art is expensive.
I FEEL LEFT OUT.

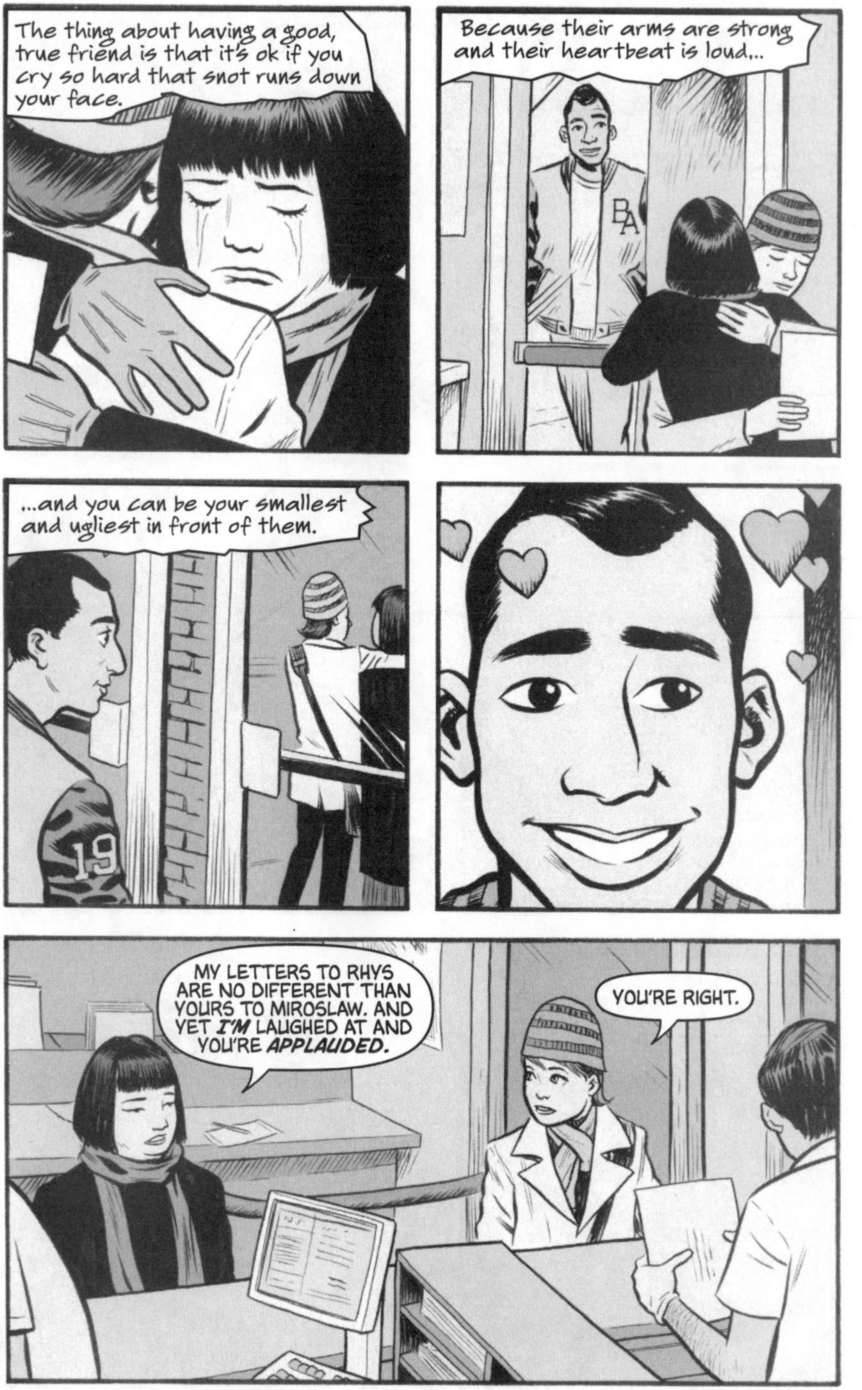
The thing about having a good, true friend is that it's ok if you cry so hard that snot runs down your face.
Because their arms are strong and their heartbeat is loud...
BA
...and you can be your smallest and ugliest in front of them.
19
MY LETTERS TO RHYS ARE NO DIFFERENT THAN YOURS TO MIROSLAW. AND YET *I'M* LAUGHED AT AND YOU'RE ***APPLAUDED***.
YOU'RE RIGHT.

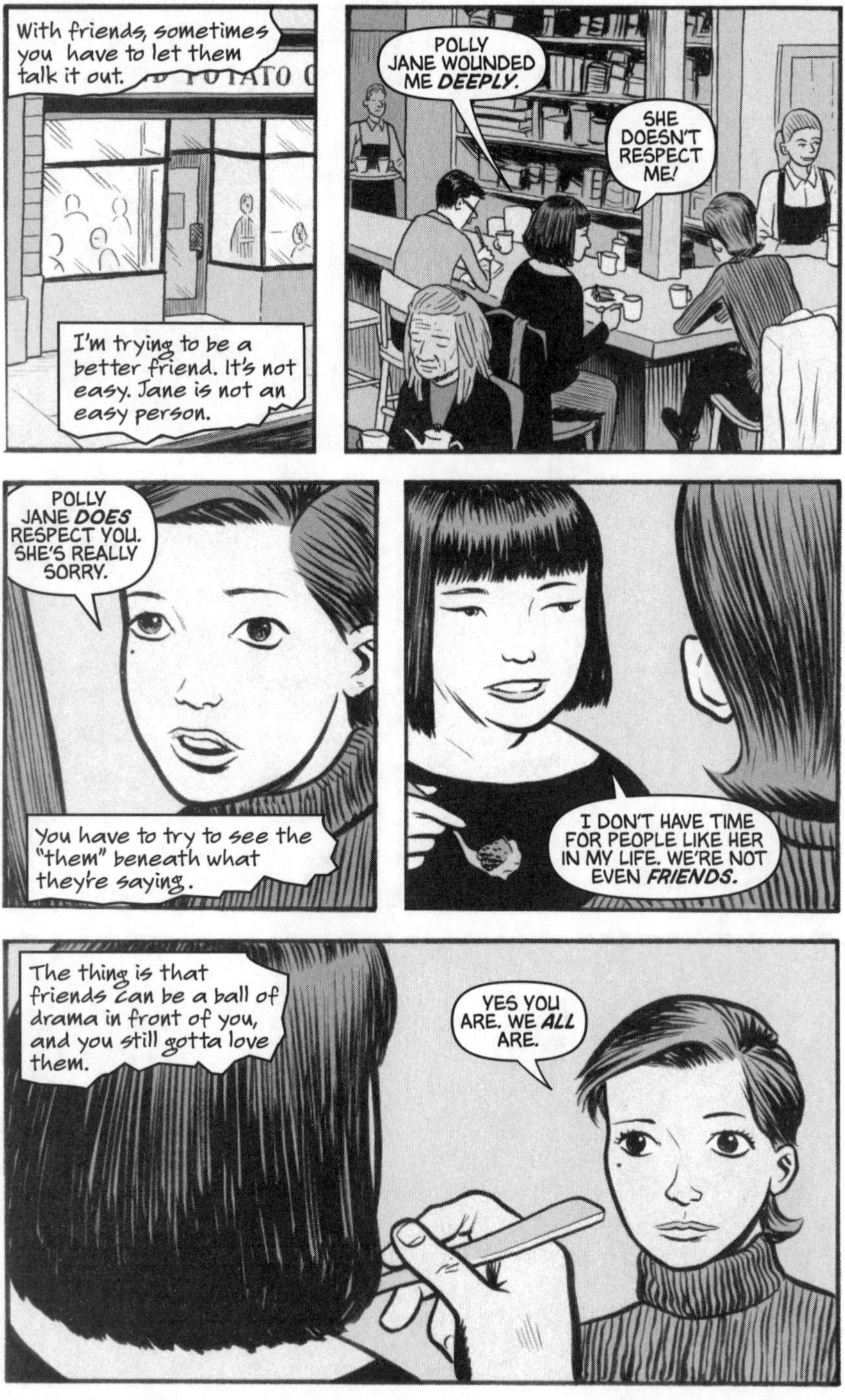
With friends, sometimes you have to let them talk it out.
I'm trying to be a better friend. It's not easy. Jane is not an easy person.
POLLY JANE WOUNDED ME DEEPLY.
SHE DOESN'T RESPECT ME!
POLLY JANE DOES RESPECT YOU. SHE'S REALLY SORRY.
You have to try to see the "them" beneath what they're saying.
I DON'T HAVE TIME FOR PEOPLE LIKE HER IN MY LIFE. WE'RE NOT EVEN FRIENDS.
The thing is that friends can be a ball of drama in front of you, and you still gotta love them.
YES YOU ARE. WE ALL ARE.

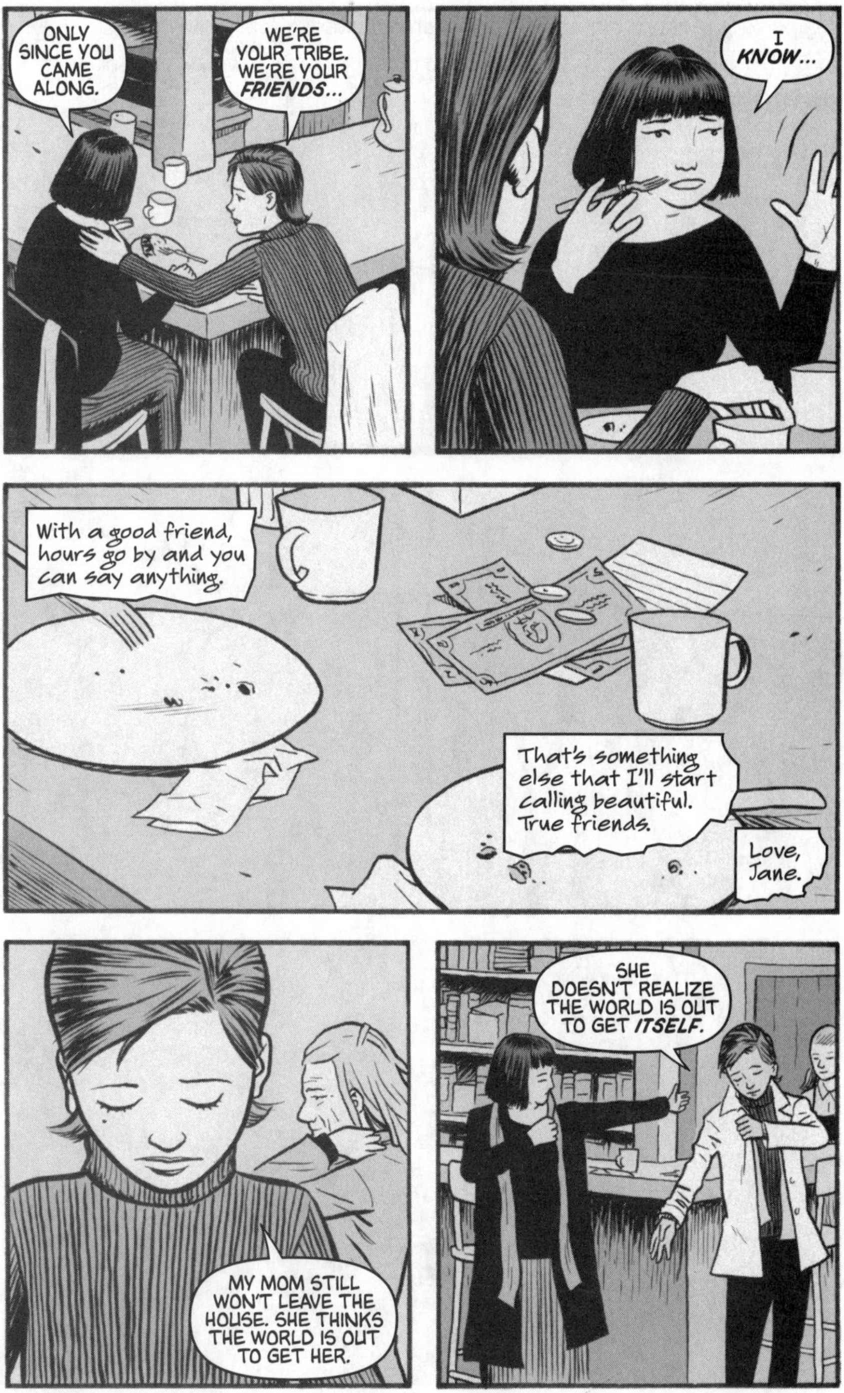
ONLY SINCE YOU CAME ALONG.
WE'RE YOUR TRIBE. WE'RE YOUR *FRIENDS...*
I *KNOW...*
With a good friend, hours go by and you can say anything.
That's something else that I'll start calling beautiful. True friends.
Love, Jane.
MY MOM STILL WON'T LEAVE THE HOUSE. SHE THINKS THE WORLD IS OUT TO GET HER.
SHE DOESN'T REALIZE THE WORLD IS OUT TO GET *ITSELF*.

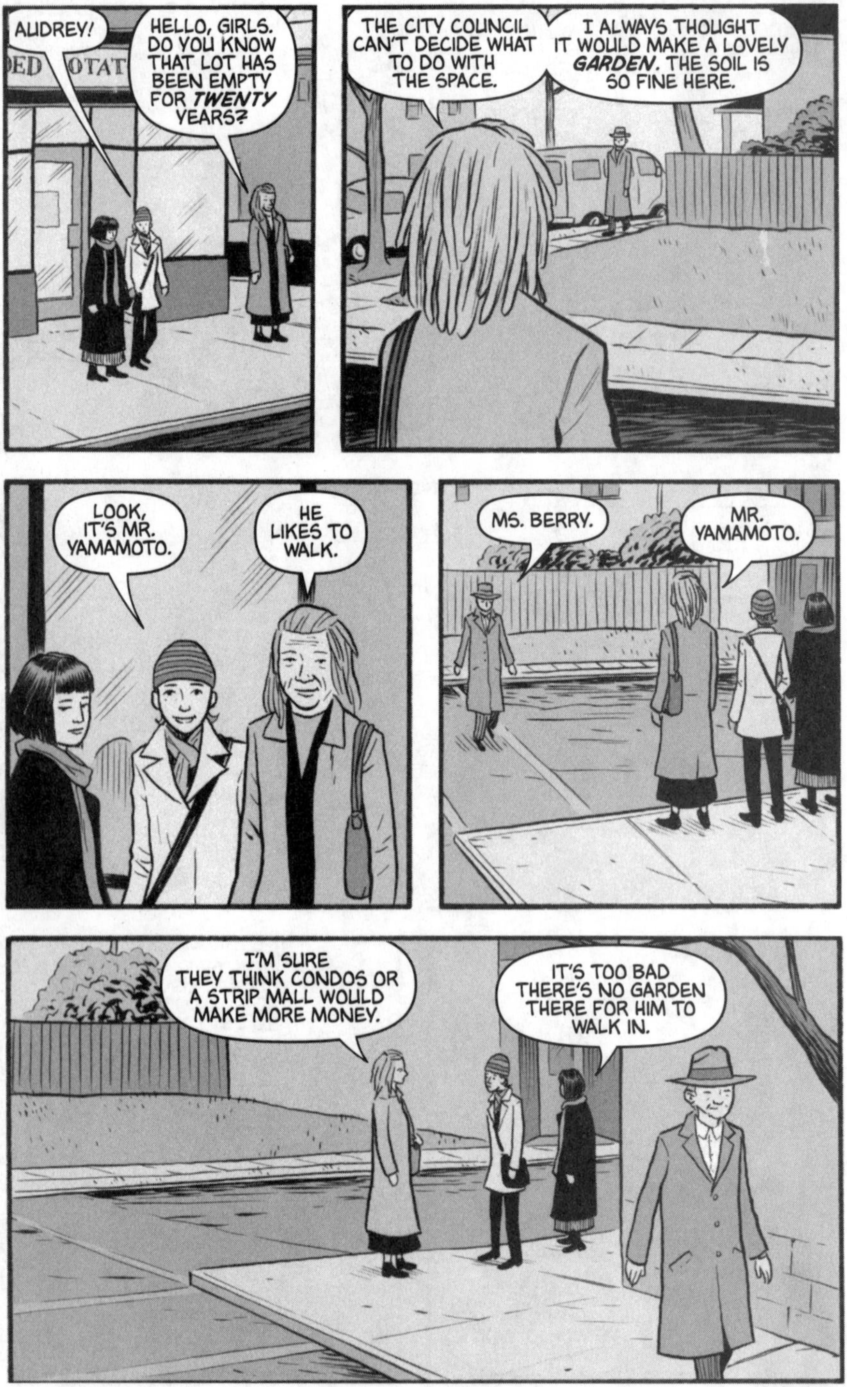
AUDREY!
HELLO, GIRLS. DO YOU KNOW THAT LOT HAS BEEN EMPTY FOR *TWENTY* YEARS?
DED
OTAT
THE CITY COUNCIL CAN'T DECIDE WHAT TO DO WITH THE SPACE.
I ALWAYS THOUGHT IT WOULD MAKE A LOVELY *GARDEN*. THE SOIL IS SO FINE HERE.
LOOK, IT'S MR. YAMAMOTO.
HE LIKES TO WALK.
MS. BERRY.
MR. YAMAMOTO.
I'M SURE THEY THINK CONDOS OR A STRIP MALL WOULD MAKE MORE MONEY.
IT'S TOO BAD THERE'S NO GARDEN THERE FOR HIM TO WALK IN.

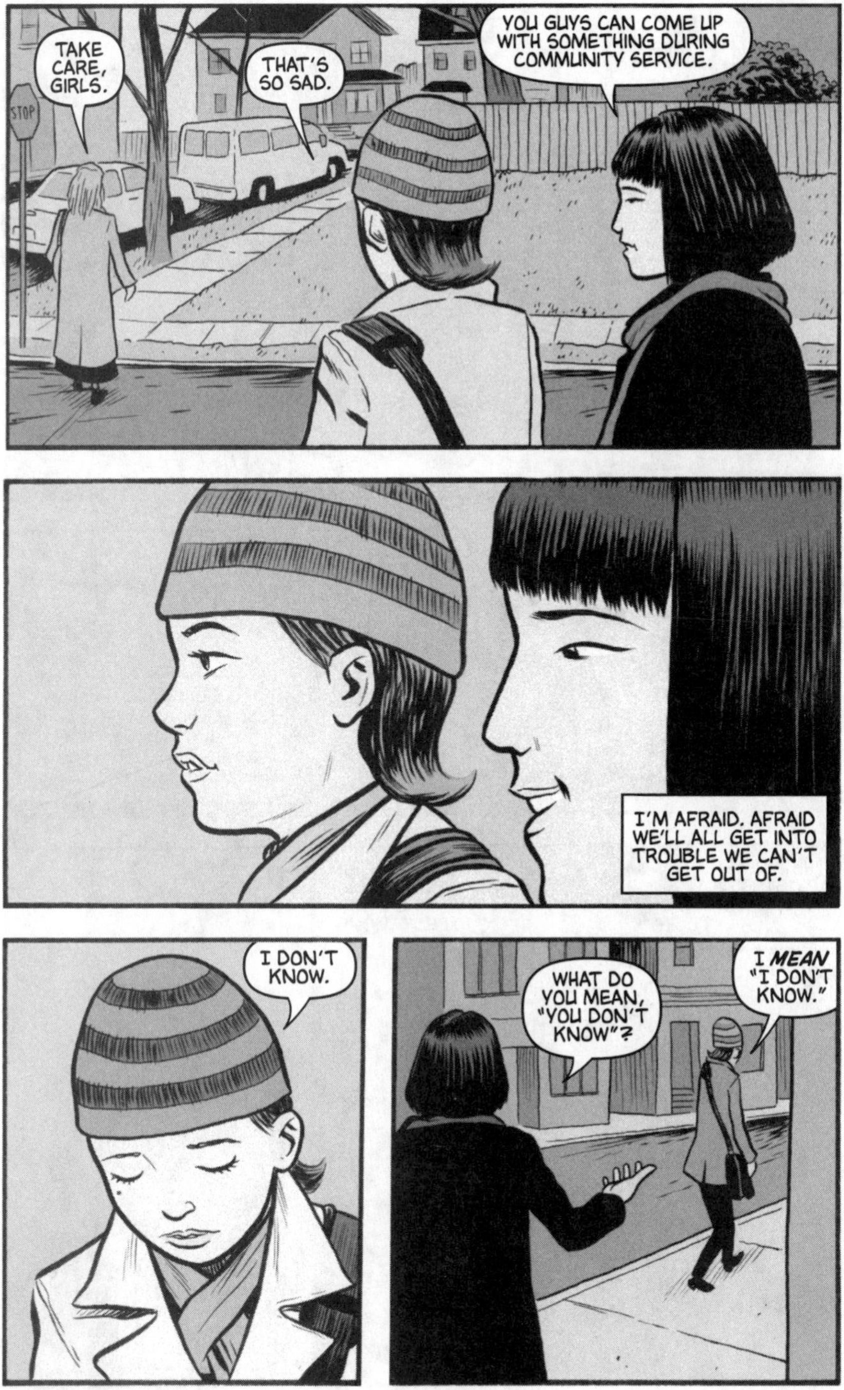

TAKE CARE, GIRLS.
THAT'S SO SAD.
YOU GUYS CAN COME UP WITH SOMETHING DURING COMMUNITY SERVICE.
I'M AFRAID. AFRAID WE'LL ALL GET INTO TROUBLE WE CAN'T GET OUT OF.
I DON'T KNOW.
WHAT DO YOU MEAN, "YOU DON'T KNOW"?
I *MEAN* "I DON'T KNOW."

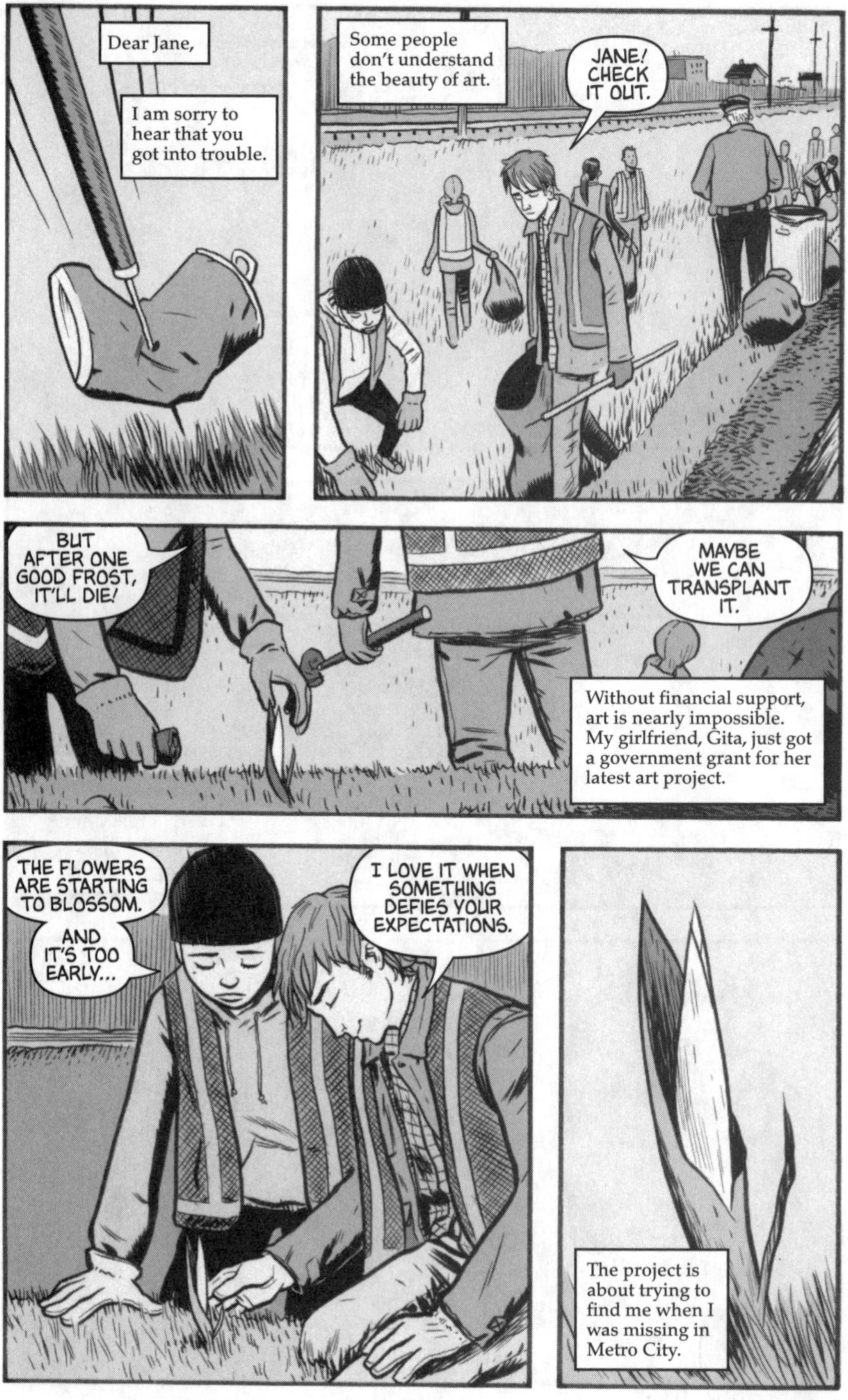
Dear Jane,
I am sorry to hear that you got into trouble.
Some people don't understand the beauty of art.
JANE! CHECK IT OUT.
BUT AFTER ONE GOOD FROST, IT'LL DIE!
MAYBE WE CAN TRANSPLANT IT.
Without financial support, art is nearly impossible. My girlfriend, Gita, just got a government grant for her latest art project.
THE FLOWERS ARE STARTING TO BLOSSOM.
AND IT'S TOO EARLY...
I LOVE IT WHEN SOMETHING DEFIES YOUR EXPECTATIONS.
The project is about trying to find me when I was missing in Metro City.

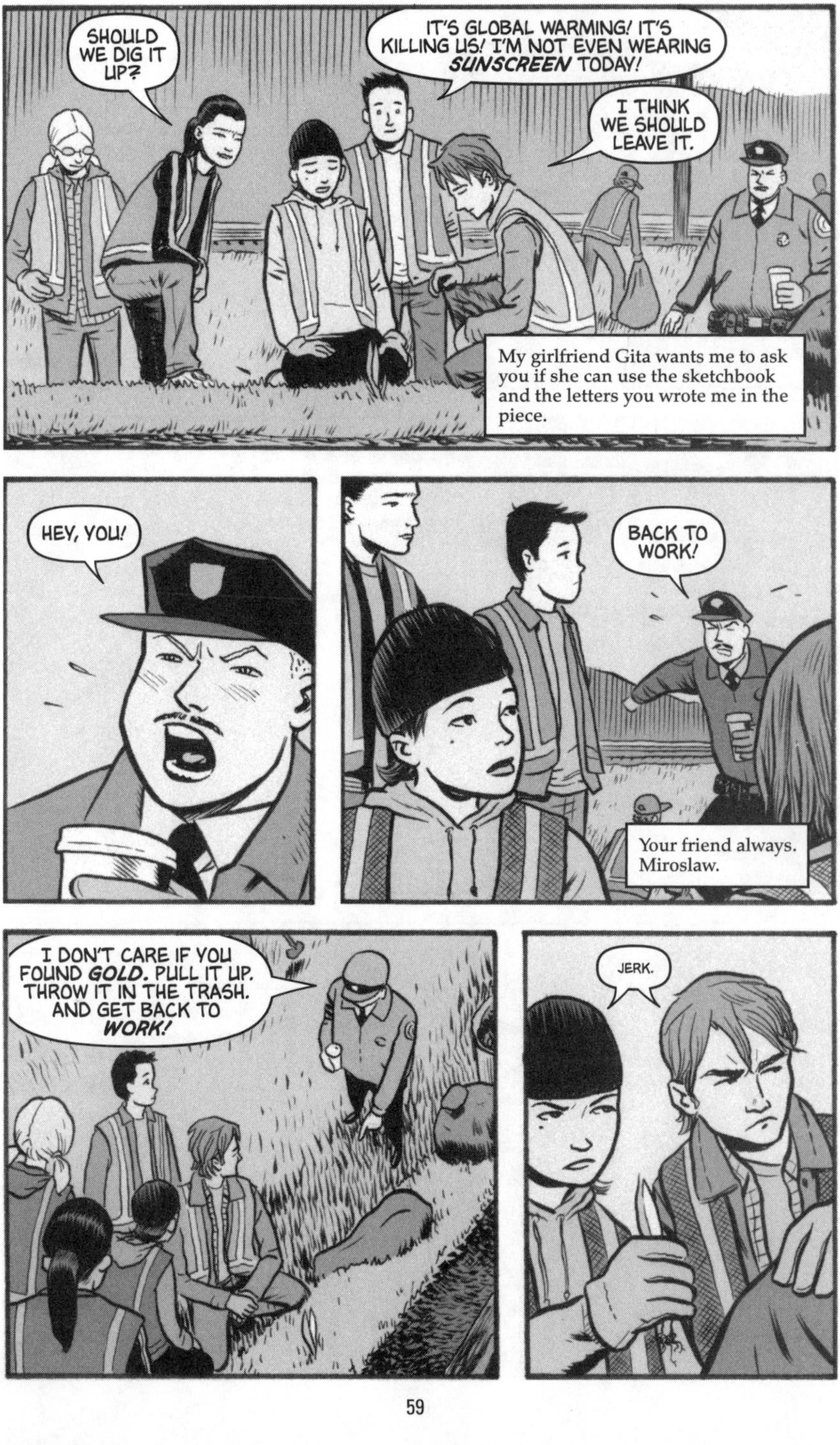
SHOULD WE DIG IT UP?
IT'S GLOBAL WARMING! IT'S KILLING US! I'M NOT EVEN WEARING SUNSCREEN TODAY!
I THINK WE SHOULD LEAVE IT.
My girlfriend Gita wants me to ask you if she can use the sketchbook and the letters you wrote me in the piece.
HEY, YOU!
BACK TO WORK!
Your friend always. Miroslaw.
I DON'T CARE IF YOU FOUND GOLD. PULL IT UP. THROW IT IN THE TRASH. AND GET BACK TO WORK!
JERK.

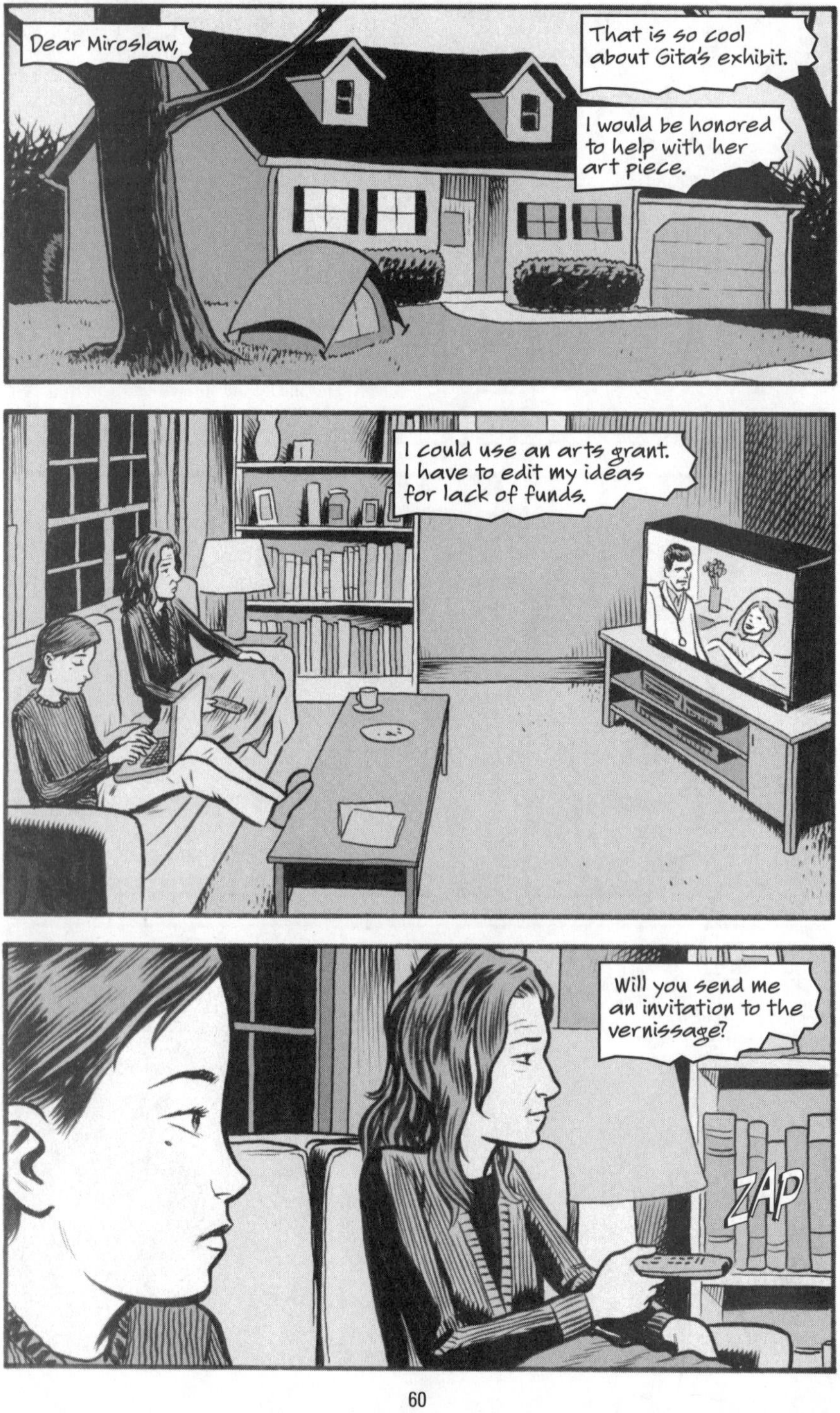
Dear Miroslaw,
That is so cool about Gita's exhibit.
I would be honored to help with her art piece.
I could use an arts grant. I have to edit my ideas for lack of funds.
Will you send me an invitation to the vernissage?
ZAP

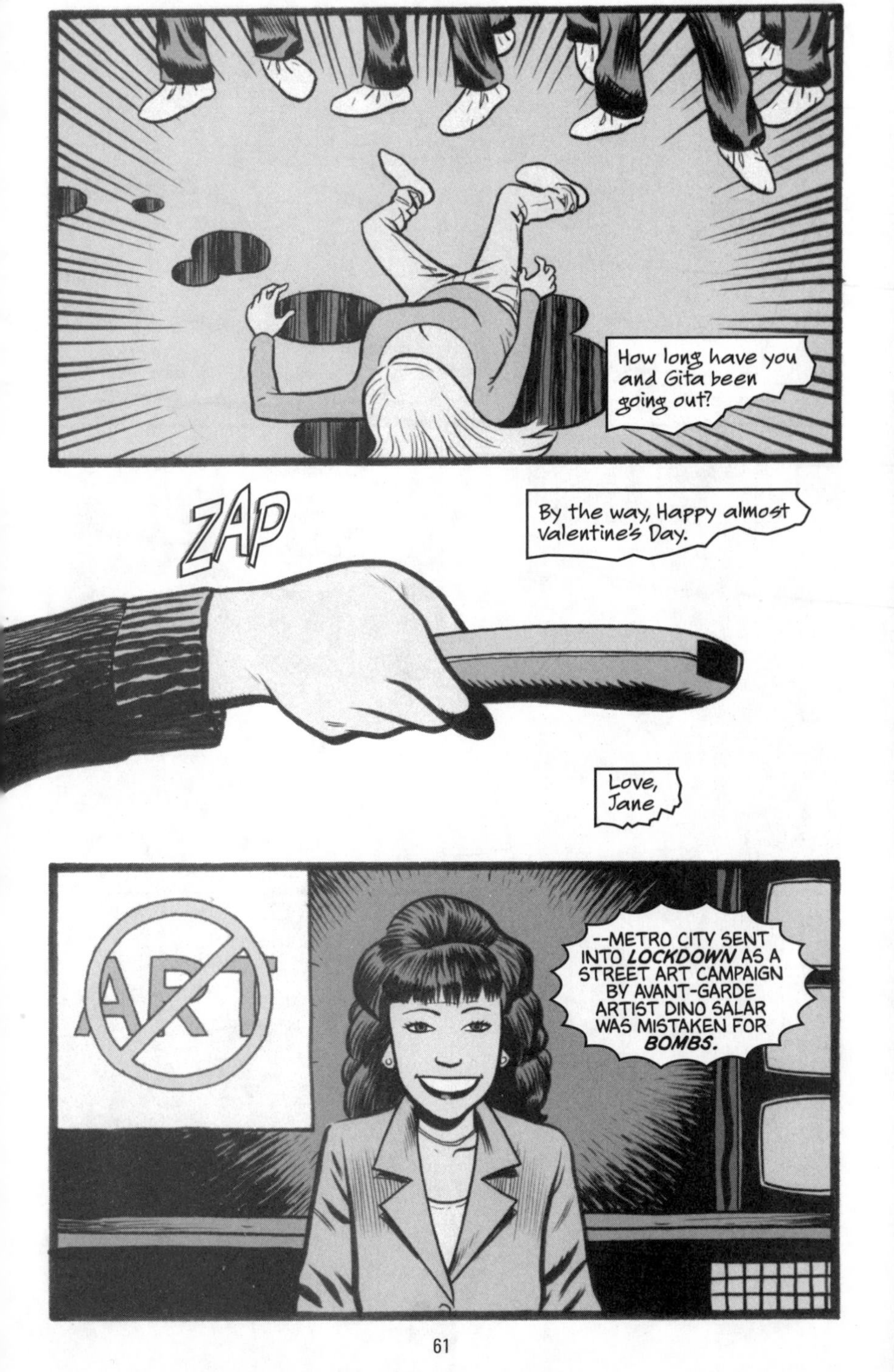
How long have you and Gita been going out?
ZAP
By the way, Happy almost Valentine's Day.
Love, Jane
--METRO CITY SENT INTO LOCKDOWN AS A STREET ART CAMPAIGN BY AVANT-GARDE ARTIST DINO SALAR WAS MISTAKEN FOR BOMBS.
ART

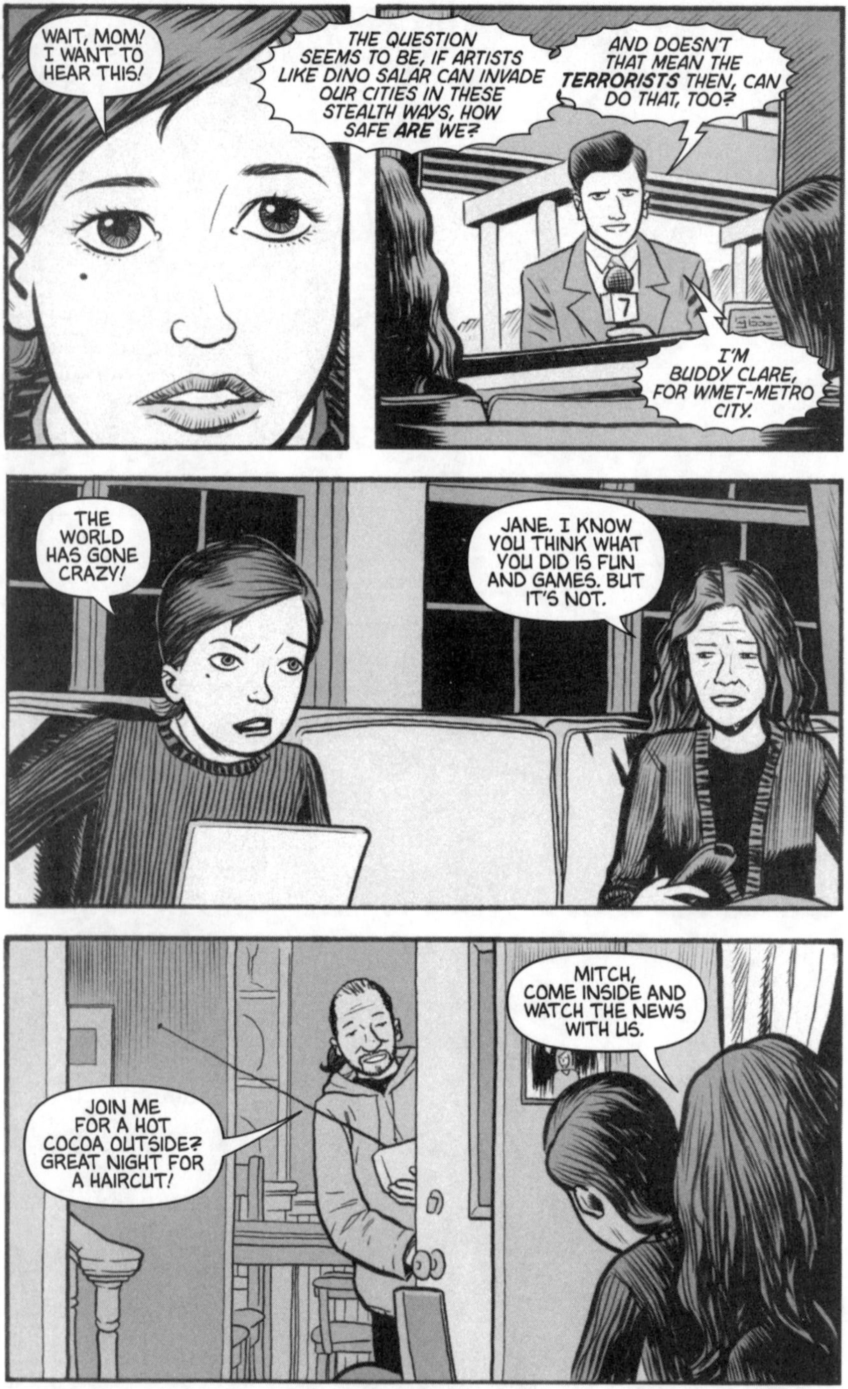
WAIT, MOM! I WANT TO HEAR THIS!
THE QUESTION SEEMS TO BE, IF ARTISTS LIKE DINO SALAR CAN INVADE OUR CITIES IN THESE STEALTH WAYS, HOW SAFE **ARE** WE?
AND DOESN'T THAT MEAN THE **TERRORISTS** THEN, CAN DO THAT, TOO?
I'M BUDDY CLARE, FOR WMET-METRO CITY.
THE WORLD HAS GONE CRAZY!
JANE. I KNOW YOU THINK WHAT YOU DID IS FUN AND GAMES. BUT IT'S NOT.
MITCH, COME INSIDE AND WATCH THE NEWS WITH US.
JOIN ME FOR A HOT COCOA OUTSIDE? GREAT NIGHT FOR A HAIRCUT!

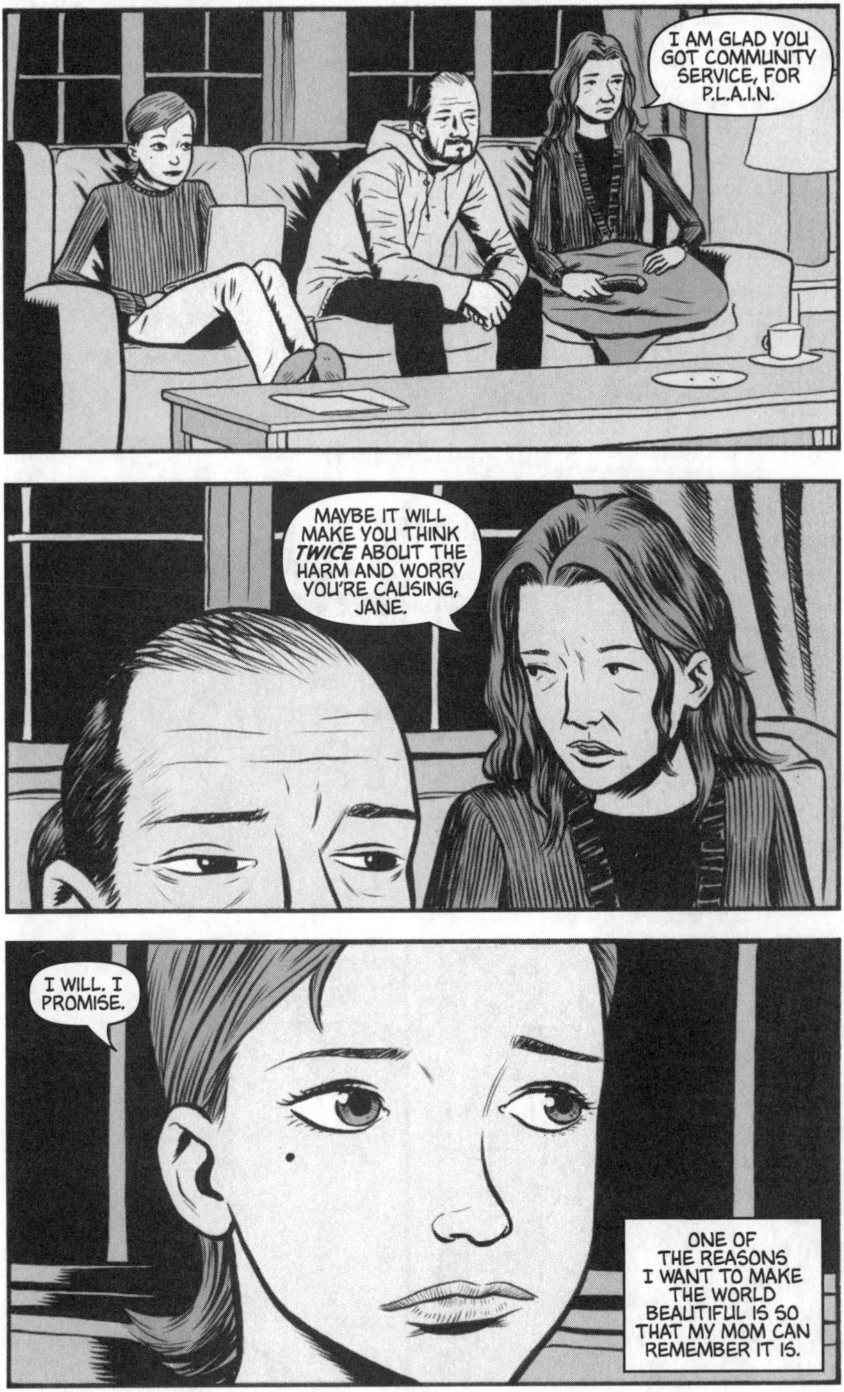
I AM GLAD YOU GOT COMMUNITY SERVICE, FOR P.L.A.I.N.
MAYBE IT WILL MAKE YOU THINK *TWICE* ABOUT THE HARM AND WORRY YOU'RE CAUSING, JANE.
I WILL. I PROMISE.
ONE OF THE REASONS I WANT TO MAKE THE WORLD BEAUTIFUL IS SO THAT MY MOM CAN REMEMBER IT IS.

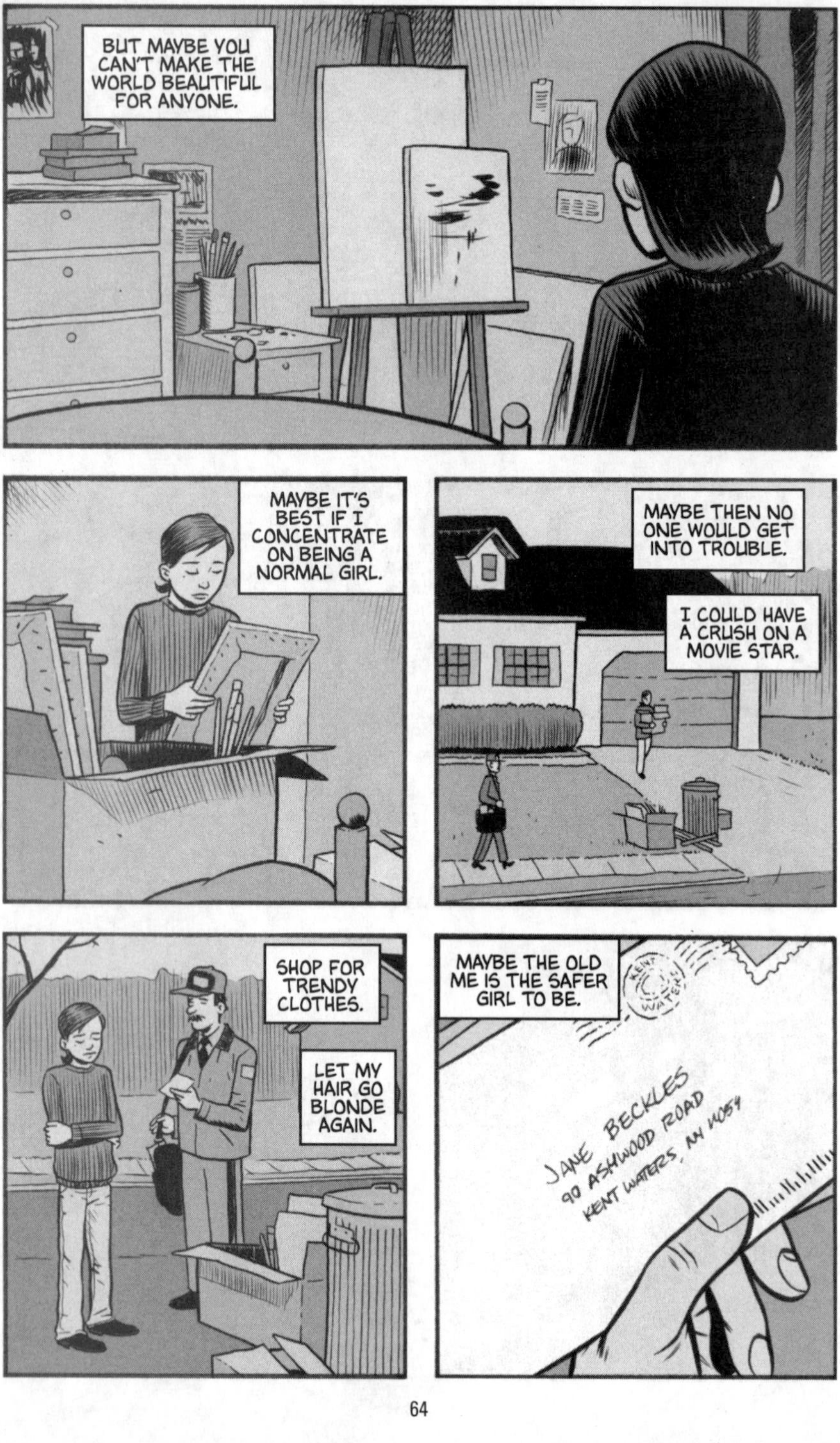

BUT MAYBE YOU CAN'T MAKE THE WORLD BEAUTIFUL FOR ANYONE.
MAYBE IT'S BEST IF I CONCENTRATE ON BEING A NORMAL GIRL.
MAYBE THEN NO ONE WOULD GET INTO TROUBLE.
I COULD HAVE A CRUSH ON A MOVIE STAR.
SHOP FOR TRENDY CLOTHES.
LET MY HAIR GO BLONDE AGAIN.
MAYBE THE OLD ME IS THE SAFER GIRL TO BE.
KENT WATERS
JANE BECKLES
90 ASHWOOD ROAD
KENT WATERS, NY 10054

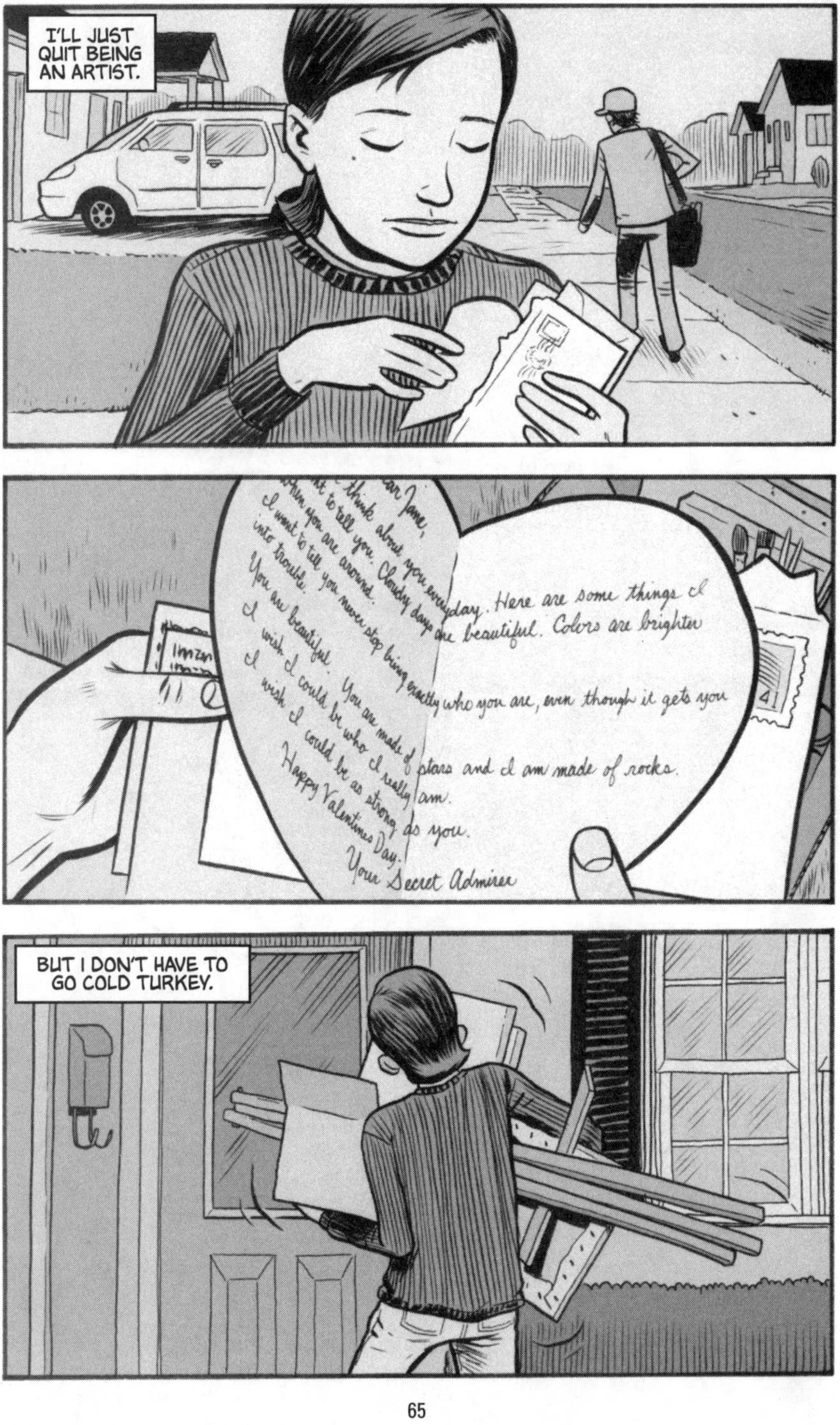
I'LL JUST QUIT BEING AN ARTIST.
Dear Jane,
I think about you everyday. Here are some things I want to tell you. Cloudy days are beautiful. Colors are brighter when you are around.
I want to tell you never stop being exactly who you are, even though it gets you into trouble.
You are beautiful. You are made of stars and I am made of rocks.
I wish I could be who I really am.
I wish I could be as strong as you.
Happy Valentines Day.
Your Secret Admirer
BUT I DON'T HAVE TO GO COLD TURKEY.

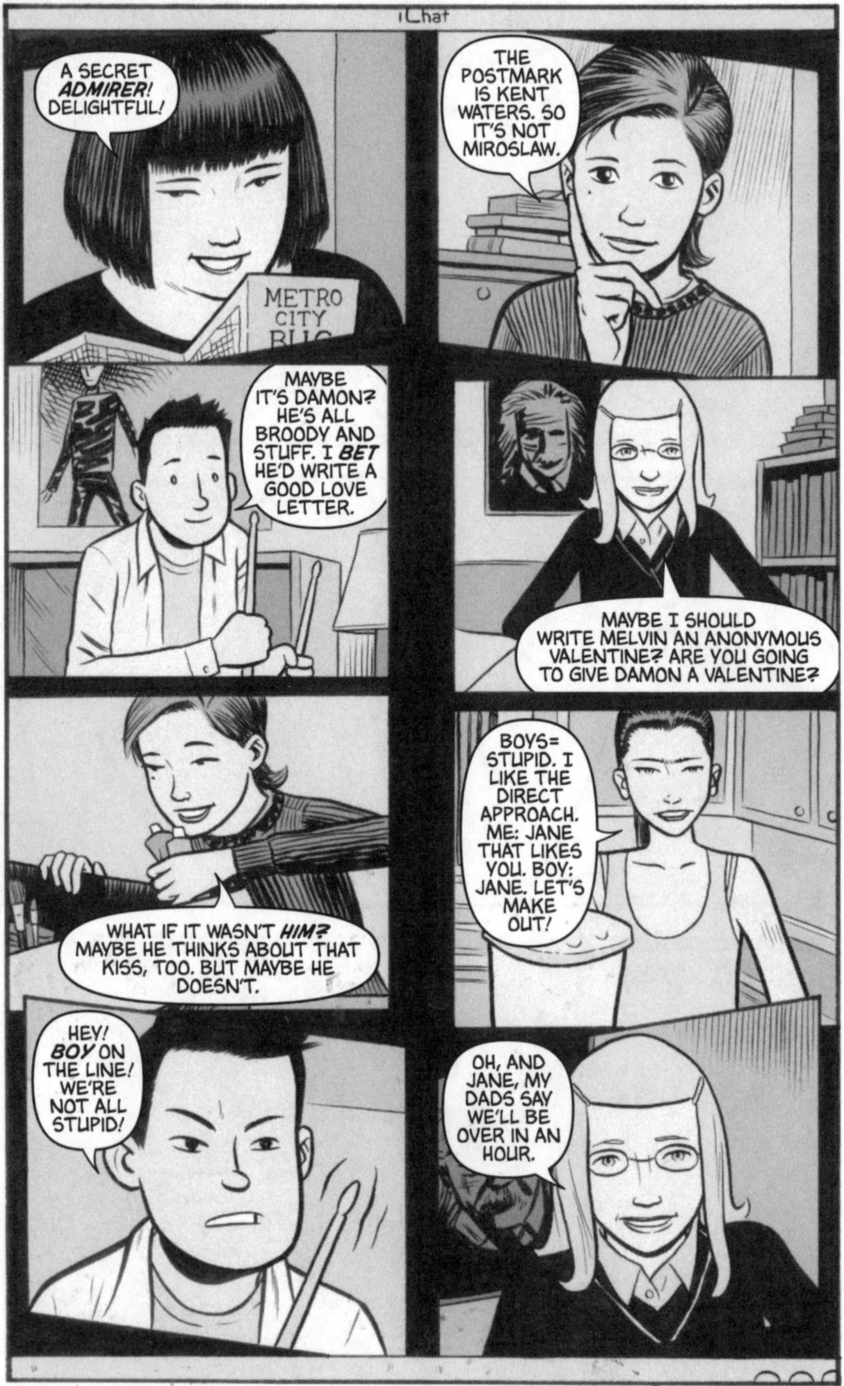
iChat
A SECRET ADMIRER! DELIGHTFUL!
METRO CITY
THE POSTMARK IS KENT WATERS. SO IT'S NOT MIROSLAW.
MAYBE IT'S DAMON? HE'S ALL BROODY AND STUFF. I BET HE'D WRITE A GOOD LOVE LETTER.
MAYBE I SHOULD WRITE MELVIN AN ANONYMOUS VALENTINE? ARE YOU GOING TO GIVE DAMON A VALENTINE?
WHAT IF IT WASN'T HIM? MAYBE HE THINKS ABOUT THAT KISS, TOO. BUT MAYBE HE DOESN'T.
BOYS= STUPID. I LIKE THE DIRECT APPROACH. ME: JANE THAT LIKES YOU. BOY: JANE. LET'S MAKE OUT!
HEY! BOY ON THE LINE! WE'RE NOT ALL STUPID!
OH, AND JANE, MY DADS SAY WE'LL BE OVER IN AN HOUR.

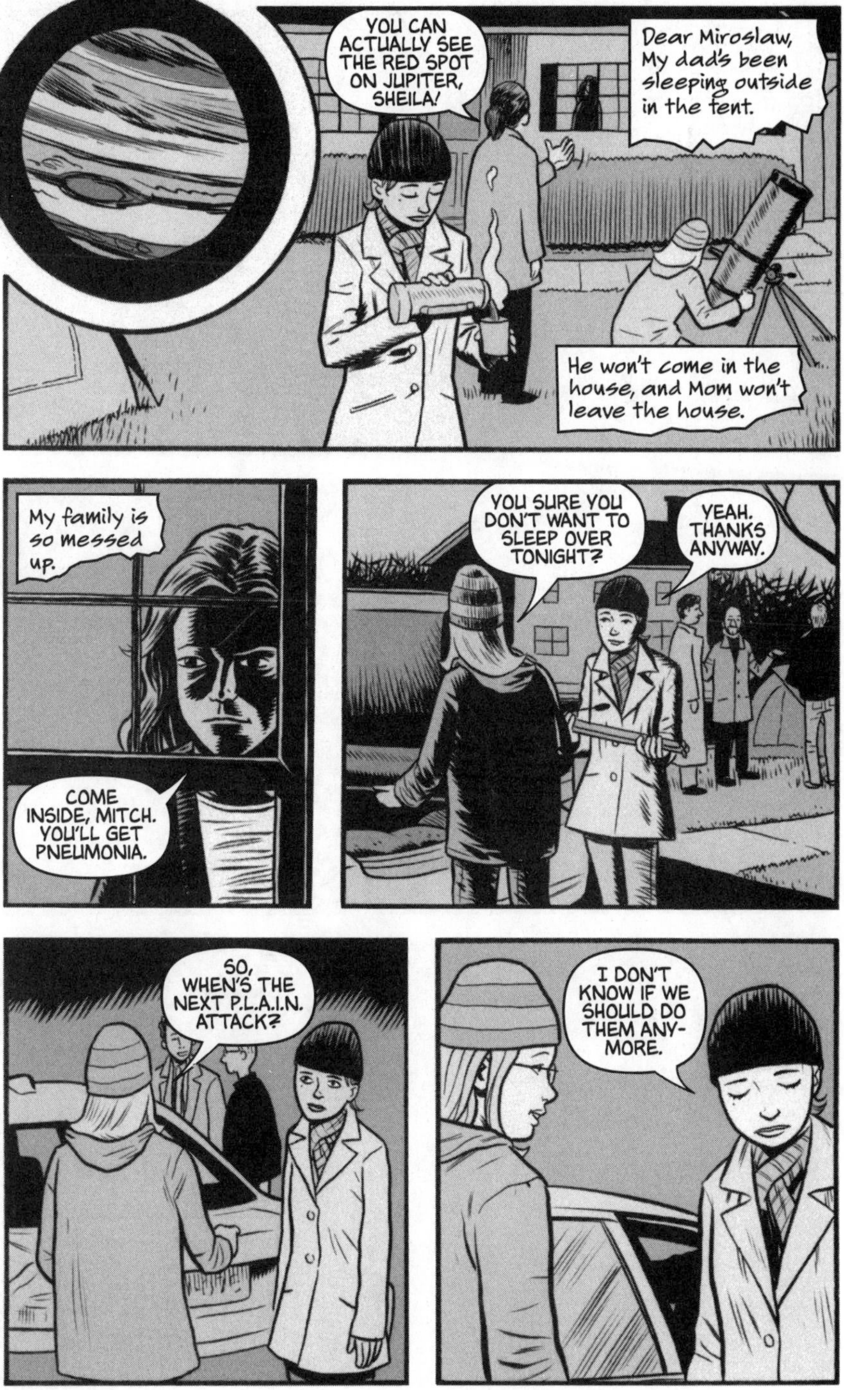

YOU CAN ACTUALLY SEE THE RED SPOT ON JUPITER, SHEILA!
Dear Miroslaw, My dad's been sleeping outside in the tent.
He won't come in the house, and Mom won't leave the house.
My family is so messed up.
COME INSIDE, MITCH. YOU'LL GET PNEUMONIA.
YOU SURE YOU DON'T WANT TO SLEEP OVER TONIGHT?
YEAH. THANKS ANYWAY.
SO, WHEN'S THE NEXT P.L.A.I.N. ATTACK?
I DON'T KNOW IF WE SHOULD DO THEM ANY-MORE.

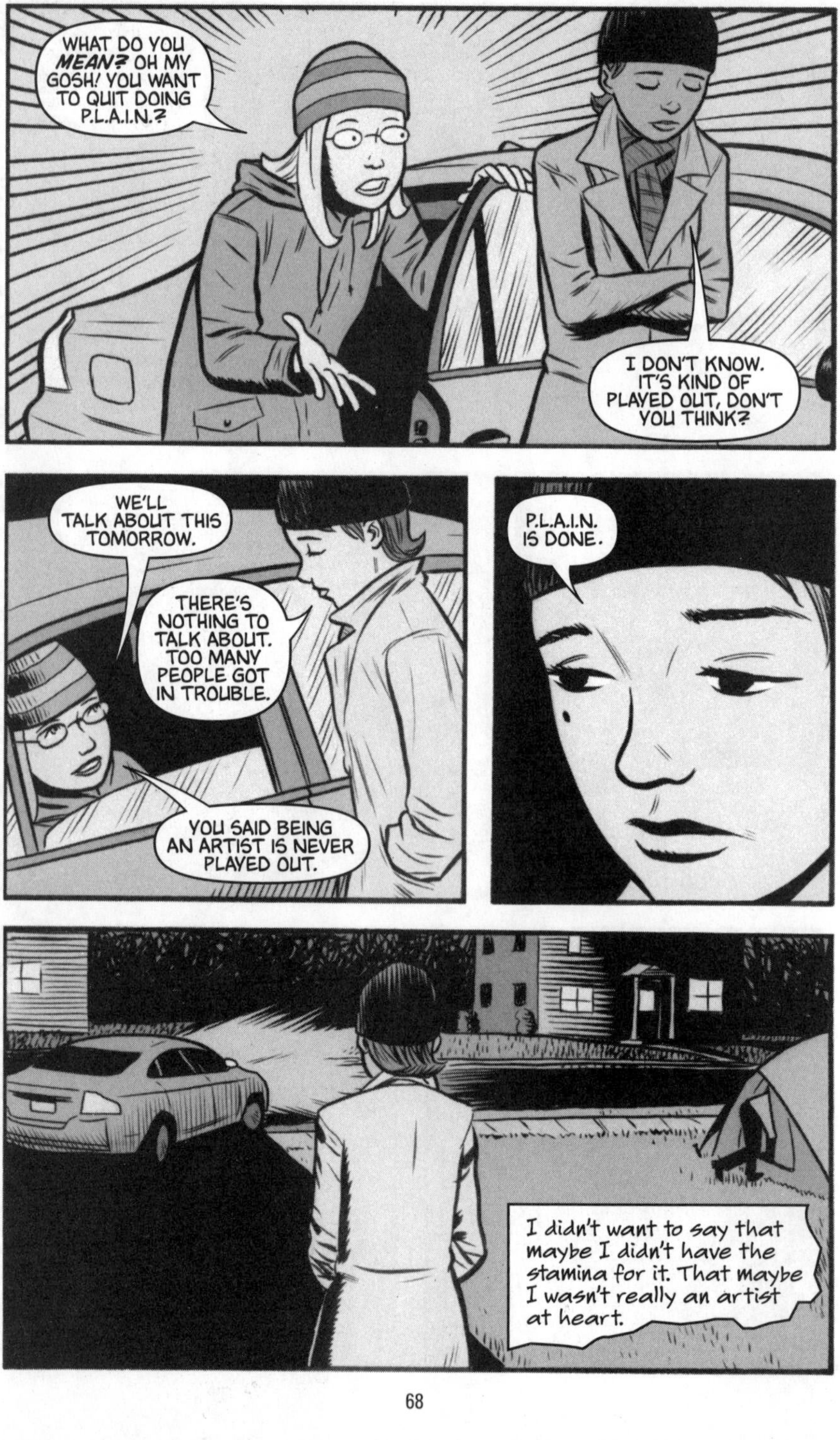
WHAT DO YOU *MEAN?* OH MY GOSH! YOU WANT TO QUIT DOING P.L.A.I.N.?
I DON'T KNOW. IT'S KIND OF PLAYED OUT, DON'T YOU THINK?
WE'LL TALK ABOUT THIS TOMORROW.
THERE'S NOTHING TO TALK ABOUT. TOO MANY PEOPLE GOT IN TROUBLE.
YOU SAID BEING AN ARTIST IS NEVER PLAYED OUT.
P.L.A.I.N. IS DONE.
I didn't want to say that maybe I didn't have the stamina for it. That maybe I wasn't really an artist at heart.

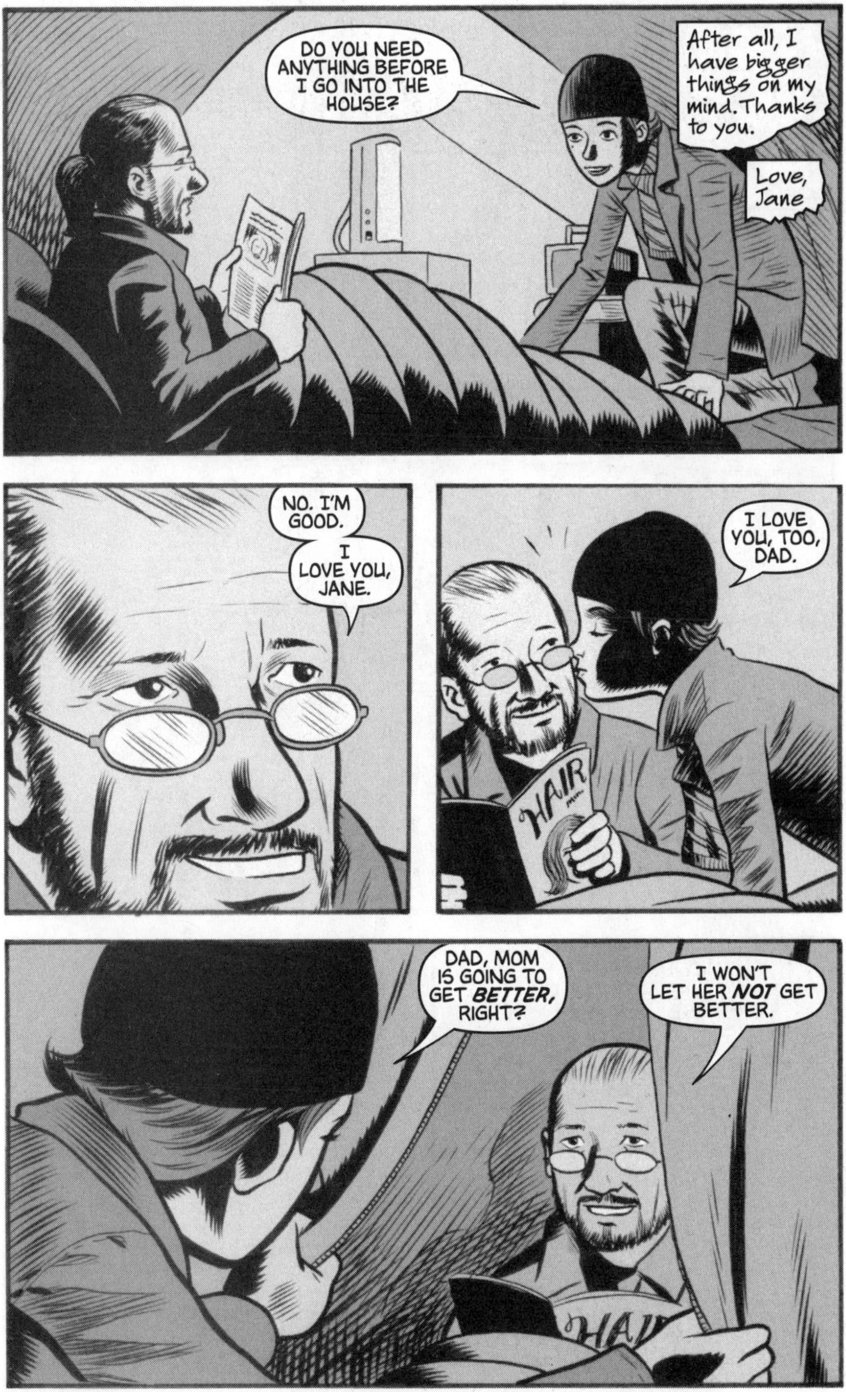
DO YOU NEED ANYTHING BEFORE I GO INTO THE HOUSE?
After all, I have bigger things on my mind. Thanks to you.
Love, Jane
NO. I'M GOOD.
I LOVE YOU, JANE.
I LOVE YOU, TOO, DAD.
HAIR
DAD, MOM IS GOING TO GET *BETTER*, RIGHT?
I WON'T LET HER *NOT* GET BETTER.

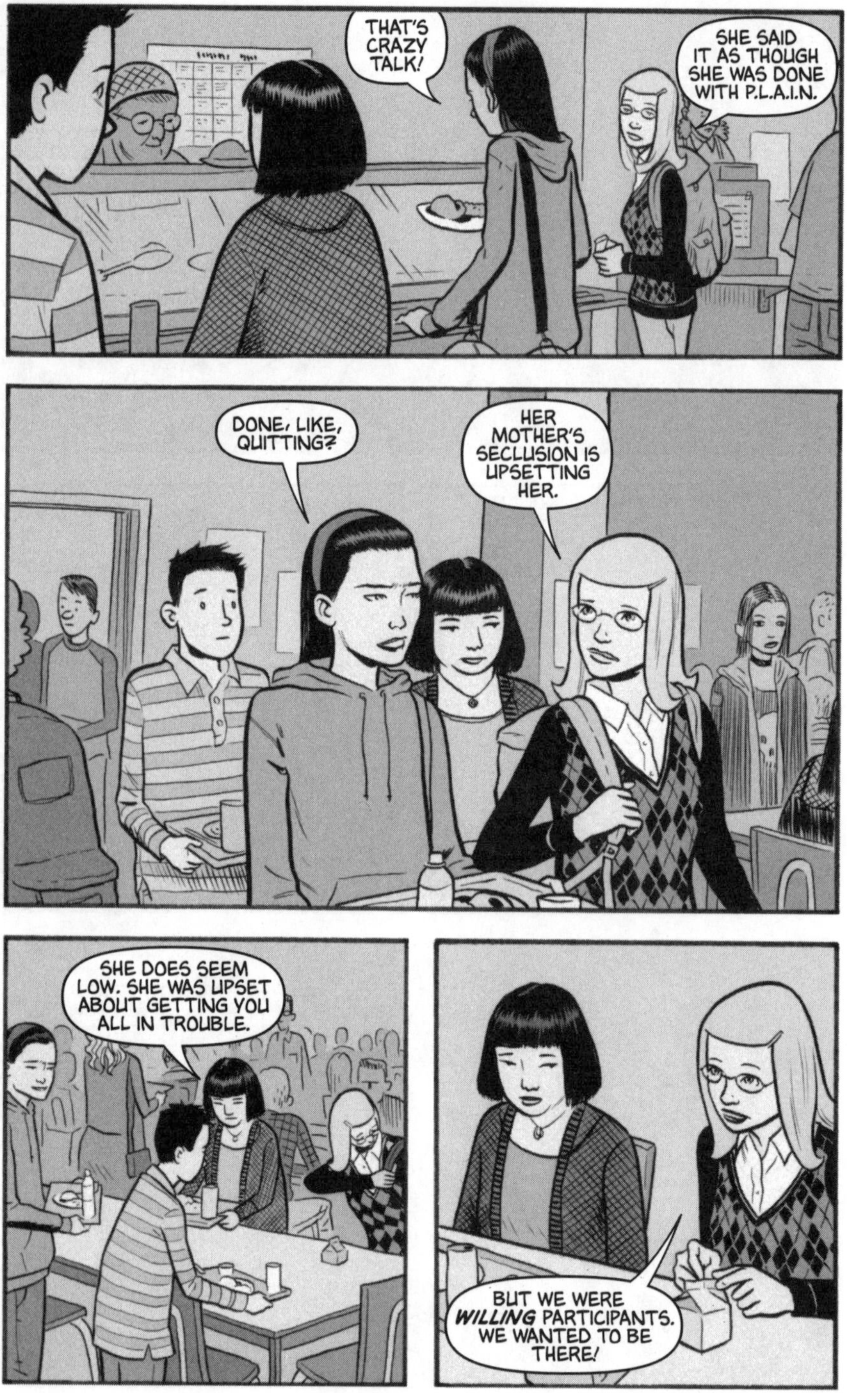
THAT'S CRAZY TALK!
SHE SAID IT AS THOUGH SHE WAS DONE WITH P.L.A.I.N.
DONE, LIKE, QUITTING?
HER MOTHER'S SECLUSION IS UPSETTING HER.
SHE DOES SEEM LOW. SHE WAS UPSET ABOUT GETTING YOU ALL IN TROUBLE.
BUT WE WERE *WILLING* PARTICIPANTS. WE WANTED TO BE THERE!

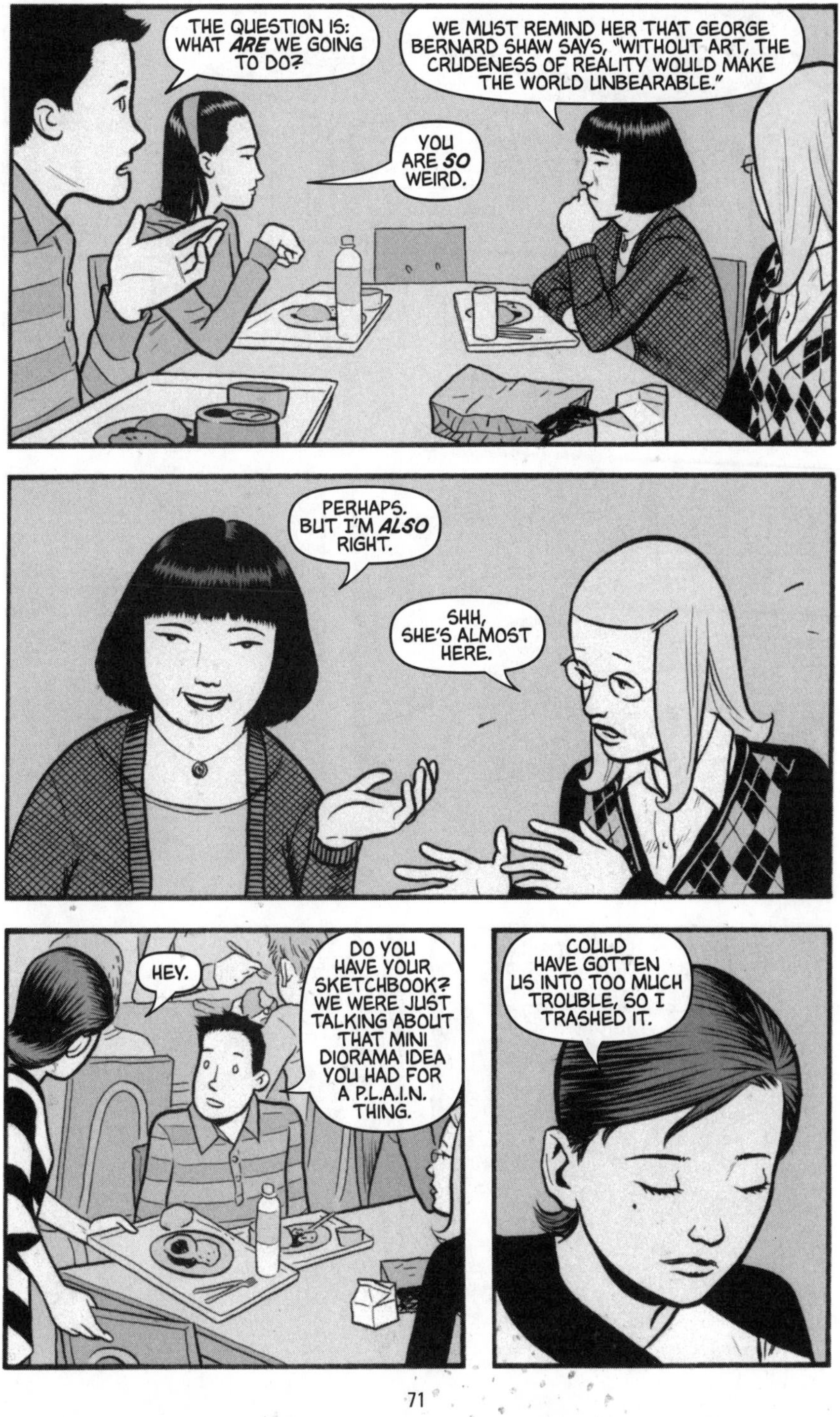
THE QUESTION IS: WHAT *ARE* WE GOING TO DO?
WE MUST REMIND HER THAT GEORGE BERNARD SHAW SAYS, "WITHOUT ART, THE CRUDENESS OF REALITY WOULD MAKE THE WORLD UNBEARABLE."
YOU ARE *SO* WEIRD.
PERHAPS. BUT I'M *ALSO* RIGHT.
SHH, SHE'S ALMOST HERE.
HEY.
DO YOU HAVE YOUR SKETCHBOOK? WE WERE JUST TALKING ABOUT THAT MINI DIORAMA IDEA YOU HAD FOR A P.L.A.I.N. THING.
COULD HAVE GOTTEN US INTO TOO MUCH TROUBLE, SO I TRASHED IT.

COMING SOON
WATER PARK ESTATES

FINAL FARMER MARKET TODAY 3 PM

COMING SOON AT THIS SITE WATER PARK ESTATES CONDOS

WHY DO PEOPLE WANT TO GET RID OF THE THINGS THAT ARE GOOD IN THE WORLD? THE THINGS THAT BRING PEOPLE TOGETHER?

WHY DOES DEVELOPMENT SEEM SO UNDEVELOPED?

MING SOON AT THS SITE WATER PAR ESTATE

AUDREY, WHAT WILL YOU DO NOW THAT THEY'RE CLOSING THE MARKET?

IT'S HARD TO START OVER AT *MY* AGE.

OH, THERE YOU ARE, DAMON.

DO YOU KNOW JANE?

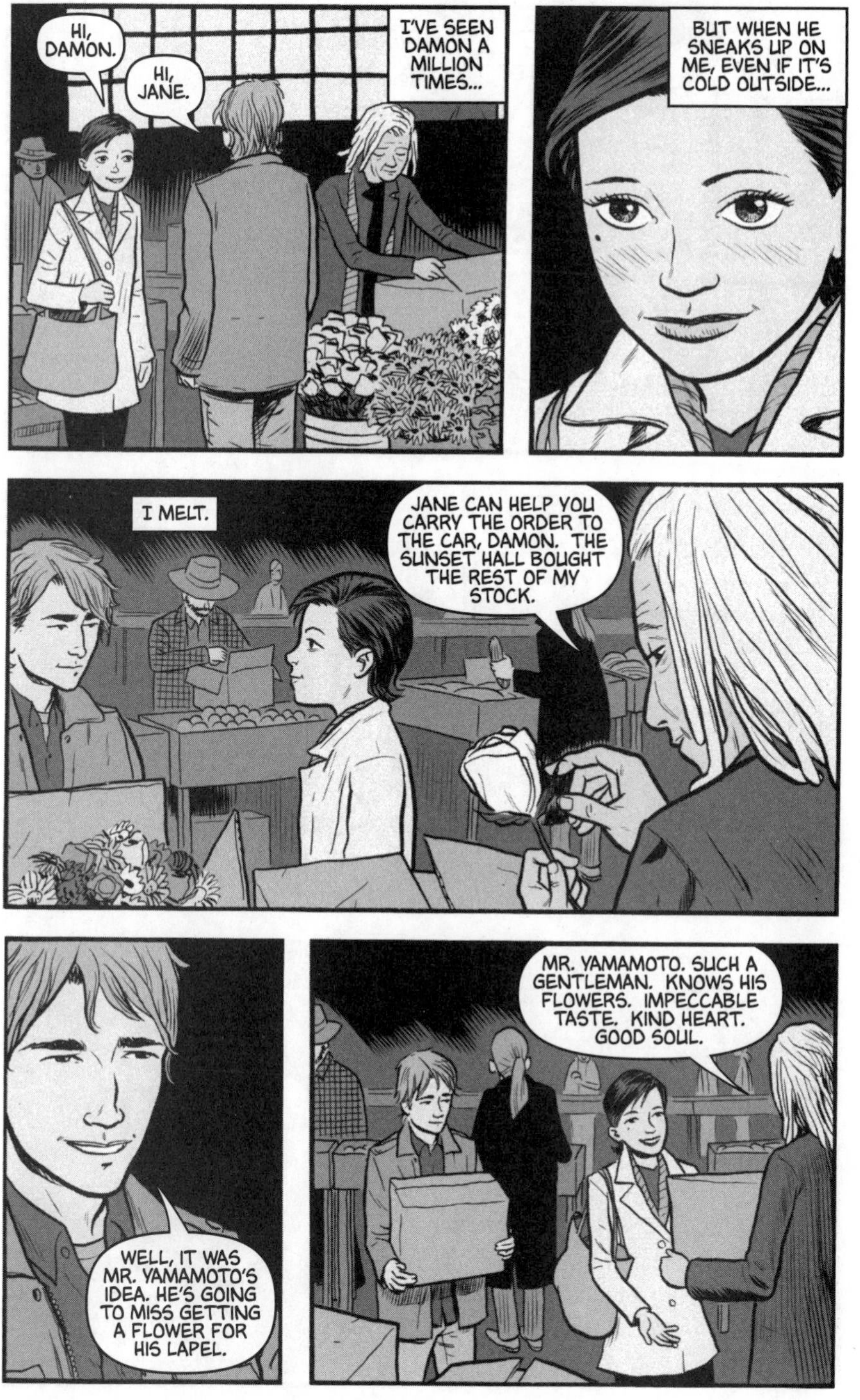
HI, DAMON.
HI, JANE.
I'VE SEEN DAMON A MILLION TIMES...
BUT WHEN HE SNEAKS UP ON ME, EVEN IF IT'S COLD OUTSIDE...
I MELT.
JANE CAN HELP YOU CARRY THE ORDER TO THE CAR, DAMON. THE SUNSET HALL BOUGHT THE REST OF MY STOCK.
WELL, IT WAS MR. YAMAMOTO'S IDEA. HE'S GOING TO MISS GETTING A FLOWER FOR HIS LAPEL.
MR. YAMAMOTO. SUCH A GENTLEMAN. KNOWS HIS FLOWERS. IMPECCABLE TASTE. KIND HEART. GOOD SOUL.

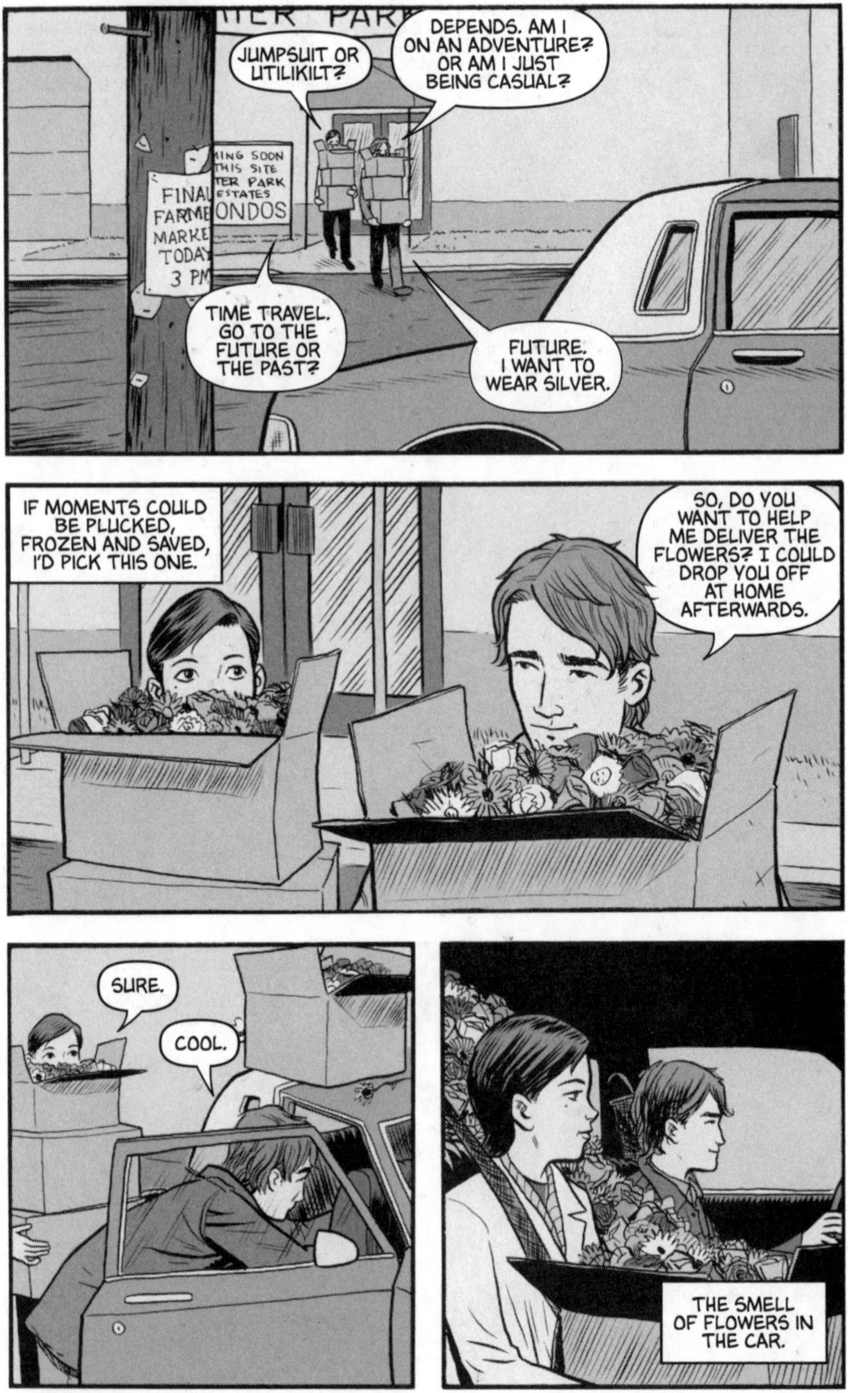
JUMPSUIT OR UTILIKILT?
DEPENDS. AM I ON AN ADVENTURE? OR AM I JUST BEING CASUAL?
FINAL FARMERS MARKET TODAY 3 PM
TIME TRAVEL. GO TO THE FUTURE OR THE PAST?
FUTURE. I WANT TO WEAR SILVER.
IF MOMENTS COULD BE PLUCKED, FROZEN AND SAVED, I'D PICK THIS ONE.
SO, DO YOU WANT TO HELP ME DELIVER THE FLOWERS? I COULD DROP YOU OFF AT HOME AFTERWARDS.
SURE.
COOL.
THE SMELL OF FLOWERS IN THE CAR.

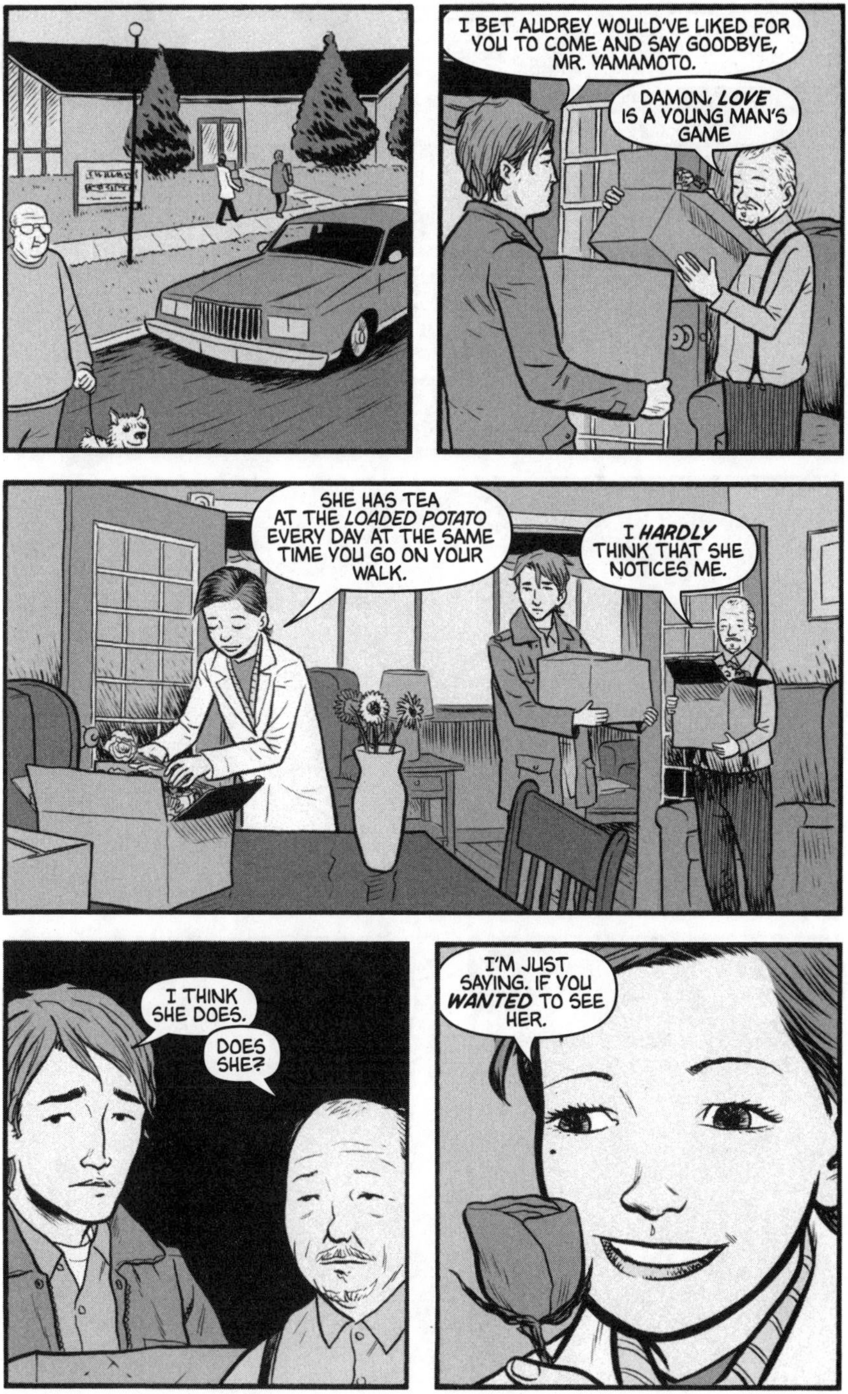
I BET AUDREY WOULD'VE LIKED FOR YOU TO COME AND SAY GOODBYE, MR. YAMAMOTO.
DAMON, *LOVE* IS A YOUNG MAN'S GAME
SHE HAS TEA AT THE *LOADED POTATO* EVERY DAY AT THE SAME TIME YOU GO ON YOUR WALK.
I *HARDLY* THINK THAT SHE NOTICES ME.
I THINK SHE DOES.
DOES SHE?
I'M JUST SAYING. IF YOU *WANTED* TO SEE HER.

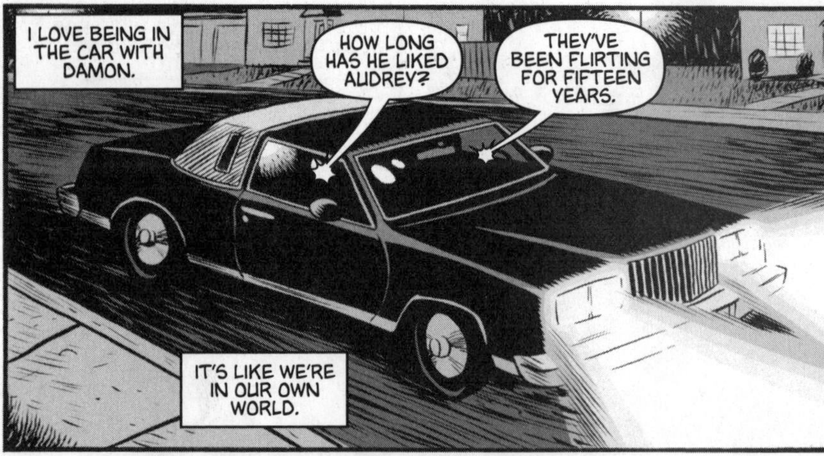

I LOVE BEING IN THE CAR WITH DAMON.
HOW LONG HAS HE LIKED AUDREY?
THEY'VE BEEN FLIRTING FOR FIFTEEN YEARS.
IT'S LIKE WE'RE IN OUR OWN WORLD.

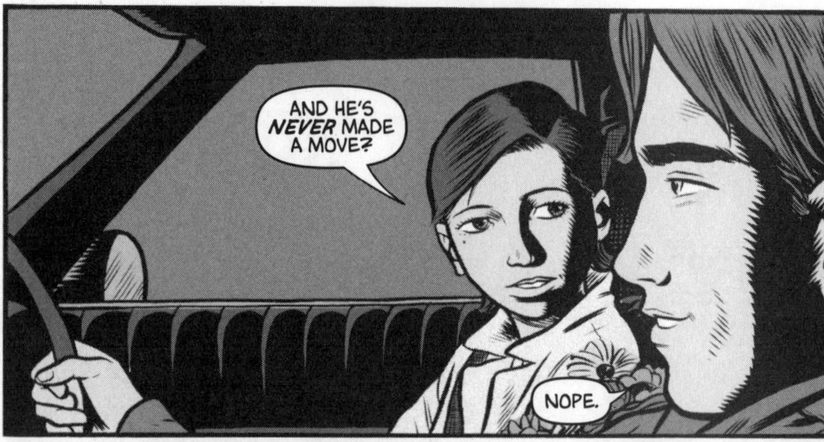

AND HE'S *NEVER* MADE A MOVE?
NOPE.

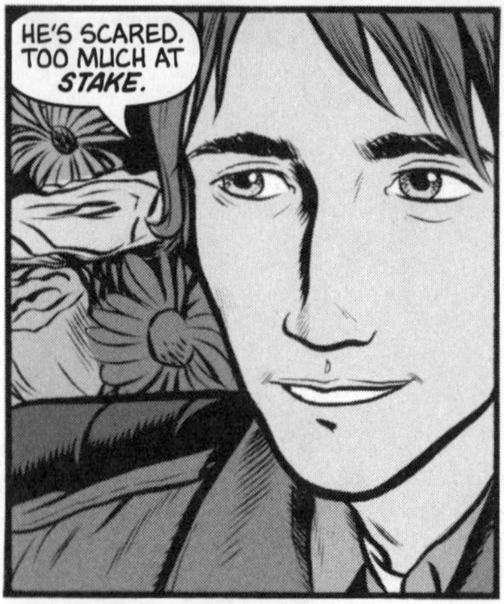

HE'S SCARED. TOO MUCH AT *STAKE*.

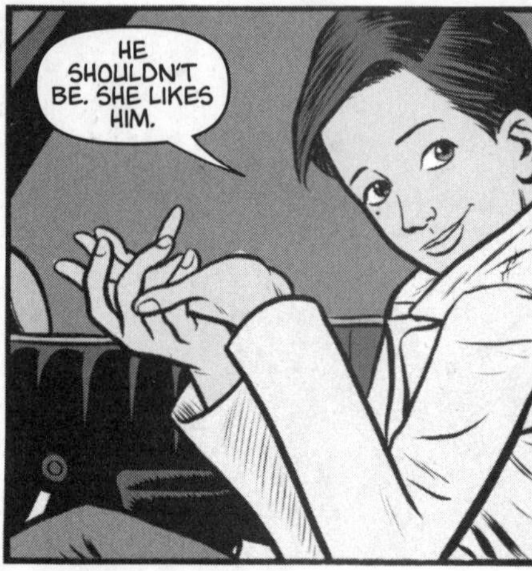

HE SHOULDN'T BE. SHE LIKES HIM.

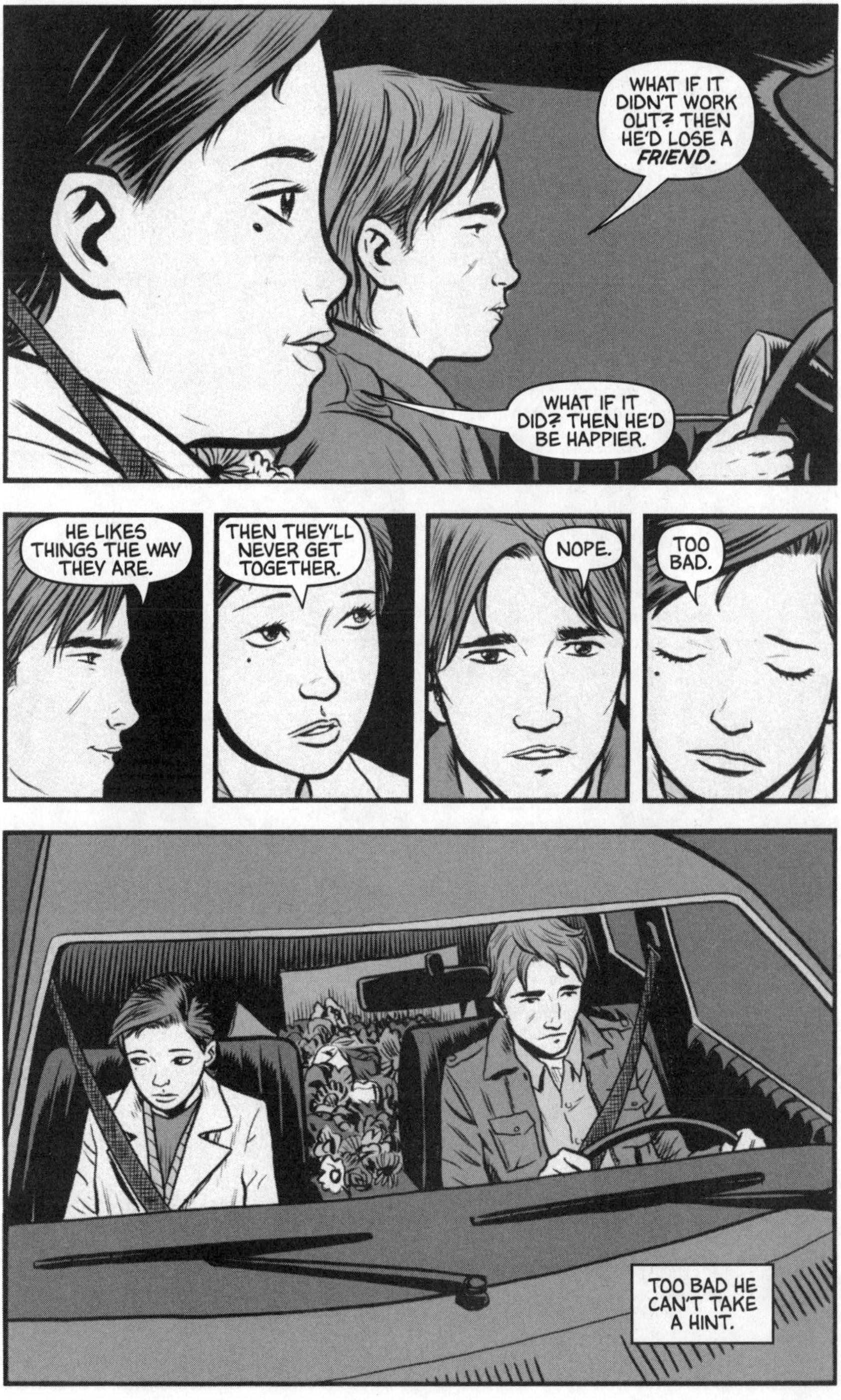
WHAT IF IT DIDN'T WORK OUT? THEN HE'D LOSE A *FRIEND*.
WHAT IF IT DID? THEN HE'D BE HAPPIER.
HE LIKES THINGS THE WAY THEY ARE.
THEN THEY'LL NEVER GET TOGETHER.
NOPE.
TOO BAD.
TOO BAD HE CAN'T TAKE A HINT.

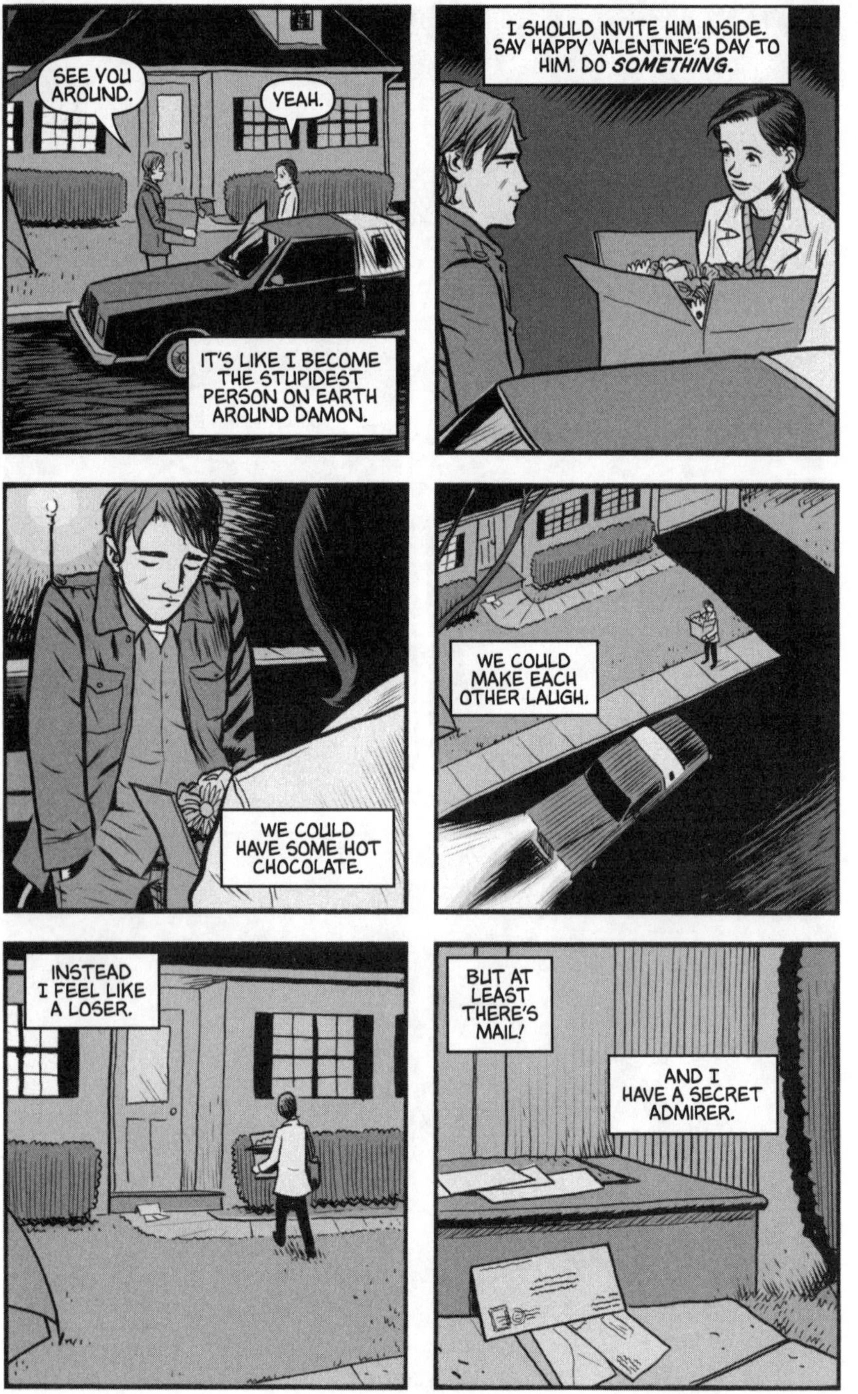
SEE YOU AROUND.
YEAH.
IT'S LIKE I BECOME THE STUPIDEST PERSON ON EARTH AROUND DAMON.
I SHOULD INVITE HIM INSIDE. SAY HAPPY VALENTINE'S DAY TO HIM. DO *SOMETHING.*
WE COULD HAVE SOME HOT CHOCOLATE.
WE COULD MAKE EACH OTHER LAUGH.
INSTEAD I FEEL LIKE A LOSER.
BUT AT LEAST THERE'S MAIL!
AND I HAVE A SECRET ADMIRER.

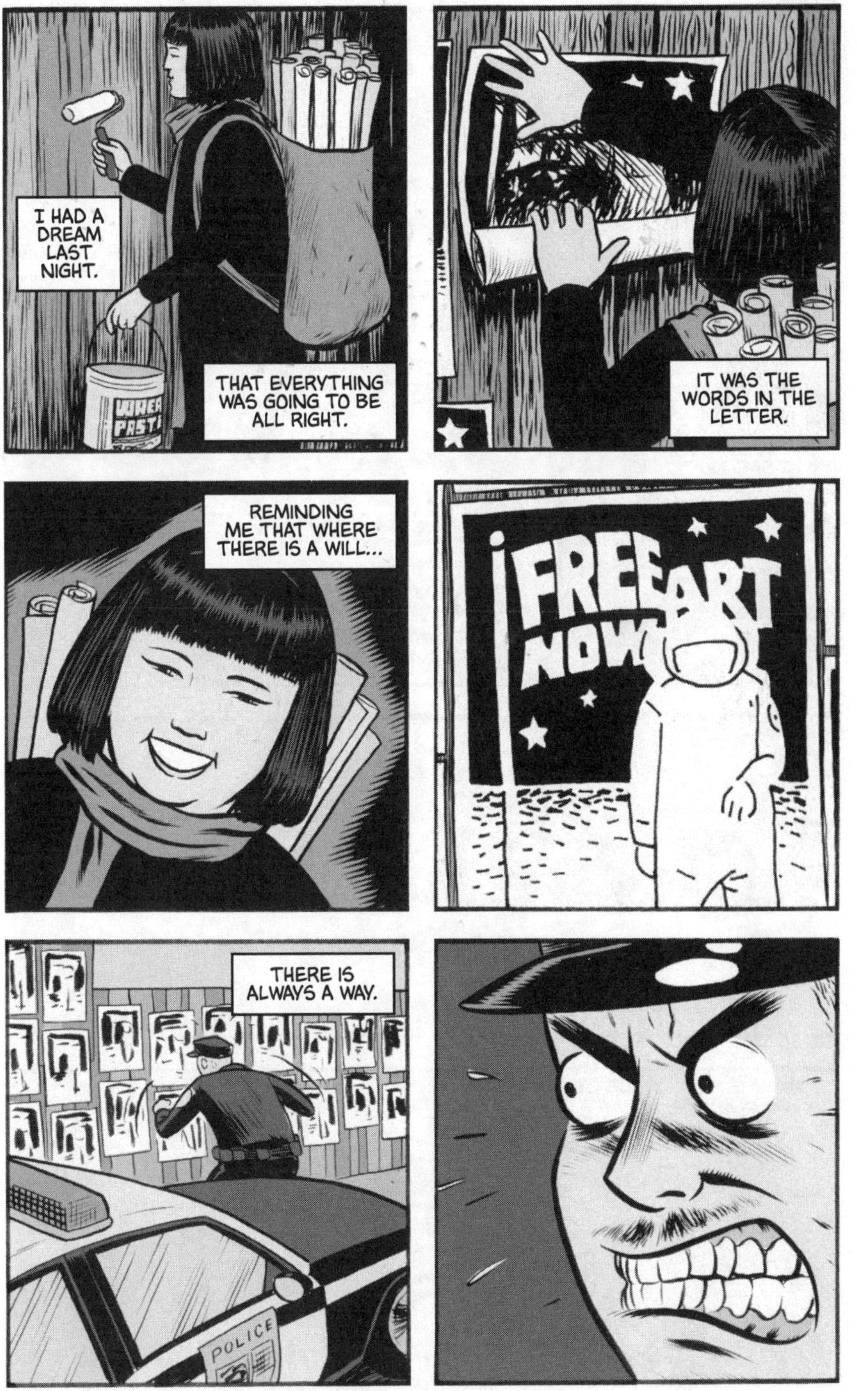
I HAD A DREAM LAST NIGHT.
THAT EVERYTHING WAS GOING TO BE ALL RIGHT.
IT WAS THE WORDS IN THE LETTER.
REMINDING ME THAT WHERE THERE IS A WILL...
¡FREE ART NOW
THERE IS ALWAYS A WAY.
POLICE

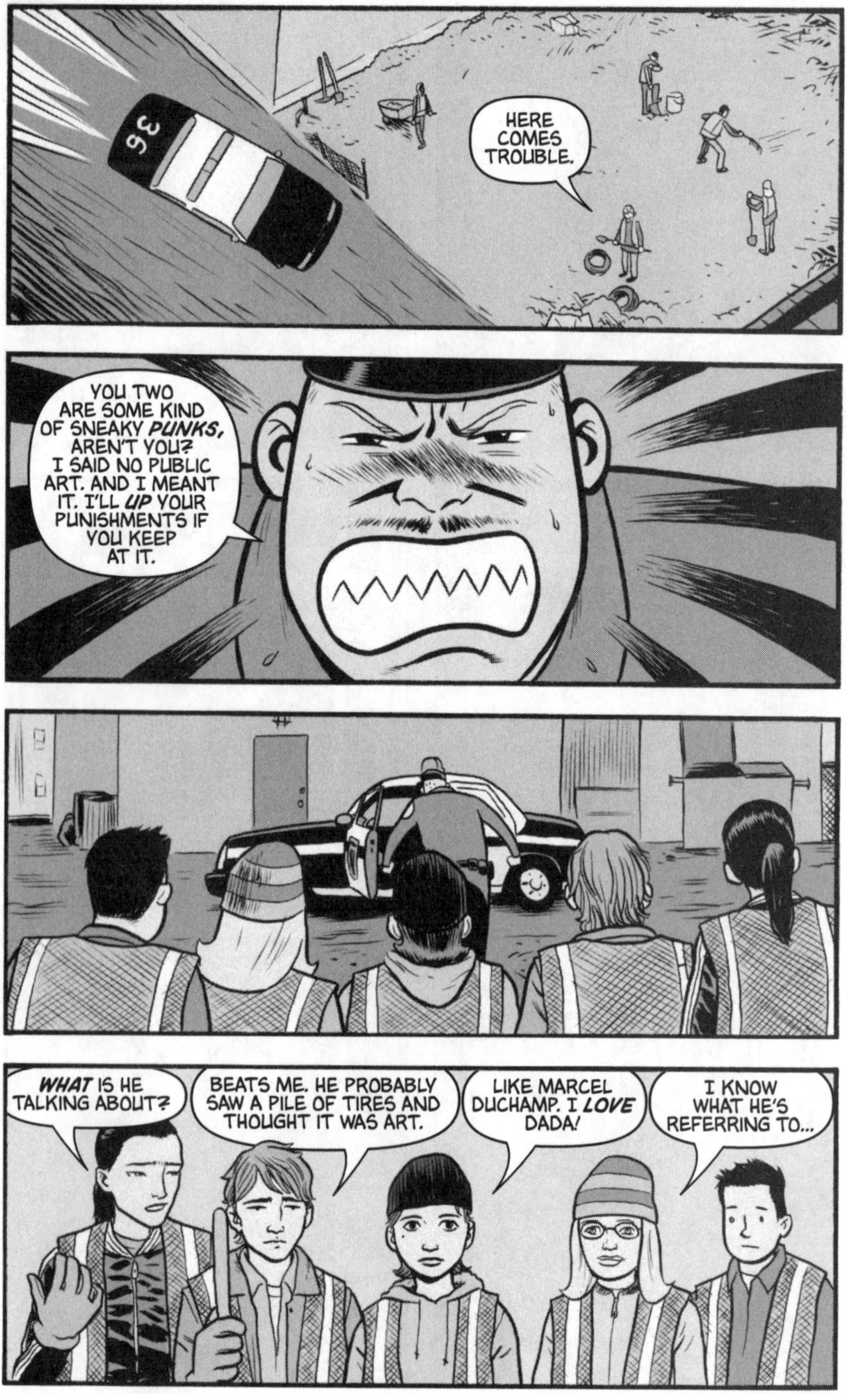
HERE COMES TROUBLE.
36
YOU TWO ARE SOME KIND OF SNEAKY PUNKS, AREN'T YOU? I SAID NO PUBLIC ART. AND I MEANT IT. I'LL UP YOUR PUNISHMENTS IF YOU KEEP AT IT.
WHAT IS HE TALKING ABOUT?
BEATS ME. HE PROBABLY SAW A PILE OF TIRES AND THOUGHT IT WAS ART.
LIKE MARCEL DUCHAMP. I LOVE DADA!
I KNOW WHAT HE'S REFERRING TO...

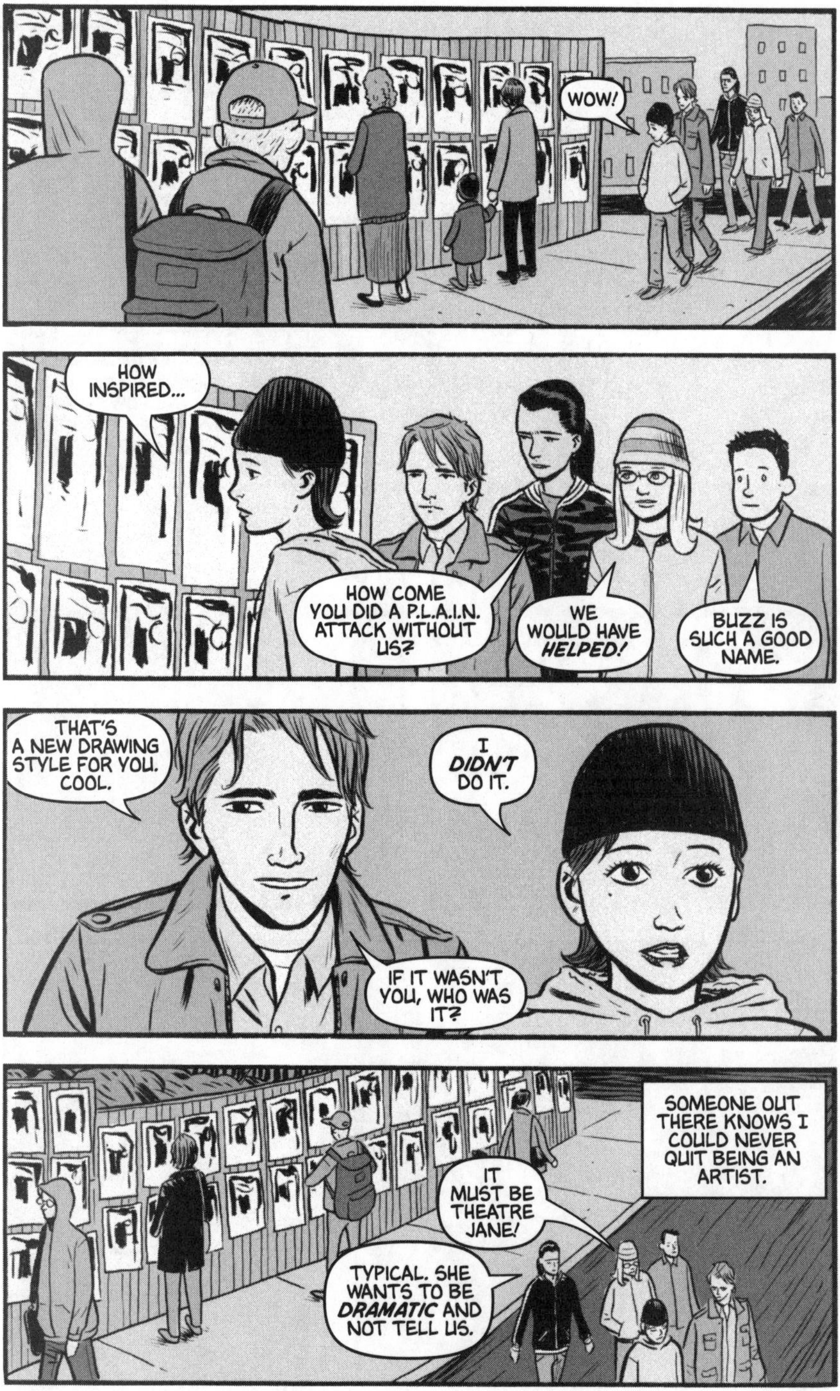
WOW!
HOW INSPIRED...
HOW COME YOU DID A P.L.A.I.N. ATTACK WITHOUT US?
WE WOULD HAVE HELPED!
BUZZ IS SUCH A GOOD NAME.
THAT'S A NEW DRAWING STYLE FOR YOU. COOL.
I DIDN'T DO IT.
IF IT WASN'T YOU, WHO WAS IT?
SOMEONE OUT THERE KNOWS I COULD NEVER QUIT BEING AN ARTIST.
IT MUST BE THEATRE JANE!
TYPICAL. SHE WANTS TO BE DRAMATIC AND NOT TELL US.

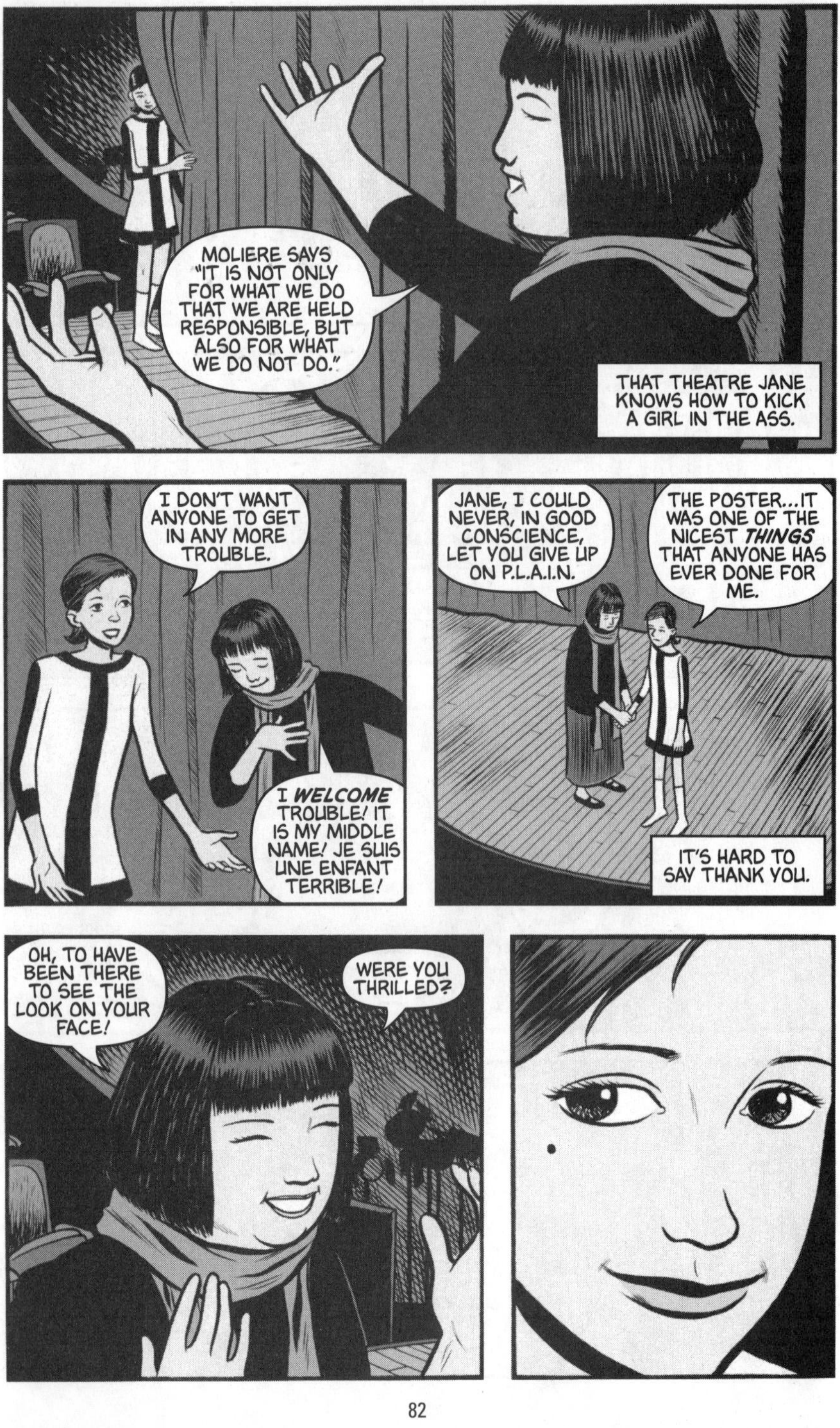
MOLIERE SAYS "IT IS NOT ONLY FOR WHAT WE DO THAT WE ARE HELD RESPONSIBLE, BUT ALSO FOR WHAT WE DO NOT DO."
THAT THEATRE JANE KNOWS HOW TO KICK A GIRL IN THE ASS.
I DON'T WANT ANYONE TO GET IN ANY MORE TROUBLE.
I *WELCOME* TROUBLE! IT IS MY MIDDLE NAME! JE SUIS UNE ENFANT TERRIBLE!
JANE, I COULD NEVER, IN GOOD CONSCIENCE, LET YOU GIVE UP ON P.L.A.I.N.
THE POSTER...IT WAS ONE OF THE NICEST *THINGS* THAT ANYONE HAS EVER DONE FOR ME.
IT'S HARD TO SAY THANK YOU.
OH, TO HAVE BEEN THERE TO SEE THE LOOK ON YOUR FACE!
WERE YOU THRILLED?

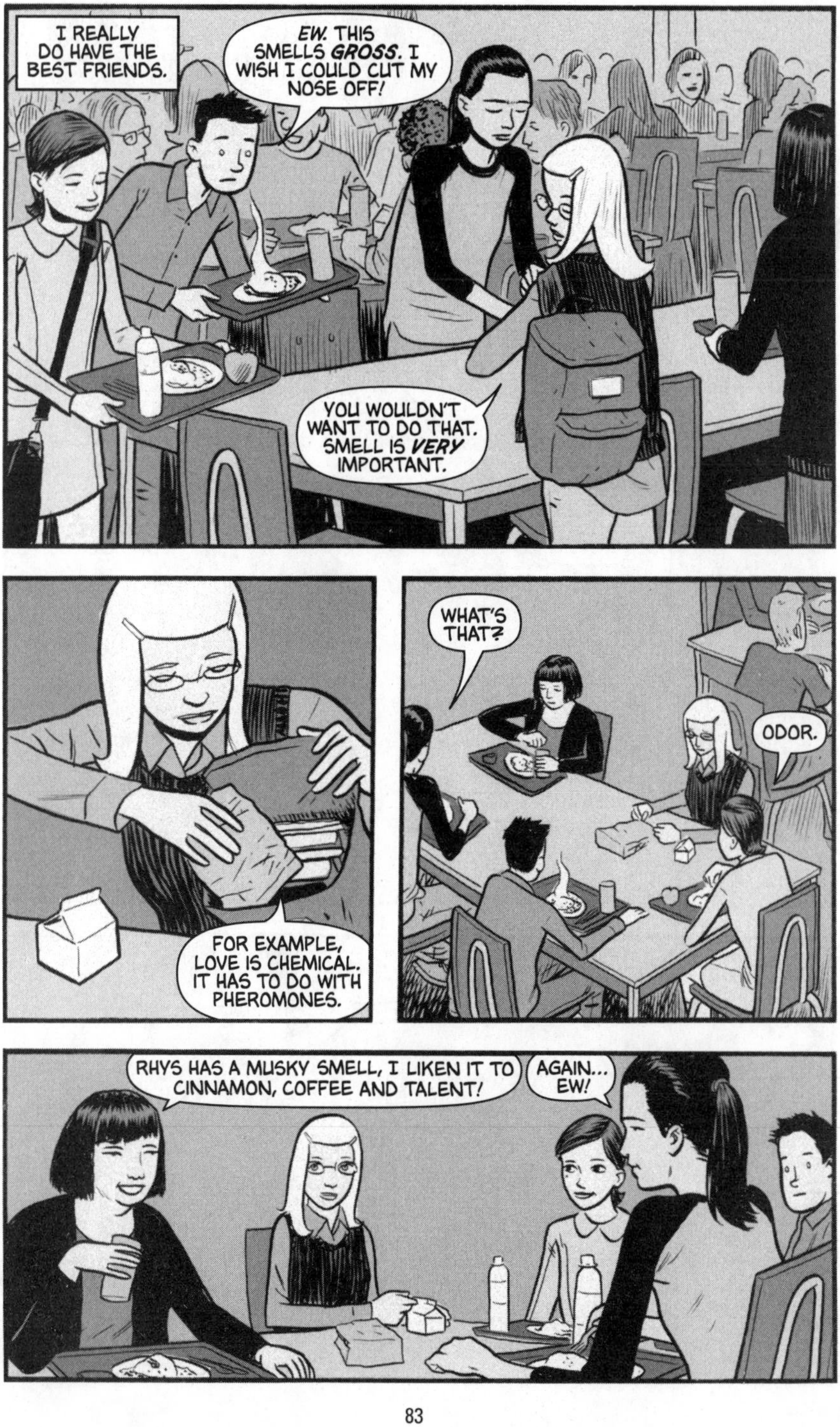

I REALLY DO HAVE THE BEST FRIENDS.
EW. THIS SMELLS GROSS. I WISH I COULD CUT MY NOSE OFF!
YOU WOULDN'T WANT TO DO THAT. SMELL IS VERY IMPORTANT.
FOR EXAMPLE, LOVE IS CHEMICAL. IT HAS TO DO WITH PHEROMONES.
WHAT'S THAT?
ODOR.
RHYS HAS A MUSKY SMELL, I LIKEN IT TO CINNAMON, COFFEE AND TALENT!
AGAIN... EW!

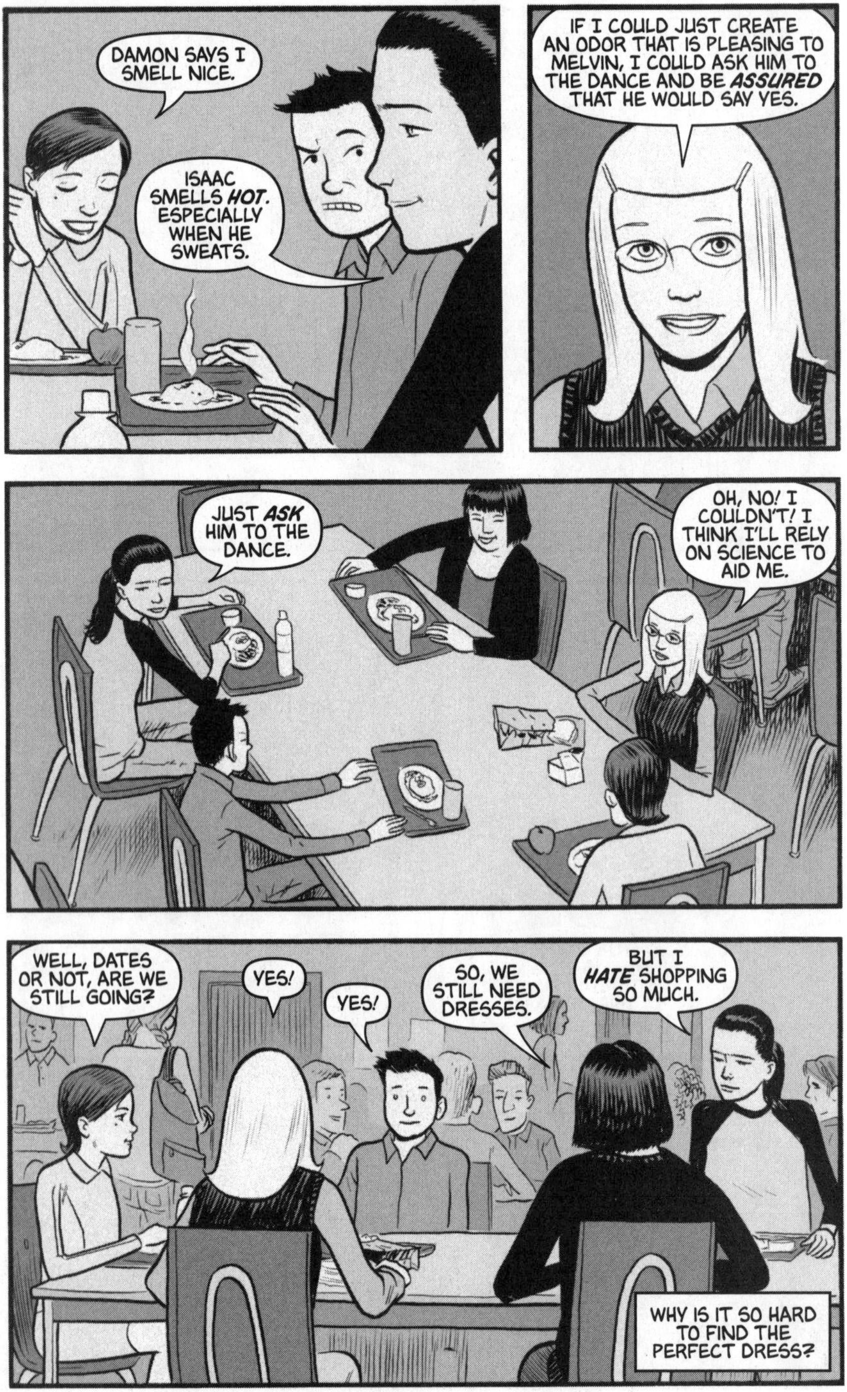
DAMON SAYS I SMELL NICE.
ISAAC SMELLS HOT. ESPECIALLY WHEN HE SWEATS.
IF I COULD JUST CREATE AN ODOR THAT IS PLEASING TO MELVIN, I COULD ASK HIM TO THE DANCE AND BE ASSURED THAT HE WOULD SAY YES.
JUST ASK HIM TO THE DANCE.
OH, NO! I COULDN'T! I THINK I'LL RELY ON SCIENCE TO AID ME.
WELL, DATES OR NOT, ARE WE STILL GOING?
YES!
YES!
SO, WE STILL NEED DRESSES.
BUT I HATE SHOPPING SO MUCH.
WHY IS IT SO HARD TO FIND THE PERFECT DRESS?

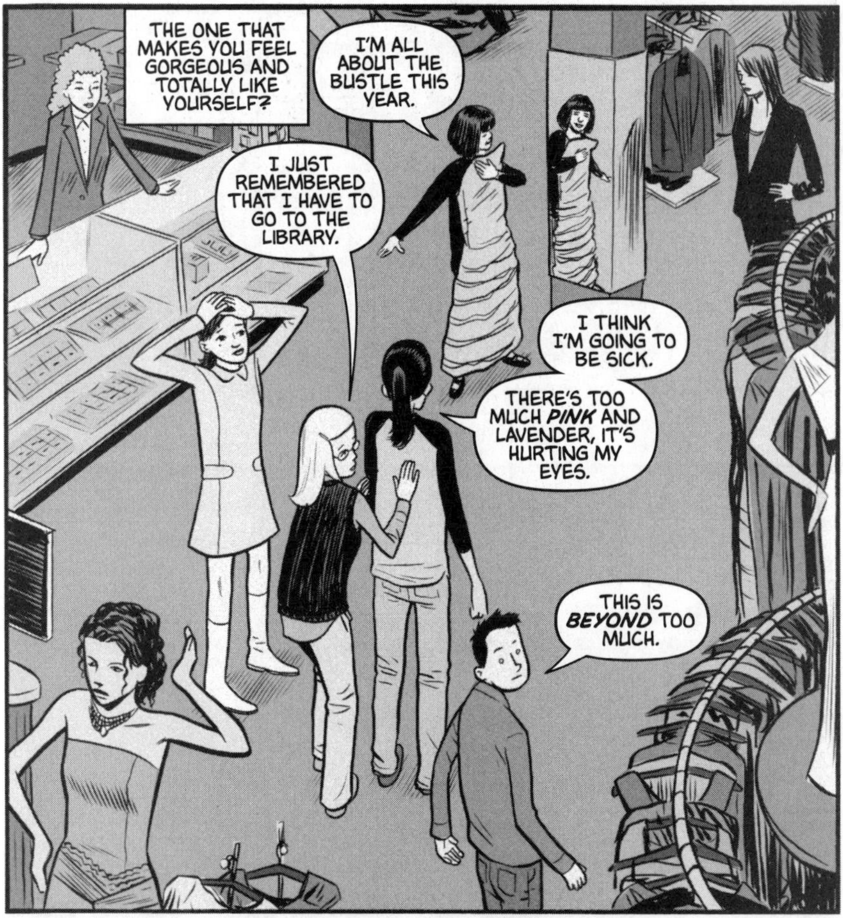
THE ONE THAT MAKES YOU FEEL GORGEOUS AND TOTALLY LIKE YOURSELF?
I'M ALL ABOUT THE BUSTLE THIS YEAR.
I JUST REMEMBERED THAT I HAVE TO GO TO THE LIBRARY.
I THINK I'M GOING TO BE SICK.
THERE'S TOO MUCH *PINK* AND LAVENDER, IT'S HURTING MY EYES.
THIS IS ***BEYOND*** TOO MUCH.

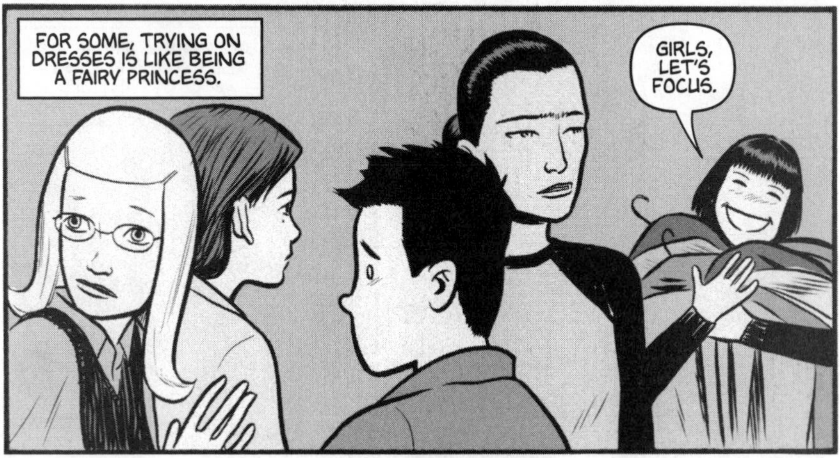
FOR SOME, TRYING ON DRESSES IS LIKE BEING A FAIRY PRINCESS.
GIRLS, LET'S FOCUS.

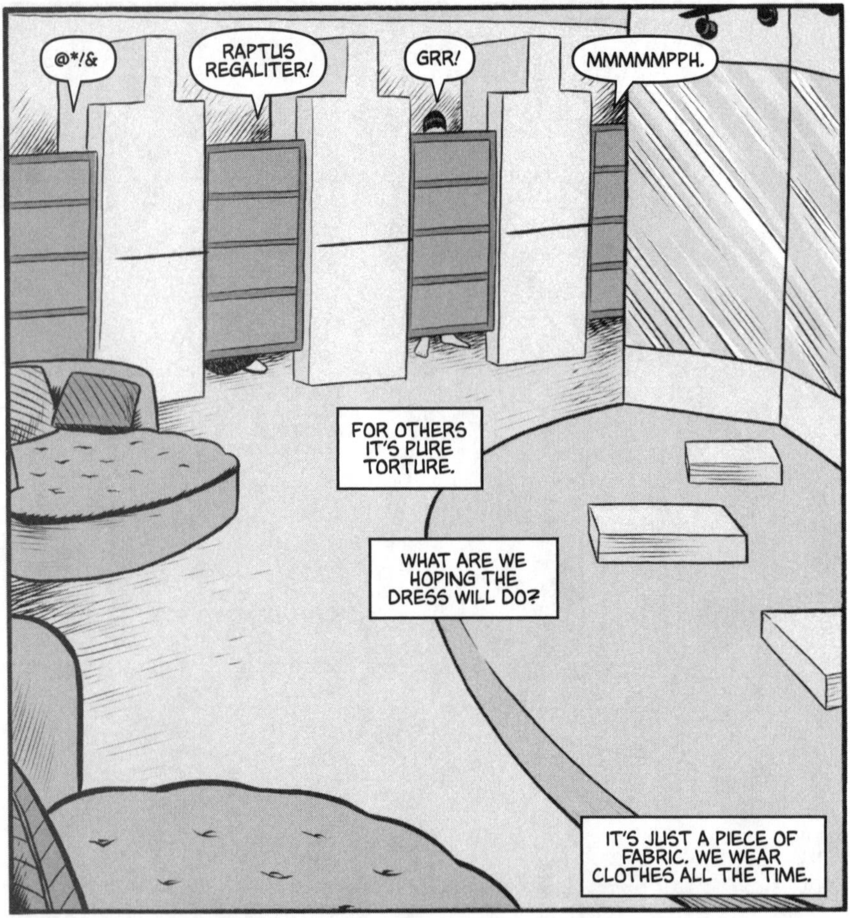
@*!&
RAPTUS REGALITER!
GRR!
MMMMMPPH.
FOR OTHERS IT'S PURE TORTURE.
WHAT ARE WE HOPING THE DRESS WILL DO?
IT'S JUST A PIECE OF FABRIC. WE WEAR CLOTHES ALL THE TIME.

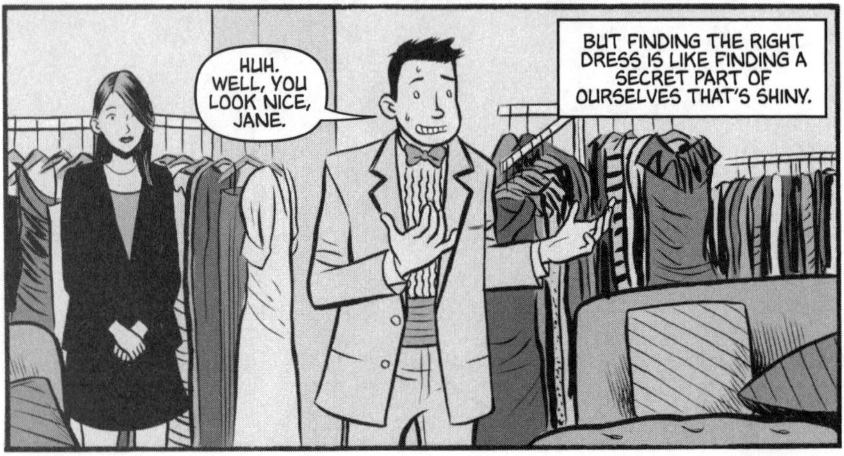
BUT FINDING THE RIGHT DRESS IS LIKE FINDING A SECRET PART OF OURSELVES THAT'S SHINY.
HUH. WELL, YOU LOOK NICE, JANE.

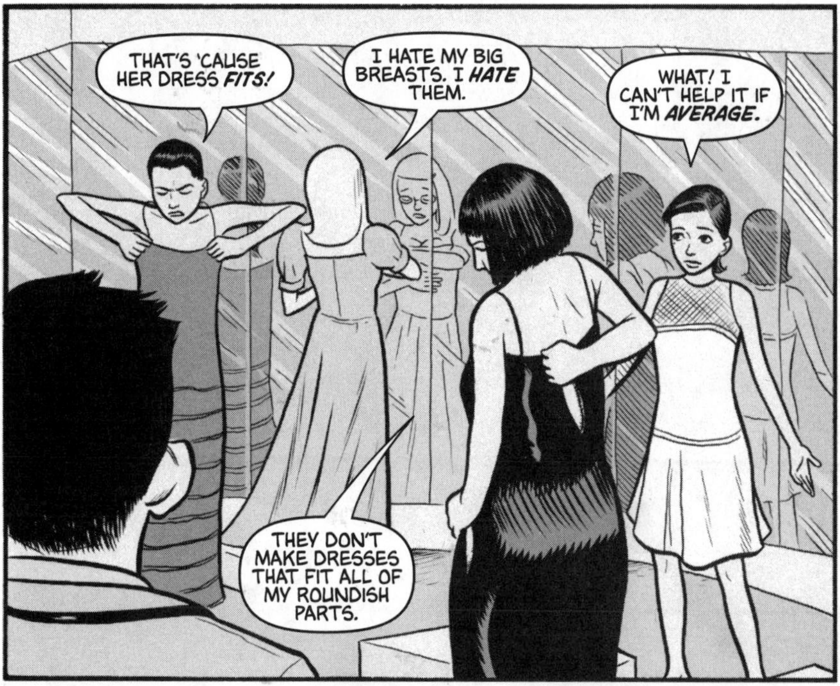
THAT'S 'CAUSE HER DRESS FITS!
I HATE MY BIG BREASTS. I HATE THEM.
WHAT! I CAN'T HELP IT IF I'M AVERAGE.
THEY DON'T MAKE DRESSES THAT FIT ALL OF MY ROUNDISH PARTS.

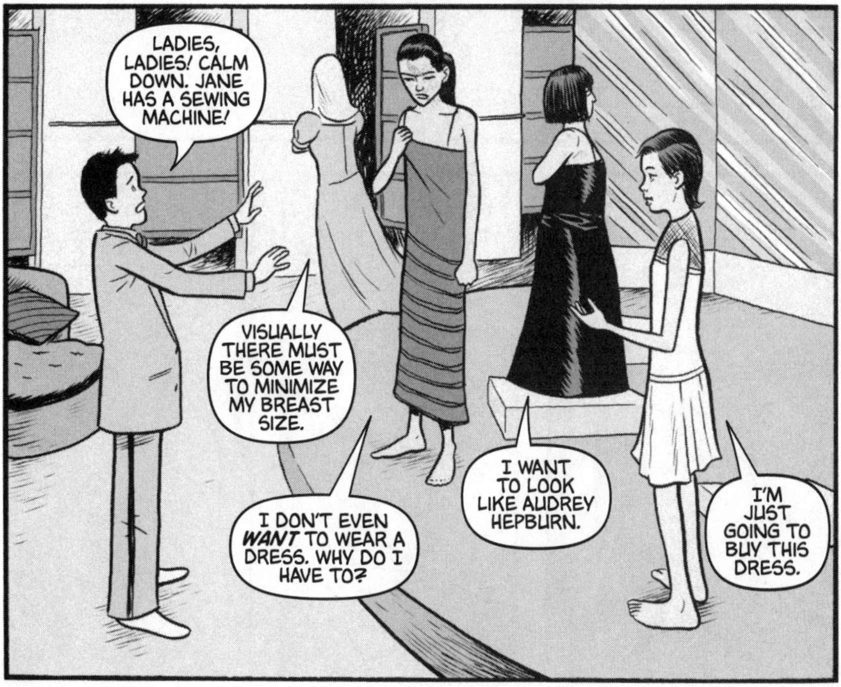
LADIES, LADIES! CALM DOWN. JANE HAS A SEWING MACHINE!
VISUALLY THERE MUST BE SOME WAY TO MINIMIZE MY BREAST SIZE.
I DON'T EVEN WANT TO WEAR A DRESS. WHY DO I HAVE TO?
I WANT TO LOOK LIKE AUDREY HEPBURN.
I'M JUST GOING TO BUY THIS DRESS.

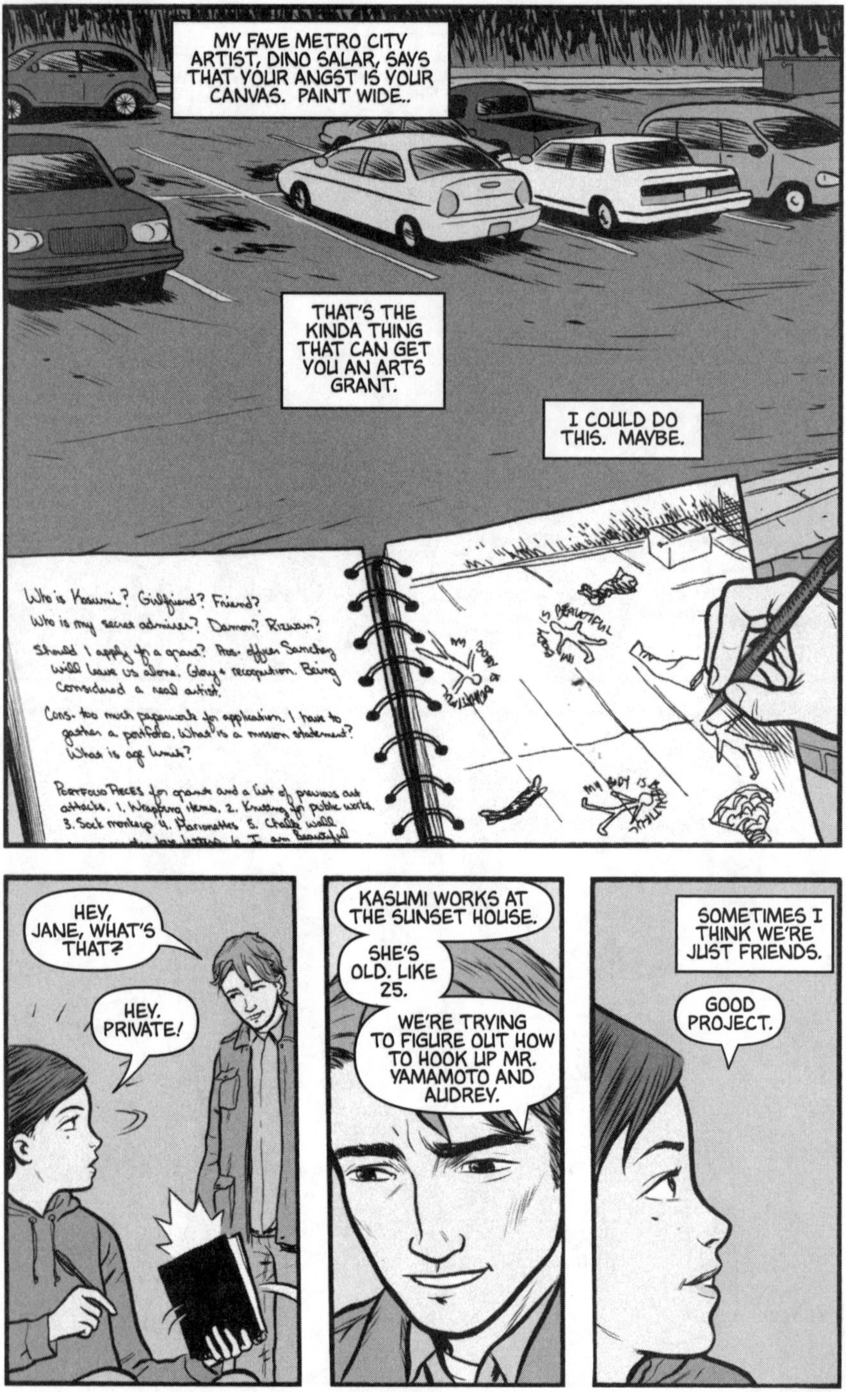
MY FAVE METRO CITY ARTIST, DINO SALAR, SAYS THAT YOUR ANGST IS YOUR CANVAS. PAINT WIDE..
THAT'S THE KINDA THING THAT CAN GET YOU AN ARTS GRANT.
I COULD DO THIS. MAYBE.
Who is Kasumi? Girlfriend? Friend?
Who is my secret admirer? Damon? Rizwan?
Should I apply for a grant? Pros- officer Sanchez will leave us alone. Glory + recognition. Being considered a real artist.
Cons- too much paperwork for application. I have to gather a portfolio. What is a mission statement? What is age limit?
Portfolio Pieces for grant and a list of previous art attacks. 1. Wrapping items. 2. Knitting for public works. 3. Sock monkeys 4. Marionettes 5. Chalk wall
HEY, JANE, WHAT'S THAT?
HEY. PRIVATE!
KASUMI WORKS AT THE SUNSET HOUSE.
SHE'S OLD. LIKE 25.
WE'RE TRYING TO FIGURE OUT HOW TO HOOK UP MR. YAMAMOTO AND AUDREY.
SOMETIMES I THINK WE'RE JUST FRIENDS.
GOOD PROJECT.

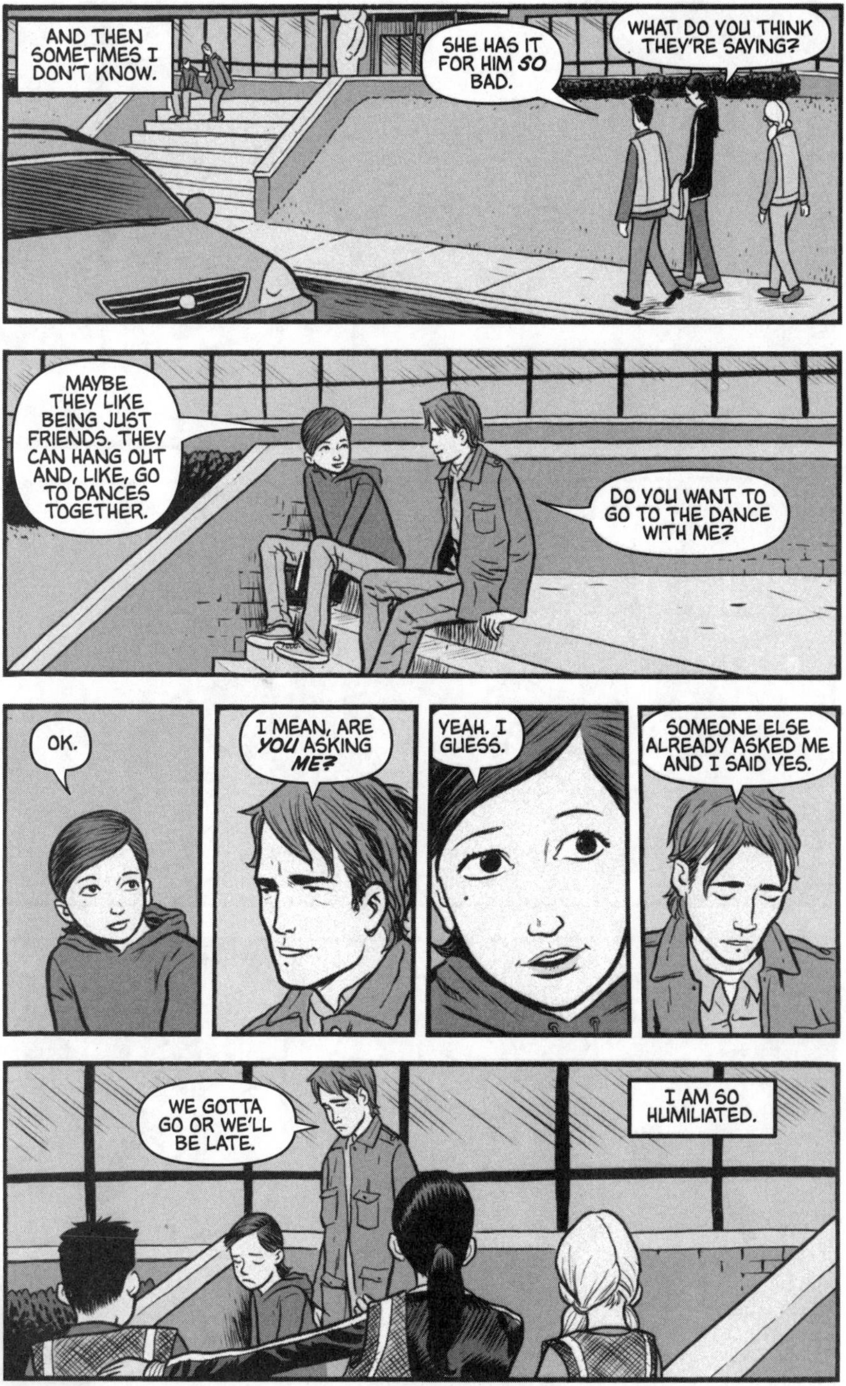
AND THEN SOMETIMES I DON'T KNOW.
SHE HAS IT FOR HIM *SO* BAD.
WHAT DO YOU THINK THEY'RE SAYING?
MAYBE THEY LIKE BEING JUST FRIENDS. THEY CAN HANG OUT AND, LIKE, GO TO DANCES TOGETHER.
DO YOU WANT TO GO TO THE DANCE WITH ME?
OK.
I MEAN, ARE *YOU* ASKING *ME?*
YEAH. I GUESS.
SOMEONE ELSE ALREADY ASKED ME AND I SAID YES.
WE GOTTA GO OR WE'LL BE LATE.
I AM SO HUMILIATED.

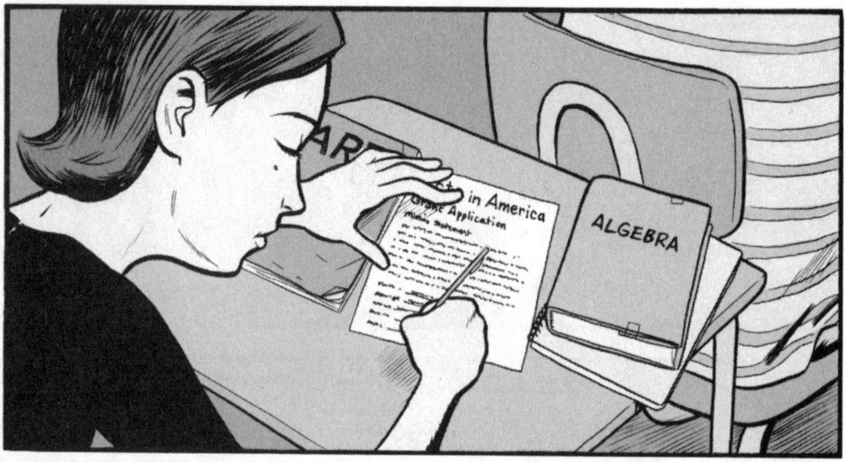
in America
Grant Application
ALGEBRA

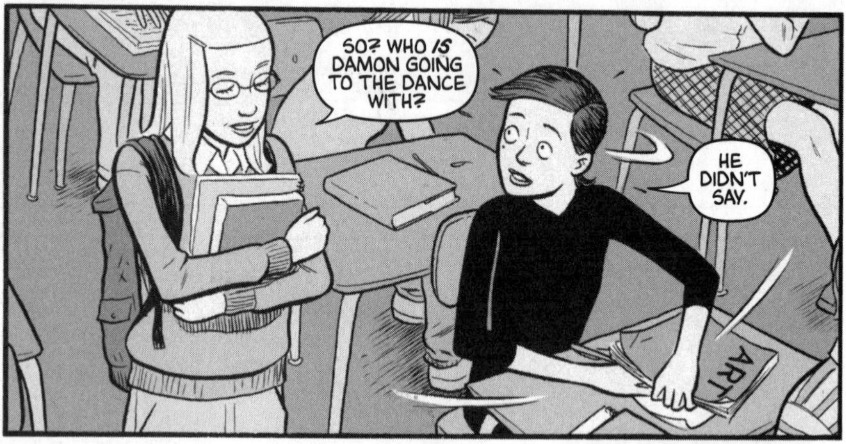
SO? WHO *IS* DAMON GOING TO THE DANCE WITH?
HE DIDN'T SAY.
ART

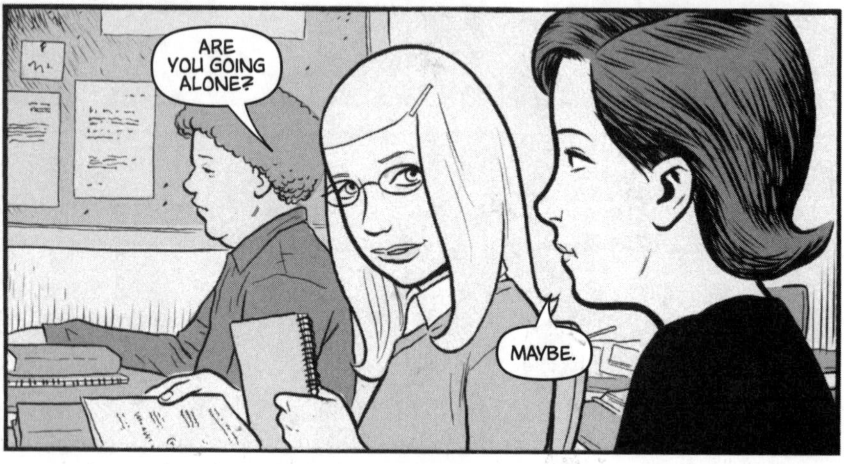
ARE YOU GOING ALONE?
MAYBE.

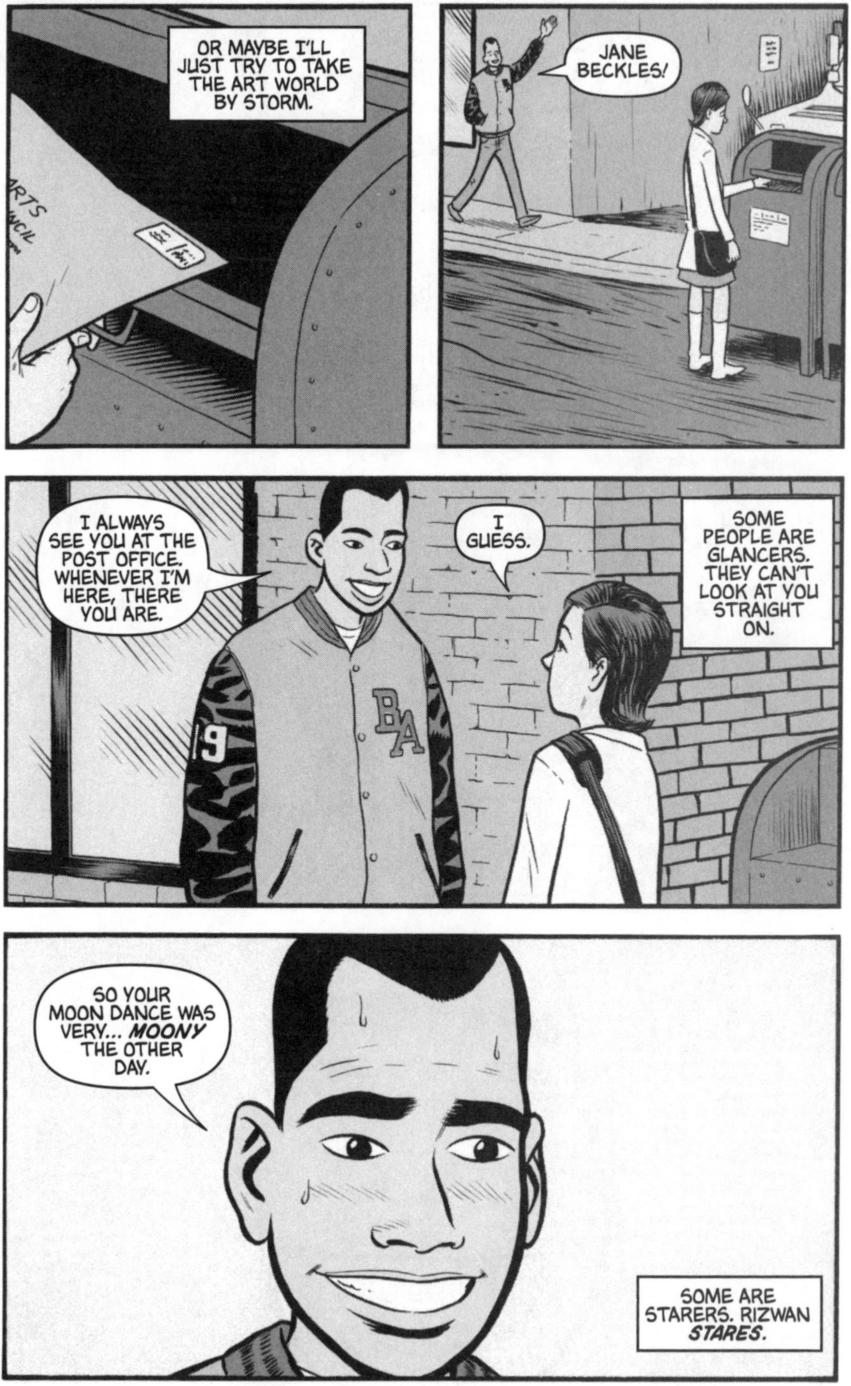
OR MAYBE I'LL JUST TRY TO TAKE THE ART WORLD BY STORM.
JANE BECKLES!
I ALWAYS SEE YOU AT THE POST OFFICE. WHENEVER I'M HERE, THERE YOU ARE.
I GUESS.
SOME PEOPLE ARE GLANCERS. THEY CAN'T LOOK AT YOU STRAIGHT ON.
SO YOUR MOON DANCE WAS VERY... ***MOONY*** THE OTHER DAY.
SOME ARE STARERS. RIZWAN ***STARES.***

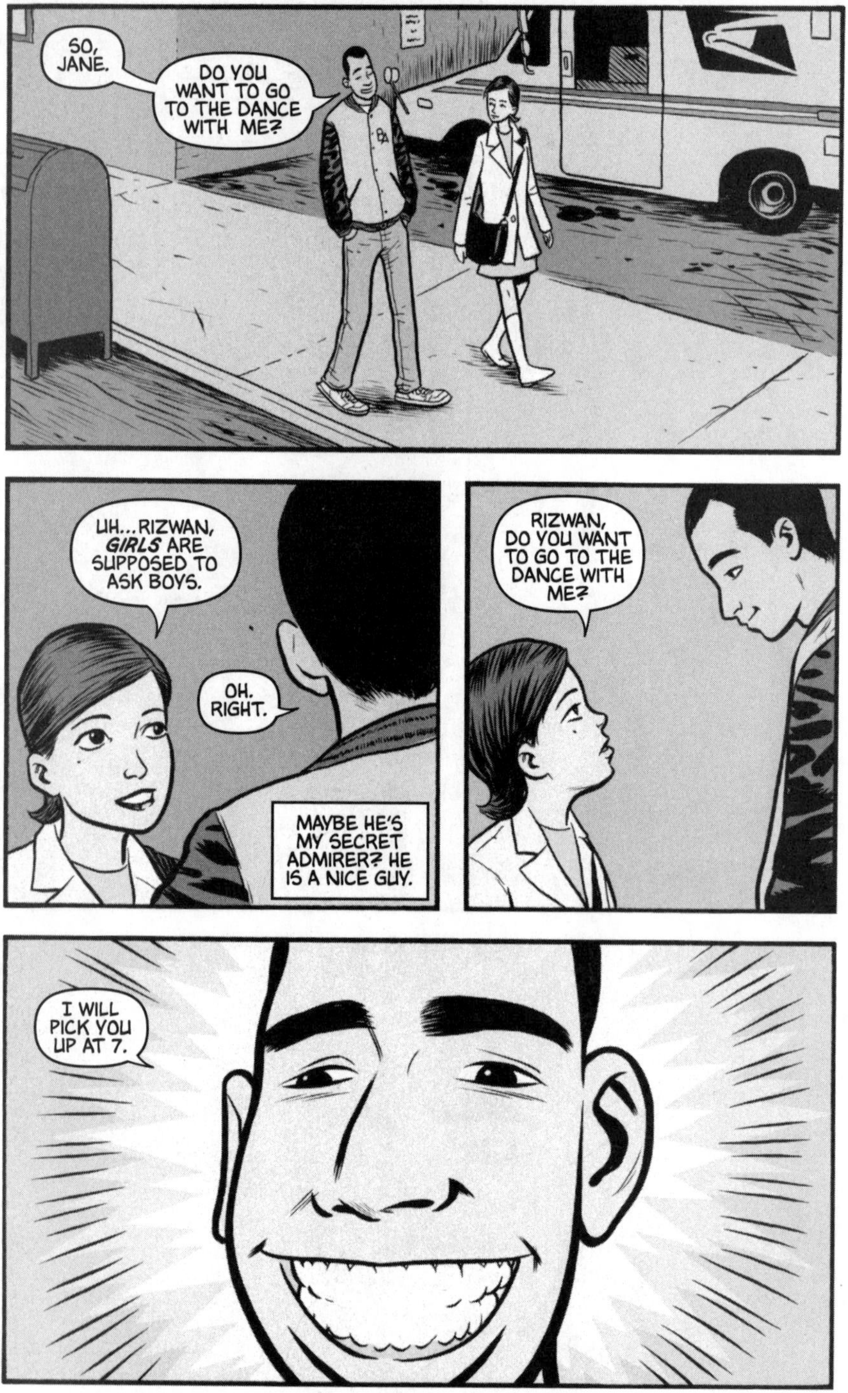
SO, JANE.
DO YOU WANT TO GO TO THE DANCE WITH ME?
UH... RIZWAN, GIRLS ARE SUPPOSED TO ASK BOYS.
OH. RIGHT.
MAYBE HE'S MY SECRET ADMIRER? HE IS A NICE GUY.
RIZWAN, DO YOU WANT TO GO TO THE DANCE WITH ME?
I WILL PICK YOU UP AT 7.

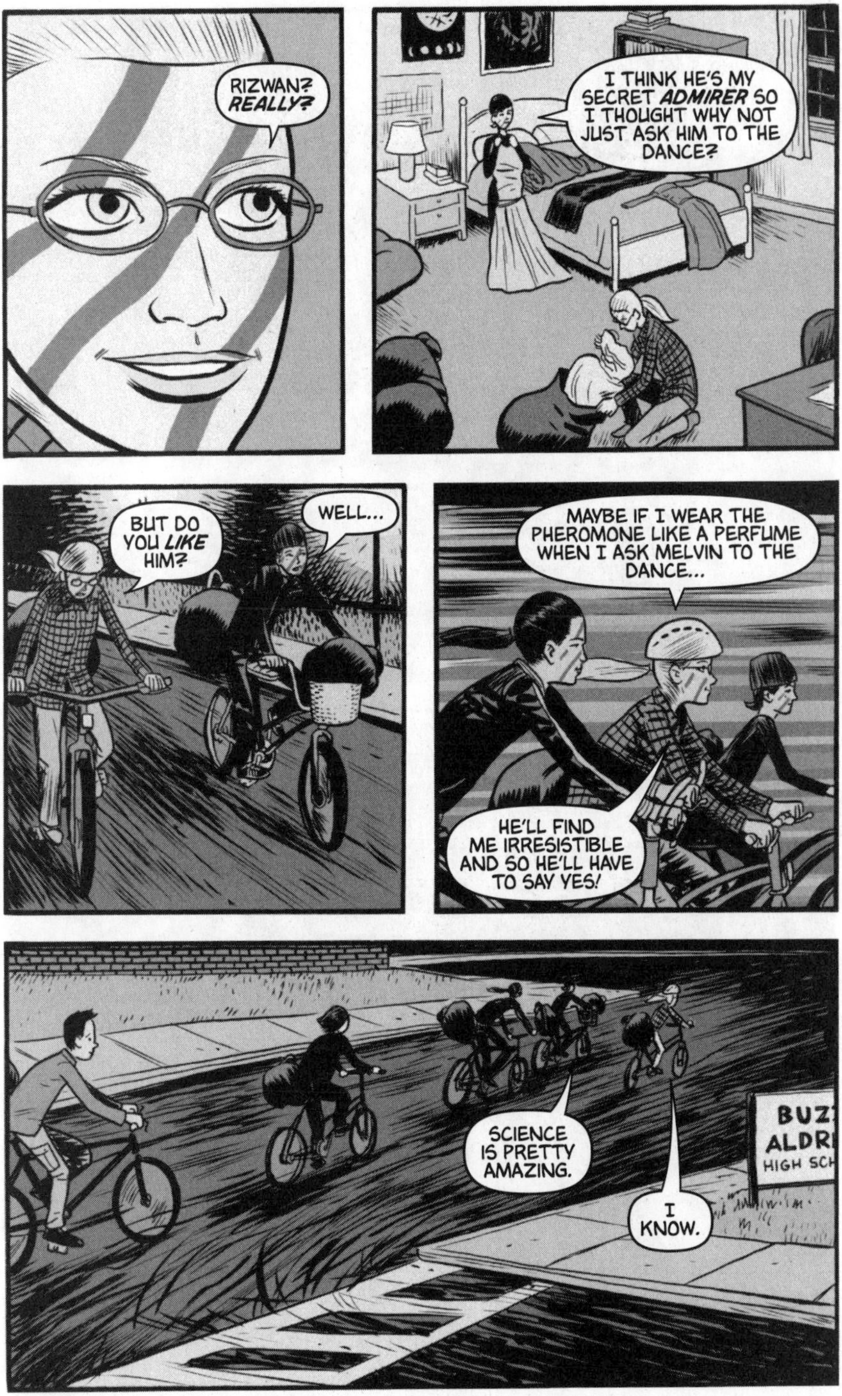
RIZWAN? *REALLY?*
I THINK HE'S MY SECRET *ADMIRER* SO I THOUGHT WHY NOT JUST ASK HIM TO THE DANCE?
BUT DO YOU *LIKE* HIM?
WELL...
MAYBE IF I WEAR THE PHEROMONE LIKE A PERFUME WHEN I ASK MELVIN TO THE DANCE...
HE'LL FIND ME IRRESISTIBLE AND SO HE'LL HAVE TO SAY YES!
SCIENCE IS PRETTY AMAZING.
I KNOW.

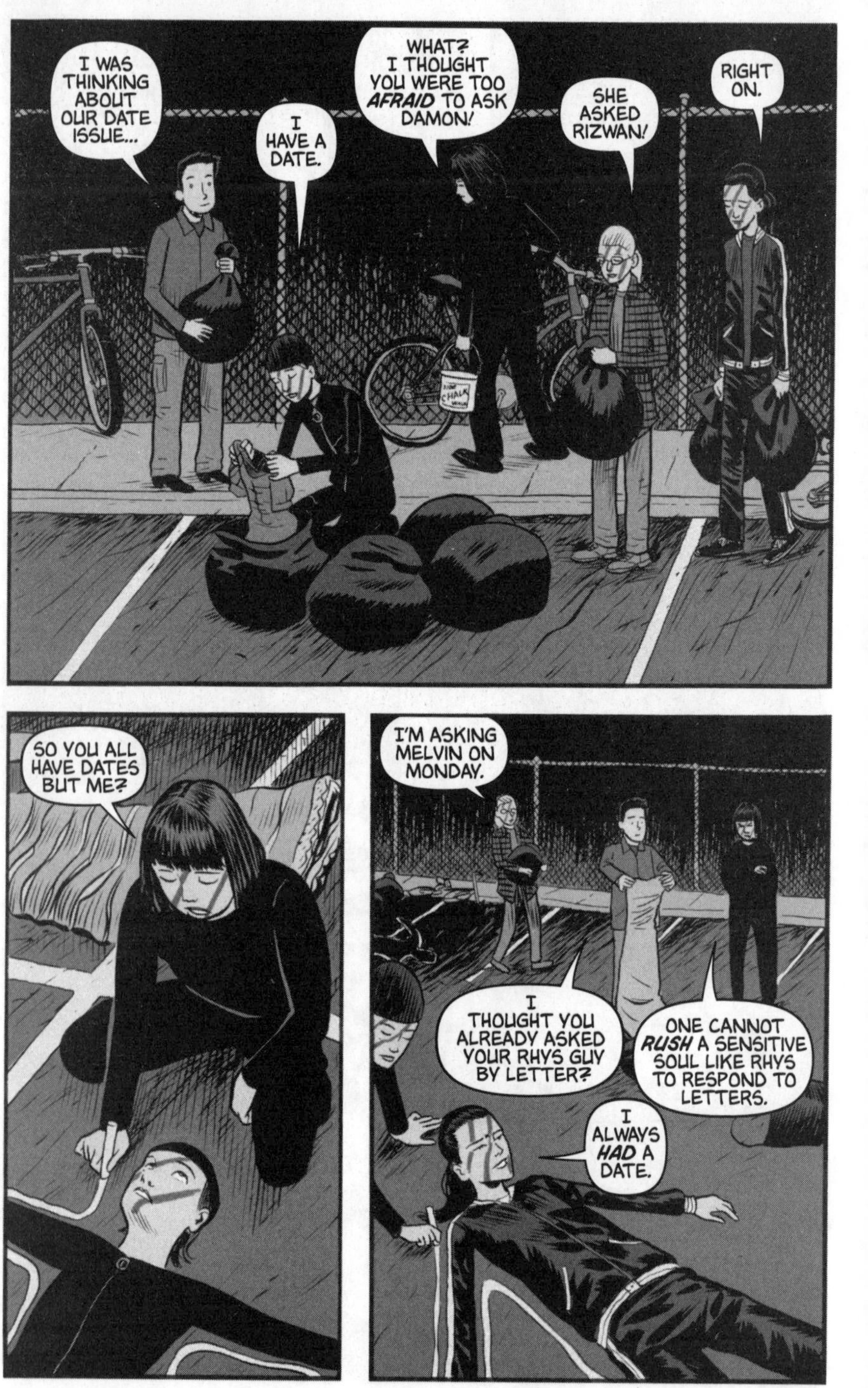
I WAS THINKING ABOUT OUR DATE ISSUE...
I HAVE A DATE.
WHAT? I THOUGHT YOU WERE TOO AFRAID TO ASK DAMON!
SHE ASKED RIZWAN!
RIGHT ON.
SO YOU ALL HAVE DATES BUT ME?
I'M ASKING MELVIN ON MONDAY.
I THOUGHT YOU ALREADY ASKED YOUR RHYS GUY BY LETTER?
ONE CANNOT RUSH A SENSITIVE SOUL LIKE RHYS TO RESPOND TO LETTERS.
I ALWAYS HAD A DATE.

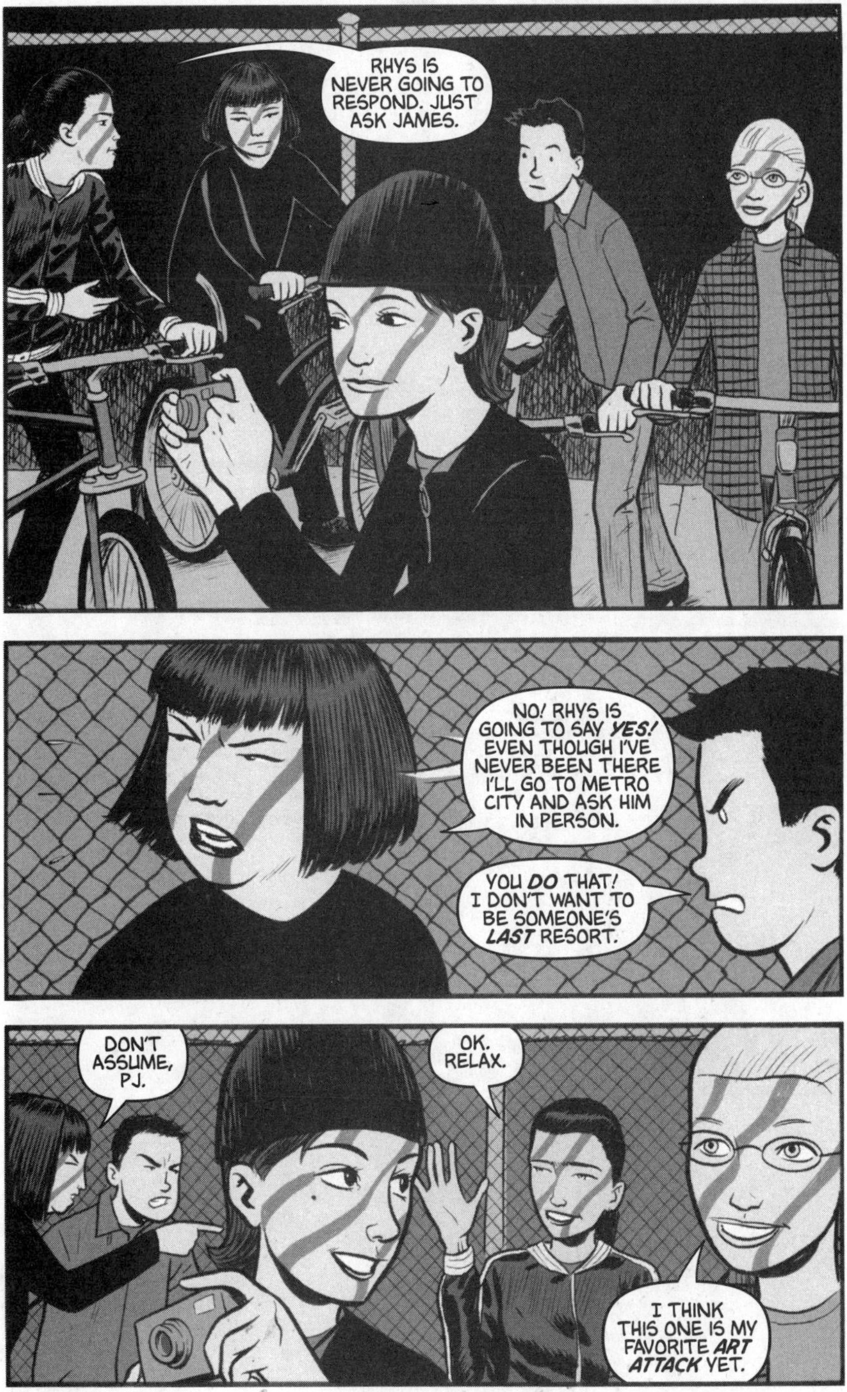
RHYS IS NEVER GOING TO RESPOND. JUST ASK JAMES.
NO! RHYS IS GOING TO SAY *YES!* EVEN THOUGH I'VE NEVER BEEN THERE I'LL GO TO METRO CITY AND ASK HIM IN PERSON.
YOU *DO* THAT! I DON'T WANT TO BE SOMEONE'S *LAST* RESORT.
DON'T ASSUME, PJ.
OK. RELAX.
I THINK THIS ONE IS MY FAVORITE *ART ATTACK* YET.

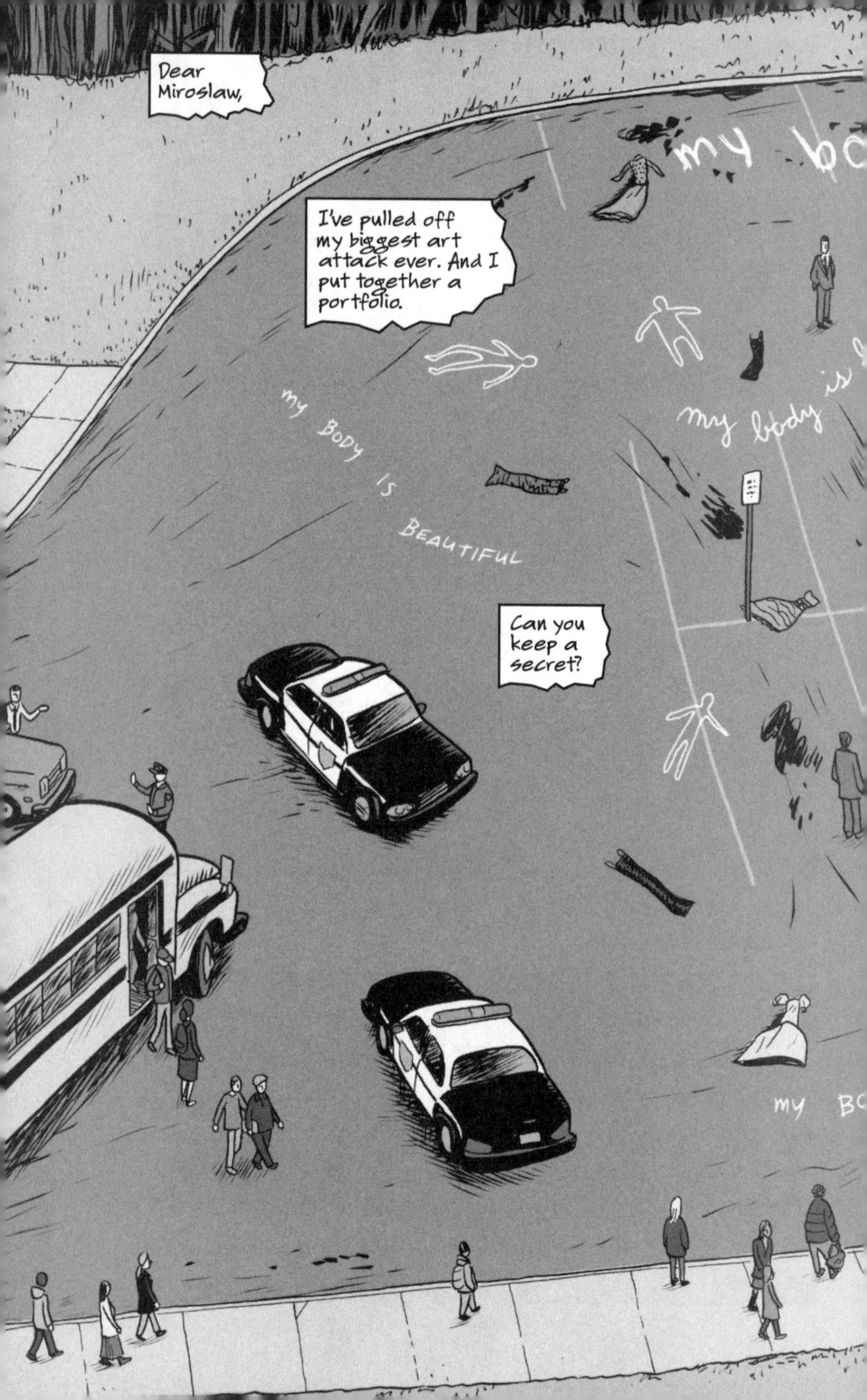
Dear Miroslaw,
I've pulled off my biggest art attack ever. And I put together a portfolio.
Can you keep a secret?
my body is beautiful
my body is
my bo
my BO

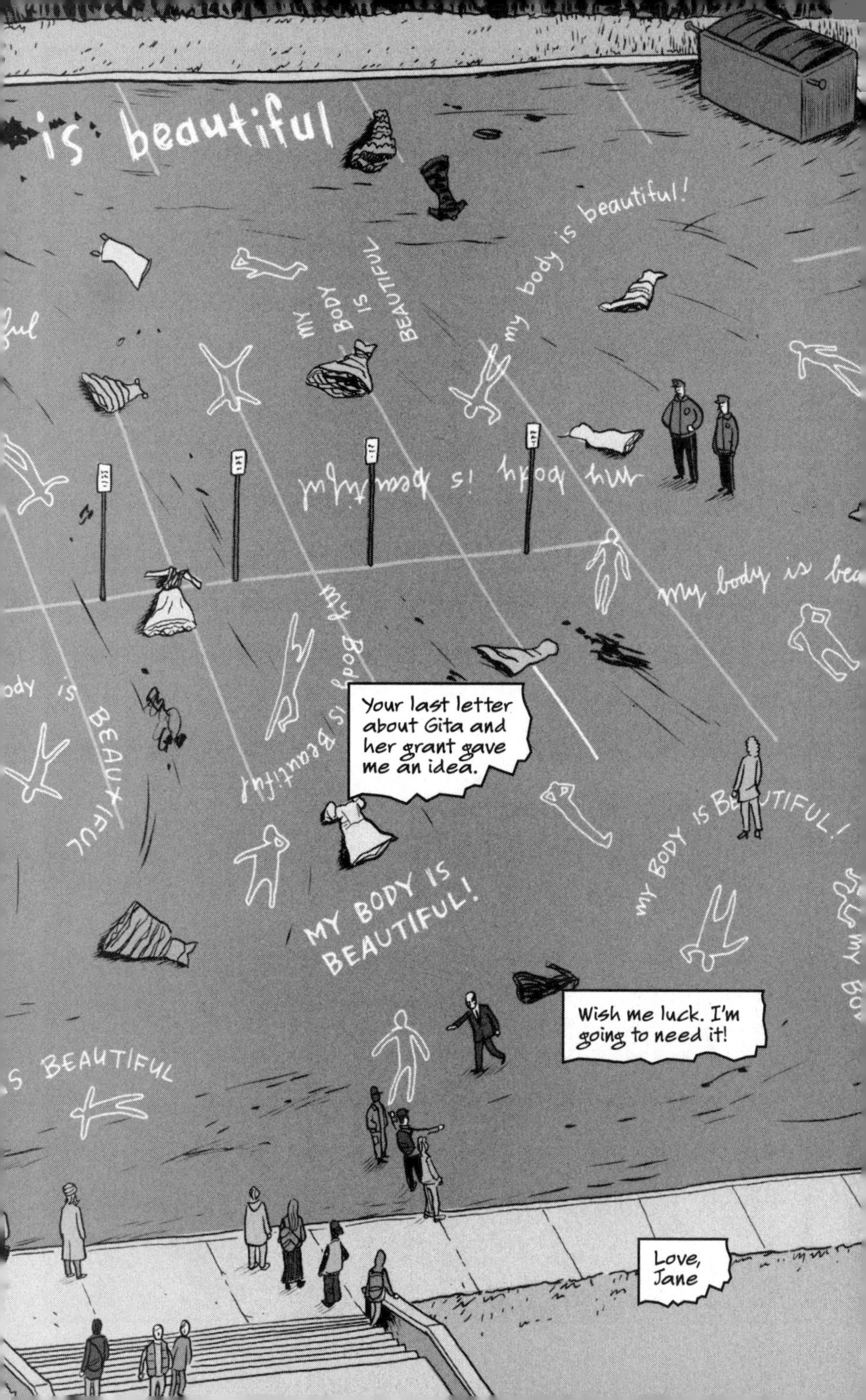

is beautiful
my body is beautiful!
MY BODY IS BEAUTIFUL
my body is beautiful
my body is beautiful
Your last letter about Gita and her grant gave me an idea.
MY BODY IS BEAUTIFUL!
MY BODY IS BEAUTIFUL!
Wish me luck. I'm going to need it!
IS BEAUTIFUL
Love, Jane

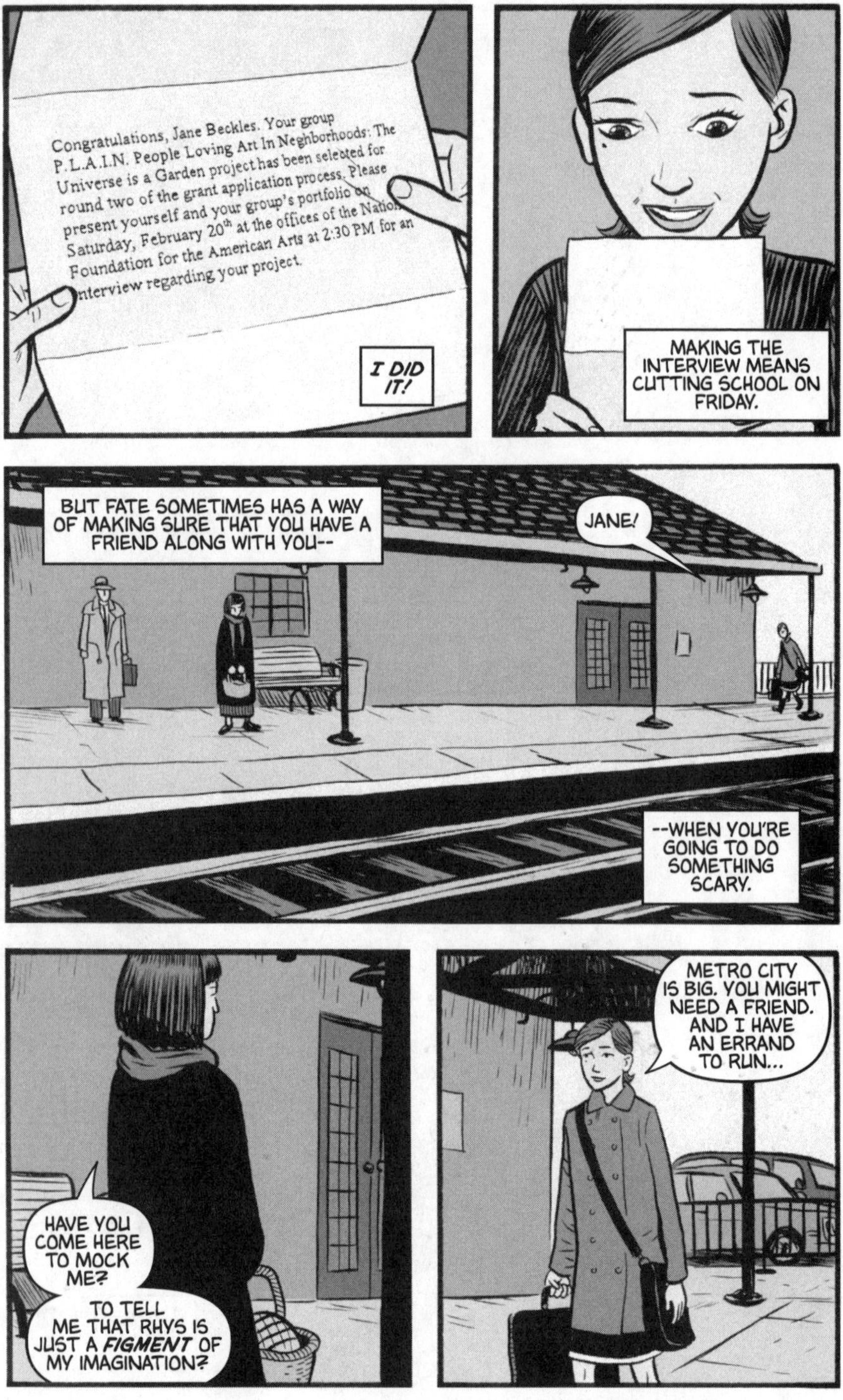
Congratulations, Jane Beckles. Your group
P.L.A.I.N. People Loving Art In Neighborhoods: The
Universe is a Garden project has been selected for
round two of the grant application process. Please
present yourself and your group's portfolio on
Saturday, February 20th at the offices of the Natio
Foundation for the American Arts at 2:30 PM for an
interview regarding your project.
I DID IT!
MAKING THE INTERVIEW MEANS CUTTING SCHOOL ON FRIDAY.
BUT FATE SOMETIMES HAS A WAY OF MAKING SURE THAT YOU HAVE A FRIEND ALONG WITH YOU--
JANE!
--WHEN YOU'RE GOING TO DO SOMETHING SCARY.
HAVE YOU COME HERE TO MOCK ME?
TO TELL ME THAT RHYS IS JUST A FIGMENT OF MY IMAGINATION?
METRO CITY IS BIG. YOU MIGHT NEED A FRIEND. AND I HAVE AN ERRAND TO RUN...

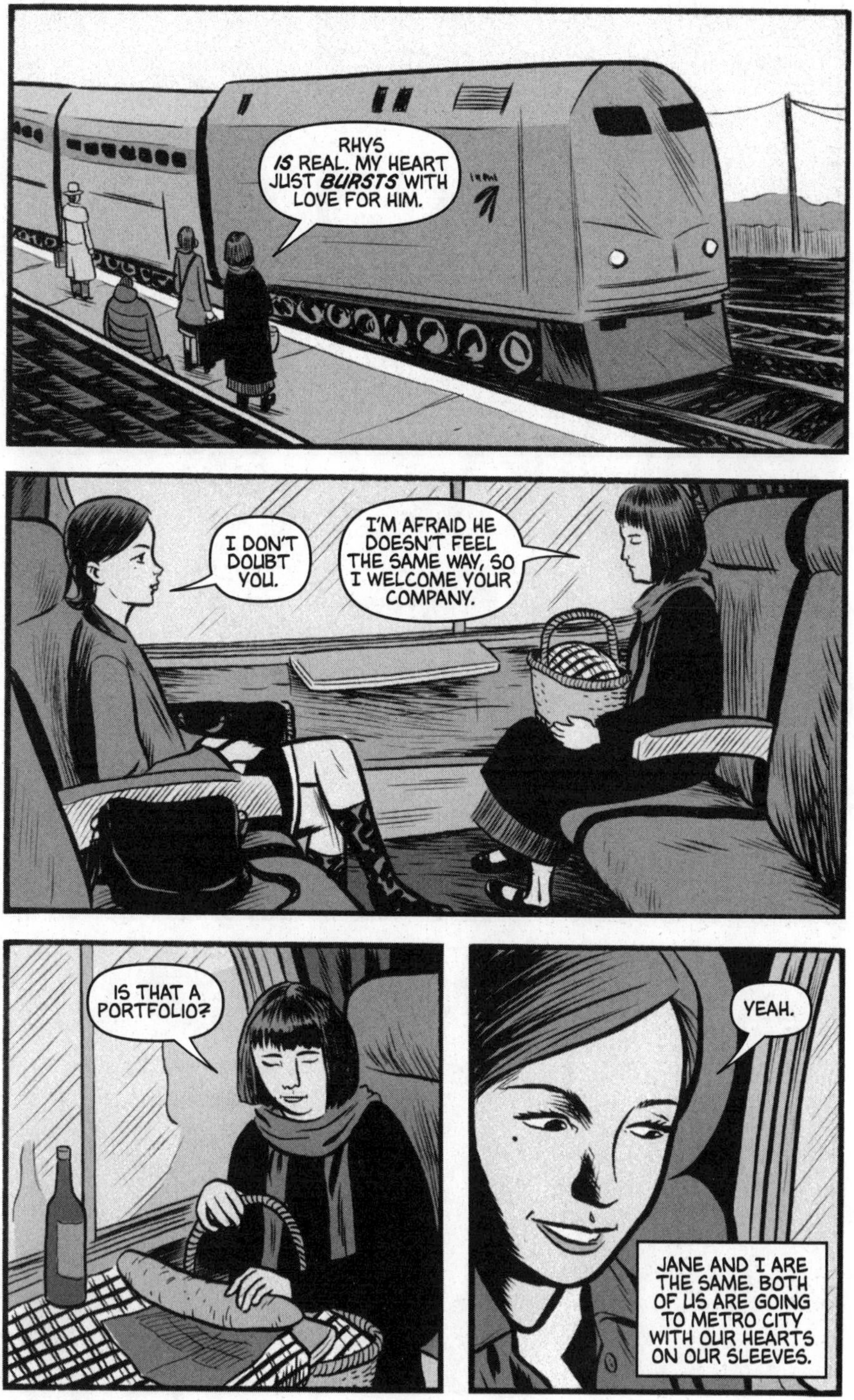
RHYS *IS* REAL. MY HEART JUST *BURSTS* WITH LOVE FOR HIM.
I DON'T DOUBT YOU.
I'M AFRAID HE DOESN'T FEEL THE SAME WAY, SO I WELCOME YOUR COMPANY.
IS THAT A PORTFOLIO?
YEAH.
JANE AND I ARE THE SAME. BOTH OF US ARE GOING TO METRO CITY WITH OUR HEARTS ON OUR SLEEVES.

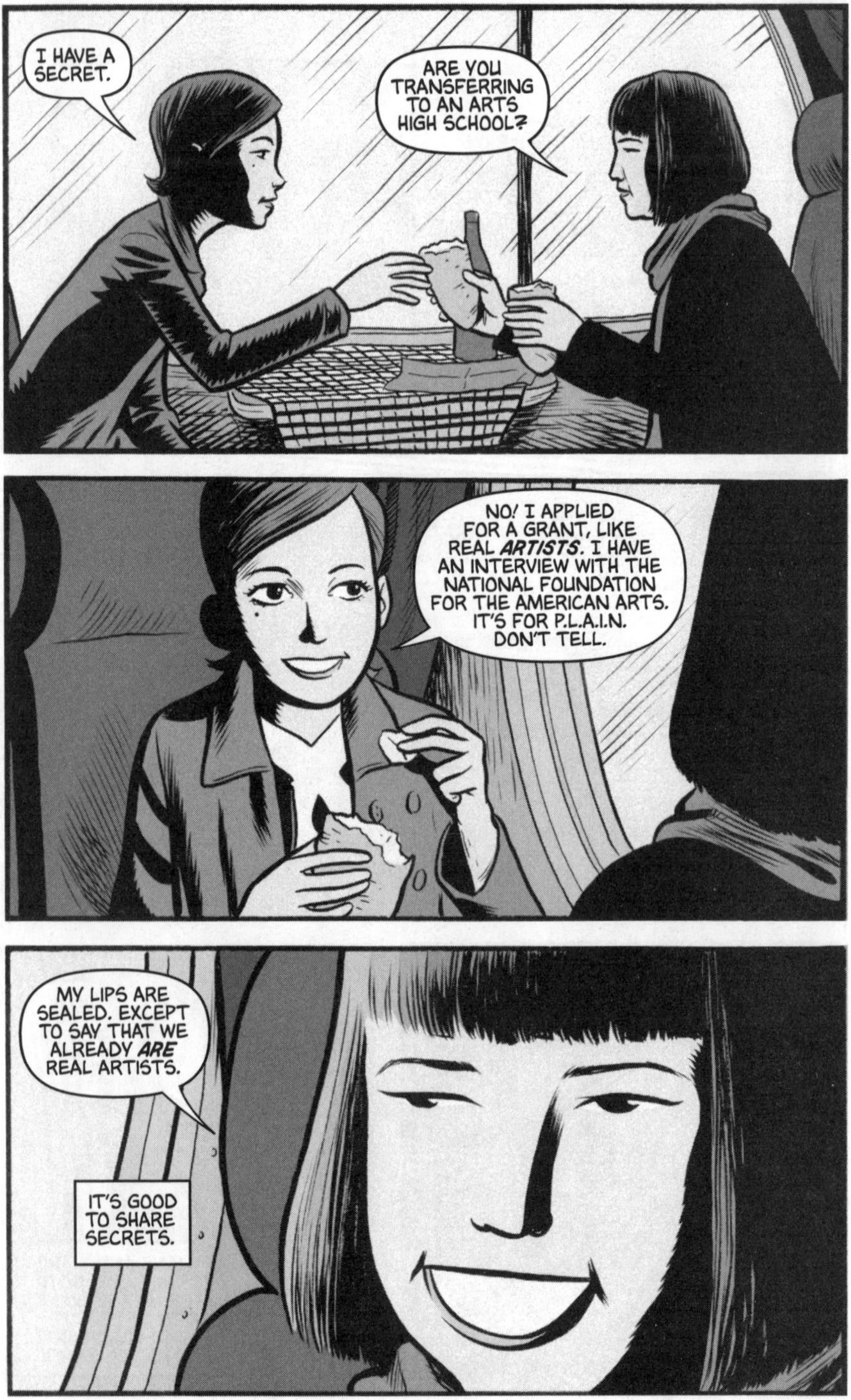
I HAVE A SECRET.
ARE YOU TRANSFERRING TO AN ARTS HIGH SCHOOL?
NO! I APPLIED FOR A GRANT, LIKE REAL *ARTISTS*. I HAVE AN INTERVIEW WITH THE NATIONAL FOUNDATION FOR THE AMERICAN ARTS. IT'S FOR P.L.A.I.N. DON'T TELL.
MY LIPS ARE SEALED. EXCEPT TO SAY THAT WE ALREADY *ARE* REAL ARTISTS.
IT'S GOOD TO SHARE SECRETS.

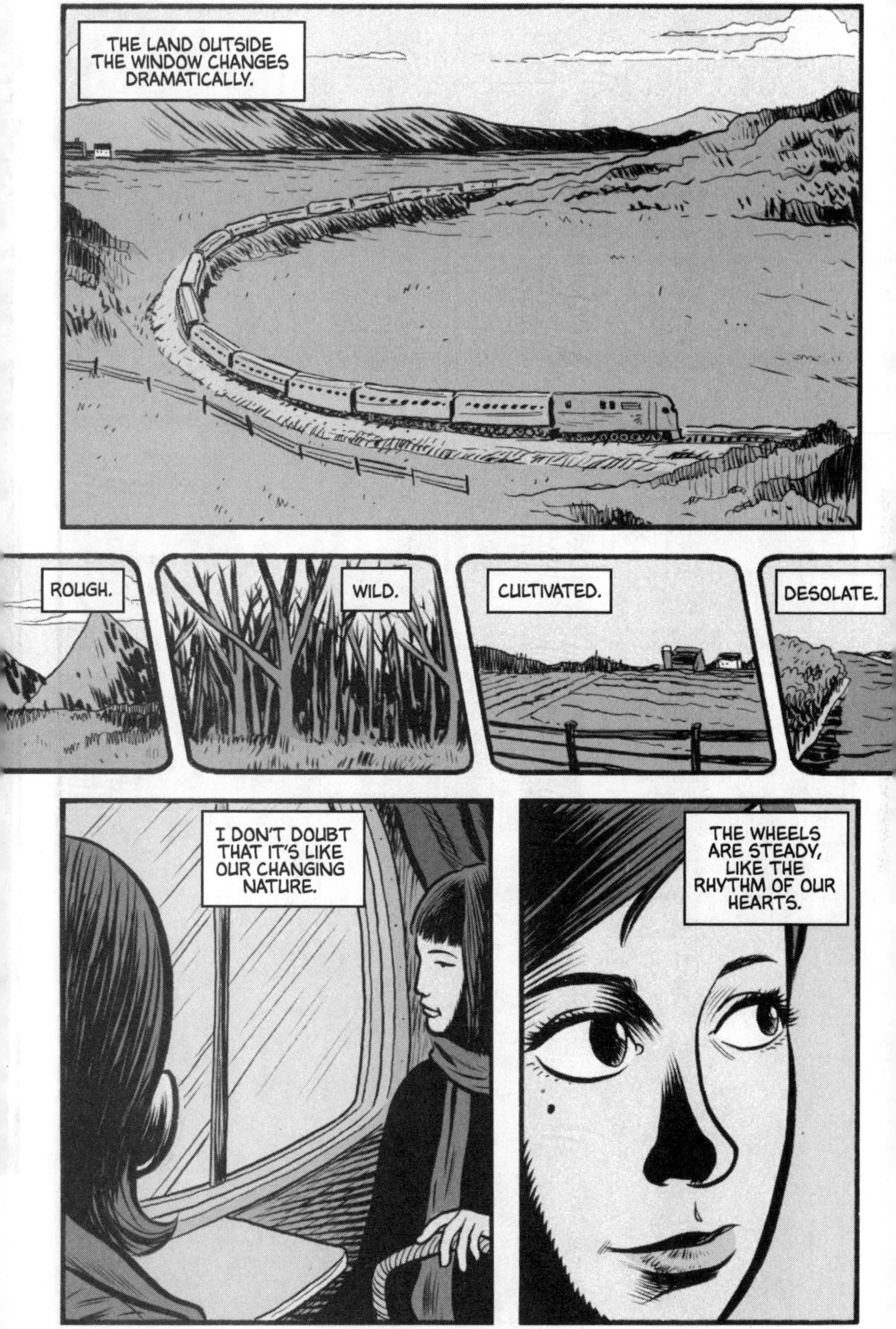
THE LAND OUTSIDE THE WINDOW CHANGES DRAMATICALLY.
ROUGH.
WILD.
CULTIVATED.
DESOLATE.
I DON'T DOUBT THAT IT'S LIKE OUR CHANGING NATURE.
THE WHEELS ARE STEADY, LIKE THE RHYTHM OF OUR HEARTS.

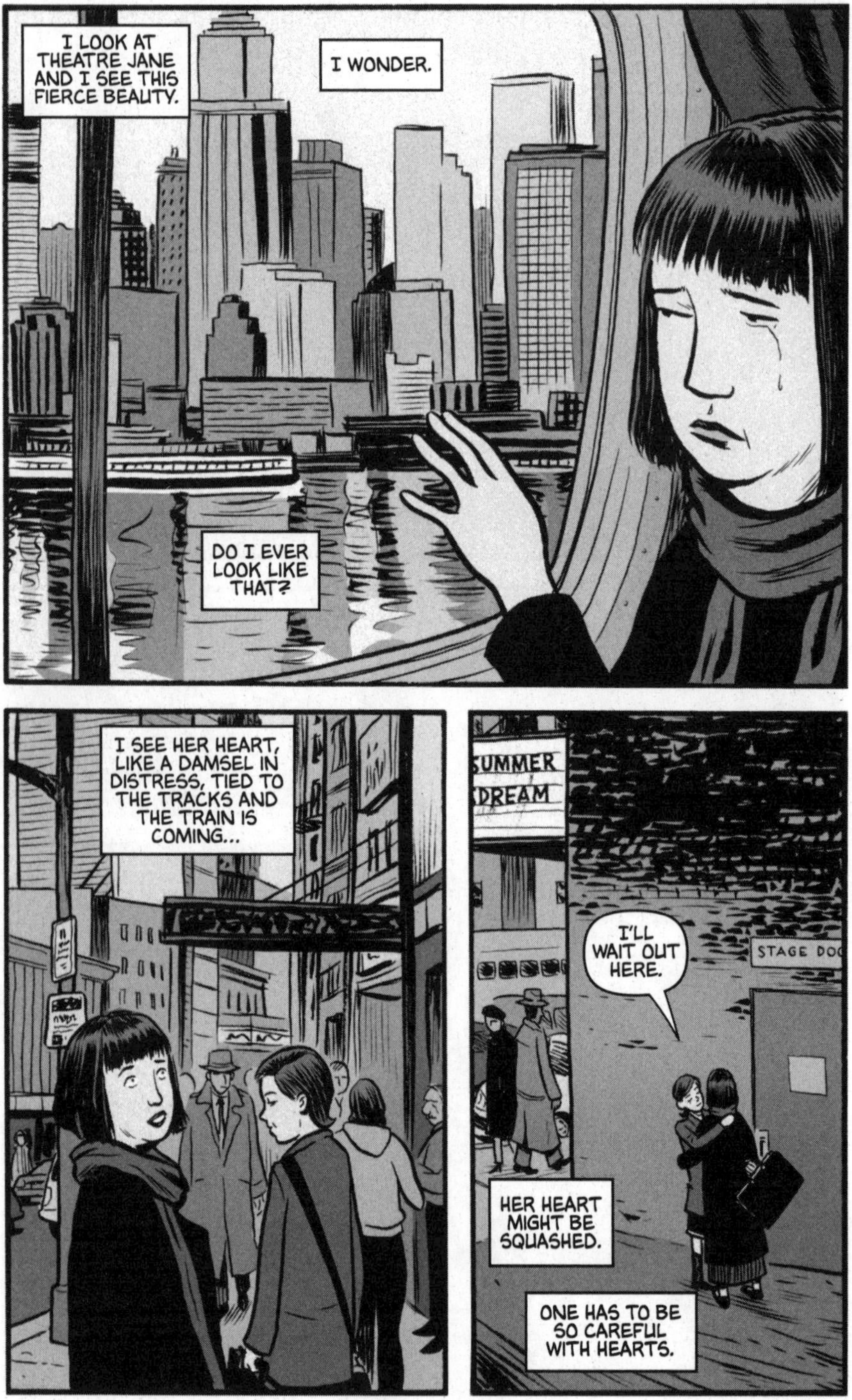
I LOOK AT THEATRE JANE AND I SEE THIS FIERCE BEAUTY.
I WONDER.
DO I EVER LOOK LIKE THAT?
I SEE HER HEART, LIKE A DAMSEL IN DISTRESS, TIED TO THE TRACKS AND THE TRAIN IS COMING...
SUMMER
DREAM
I'LL WAIT OUT HERE.
STAGE DOO
HER HEART MIGHT BE SQUASHED.
ONE HAS TO BE SO CAREFUL WITH HEARTS.

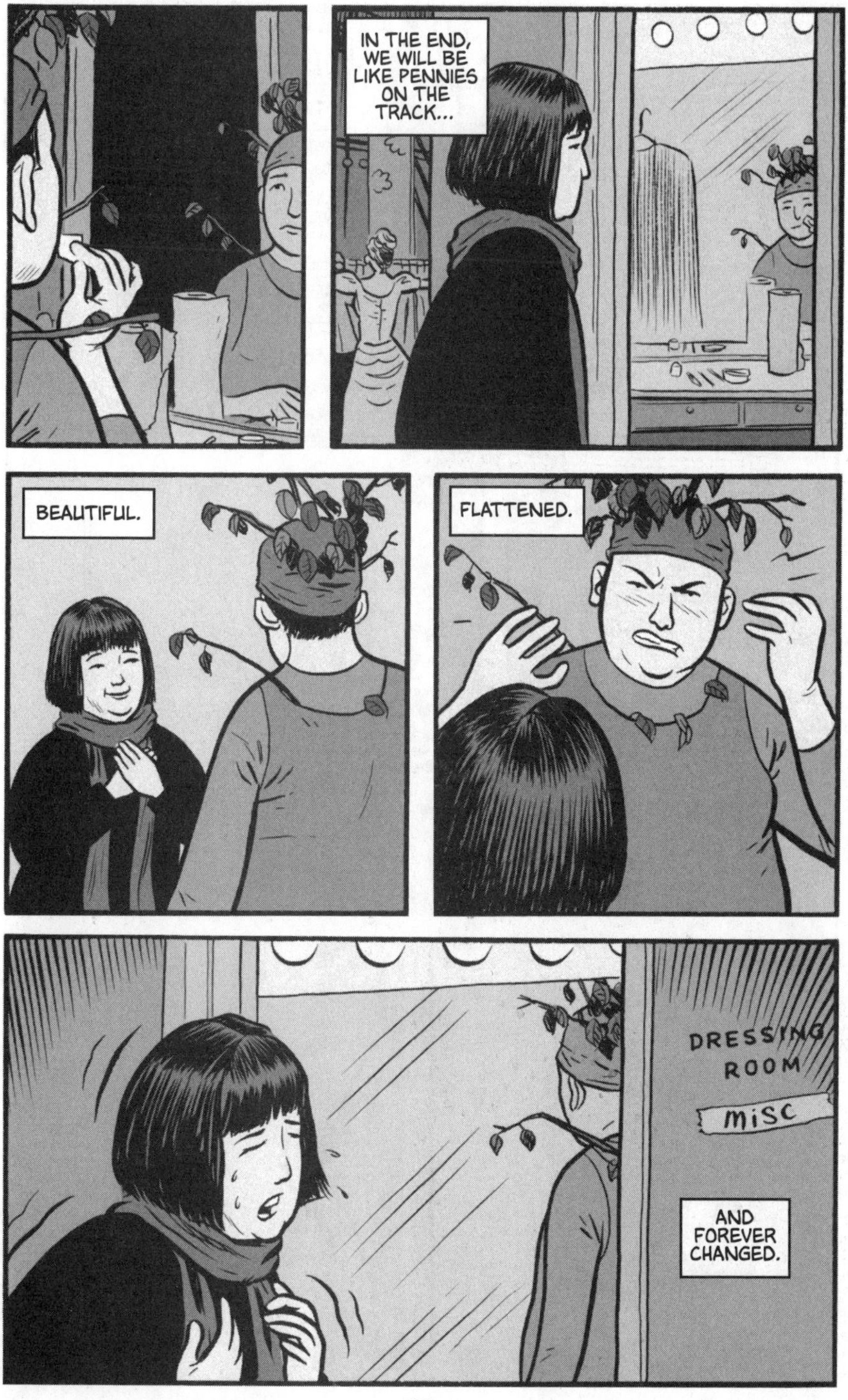
IN THE END, WE WILL BE LIKE PENNIES ON THE TRACK...
BEAUTIFUL.
FLATTENED.
DRESSING ROOM
MISC
AND FOREVER CHANGED.

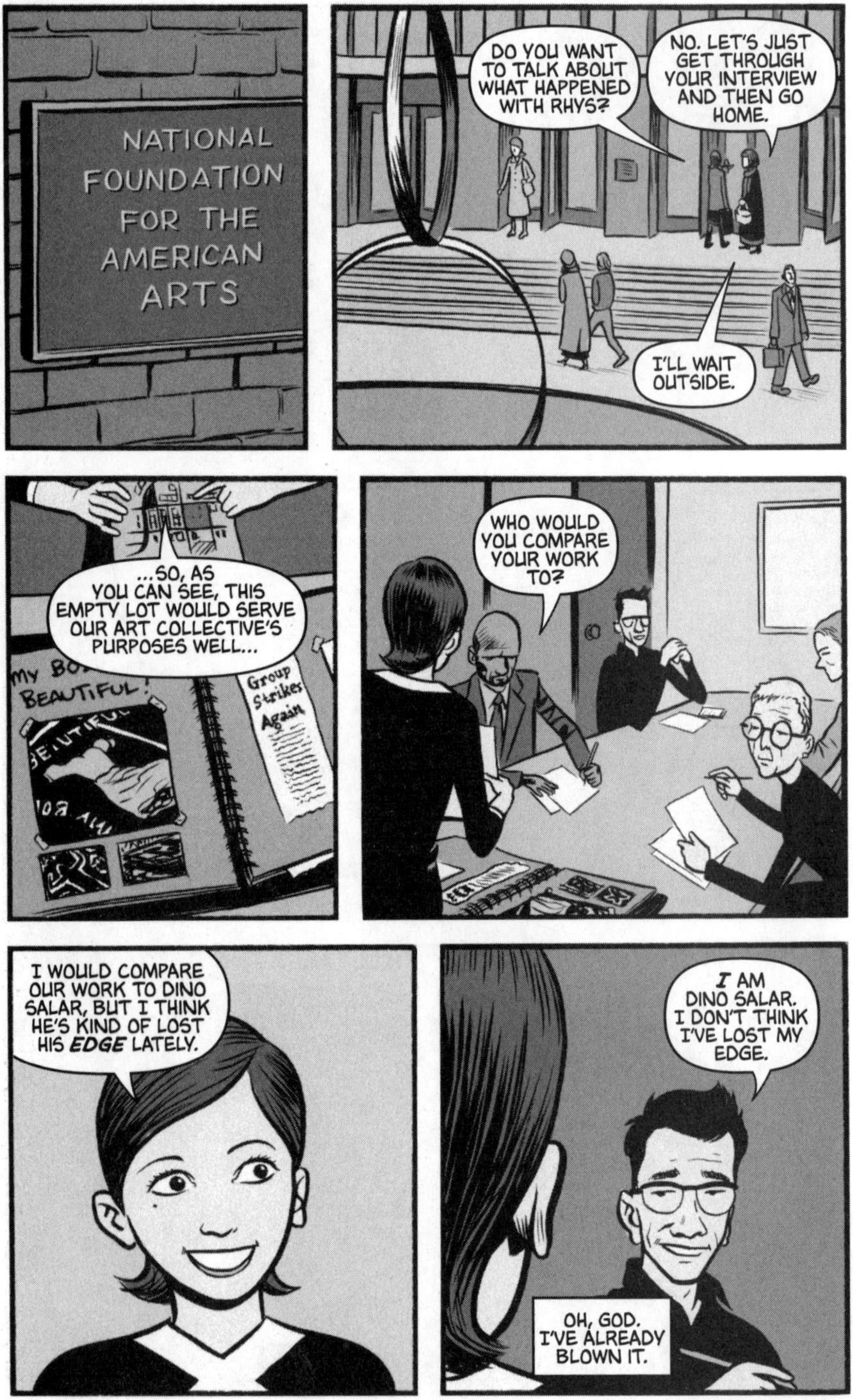
NATIONAL FOUNDATION FOR THE AMERICAN ARTS
DO YOU WANT TO TALK ABOUT WHAT HAPPENED WITH RHYS?
NO. LET'S JUST GET THROUGH YOUR INTERVIEW AND THEN GO HOME.
I'LL WAIT OUTSIDE.
...SO, AS YOU CAN SEE, THIS EMPTY LOT WOULD SERVE OUR ART COLLECTIVE'S PURPOSES WELL...
Group Strikes Again
WHO WOULD YOU COMPARE YOUR WORK TO?
I WOULD COMPARE OUR WORK TO DINO SALAR, BUT I THINK HE'S KIND OF LOST HIS *EDGE* LATELY.
I AM DINO SALAR. I DON'T THINK I'VE LOST MY EDGE.
OH, GOD. I'VE ALREADY BLOWN IT.

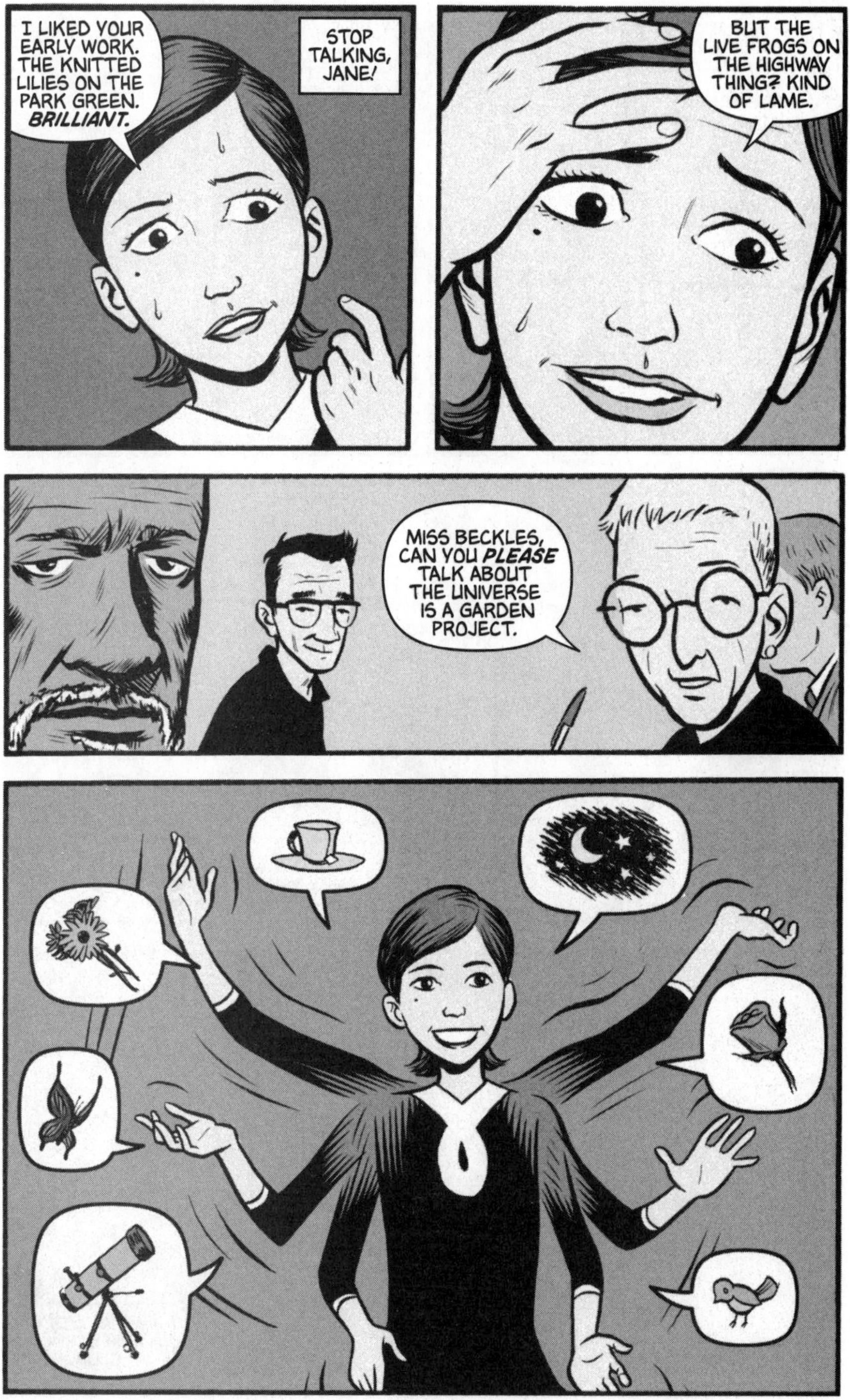
I LIKED YOUR EARLY WORK. THE KNITTED LILIES ON THE PARK GREEN. *BRILLIANT.*
STOP TALKING, JANE!
BUT THE LIVE FROGS ON THE HIGHWAY THING? KIND OF LAME.
MISS BECKLES, CAN YOU *PLEASE* TALK ABOUT THE UNIVERSE IS A GARDEN PROJECT.

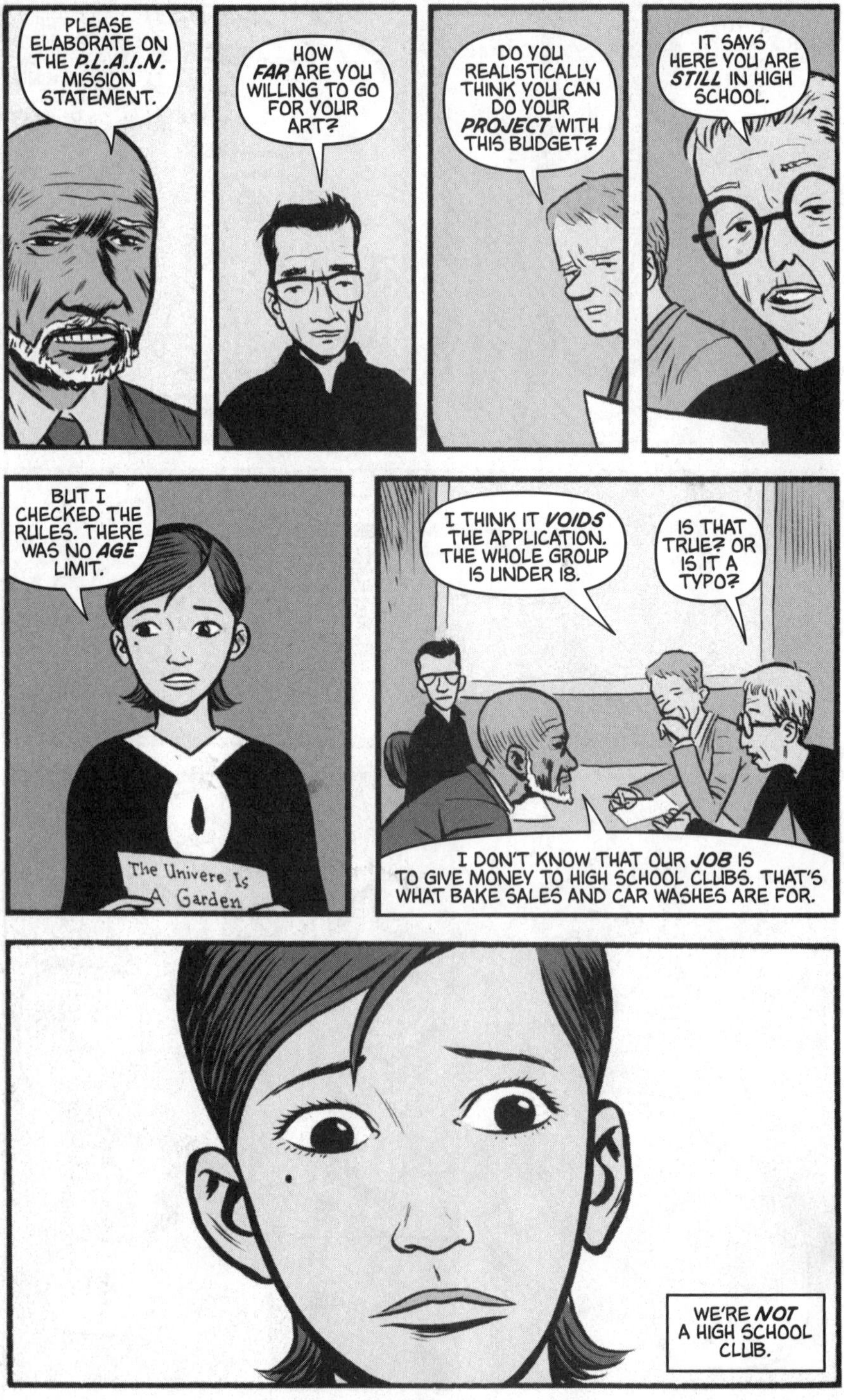

PLEASE ELABORATE ON THE P.L.A.I.N. MISSION STATEMENT.
HOW FAR ARE YOU WILLING TO GO FOR YOUR ART?
DO YOU REALISTICALLY THINK YOU CAN DO YOUR PROJECT WITH THIS BUDGET?
IT SAYS HERE YOU ARE STILL IN HIGH SCHOOL.
BUT I CHECKED THE RULES. THERE WAS NO AGE LIMIT.
The Univere Is A Garden
I THINK IT VOIDS THE APPLICATION. THE WHOLE GROUP IS UNDER 18.
IS THAT TRUE? OR IS IT A TYPO?
I DON'T KNOW THAT OUR JOB IS TO GIVE MONEY TO HIGH SCHOOL CLUBS. THAT'S WHAT BAKE SALES AND CAR WASHES ARE FOR.
WE'RE NOT A HIGH SCHOOL CLUB.

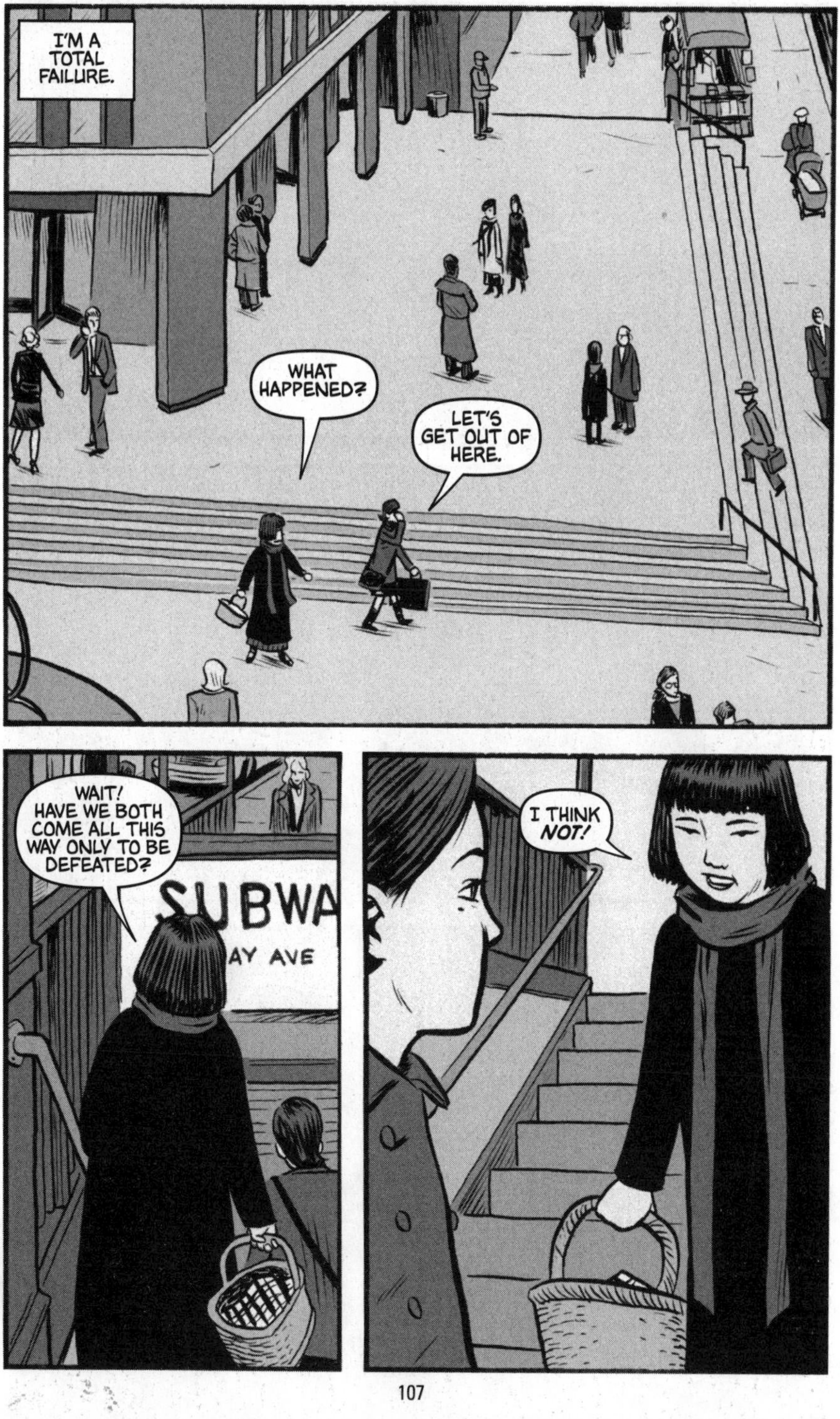
I'M A TOTAL FAILURE.
WHAT HAPPENED?
LET'S GET OUT OF HERE.
WAIT! HAVE WE BOTH COME ALL THIS WAY ONLY TO BE DEFEATED?
SUBWA
AY AVE
I THINK *NOT!*

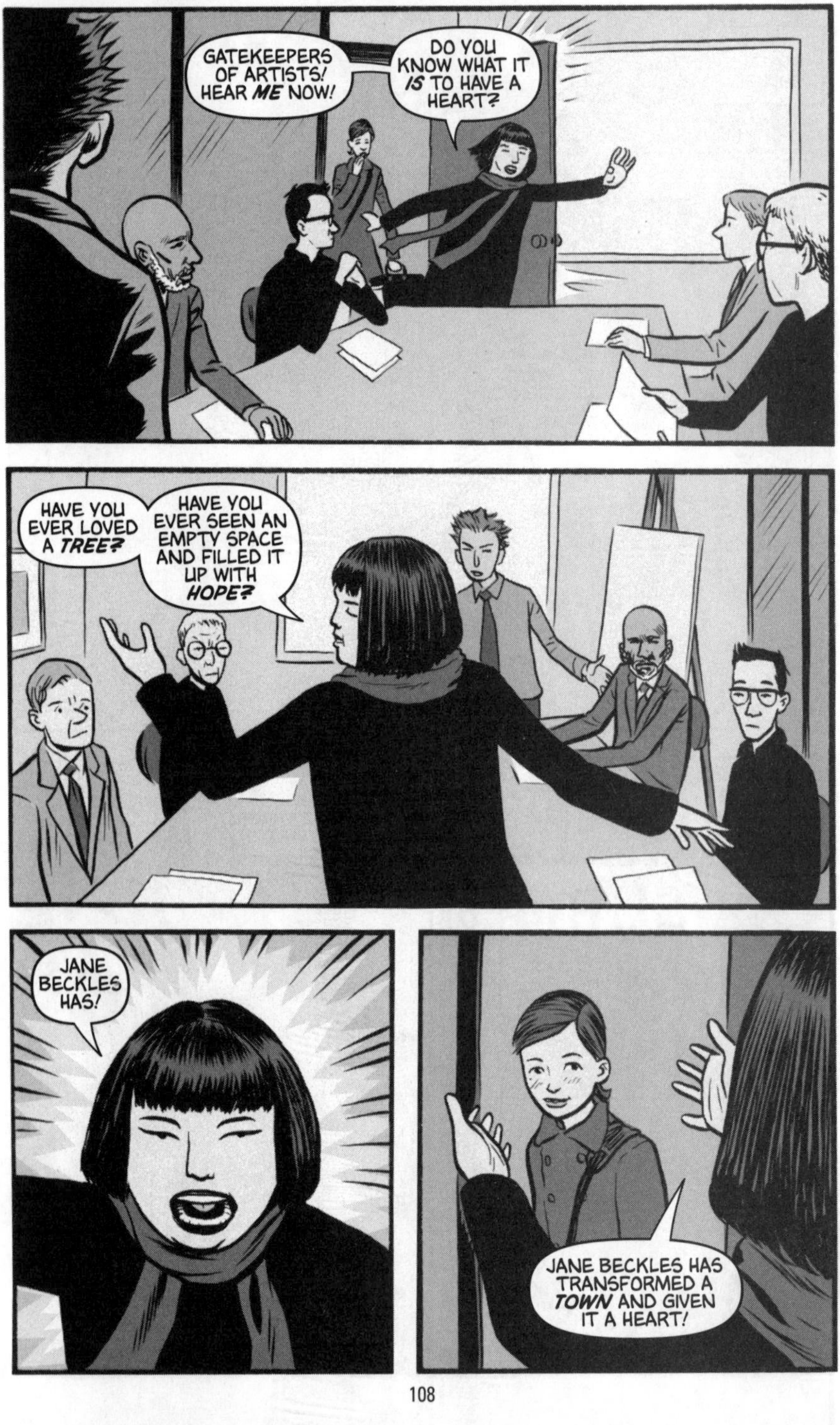
GATEKEEPERS OF ARTISTS! HEAR *ME* NOW!
DO YOU KNOW WHAT IT *IS* TO HAVE A HEART?
HAVE YOU EVER LOVED A *TREE?*
HAVE YOU EVER SEEN AN EMPTY SPACE AND FILLED IT UP WITH *HOPE?*
JANE BECKLES HAS!
JANE BECKLES HAS TRANSFORMED A *TOWN* AND GIVEN IT A HEART!

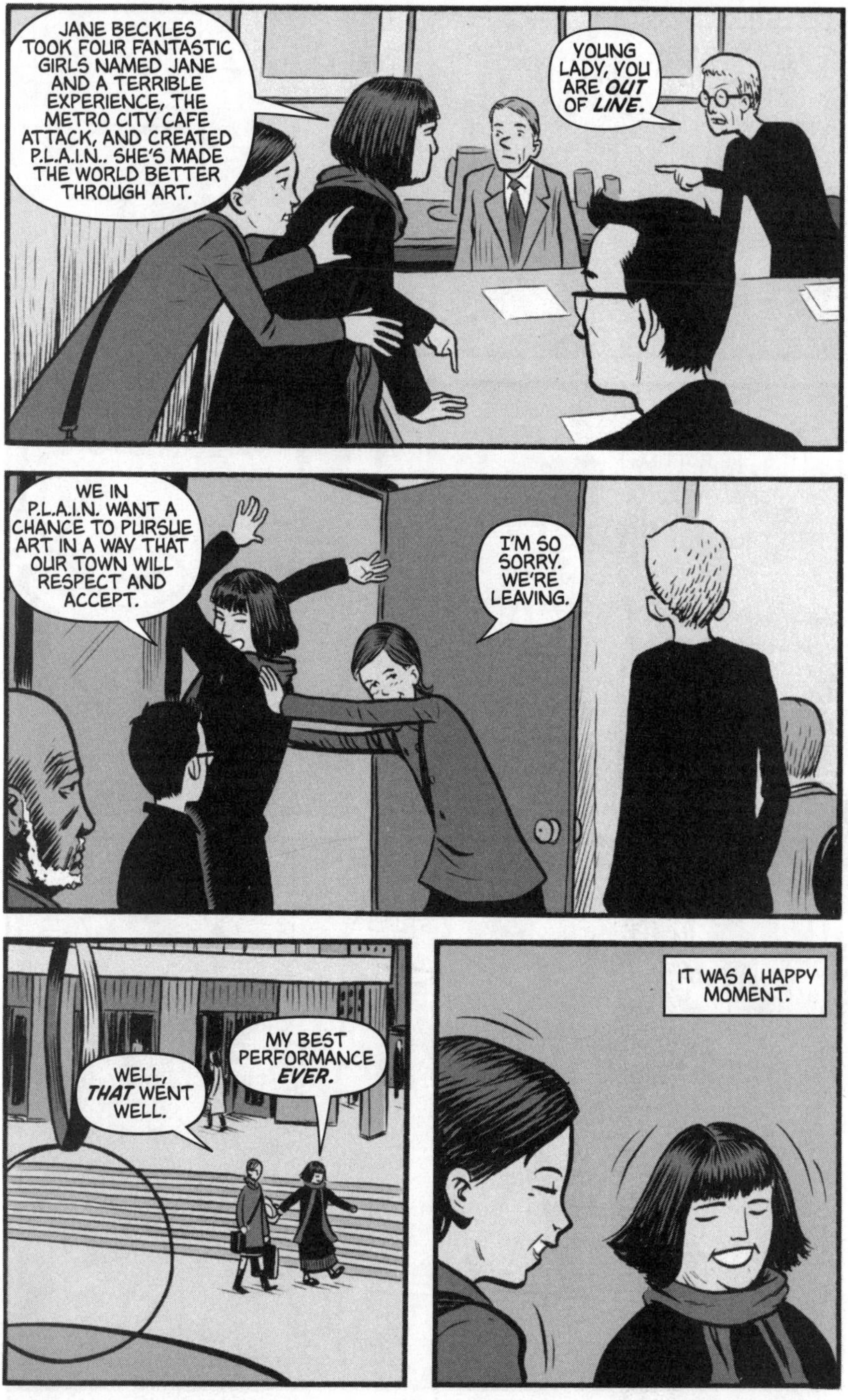
JANE BECKLES TOOK FOUR FANTASTIC GIRLS NAMED JANE AND A TERRIBLE EXPERIENCE, THE METRO CITY CAFE ATTACK, AND CREATED P.L.A.I.N.. SHE'S MADE THE WORLD BETTER THROUGH ART.
YOUNG LADY, YOU ARE *OUT* OF *LINE.*
WE IN P.L.A.I.N. WANT A CHANCE TO PURSUE ART IN A WAY THAT OUR TOWN WILL RESPECT AND ACCEPT.
I'M SO SORRY. WE'RE LEAVING.
WELL, *THAT* WENT WELL.
MY BEST PERFORMANCE *EVER.*
IT WAS A HAPPY MOMENT.

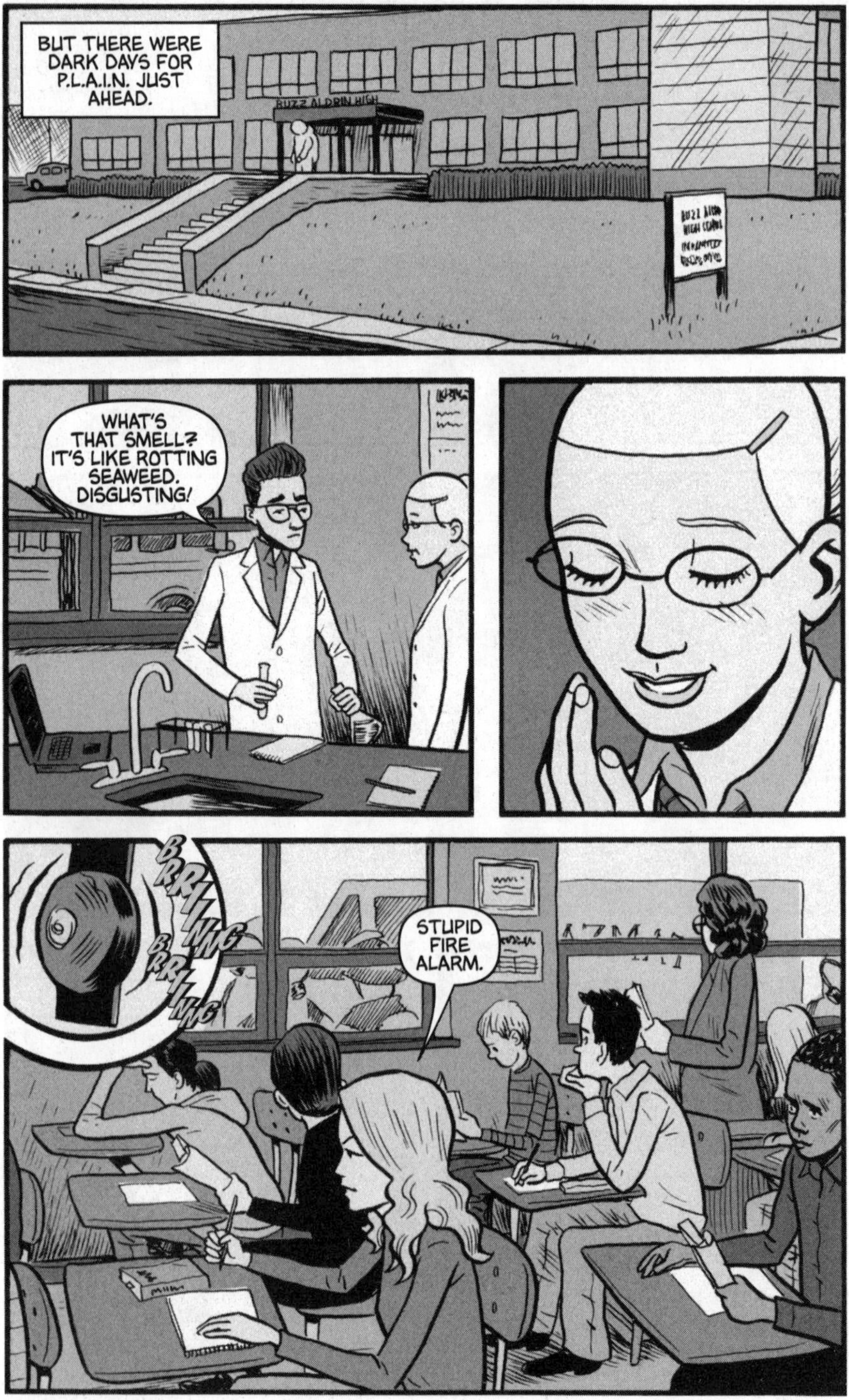
BUT THERE WERE DARK DAYS FOR P.L.A.I.N. JUST AHEAD.
BUZZ ALDRIN HIGH
WHAT'S THAT SMELL? IT'S LIKE ROTTING SEAWEED. DISGUSTING!
BRRIING
BRRIING
STUPID FIRE ALARM.

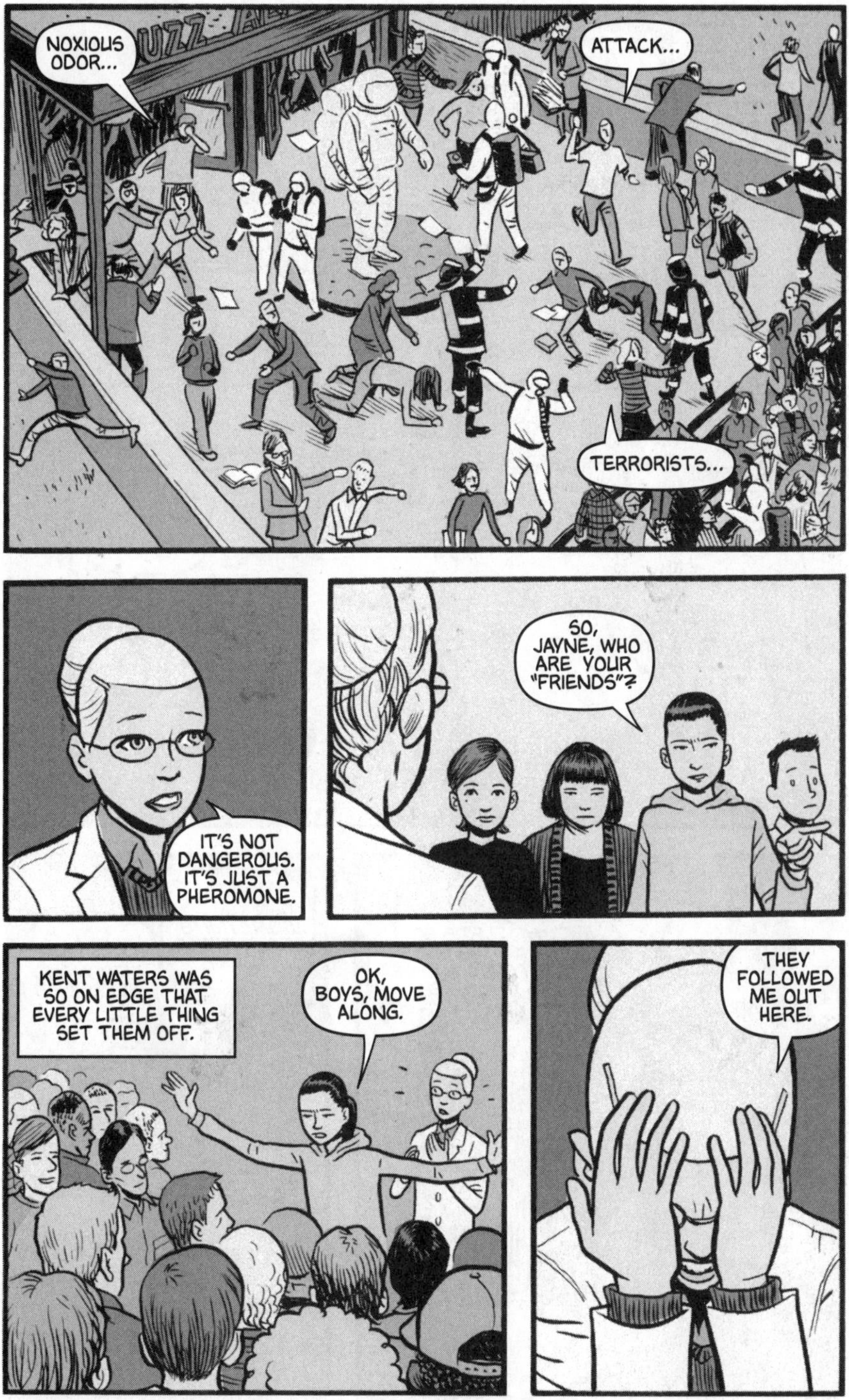
NOXIOUS ODOR...
ATTACK...
TERRORISTS...
IT'S NOT DANGEROUS. IT'S JUST A PHEROMONE.
SO, JAYNE, WHO ARE YOUR "FRIENDS"?
KENT WATERS WAS SO ON EDGE THAT EVERY LITTLE THING SET THEM OFF.
OK, BOYS, MOVE ALONG.
THEY FOLLOWED ME OUT HERE.

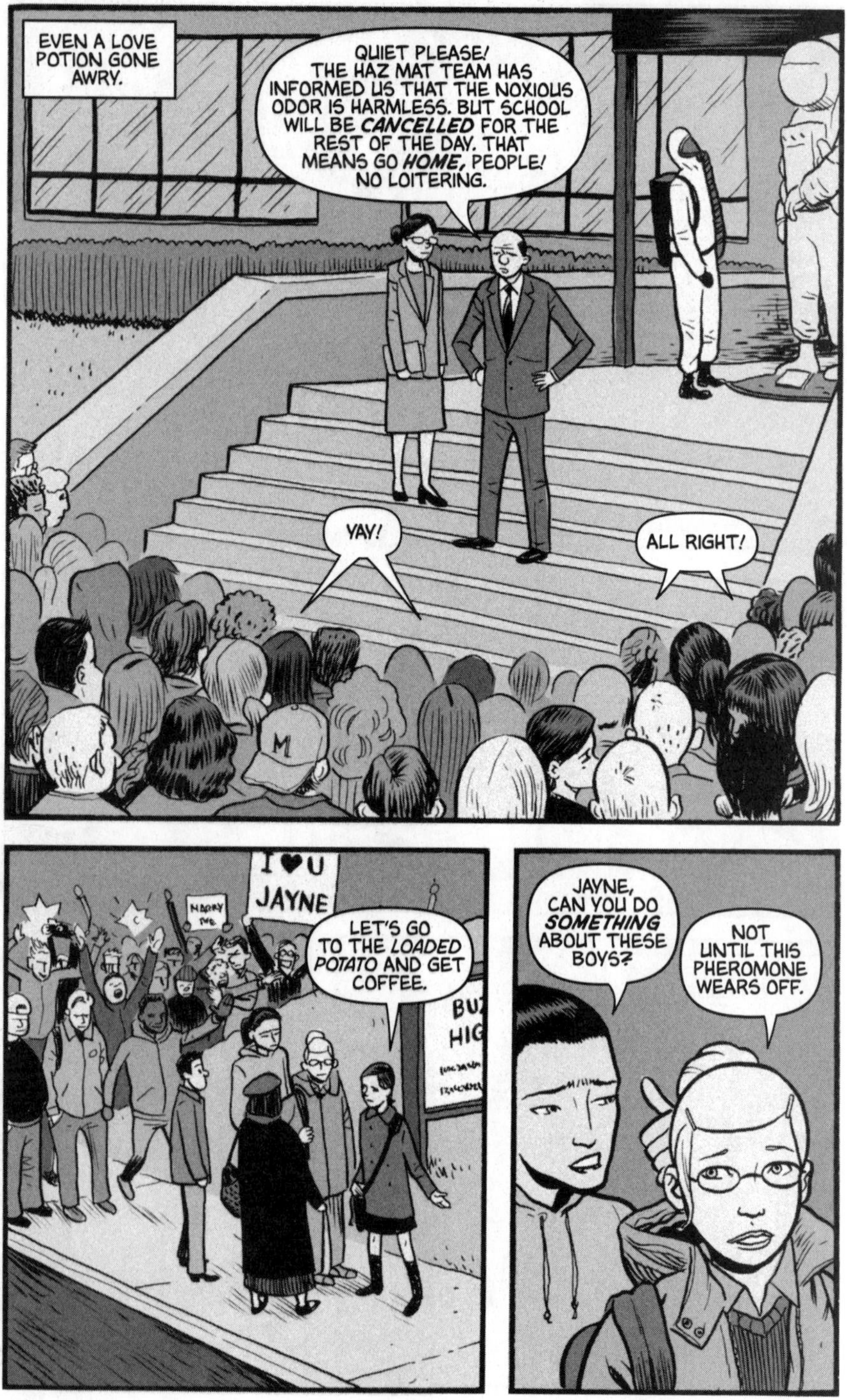

EVEN A LOVE POTION GONE AWRY.
QUIET PLEASE! THE HAZ MAT TEAM HAS INFORMED US THAT THE NOXIOUS ODOR IS HARMLESS. BUT SCHOOL WILL BE ***CANCELLED*** FOR THE REST OF THE DAY. THAT MEANS GO ***HOME,*** PEOPLE! NO LOITERING.
YAY!
ALL RIGHT!
I ♥ U JAYNE
LET'S GO TO THE *LOADED POTATO* AND GET COFFEE.
JAYNE, CAN YOU DO ***SOMETHING*** ABOUT THESE BOYS?
NOT UNTIL THIS PHEROMONE WEARS OFF.

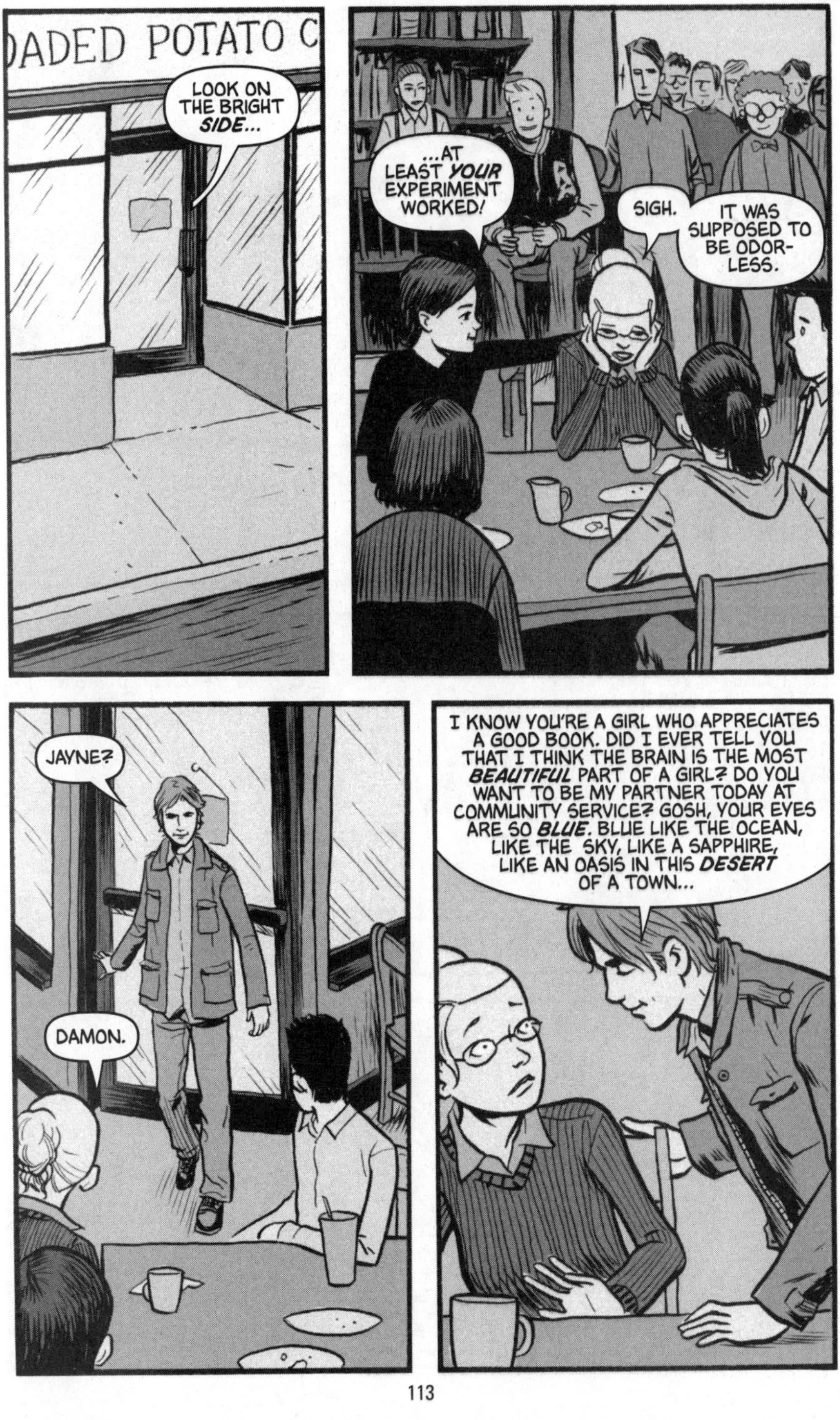
DADED POTATO C
LOOK ON THE BRIGHT SIDE...
...AT LEAST YOUR EXPERIMENT WORKED!
SIGH.
IT WAS SUPPOSED TO BE ODOR-LESS.
JAYNE?
DAMON.
I KNOW YOU'RE A GIRL WHO APPRECIATES A GOOD BOOK. DID I EVER TELL YOU THAT I THINK THE BRAIN IS THE MOST BEAUTIFUL PART OF A GIRL? DO YOU WANT TO BE MY PARTNER TODAY AT COMMUNITY SERVICE? GOSH, YOUR EYES ARE SO BLUE. BLUE LIKE THE OCEAN, LIKE THE SKY, LIKE A SAPPHIRE, LIKE AN OASIS IN THIS DESERT OF A TOWN...

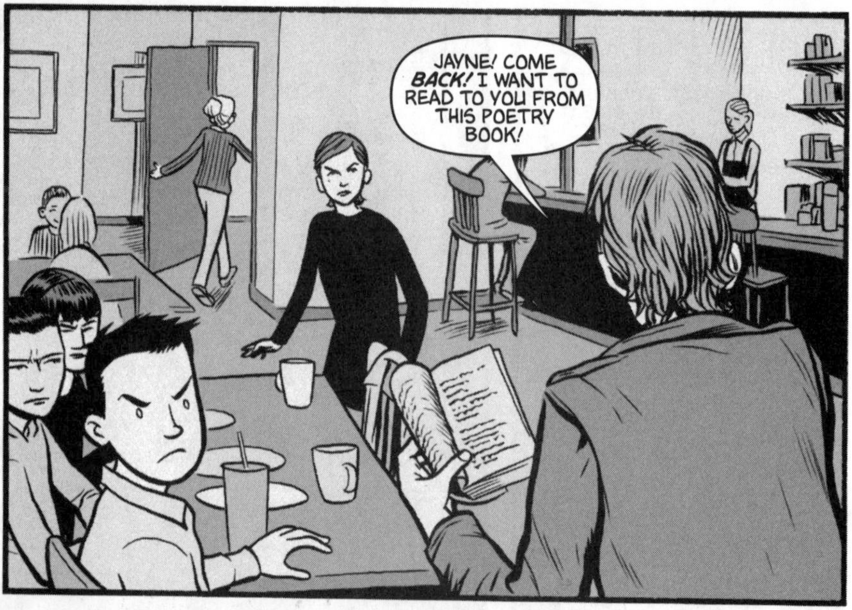
JAYNE! COME *BACK!* I WANT TO READ TO YOU FROM THIS POETRY BOOK!

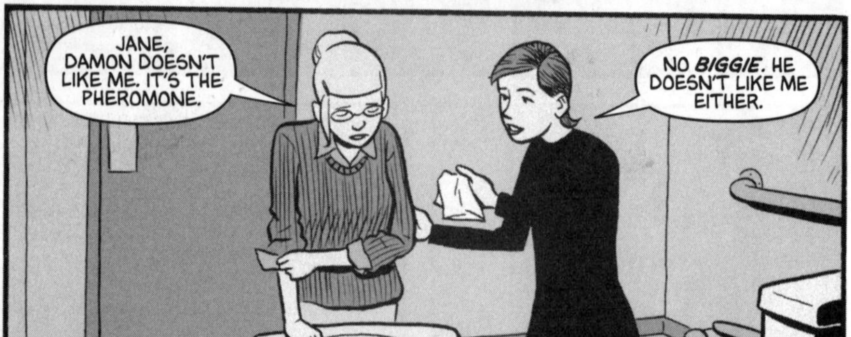
JANE, DAMON DOESN'T LIKE ME. IT'S THE PHEROMONE.
NO *BIGGIE*. HE DOESN'T LIKE ME EITHER.

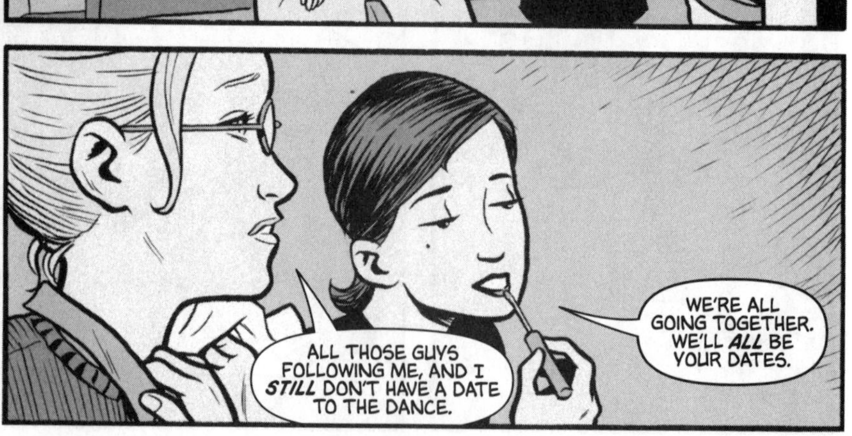
ALL THOSE GUYS FOLLOWING ME, AND I *STILL* DON'T HAVE A DATE TO THE DANCE.
WE'RE ALL GOING TOGETHER. WE'LL *ALL* BE YOUR DATES.

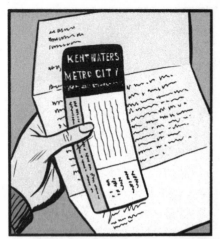

MOM, I'M HOME.

I DON'T KNOW WHICH WAY IS UP ANYMORE.

REMEMBER WHEN MY DAD FLIPPED OUT BECAUSE I WENT TO BEAUTY SCHOOL?

I HATED HIM FOR WANTING TO STOP ME.

THIS ART THING IS IMPORTANT TO JANE.

I DON'T WANT TO STOP HER FROM BEING WHO SHE WANTS TO BE.

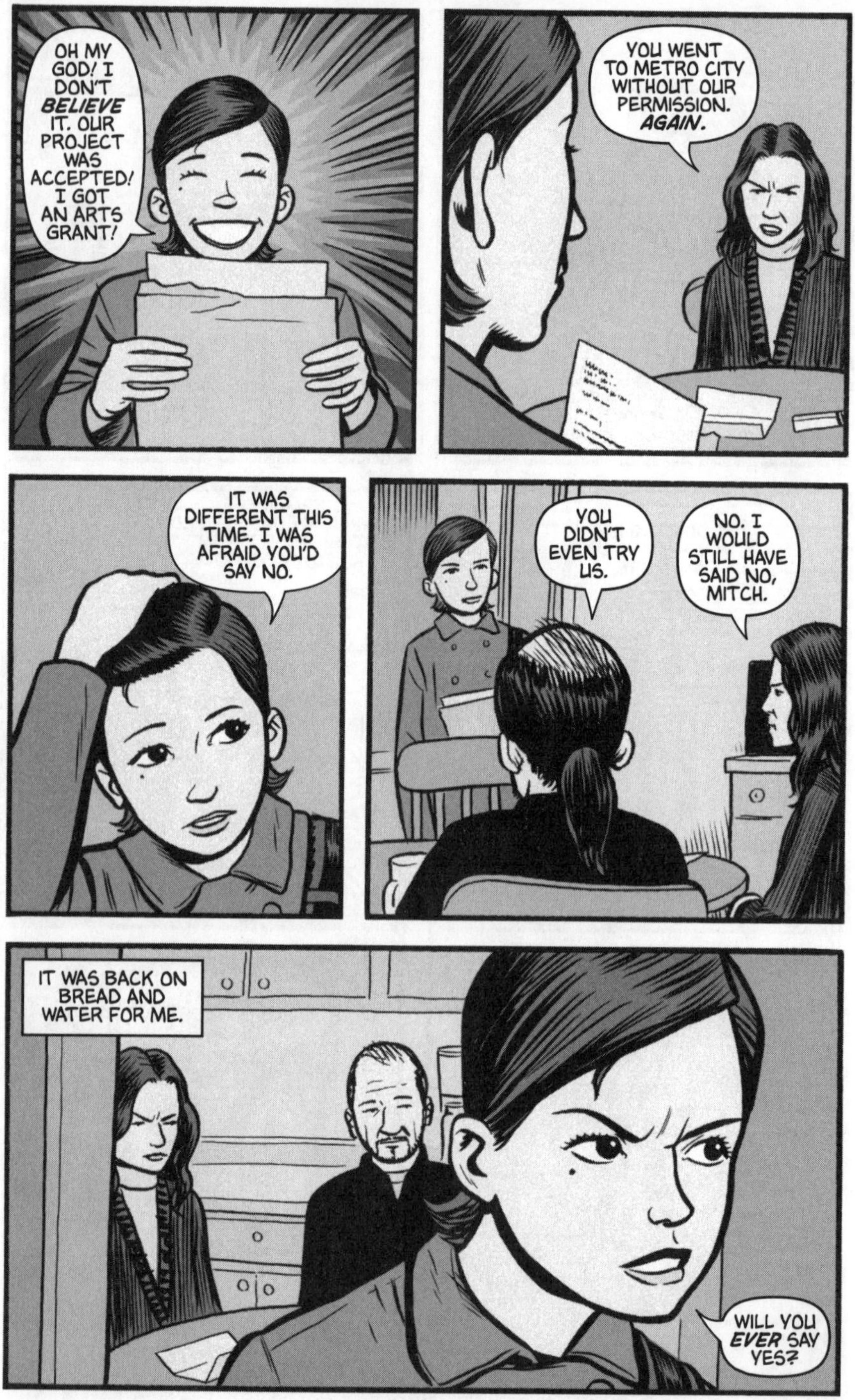
OH MY GOD! I DON'T BELIEVE IT. OUR PROJECT WAS ACCEPTED! I GOT AN ARTS GRANT!
YOU WENT TO METRO CITY WITHOUT OUR PERMISSION. AGAIN.
IT WAS DIFFERENT THIS TIME. I WAS AFRAID YOU'D SAY NO.
YOU DIDN'T EVEN TRY US.
NO. I WOULD STILL HAVE SAID NO, MITCH.
IT WAS BACK ON BREAD AND WATER FOR ME.
WILL YOU EVER SAY YES?

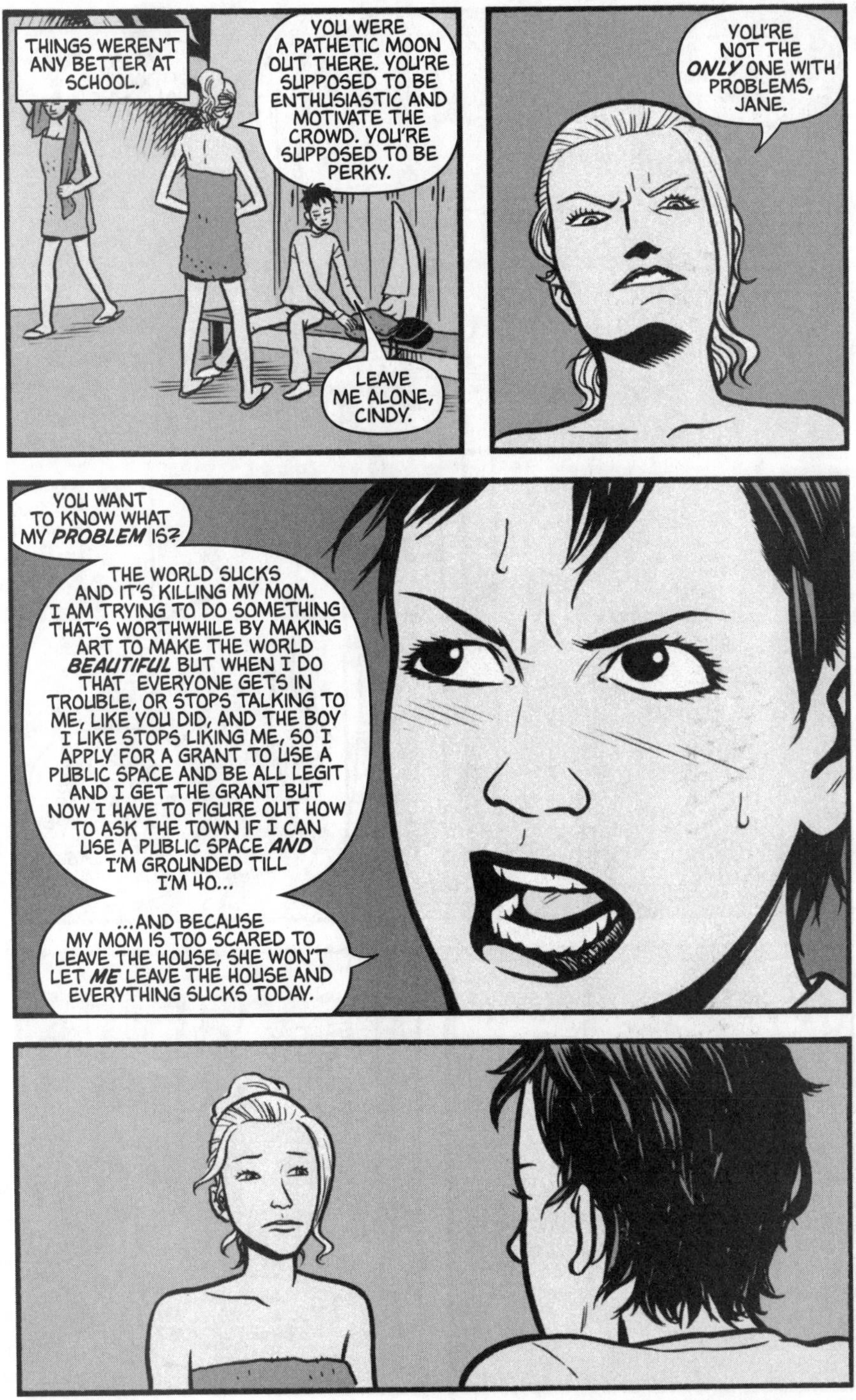
THINGS WEREN'T ANY BETTER AT SCHOOL.
YOU WERE A PATHETIC MOON OUT THERE. YOU'RE SUPPOSED TO BE ENTHUSIASTIC AND MOTIVATE THE CROWD. YOU'RE SUPPOSED TO BE PERKY.
LEAVE ME ALONE, CINDY.
YOU'RE NOT THE *ONLY* ONE WITH PROBLEMS, JANE.
YOU WANT TO KNOW WHAT MY *PROBLEM* IS?
THE WORLD SUCKS AND IT'S KILLING MY MOM. I AM TRYING TO DO SOMETHING THAT'S WORTHWHILE BY MAKING ART TO MAKE THE WORLD *BEAUTIFUL* BUT WHEN I DO THAT EVERYONE GETS IN TROUBLE, OR STOPS TALKING TO ME, LIKE YOU DID, AND THE BOY I LIKE STOPS LIKING ME, SO I APPLY FOR A GRANT TO USE A PUBLIC SPACE AND BE ALL LEGIT AND I GET THE GRANT BUT NOW I HAVE TO FIGURE OUT HOW TO ASK THE TOWN IF I CAN USE A PUBLIC SPACE *AND* I'M GROUNDED TILL I'M 40...
...AND BECAUSE MY MOM IS TOO SCARED TO LEAVE THE HOUSE, SHE WON'T LET *ME* LEAVE THE HOUSE AND EVERYTHING SUCKS TODAY.

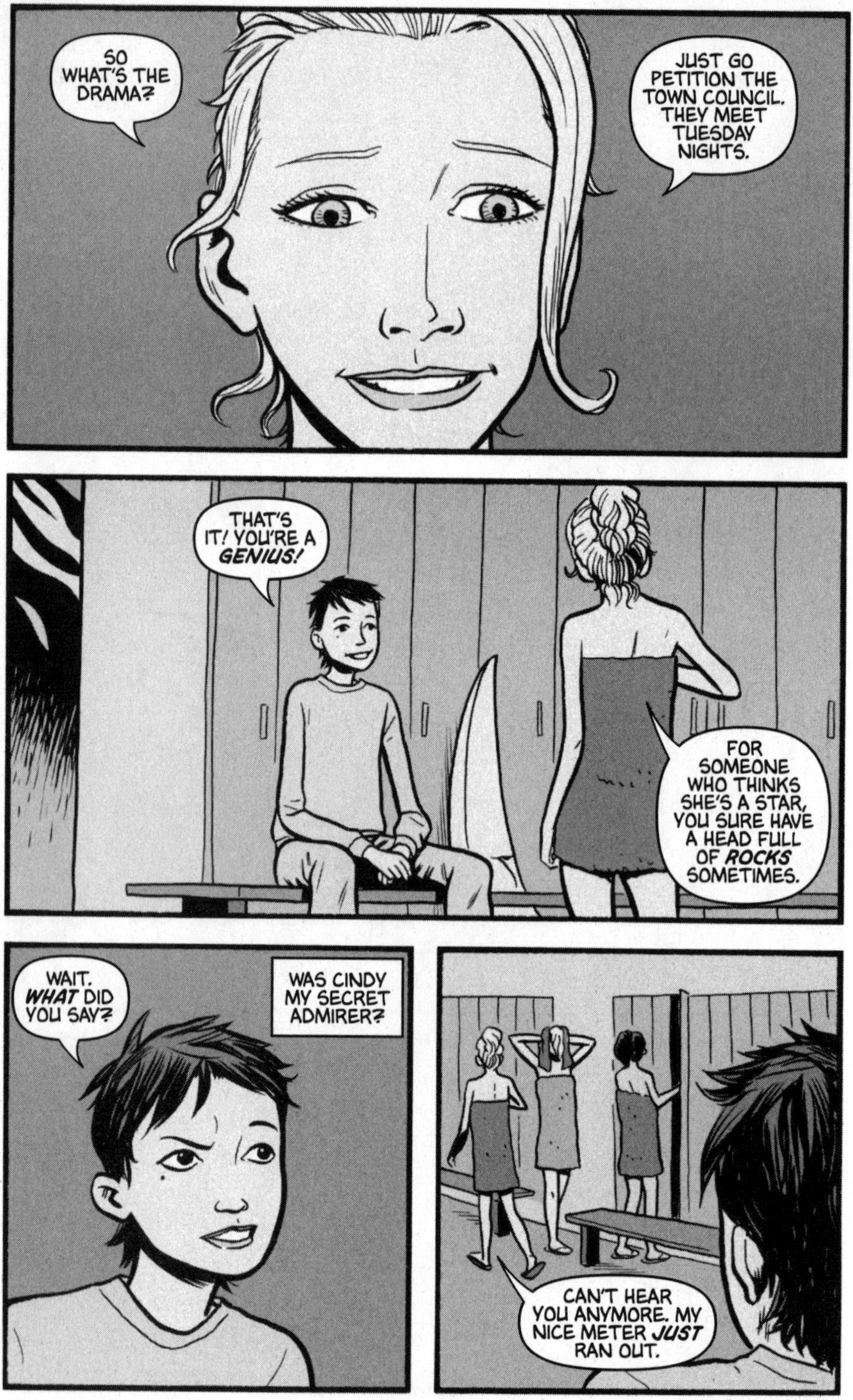
SO WHAT'S THE DRAMA?
JUST GO PETITION THE TOWN COUNCIL. THEY MEET TUESDAY NIGHTS.
THAT'S IT! YOU'RE A *GENIUS!*
FOR SOMEONE WHO THINKS SHE'S A STAR, YOU SURE HAVE A HEAD FULL OF *ROCKS* SOMETIMES.
WAIT. *WHAT* DID YOU SAY?
WAS CINDY MY SECRET ADMIRER?
CAN'T HEAR YOU ANYMORE. MY NICE METER *JUST* RAN OUT.

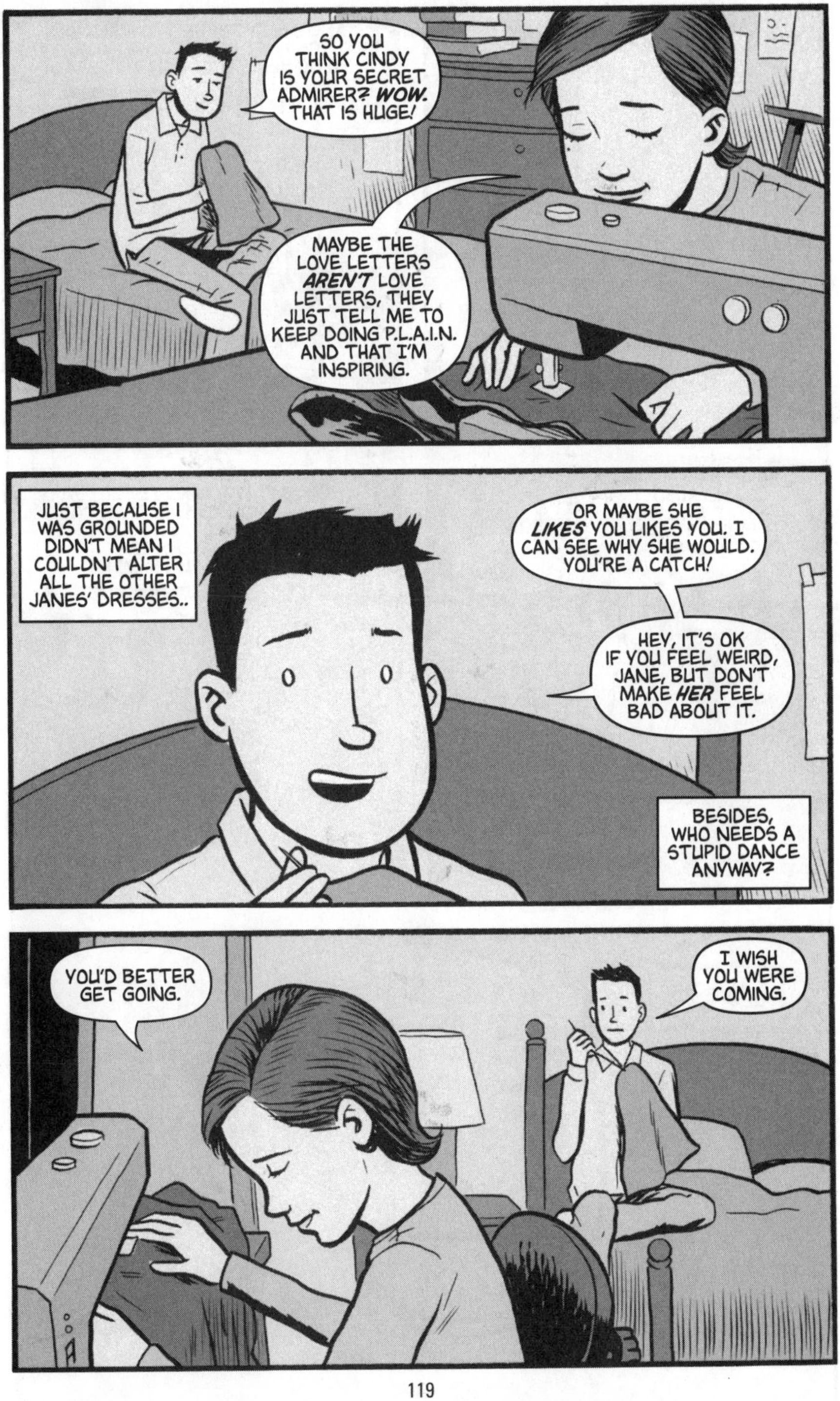
SO YOU THINK CINDY IS YOUR SECRET ADMIRER? WOW. THAT IS HUGE!
MAYBE THE LOVE LETTERS AREN'T LOVE LETTERS, THEY JUST TELL ME TO KEEP DOING P.L.A.I.N. AND THAT I'M INSPIRING.
JUST BECAUSE I WAS GROUNDED DIDN'T MEAN I COULDN'T ALTER ALL THE OTHER JANES' DRESSES..
OR MAYBE SHE LIKES YOU LIKES YOU. I CAN SEE WHY SHE WOULD. YOU'RE A CATCH!
HEY, IT'S OK IF YOU FEEL WEIRD, JANE, BUT DON'T MAKE HER FEEL BAD ABOUT IT.
BESIDES, WHO NEEDS A STUPID DANCE ANYWAY?
YOU'D BETTER GET GOING.
I WISH YOU WERE COMING.

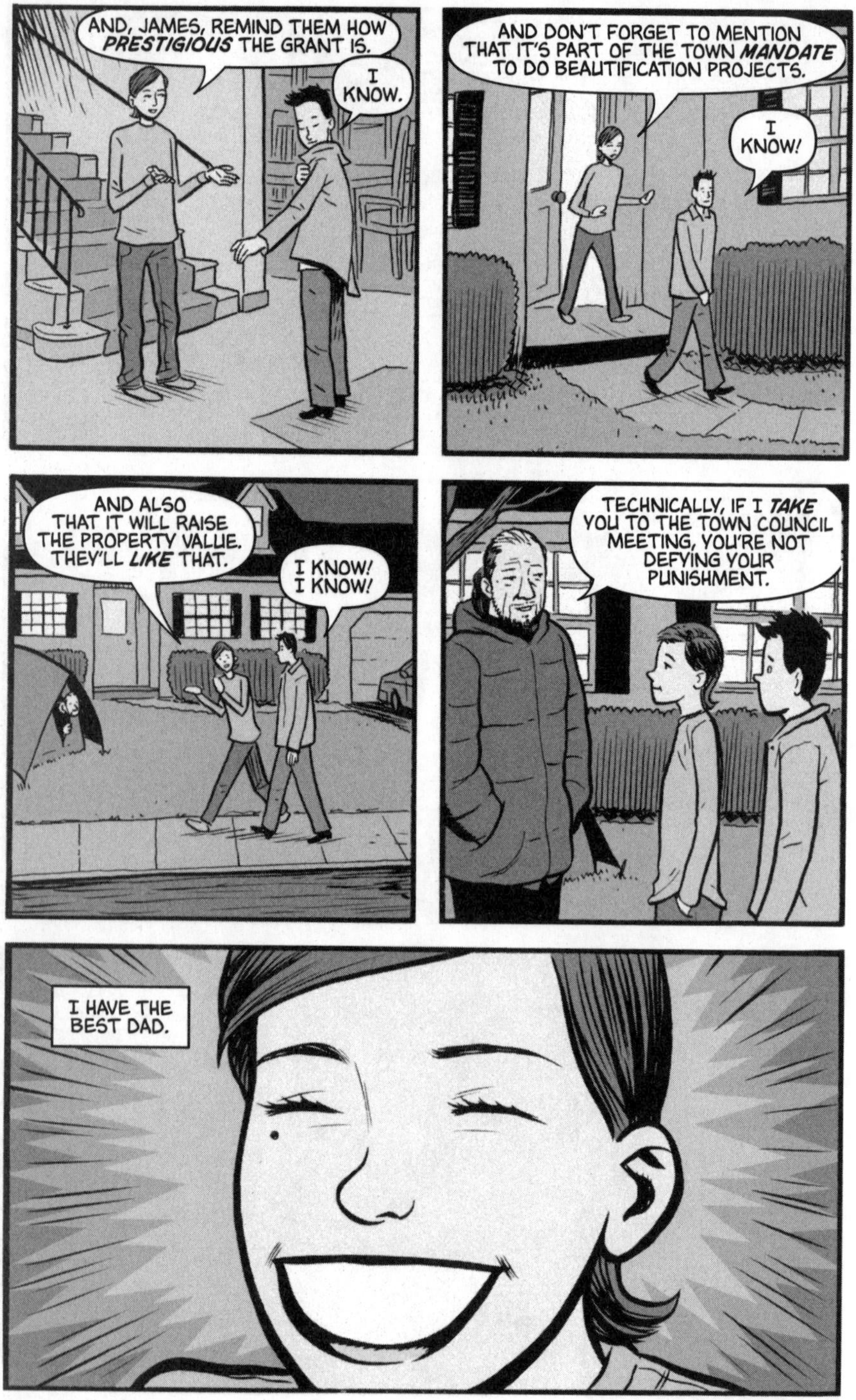
AND, JAMES, REMIND THEM HOW PRESTIGIOUS THE GRANT IS.
I KNOW.
AND DON'T FORGET TO MENTION THAT IT'S PART OF THE TOWN MANDATE TO DO BEAUTIFICATION PROJECTS.
I KNOW!
AND ALSO THAT IT WILL RAISE THE PROPERTY VALUE. THEY'LL LIKE THAT.
I KNOW! I KNOW!
TECHNICALLY, IF I TAKE YOU TO THE TOWN COUNCIL MEETING, YOU'RE NOT DEFYING YOUR PUNISHMENT.
I HAVE THE BEST DAD.

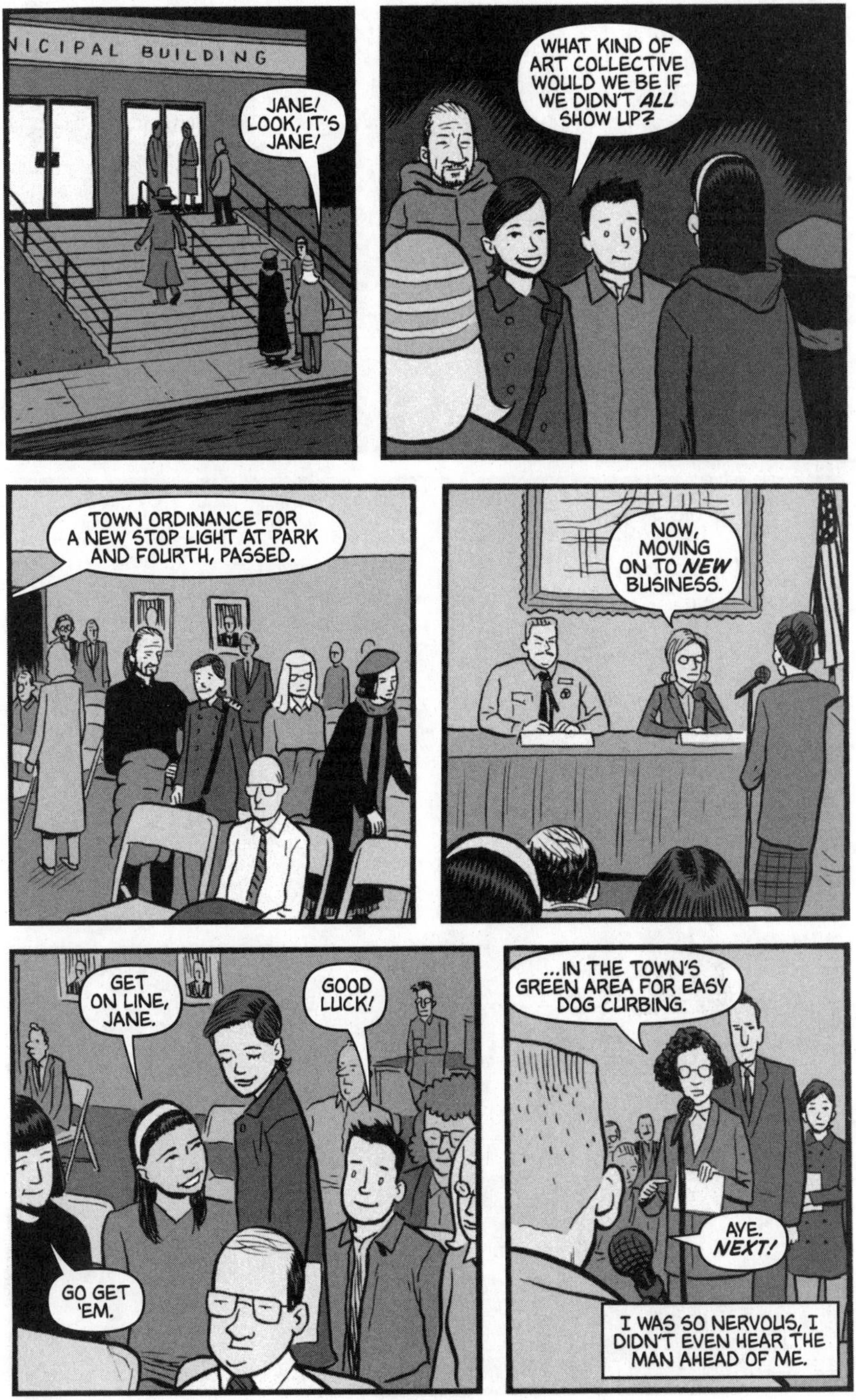
NICIPAL BUILDING
JANE! LOOK, IT'S JANE!
WHAT KIND OF ART COLLECTIVE WOULD WE BE IF WE DIDN'T ALL SHOW UP?
TOWN ORDINANCE FOR A NEW STOP LIGHT AT PARK AND FOURTH, PASSED.
NOW, MOVING ON TO NEW BUSINESS.
GET ON LINE, JANE.
GOOD LUCK!
GO GET 'EM.
...IN THE TOWN'S GREEN AREA FOR EASY DOG CURBING.
AYE. NEXT!
I WAS SO NERVOUS, I DIDN'T EVEN HEAR THE MAN AHEAD OF ME.

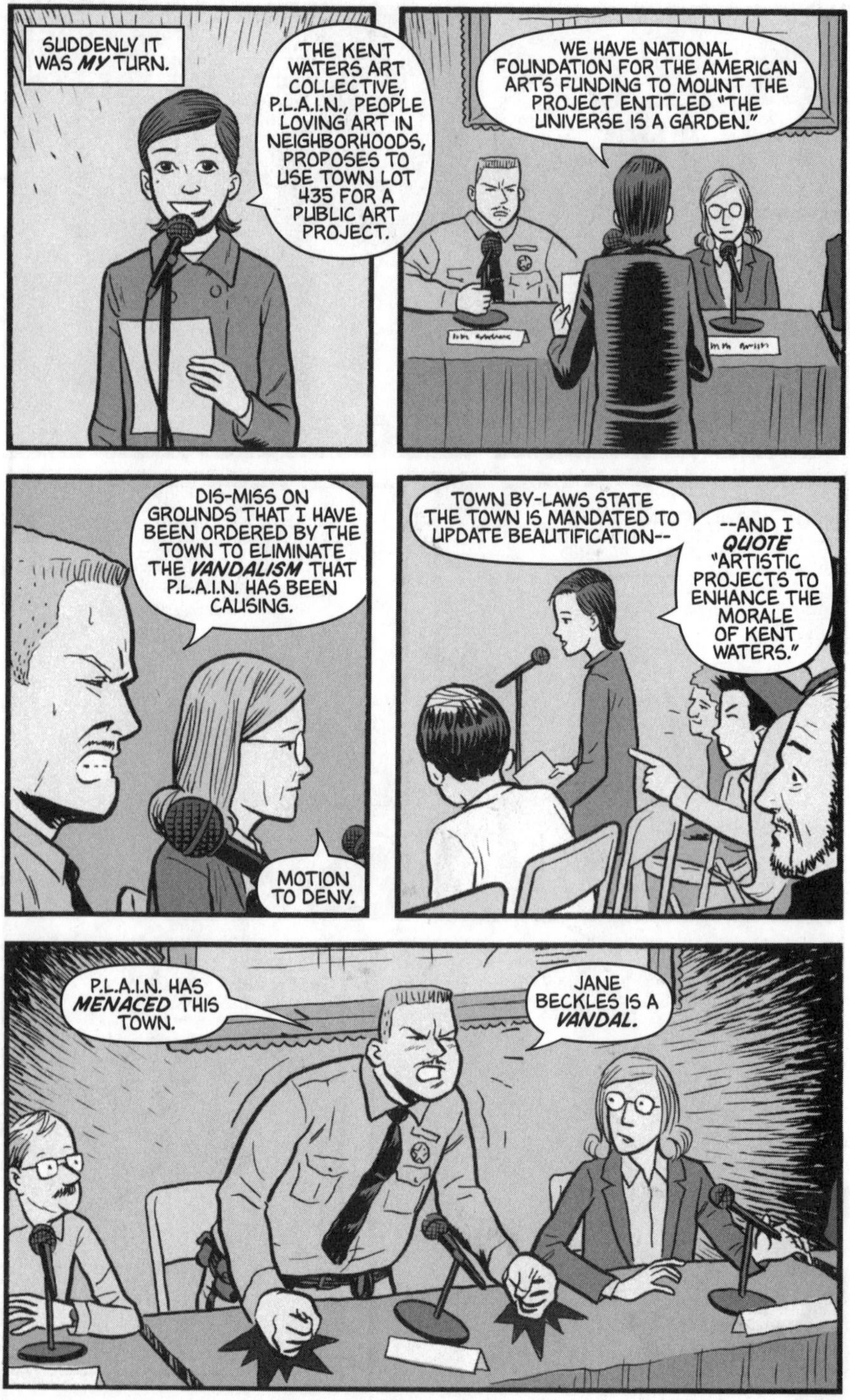

SUDDENLY IT WAS *MY* TURN.
THE KENT WATERS ART COLLECTIVE, P.L.A.I.N., PEOPLE LOVING ART IN NEIGHBORHOODS, PROPOSES TO USE TOWN LOT 435 FOR A PUBLIC ART PROJECT.
WE HAVE NATIONAL FOUNDATION FOR THE AMERICAN ARTS FUNDING TO MOUNT THE PROJECT ENTITLED "THE UNIVERSE IS A GARDEN."
DIS-MISS ON GROUNDS THAT I HAVE BEEN ORDERED BY THE TOWN TO ELIMINATE THE *VANDALISM* THAT P.L.A.I.N. HAS BEEN CAUSING.
MOTION TO DENY.
TOWN BY-LAWS STATE THE TOWN IS MANDATED TO UPDATE BEAUTIFICATION--
--AND I *QUOTE* "ARTISTIC PROJECTS TO ENHANCE THE MORALE OF KENT WATERS."
P.L.A.I.N. HAS *MENACED* THIS TOWN.
JANE BECKLES IS A *VANDAL.*

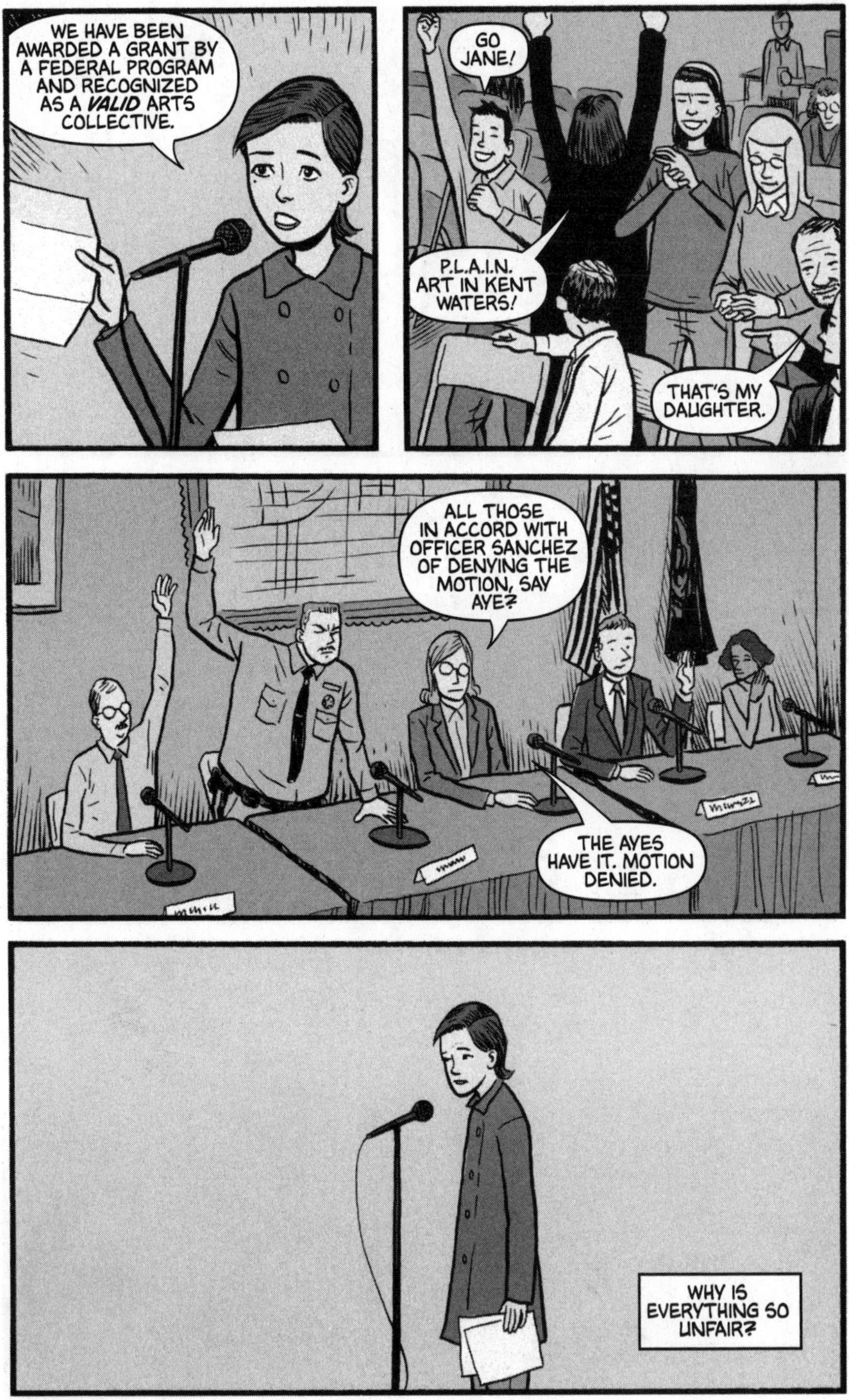
WE HAVE BEEN AWARDED A GRANT BY A FEDERAL PROGRAM AND RECOGNIZED AS A *VALID* ARTS COLLECTIVE.
GO JANE!
P.L.A.I.N. ART IN KENT WATERS!
THAT'S MY DAUGHTER.
ALL THOSE IN ACCORD WITH OFFICER SANCHEZ OF DENYING THE MOTION, SAY AYE?
THE AYES HAVE IT. MOTION DENIED.
WHY IS EVERYTHING SO UNFAIR?

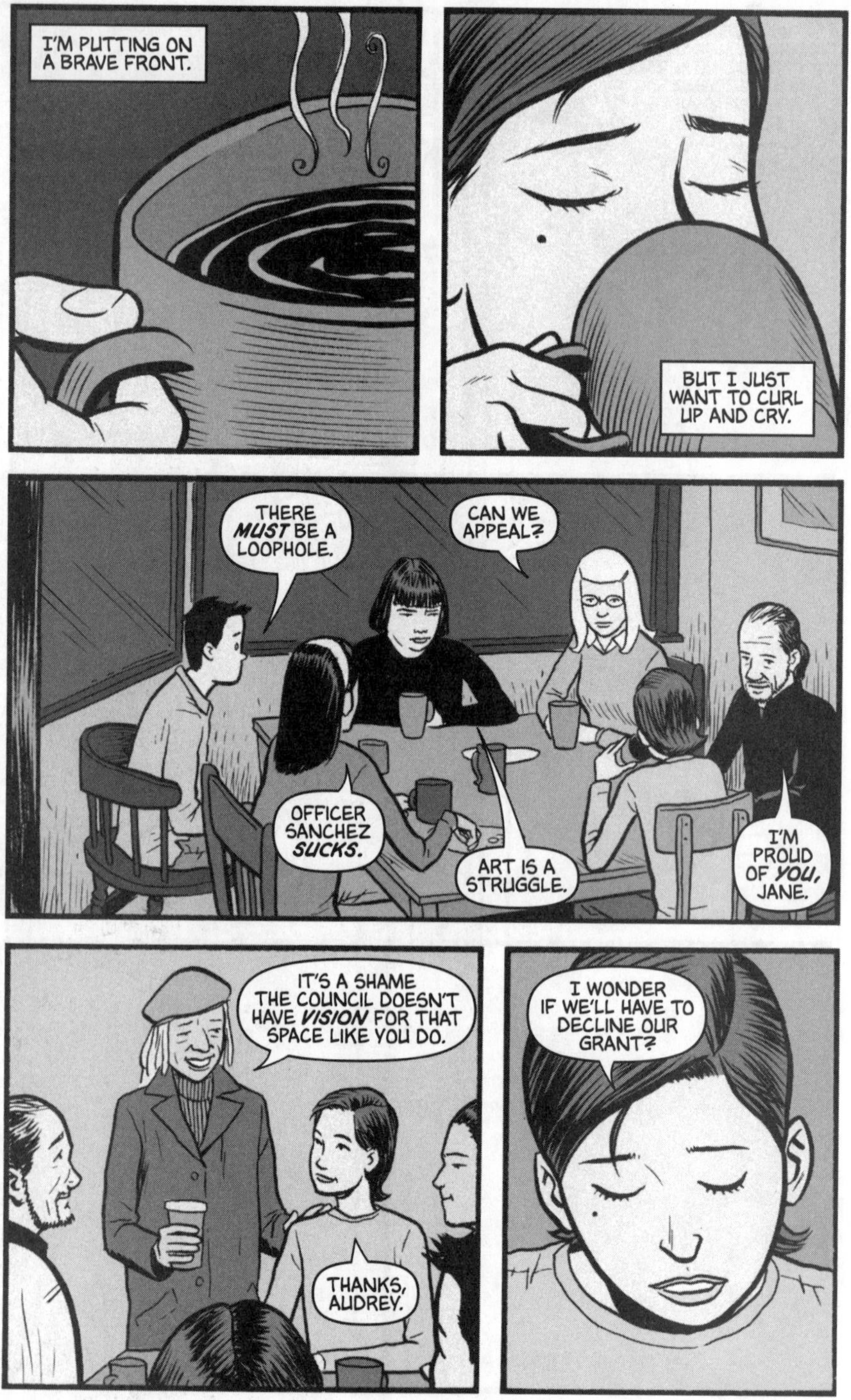

I'M PUTTING ON A BRAVE FRONT.
BUT I JUST WANT TO CURL UP AND CRY.
THERE MUST BE A LOOPHOLE.
CAN WE APPEAL?
OFFICER SANCHEZ SUCKS.
ART IS A STRUGGLE.
I'M PROUD OF YOU, JANE.
IT'S A SHAME THE COUNCIL DOESN'T HAVE VISION FOR THAT SPACE LIKE YOU DO.
THANKS, AUDREY.
I WONDER IF WE'LL HAVE TO DECLINE OUR GRANT?

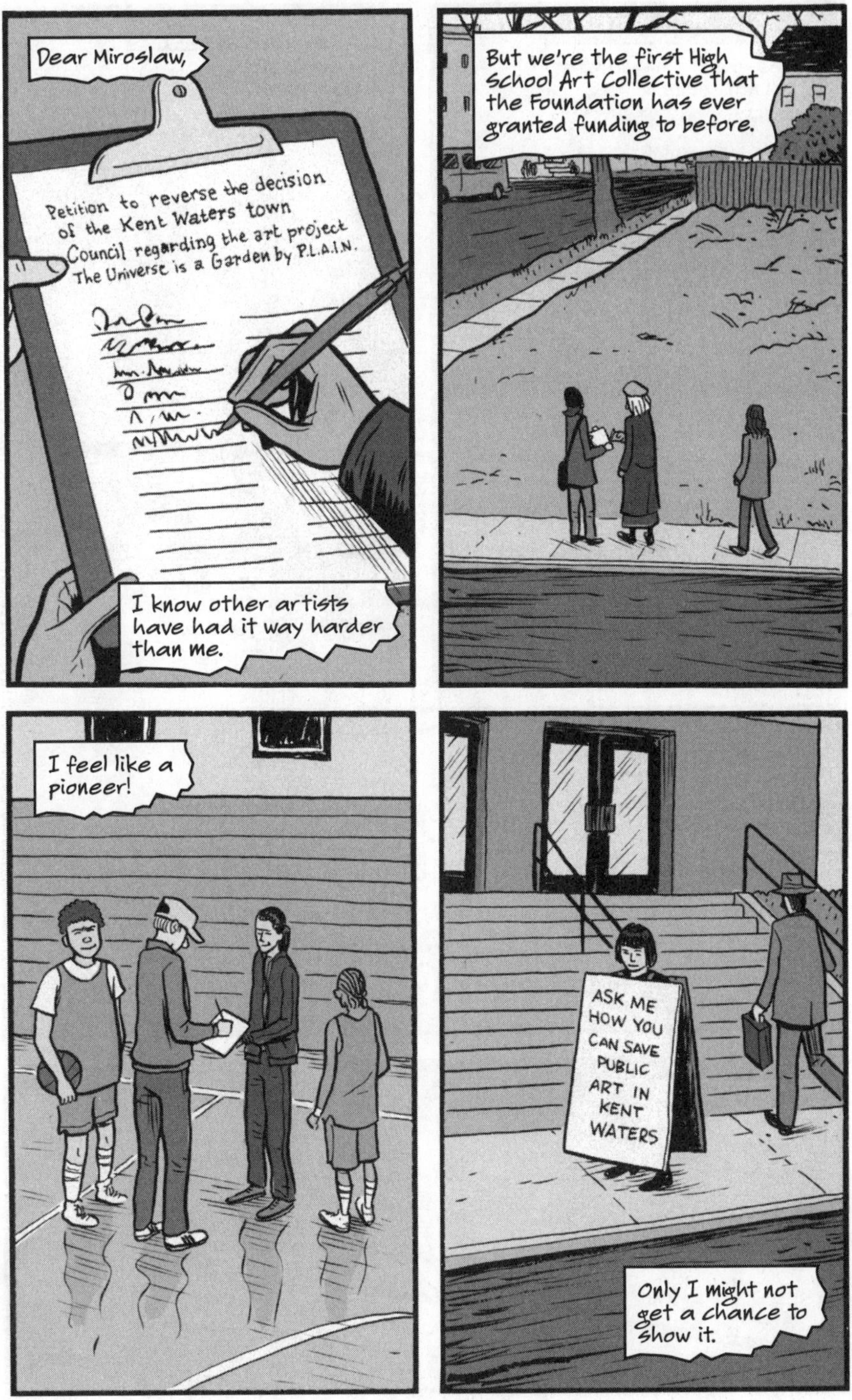
Dear Miroslaw,
Petition to reverse the decision of the Kent Waters town Council regarding the art project The Universe is a Garden by P.L.A.I.N.
I know other artists have had it way harder than me.
But we're the first High School Art Collective that the Foundation has ever granted funding to before.
I feel like a pioneer!
ASK ME HOW YOU CAN SAVE PUBLIC ART IN KENT WATERS
Only I might not get a chance to show it.

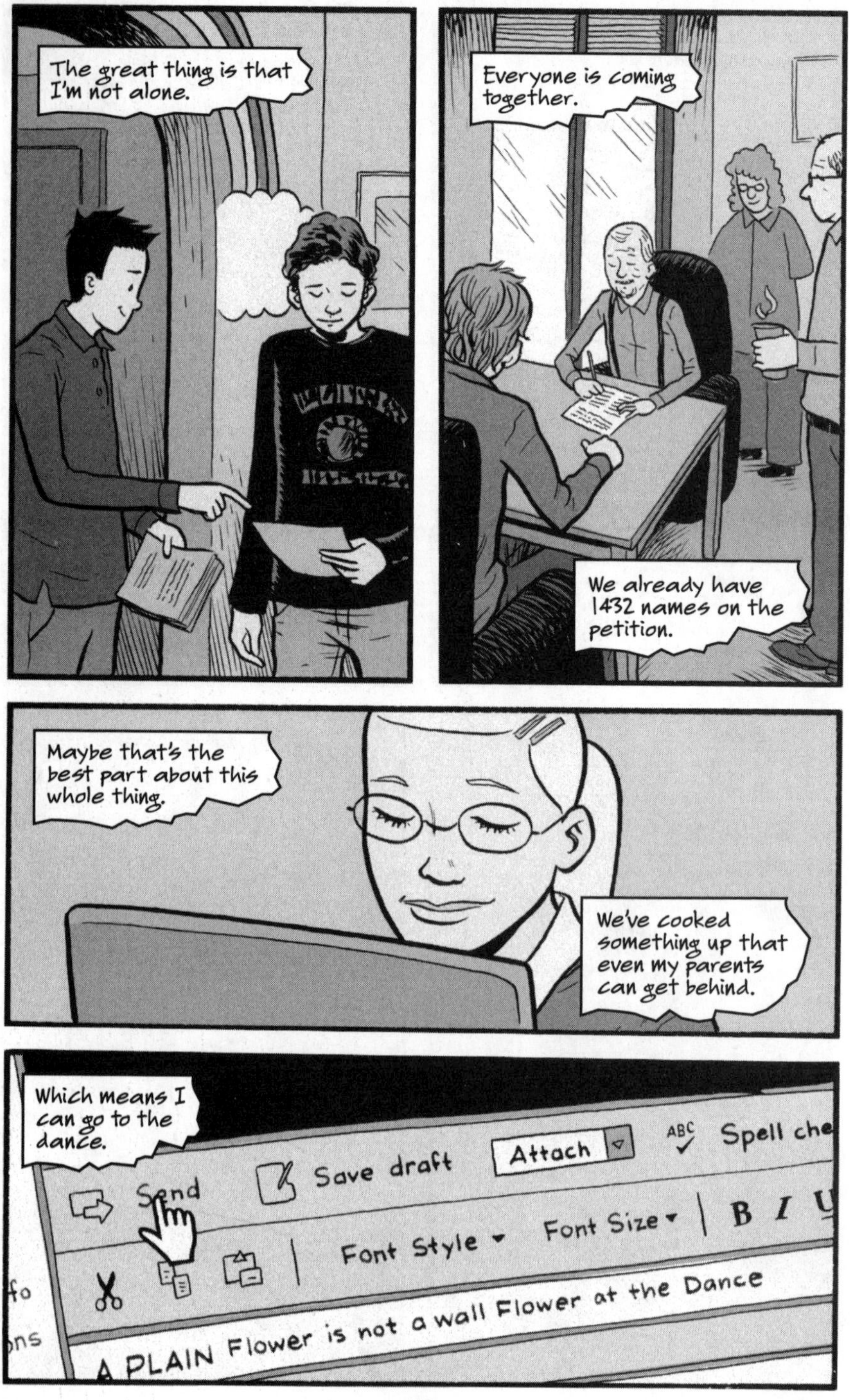
The great thing is that I'm not alone.
Everyone is coming together.
We already have 1432 names on the petition.
Maybe that's the best part about this whole thing.
We've cooked something up that even my parents can get behind.
Which means I can go to the dance.
Save draft
Attach
Spell che
Send
Font Style
Font Size
B I U
A PLAIN Flower is not a wall Flower at the Dance

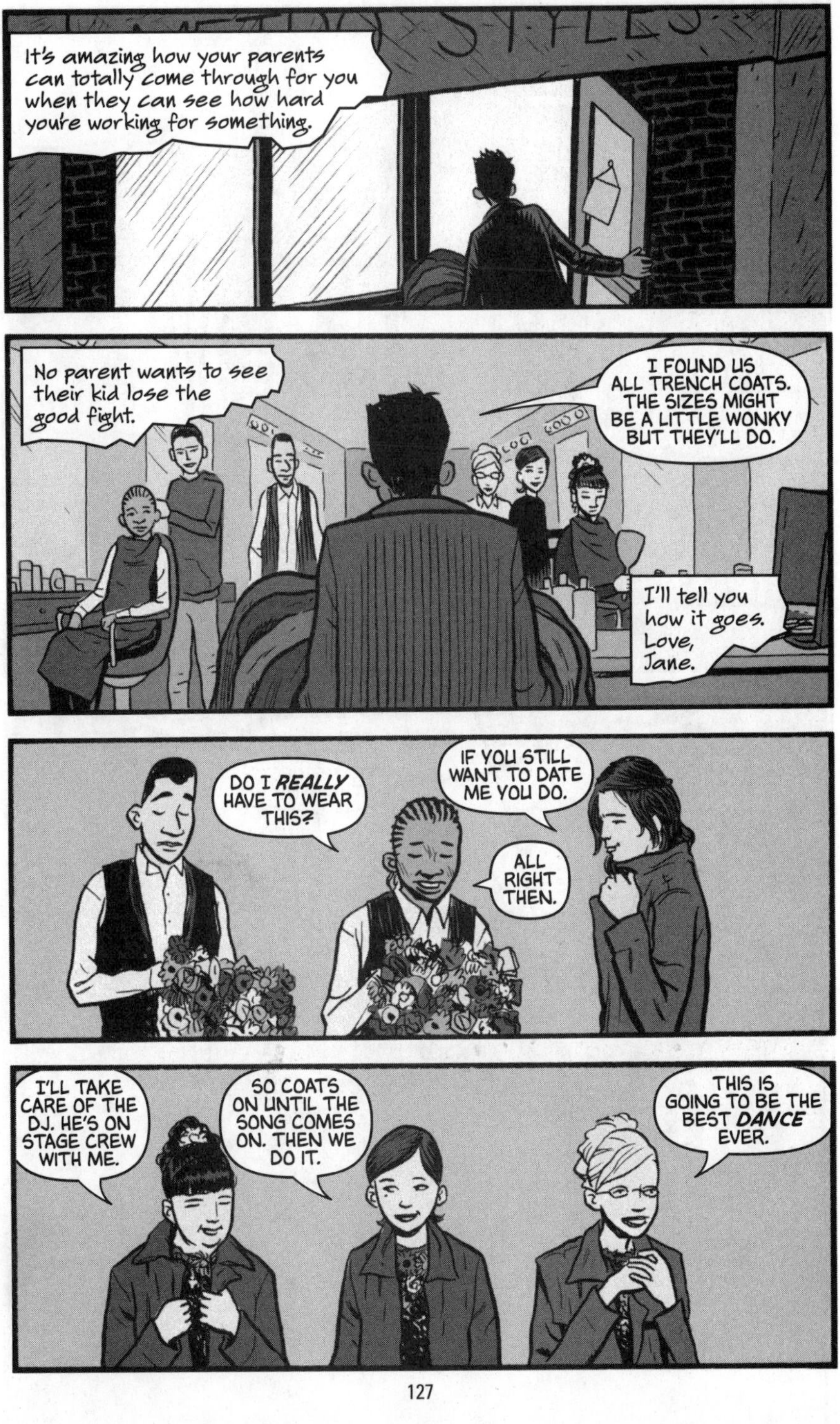
It's amazing how your parents can totally come through for you when they can see how hard you're working for something.
No parent wants to see their kid lose the good fight.
I FOUND US ALL TRENCH COATS. THE SIZES MIGHT BE A LITTLE WONKY BUT THEY'LL DO.
I'll tell you how it goes. Love, Jane.
DO I REALLY HAVE TO WEAR THIS?
IF YOU STILL WANT TO DATE ME YOU DO.
ALL RIGHT THEN.
I'LL TAKE CARE OF THE DJ. HE'S ON STAGE CREW WITH ME.
SO COATS ON UNTIL THE SONG COMES ON. THEN WE DO IT.
THIS IS GOING TO BE THE BEST DANCE EVER.

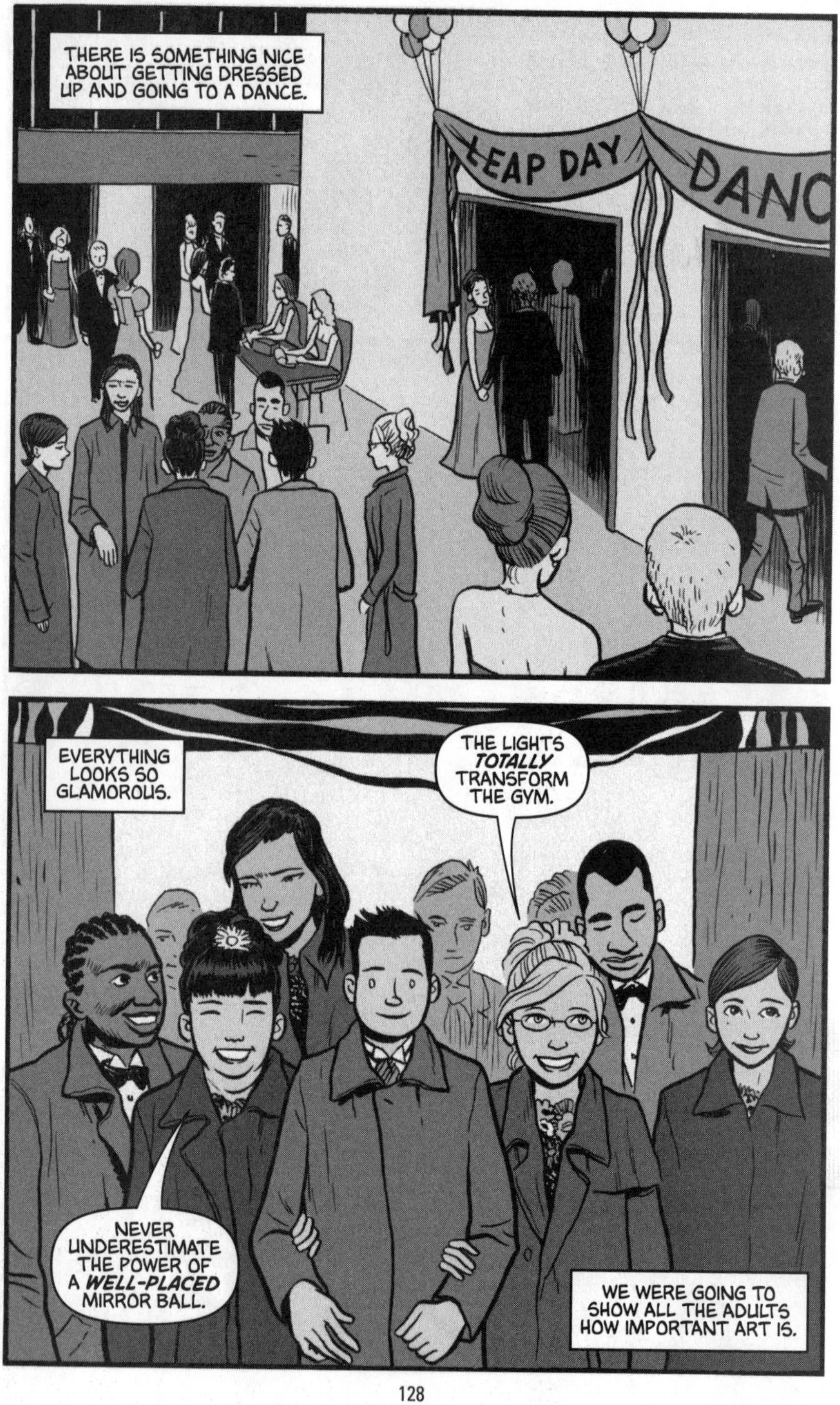
THERE IS SOMETHING NICE ABOUT GETTING DRESSED UP AND GOING TO A DANCE.
LEAP DAY DANC
EVERYTHING LOOKS SO GLAMOROUS.
THE LIGHTS *TOTALLY* TRANSFORM THE GYM.
NEVER UNDERESTIMATE THE POWER OF A ***WELL-PLACED*** MIRROR BALL.
WE WERE GOING TO SHOW ALL THE ADULTS HOW IMPORTANT ART IS.

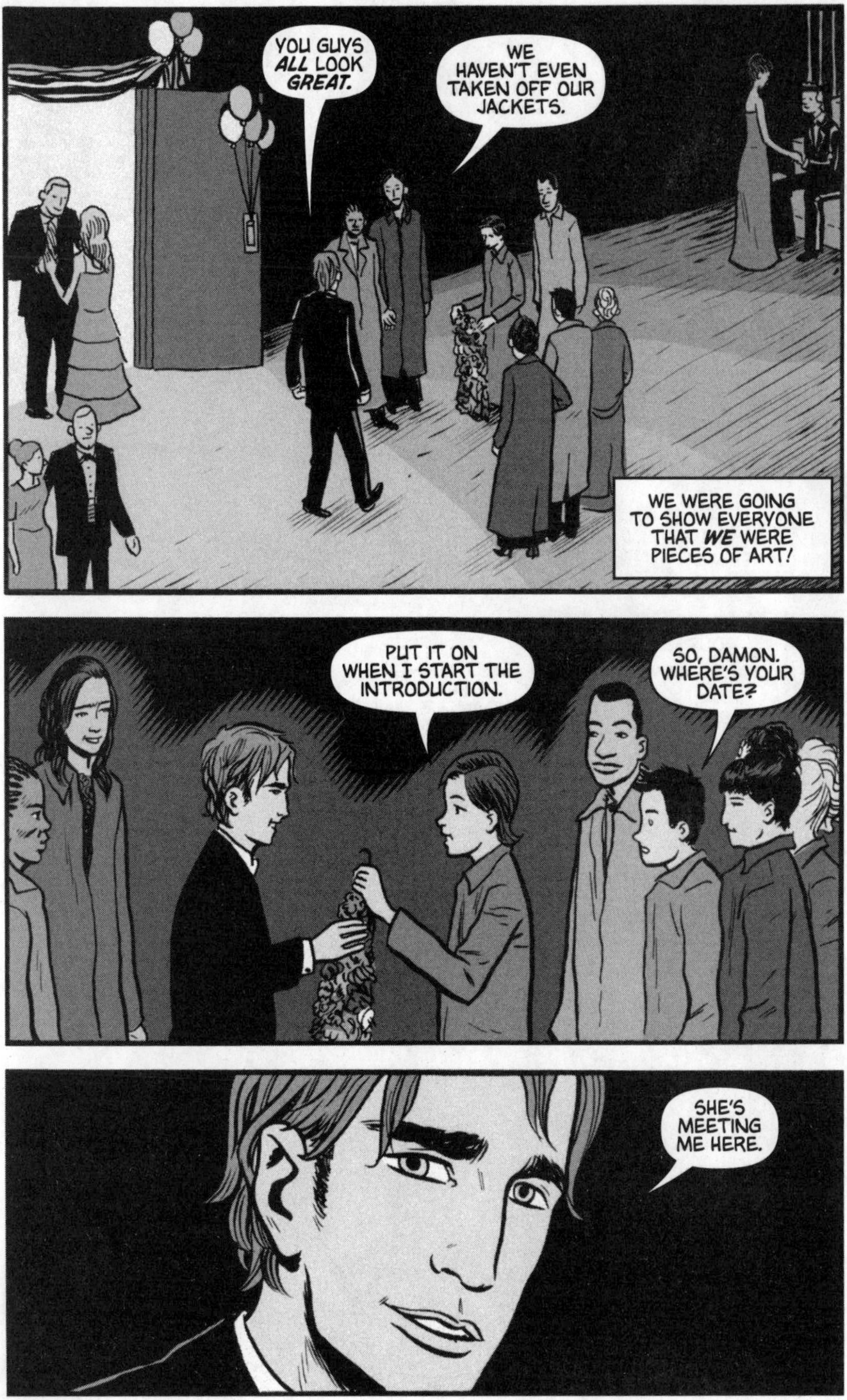
YOU GUYS ALL LOOK GREAT.
WE HAVEN'T EVEN TAKEN OFF OUR JACKETS.
WE WERE GOING TO SHOW EVERYONE THAT WE WERE PIECES OF ART!
PUT IT ON WHEN I START THE INTRODUCTION.
SO, DAMON. WHERE'S YOUR DATE?
SHE'S MEETING ME HERE.

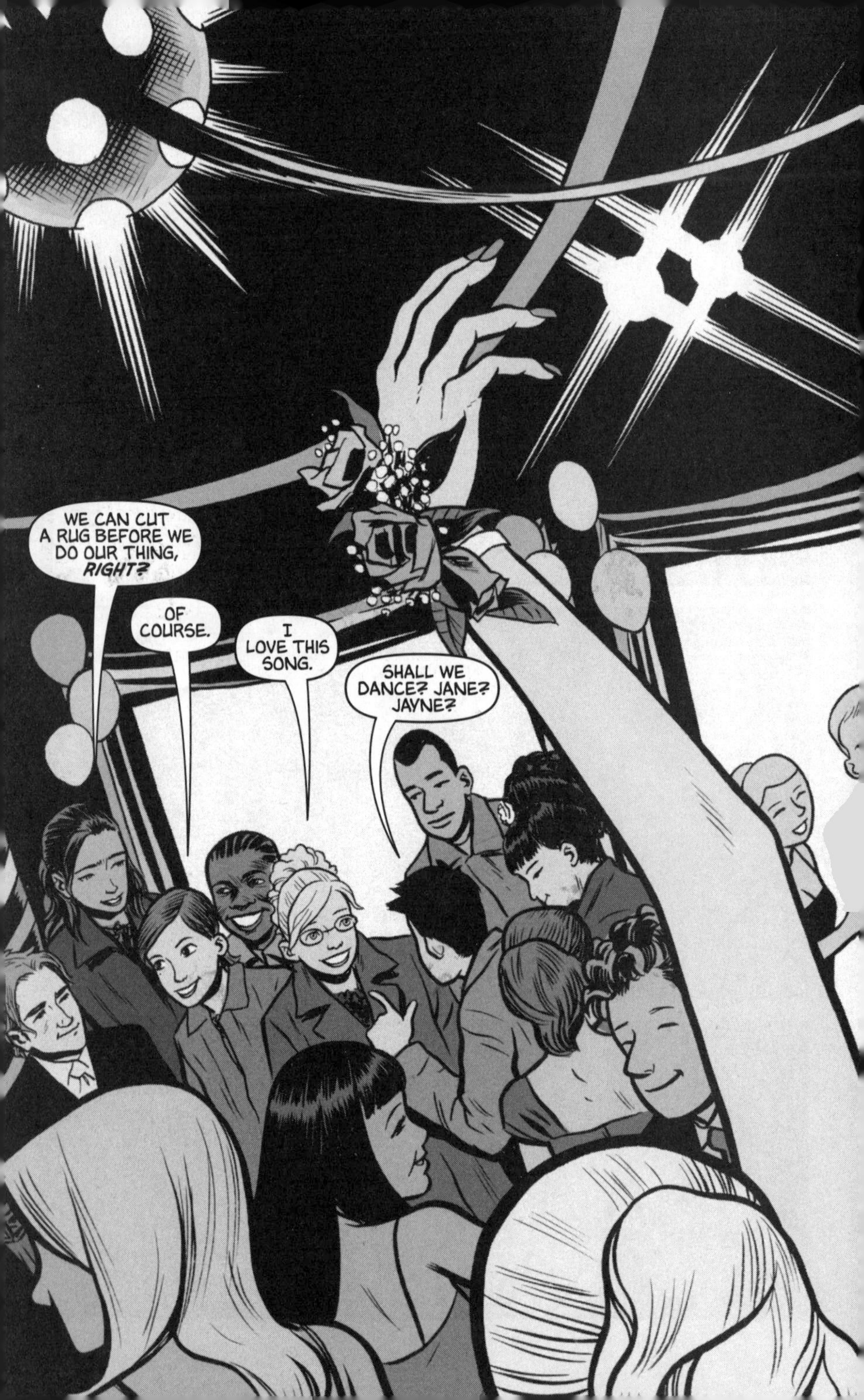
WE CAN CUT A RUG BEFORE WE DO OUR THING, *RIGHT?*
OF COURSE.
I LOVE THIS SONG.
SHALL WE DANCE? JANE? JAYNE?

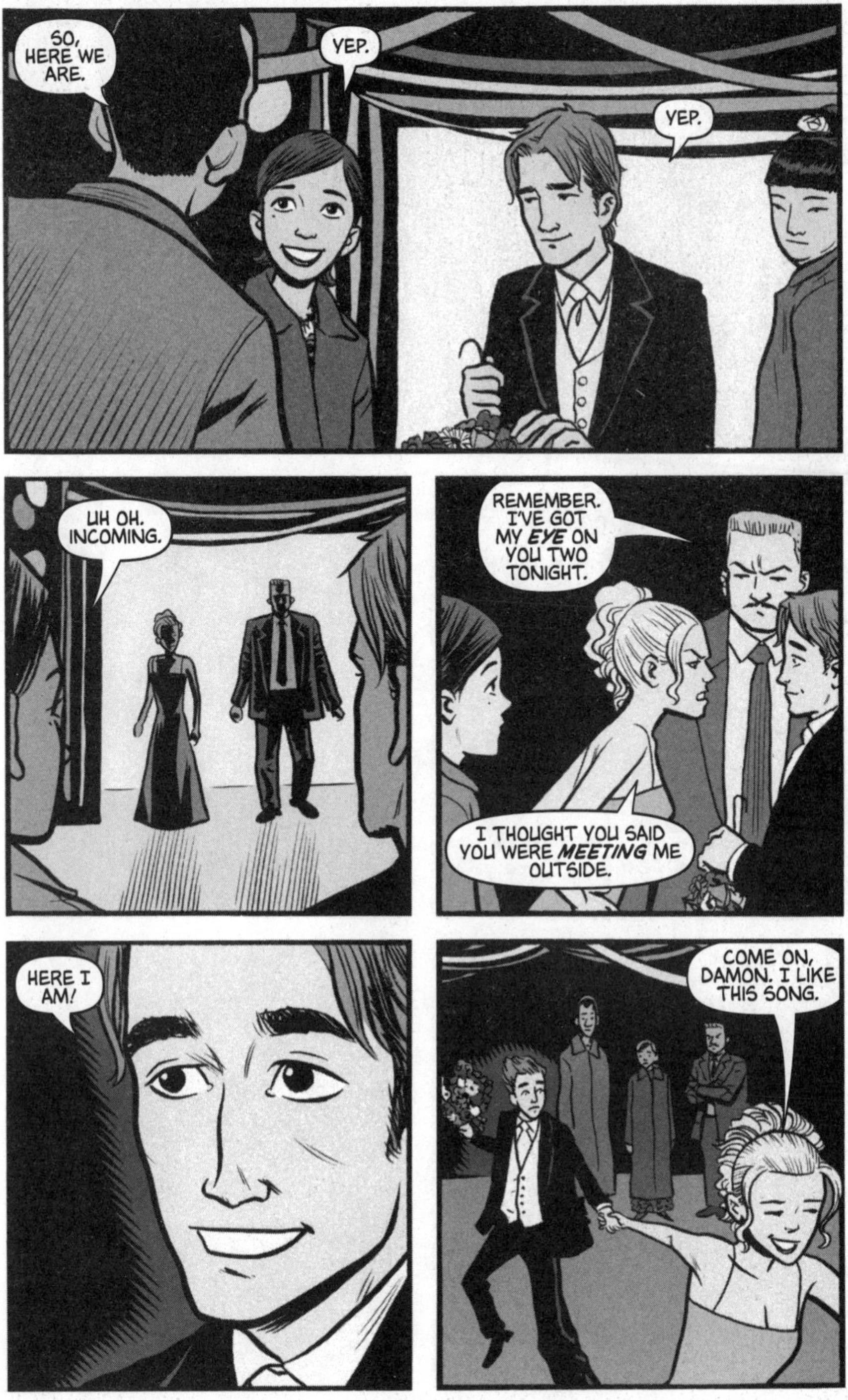
SO, HERE WE ARE.
YEP.
YEP.
UH OH. INCOMING.
REMEMBER. I'VE GOT MY *EYE* ON YOU TWO TONIGHT.
I THOUGHT YOU SAID YOU WERE *MEETING* ME OUTSIDE.
HERE I AM!
COME ON, DAMON. I LIKE THIS SONG.

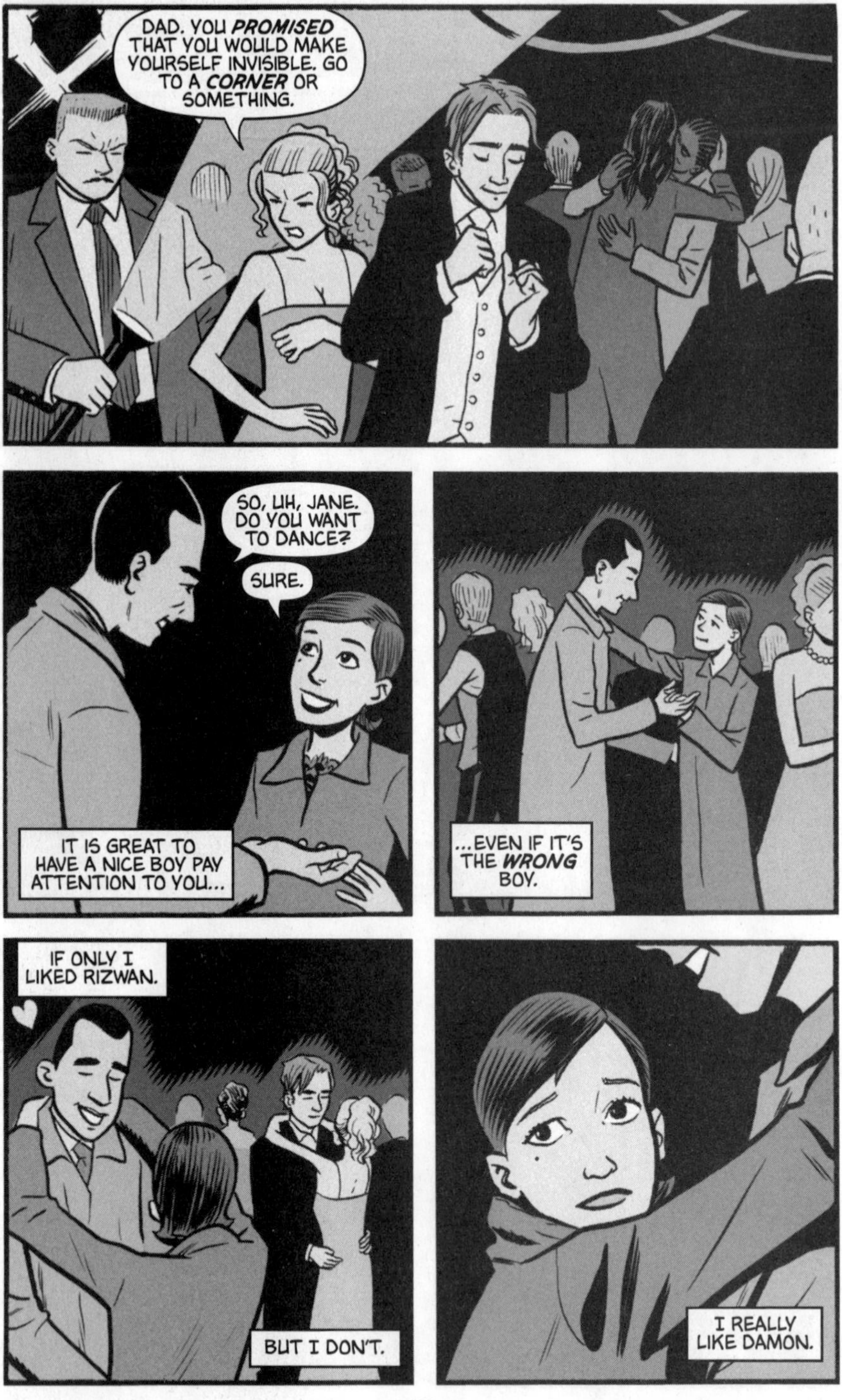
DAD. YOU *PROMISED* THAT YOU WOULD MAKE YOURSELF INVISIBLE. GO TO A *CORNER* OR SOMETHING.
SO, UH, JANE. DO YOU WANT TO DANCE?
SURE.
IT IS GREAT TO HAVE A NICE BOY PAY ATTENTION TO YOU...
...EVEN IF IT'S THE *WRONG* BOY.
IF ONLY I LIKED RIZWAN.
BUT I DON'T.
I REALLY LIKE DAMON.

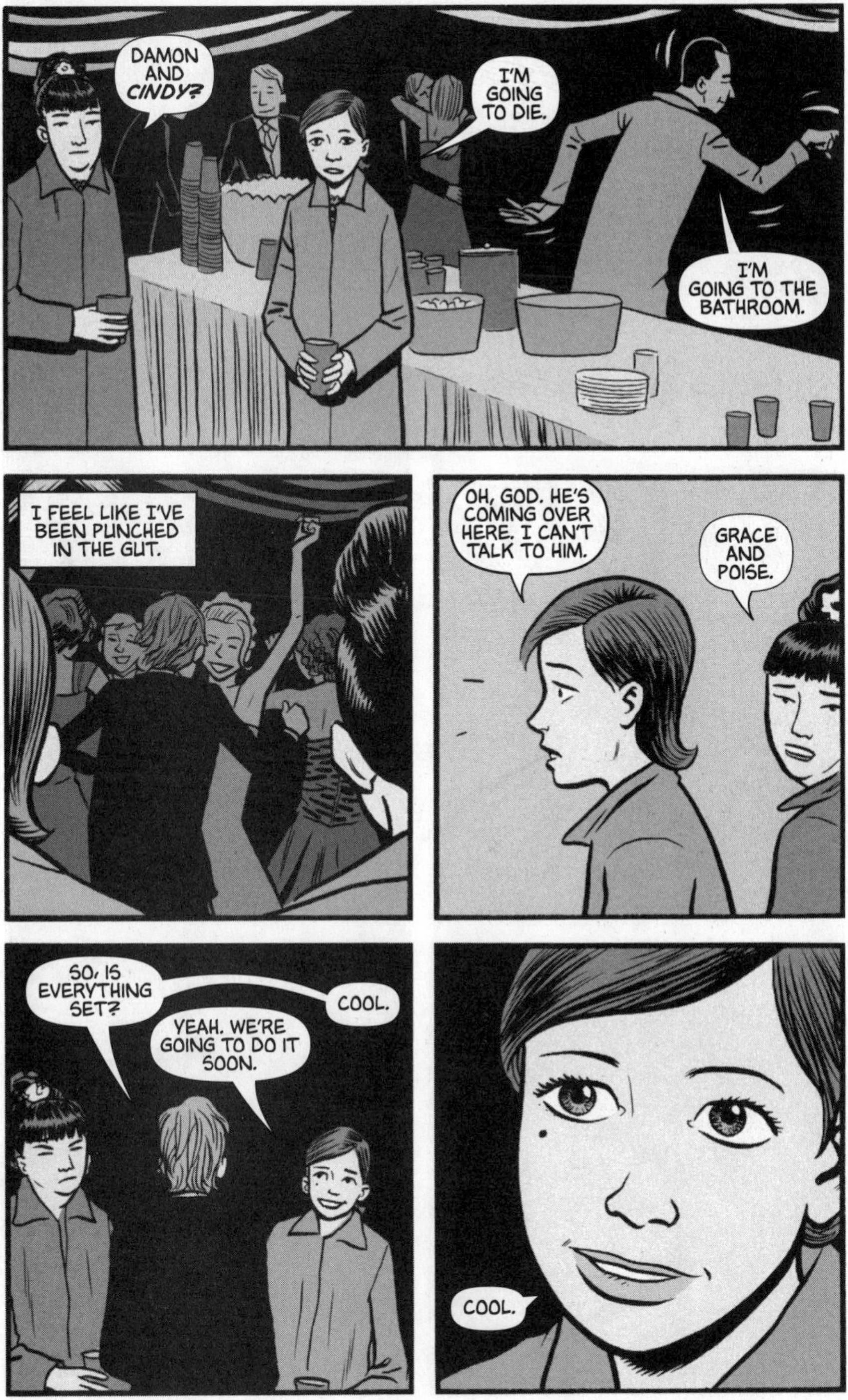
DAMON AND CINDY?
I'M GOING TO DIE.
I'M GOING TO THE BATHROOM.
I FEEL LIKE I'VE BEEN PUNCHED IN THE GUT.
OH, GOD. HE'S COMING OVER HERE. I CAN'T TALK TO HIM.
GRACE AND POISE.
SO, IS EVERYTHING SET?
YEAH. WE'RE GOING TO DO IT SOON.
COOL.
COOL.

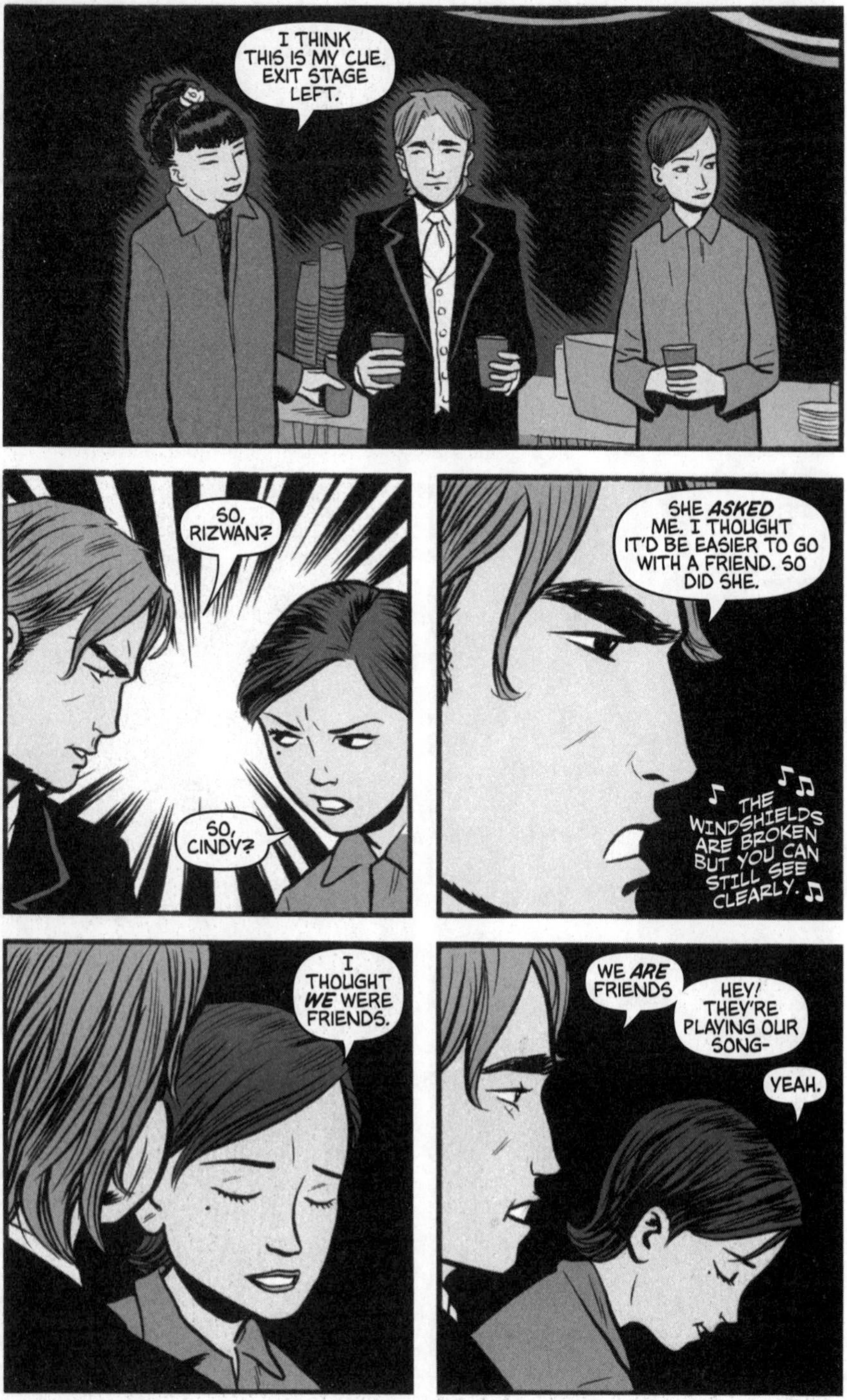
I THINK THIS IS MY CUE. EXIT STAGE LEFT.
SO, RIZWAN?
SO, CINDY?
SHE *ASKED* ME. I THOUGHT IT'D BE EASIER TO GO WITH A FRIEND. SO DID SHE.
♪ THE WINDSHIELDS ARE BROKEN BUT YOU CAN STILL SEE CLEARLY. ♫
I THOUGHT *WE* WERE FRIENDS.
WE *ARE* FRIENDS
HEY! THEY'RE PLAYING OUR SONG-
YEAH.

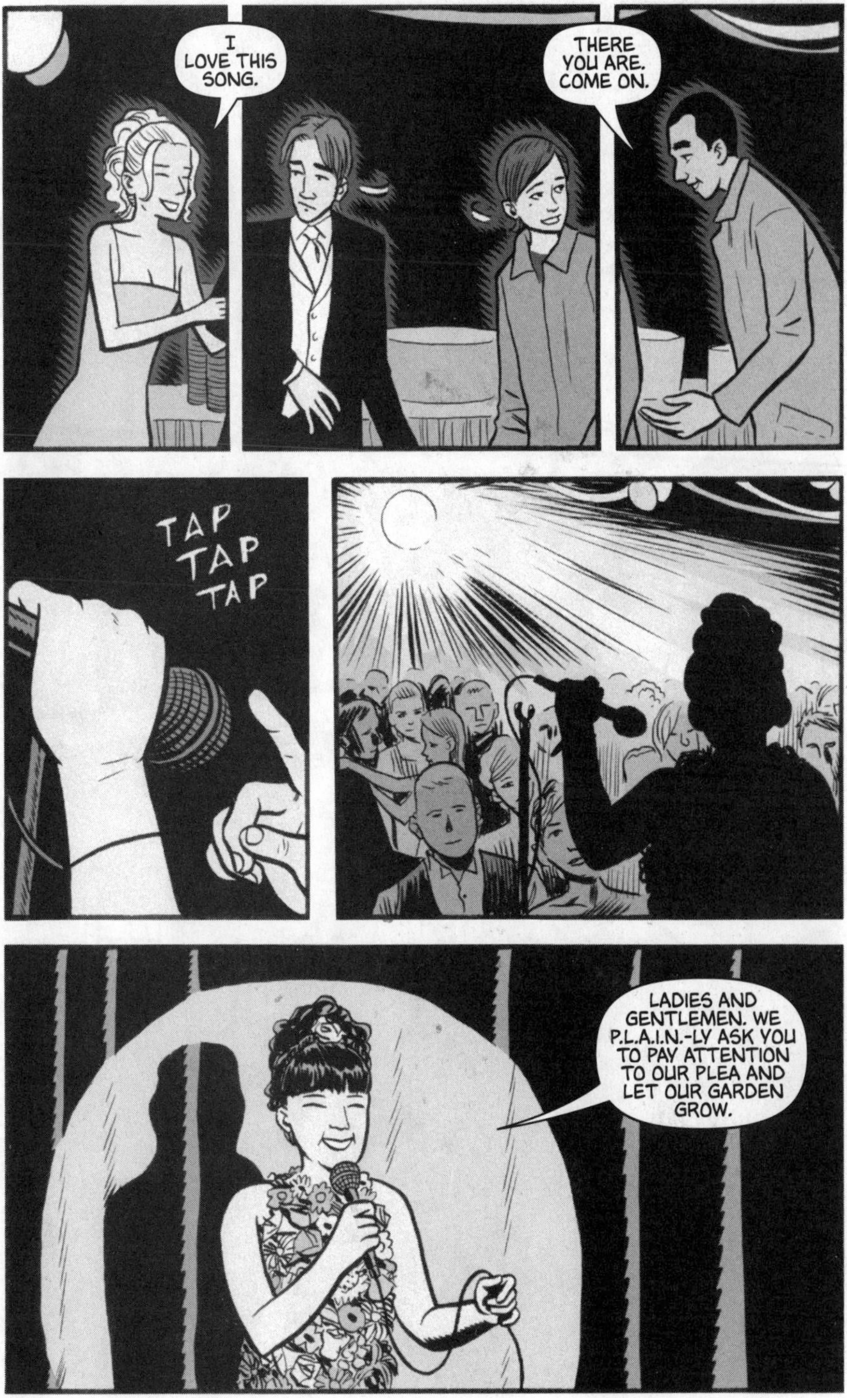
I LOVE THIS SONG.
THERE YOU ARE. COME ON.
TAP TAP TAP
LADIES AND GENTLEMEN. WE P.L.A.I.N.-LY ASK YOU TO PAY ATTENTION TO OUR PLEA AND LET OUR GARDEN GROW.

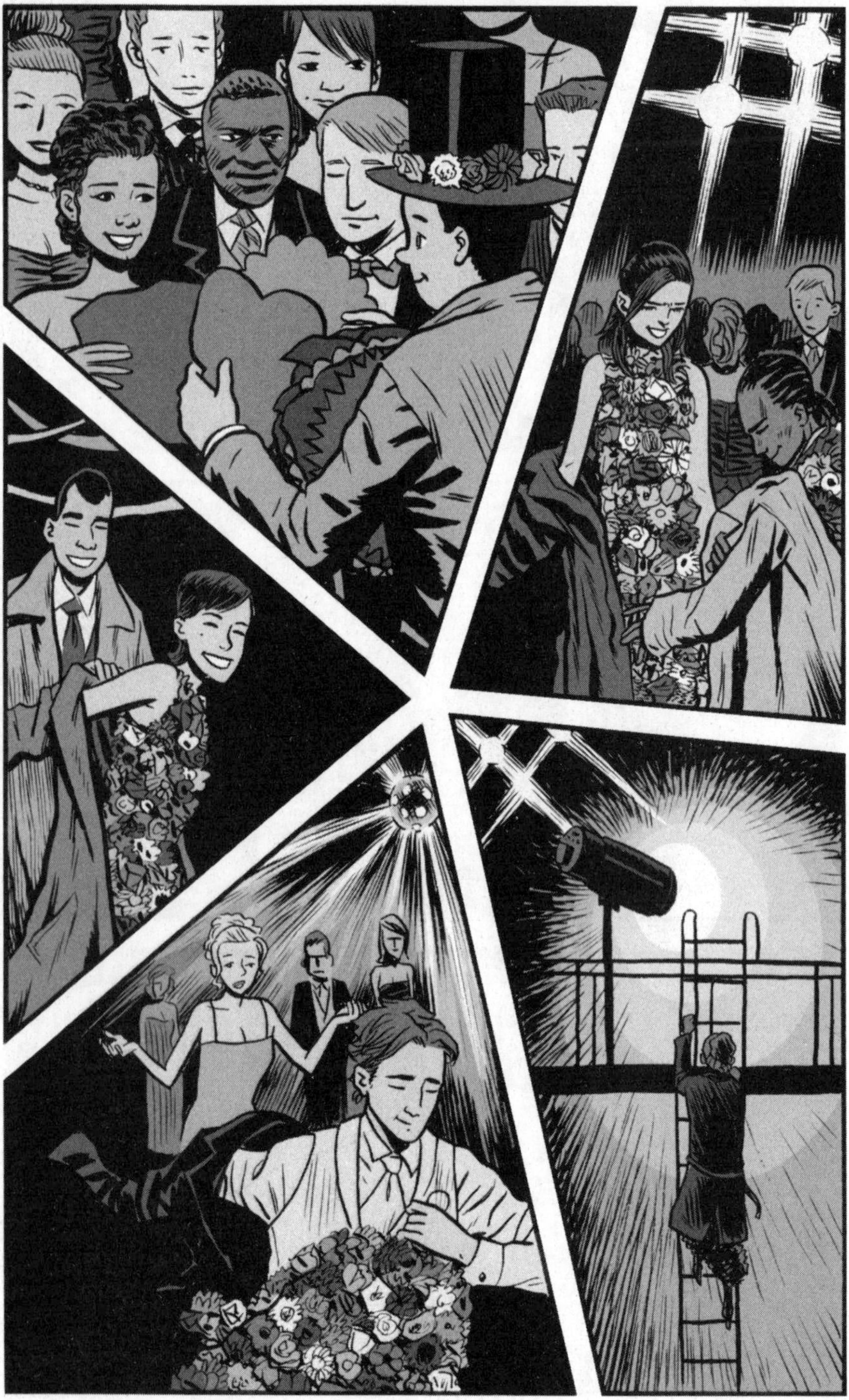

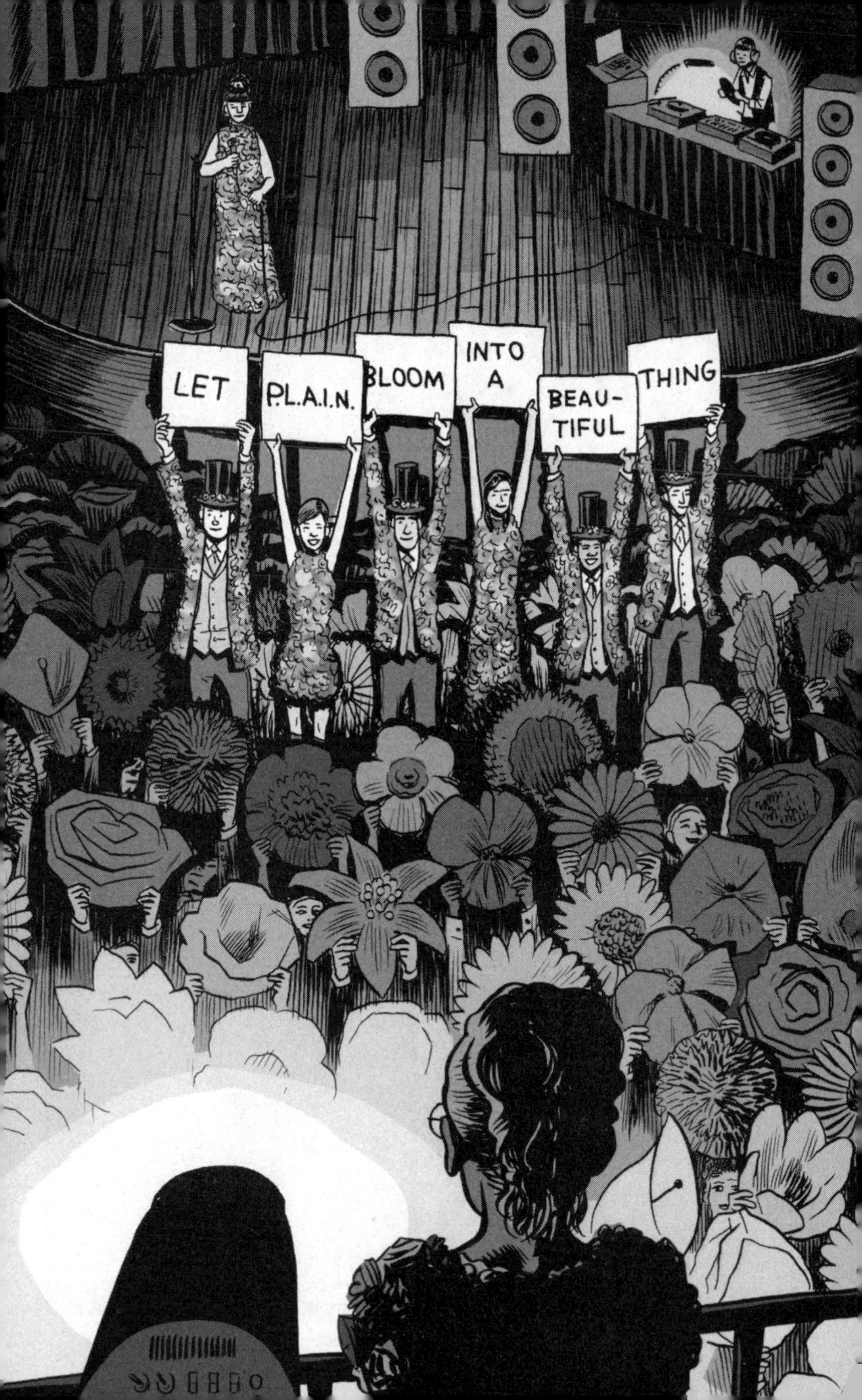
LET
P.L.A.I.N.
BLOOM
INTO
A
BEAU-
TIFUL
THING

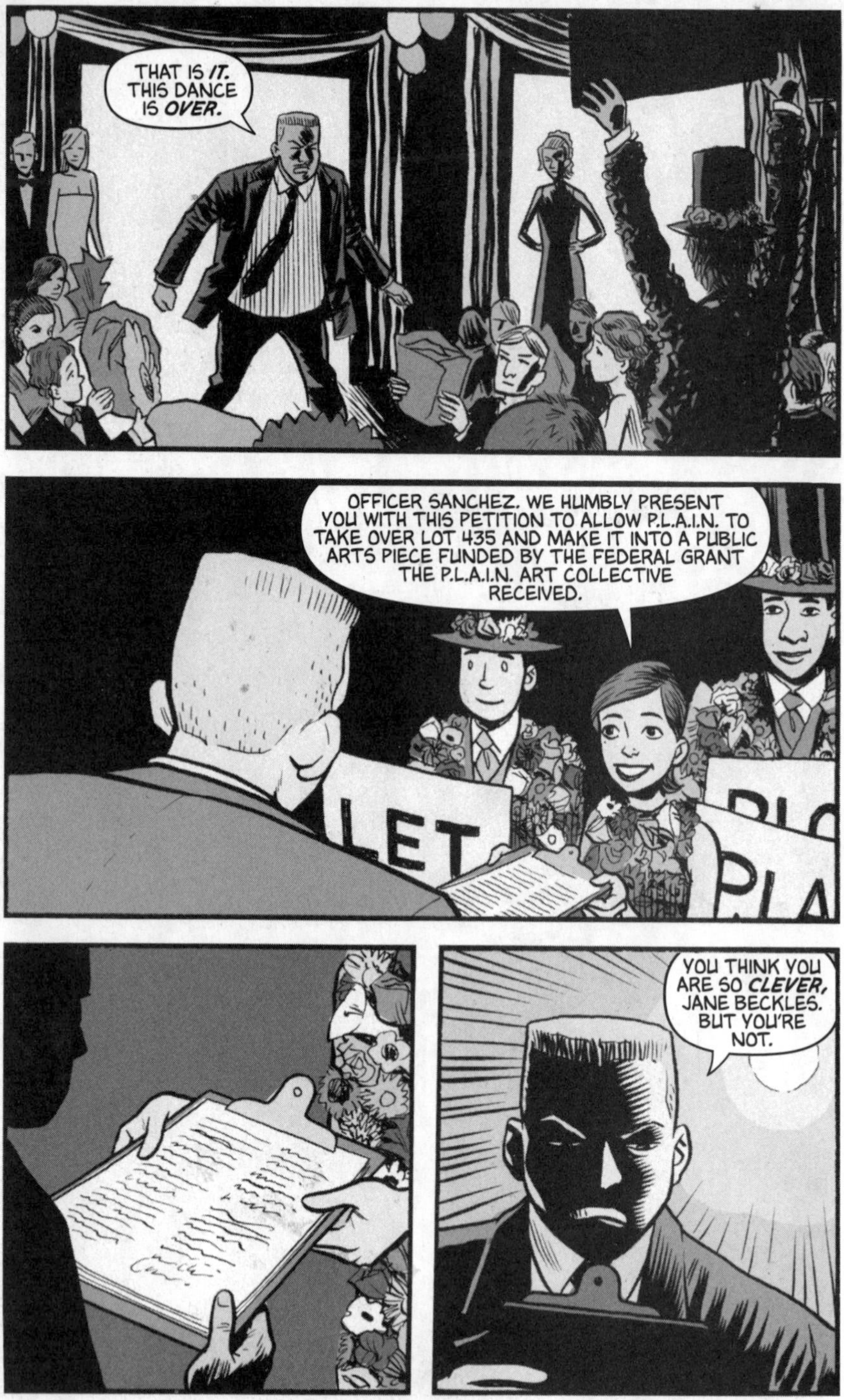
THAT IS *IT.* THIS DANCE IS *OVER.*
OFFICER SANCHEZ. WE HUMBLY PRESENT YOU WITH THIS PETITION TO ALLOW P.L.A.I.N. TO TAKE OVER LOT 435 AND MAKE IT INTO A PUBLIC ARTS PIECE FUNDED BY THE FEDERAL GRANT THE P.L.A.I.N. ART COLLECTIVE RECEIVED.
LET
YOU THINK YOU ARE SO *CLEVER,* JANE BECKLES. BUT YOU'RE NOT.

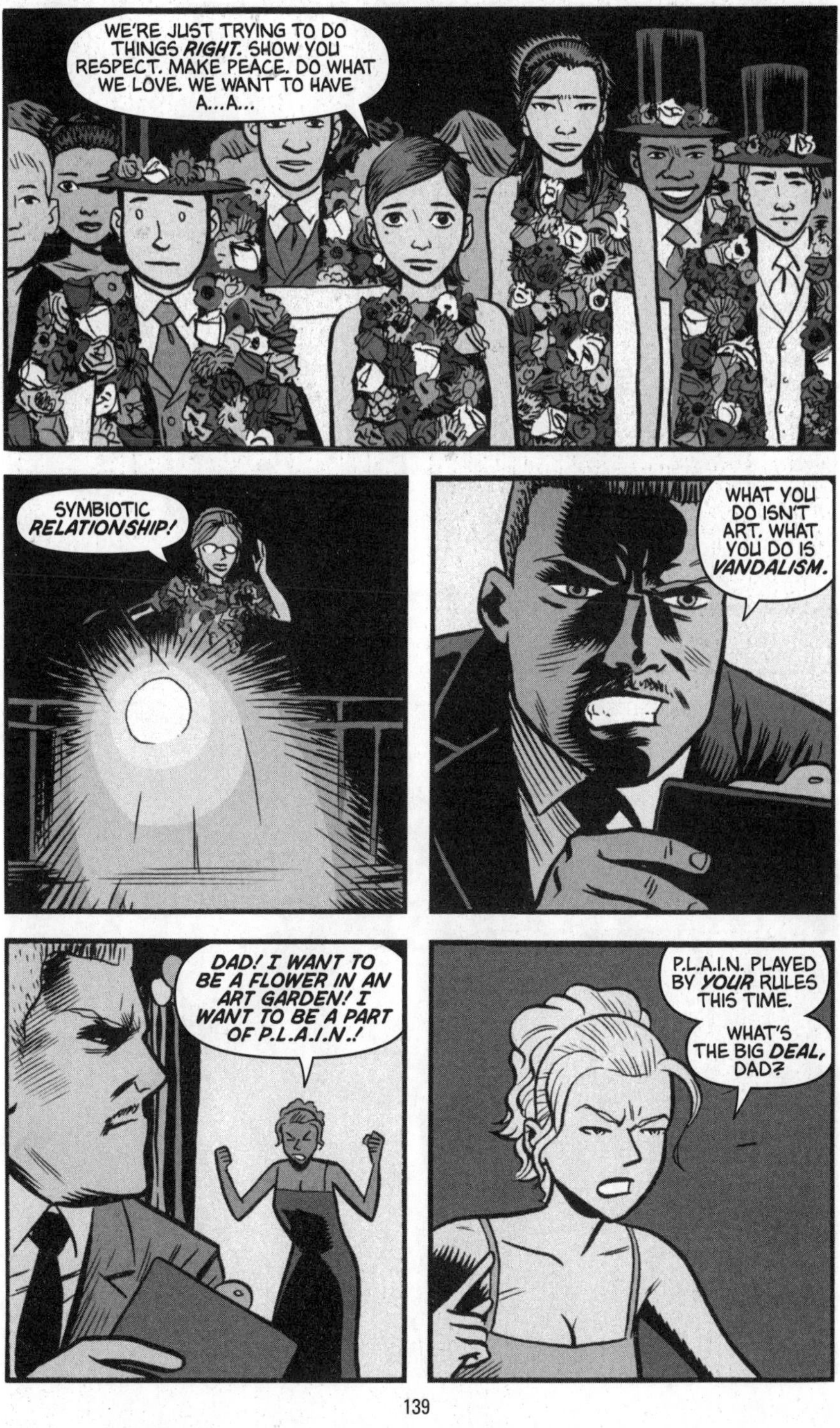
WE'RE JUST TRYING TO DO THINGS RIGHT. SHOW YOU RESPECT. MAKE PEACE. DO WHAT WE LOVE. WE WANT TO HAVE A...A...
SYMBIOTIC RELATIONSHIP!
WHAT YOU DO ISN'T ART. WHAT YOU DO IS VANDALISM.
DAD! I WANT TO BE A FLOWER IN AN ART GARDEN! I WANT TO BE A PART OF P.L.A.I.N.!
P.L.A.I.N. PLAYED BY YOUR RULES THIS TIME.
WHAT'S THE BIG DEAL, DAD?

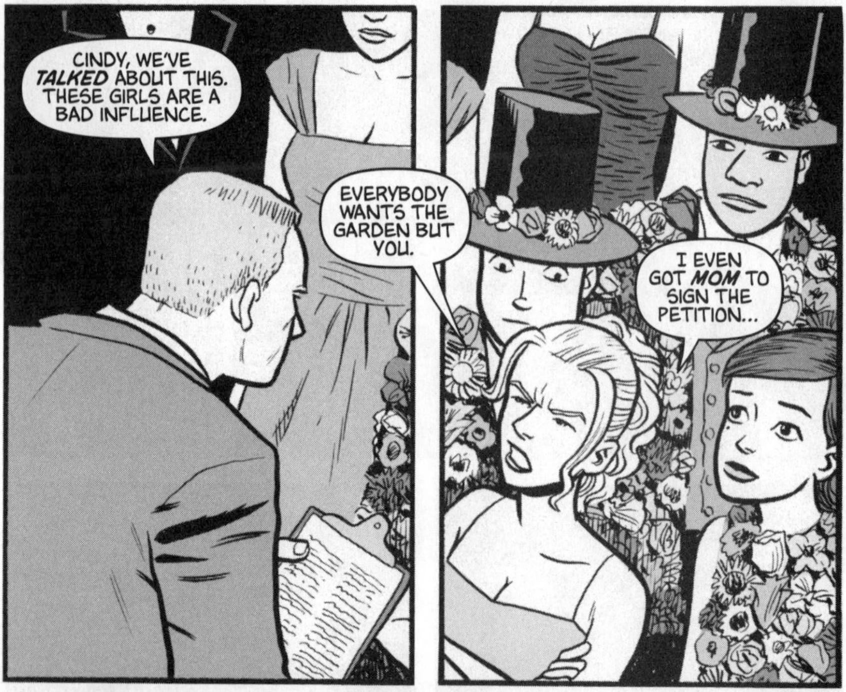
CINDY, WE'VE TALKED ABOUT THIS. THESE GIRLS ARE A BAD INFLUENCE.
EVERYBODY WANTS THE GARDEN BUT YOU.
I EVEN GOT MOM TO SIGN THE PETITION...

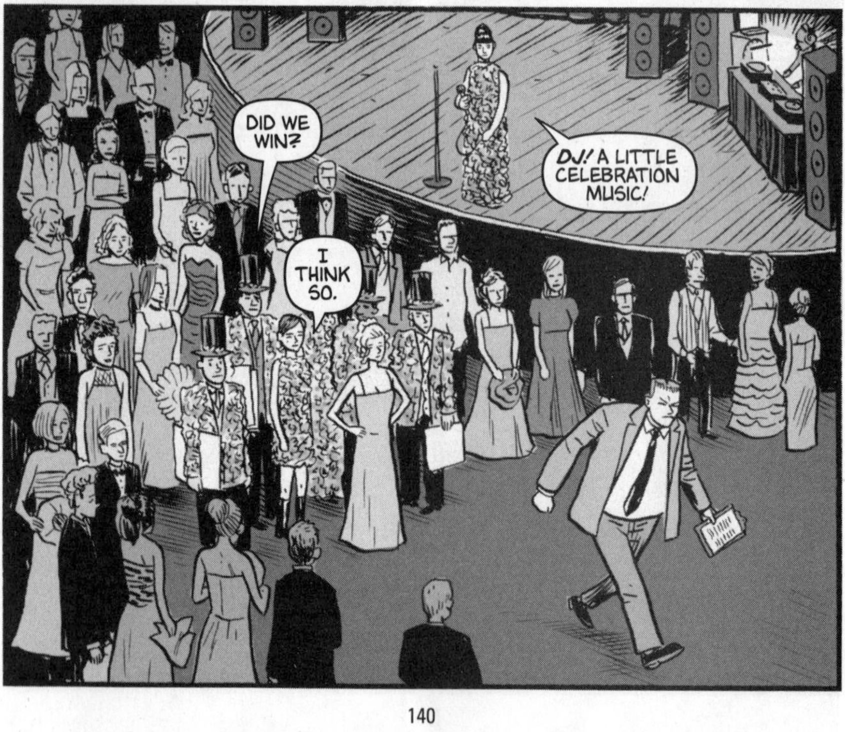
DID WE WIN?
DJ! A LITTLE CELEBRATION MUSIC!
I THINK SO.

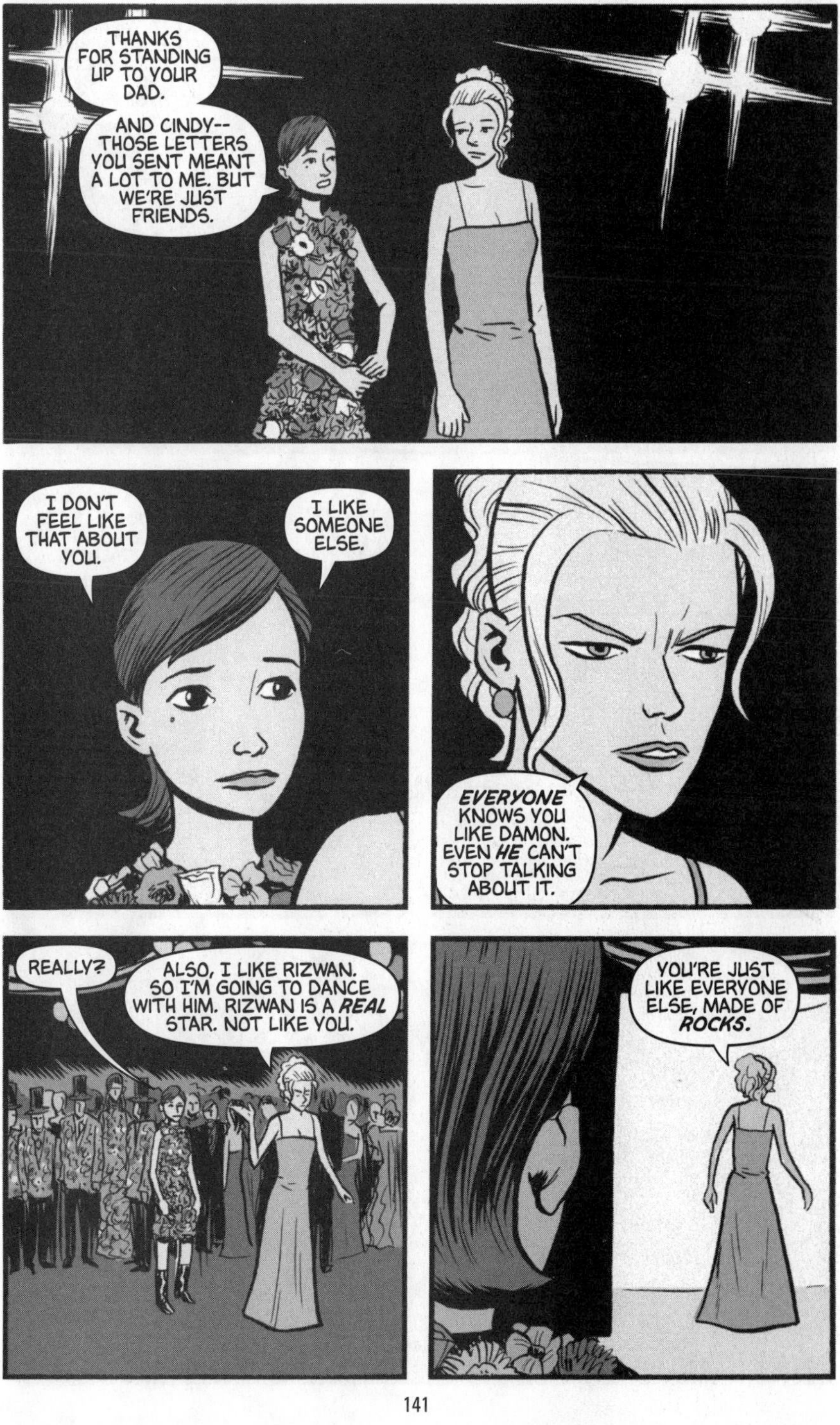
THANKS FOR STANDING UP TO YOUR DAD.
AND CINDY-- THOSE LETTERS YOU SENT MEANT A LOT TO ME. BUT WE'RE JUST FRIENDS.
I DON'T FEEL LIKE THAT ABOUT YOU.
I LIKE SOMEONE ELSE.
EVERYONE KNOWS YOU LIKE DAMON. EVEN *HE* CAN'T STOP TALKING ABOUT IT.
REALLY?
ALSO, I LIKE RIZWAN. SO I'M GOING TO DANCE WITH HIM. RIZWAN IS A *REAL* STAR. NOT LIKE YOU.
YOU'RE JUST LIKE EVERYONE ELSE, MADE OF *ROCKS*.

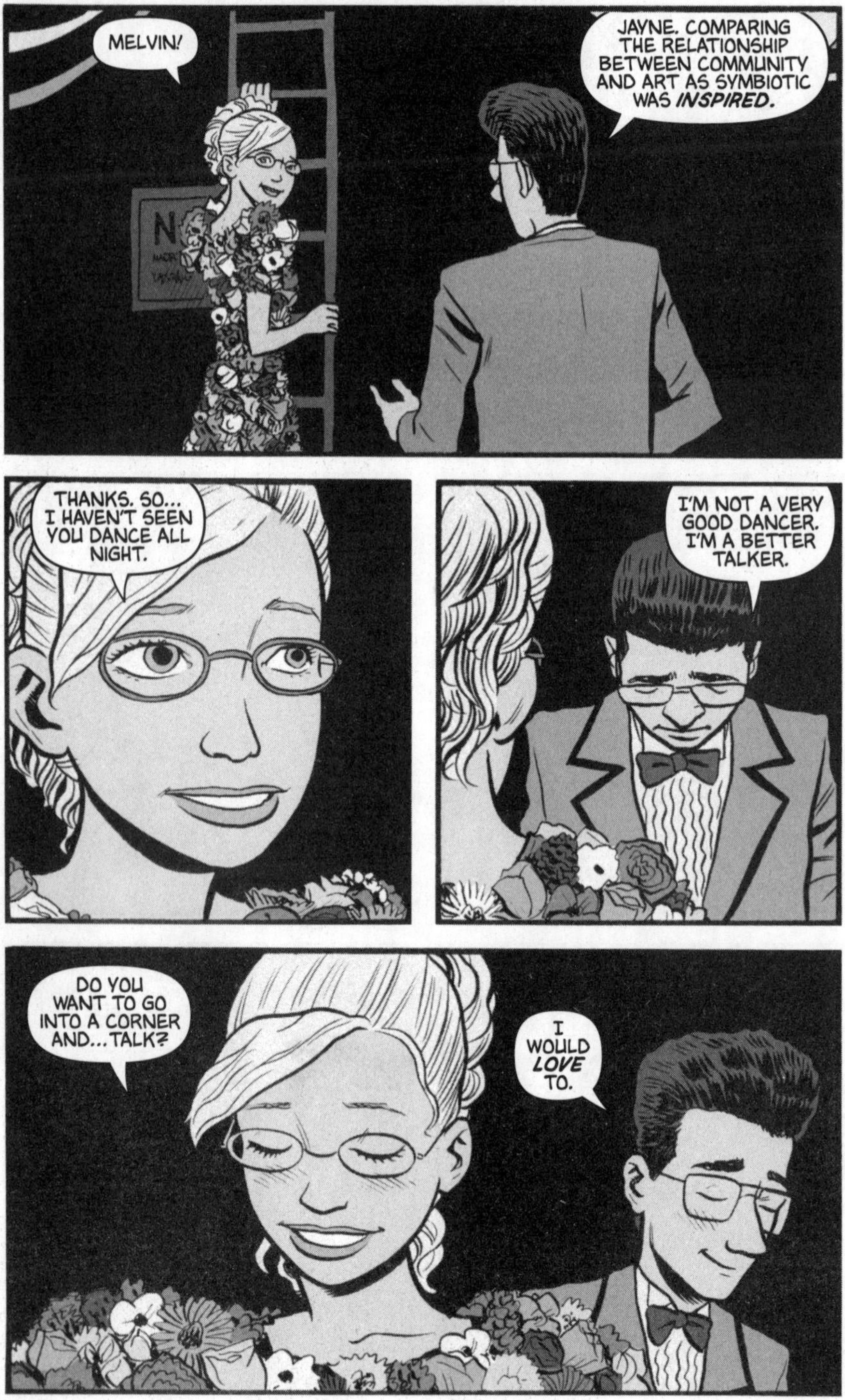

MELVIN!
JAYNE. COMPARING THE RELATIONSHIP BETWEEN COMMUNITY AND ART AS SYMBIOTIC WAS *INSPIRED.*
THANKS. SO... I HAVEN'T SEEN YOU DANCE ALL NIGHT.
I'M NOT A VERY GOOD DANCER. I'M A BETTER TALKER.
DO YOU WANT TO GO INTO A CORNER AND... TALK?
I WOULD *LOVE* TO.

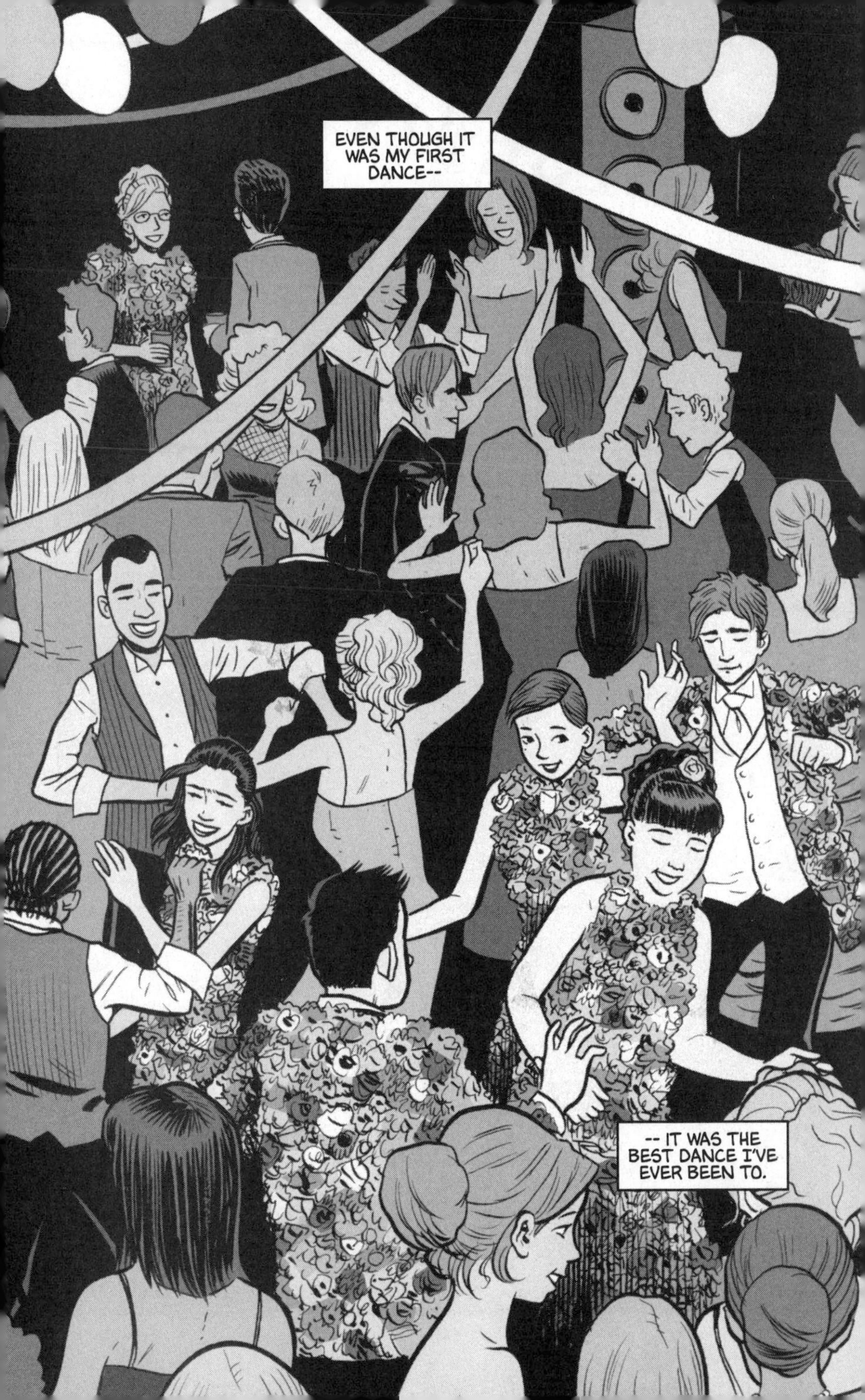
EVEN THOUGH IT WAS MY FIRST DANCE--
-- IT WAS THE BEST DANCE I'VE EVER BEEN TO.

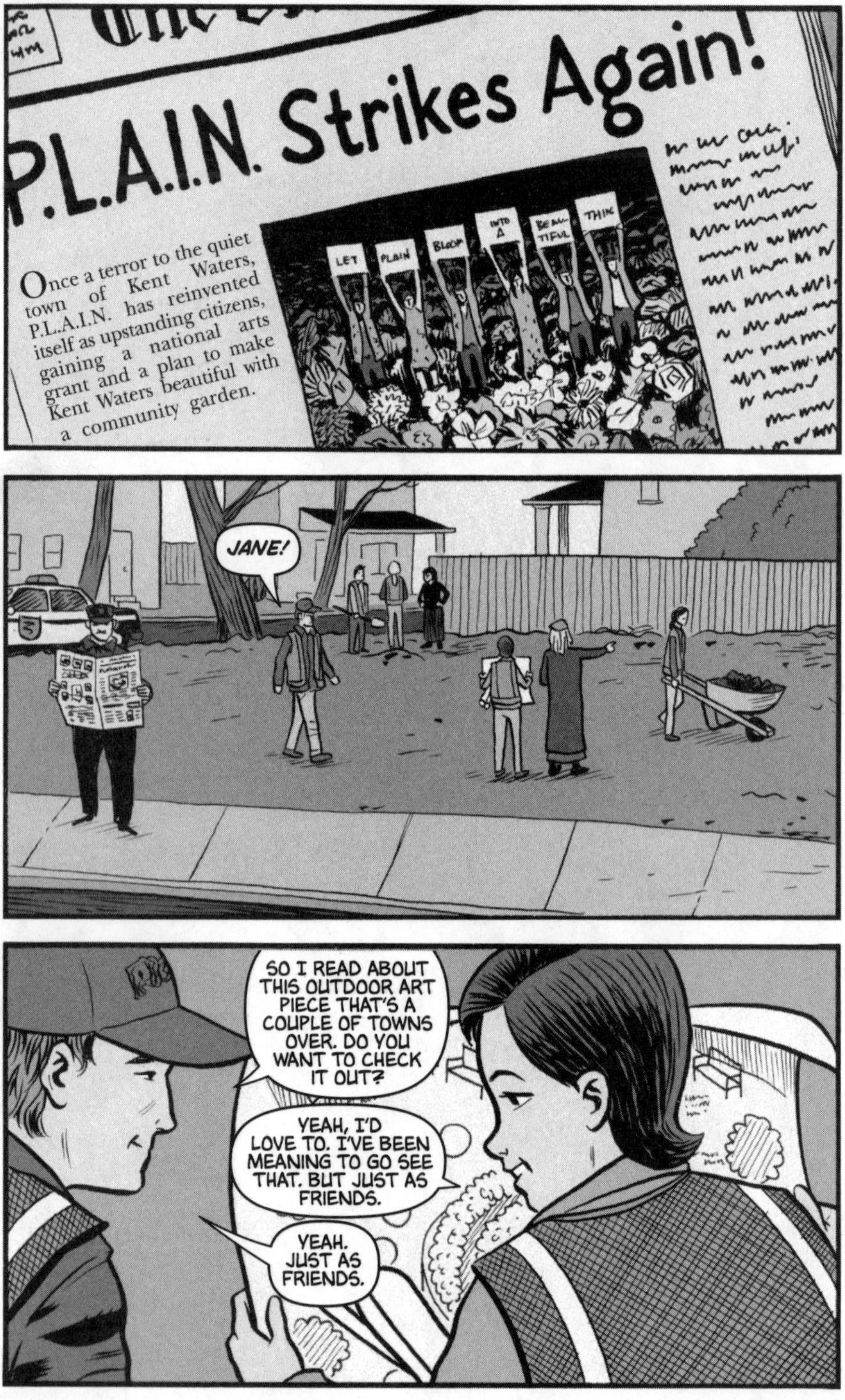
P.L.A.I.N. Strikes Again!
Once a terror to the quiet town of Kent Waters, P.L.A.I.N. has reinvented itself as upstanding citizens, gaining a national arts grant and a plan to make Kent Waters beautiful with a community garden.
LET PLAIN BLOOM INTO A BEAUTIFUL THINK
JANE!
SO I READ ABOUT THIS OUTDOOR ART PIECE THAT'S A COUPLE OF TOWNS OVER. DO YOU WANT TO CHECK IT OUT?
YEAH, I'D LOVE TO. I'VE BEEN MEANING TO GO SEE THAT. BUT JUST AS FRIENDS.
YEAH. JUST AS FRIENDS.

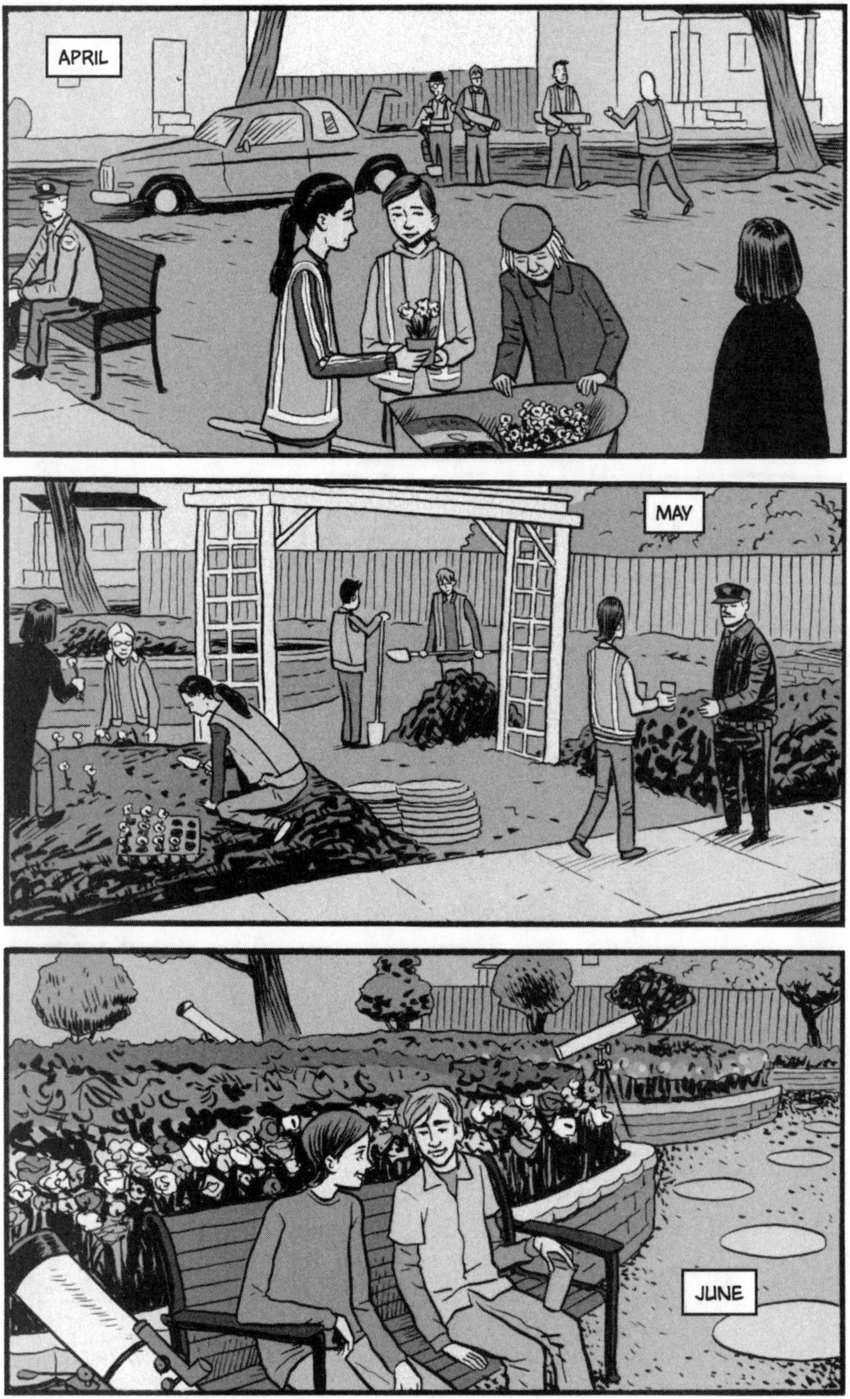
APRIL
MAY
JUNE

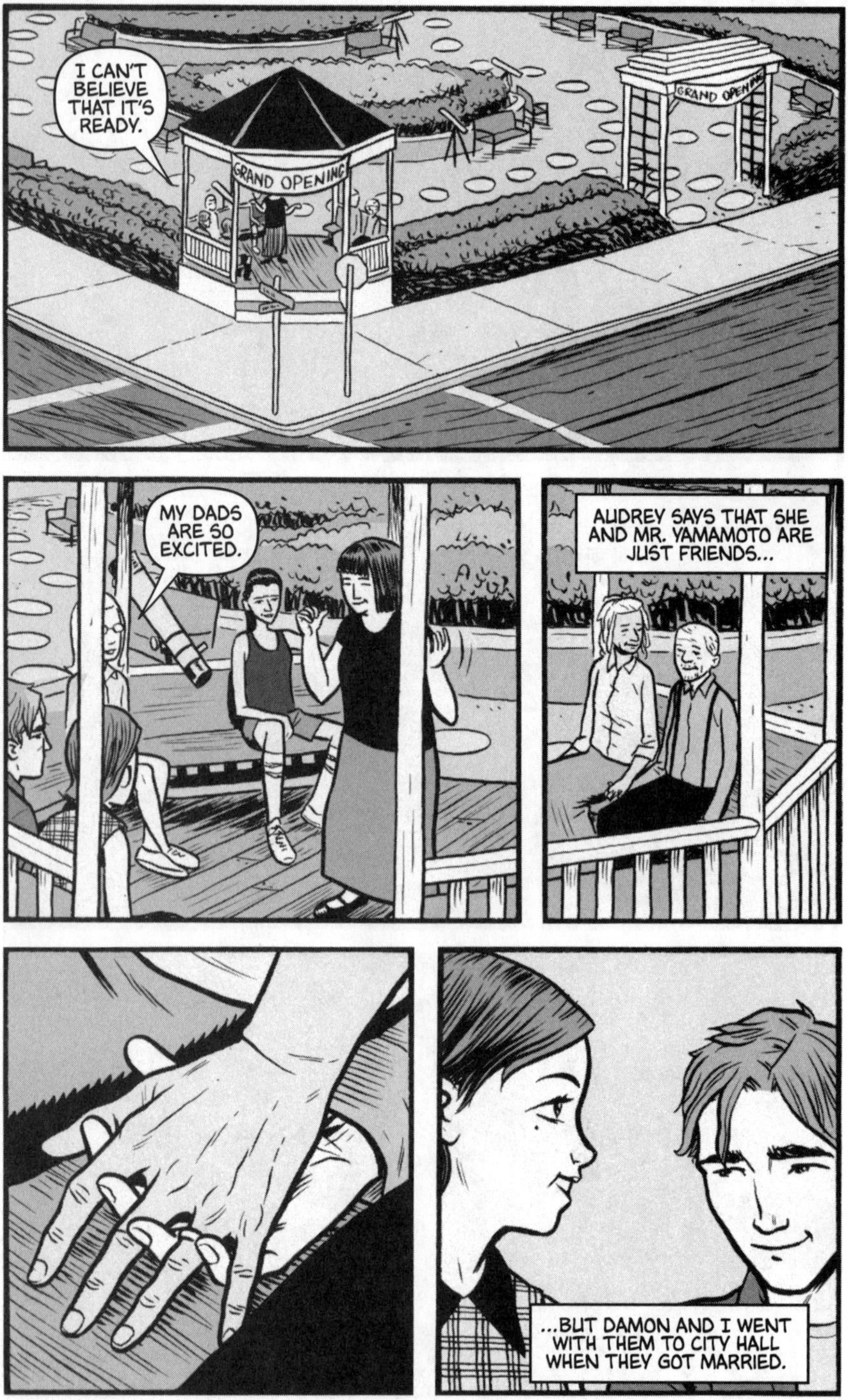
I CAN'T BELIEVE THAT IT'S READY.
GRAND OPENING
GRAND OPENING
MY DADS ARE SO EXCITED.
AUDREY SAYS THAT SHE AND MR. YAMAMOTO ARE JUST FRIENDS...
...BUT DAMON AND I WENT WITH THEM TO CITY HALL WHEN THEY GOT MARRIED.

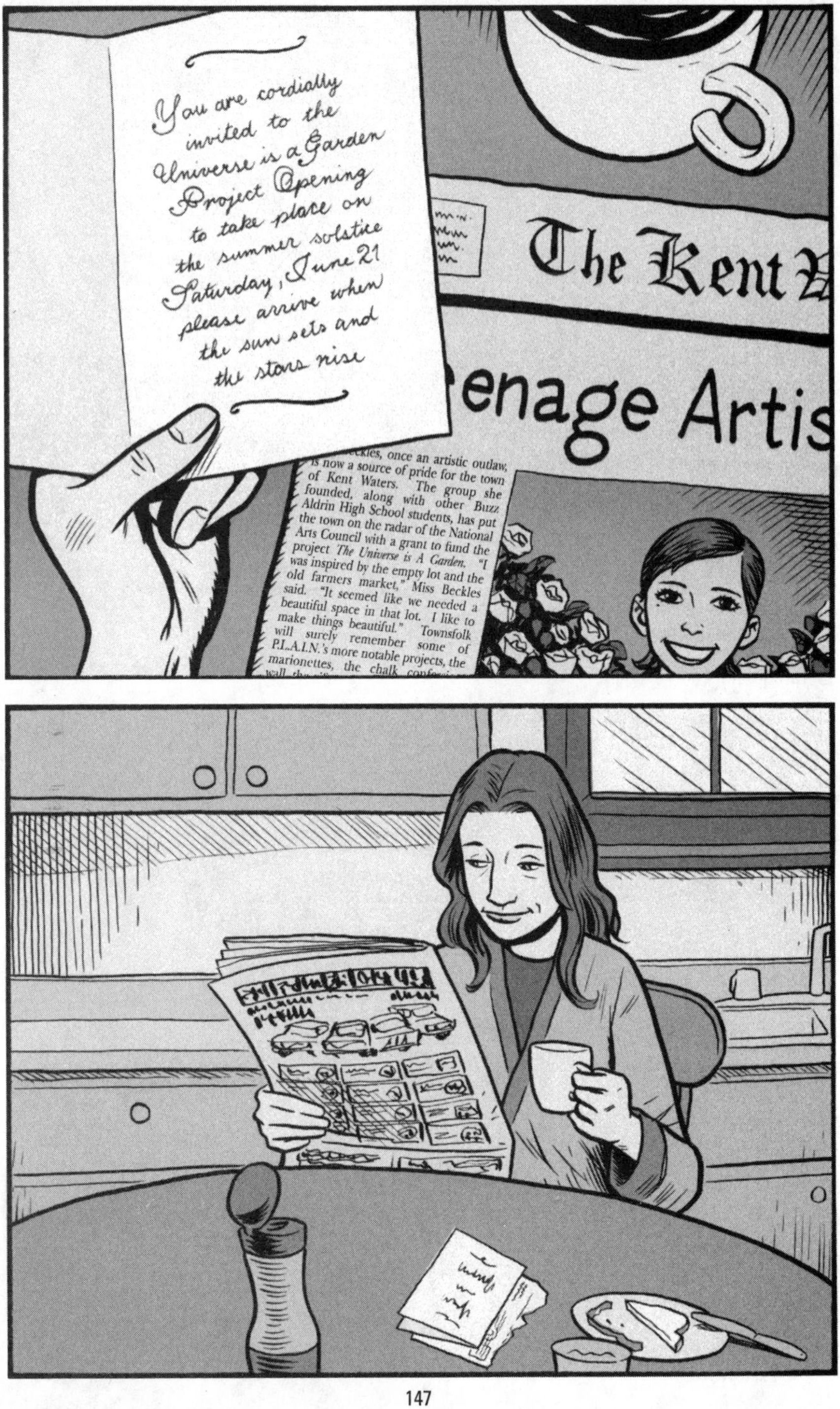

You are cordially invited to the Universe is a Garden Project Opening to take place on the summer solstice Saturday, June 21 please arrive when the sun sets and the stars rise
The Kent
once an artistic outlaw, is now a source of pride for the town of Kent Waters. The group she founded, along with other Buzz Aldrin High School students, has put the town on the radar of the National Arts Council with a grant to fund the project *The Universe is A Garden*. "I was inspired by the empty lot and the old farmers market," Miss Beckles said. "It seemed like we needed a beautiful space in that lot. I like to make things beautiful." Townsfolk will surely remember some of P.L.A.I.N.'s more notable projects, the marionettes, the chalk

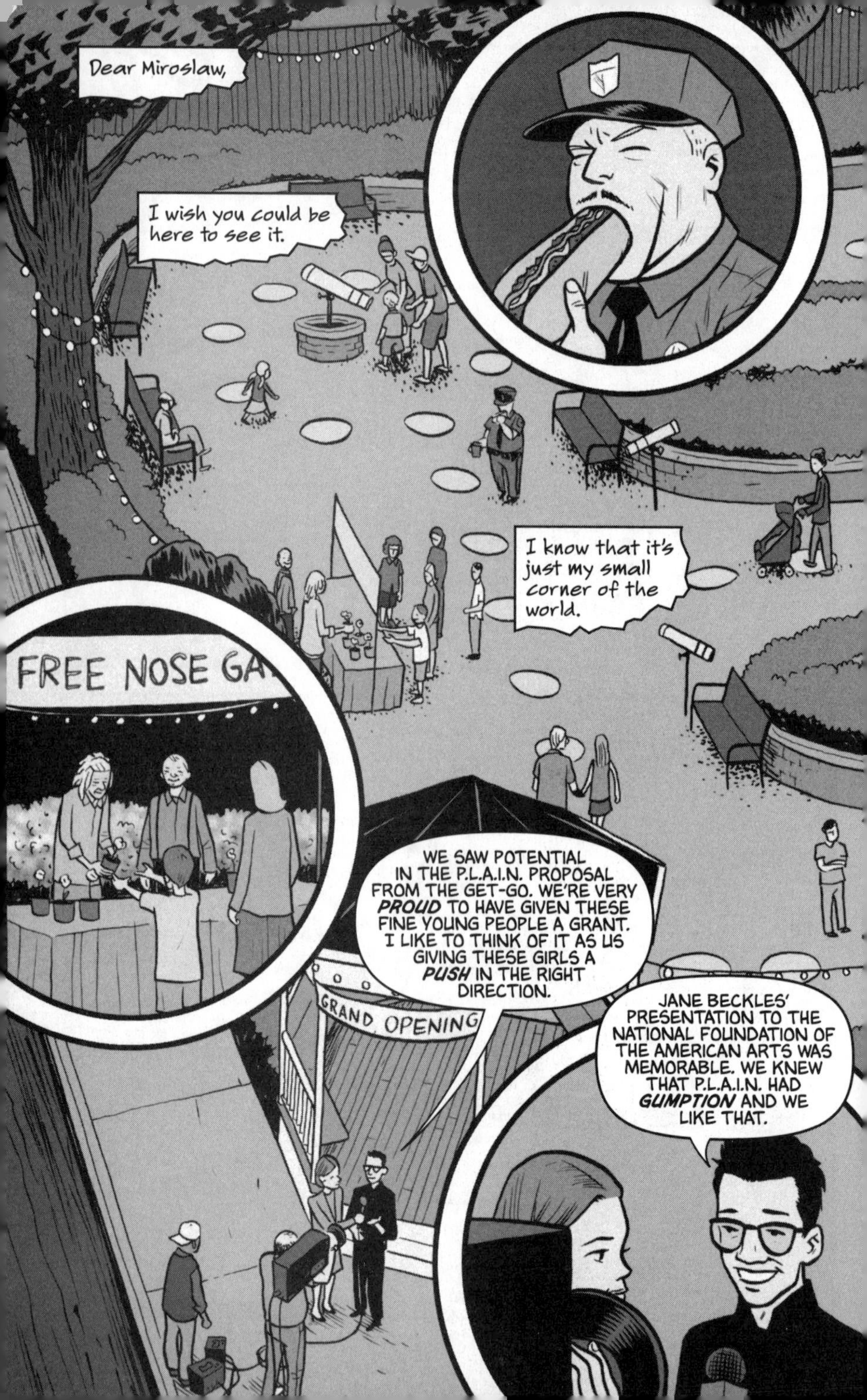
Dear Miroslaw,
I wish you could be here to see it.
I know that it's just my small corner of the world.
FREE NOSE GA
GRAND OPENING
WE SAW POTENTIAL IN THE P.L.A.I.N. PROPOSAL FROM THE GET-GO. WE'RE VERY PROUD TO HAVE GIVEN THESE FINE YOUNG PEOPLE A GRANT. I LIKE TO THINK OF IT AS US GIVING THESE GIRLS A PUSH IN THE RIGHT DIRECTION.
JANE BECKLES' PRESENTATION TO THE NATIONAL FOUNDATION OF THE AMERICAN ARTS WAS MEMORABLE. WE KNEW THAT P.L.A.I.N. HAD GUMPTION AND WE LIKE THAT.

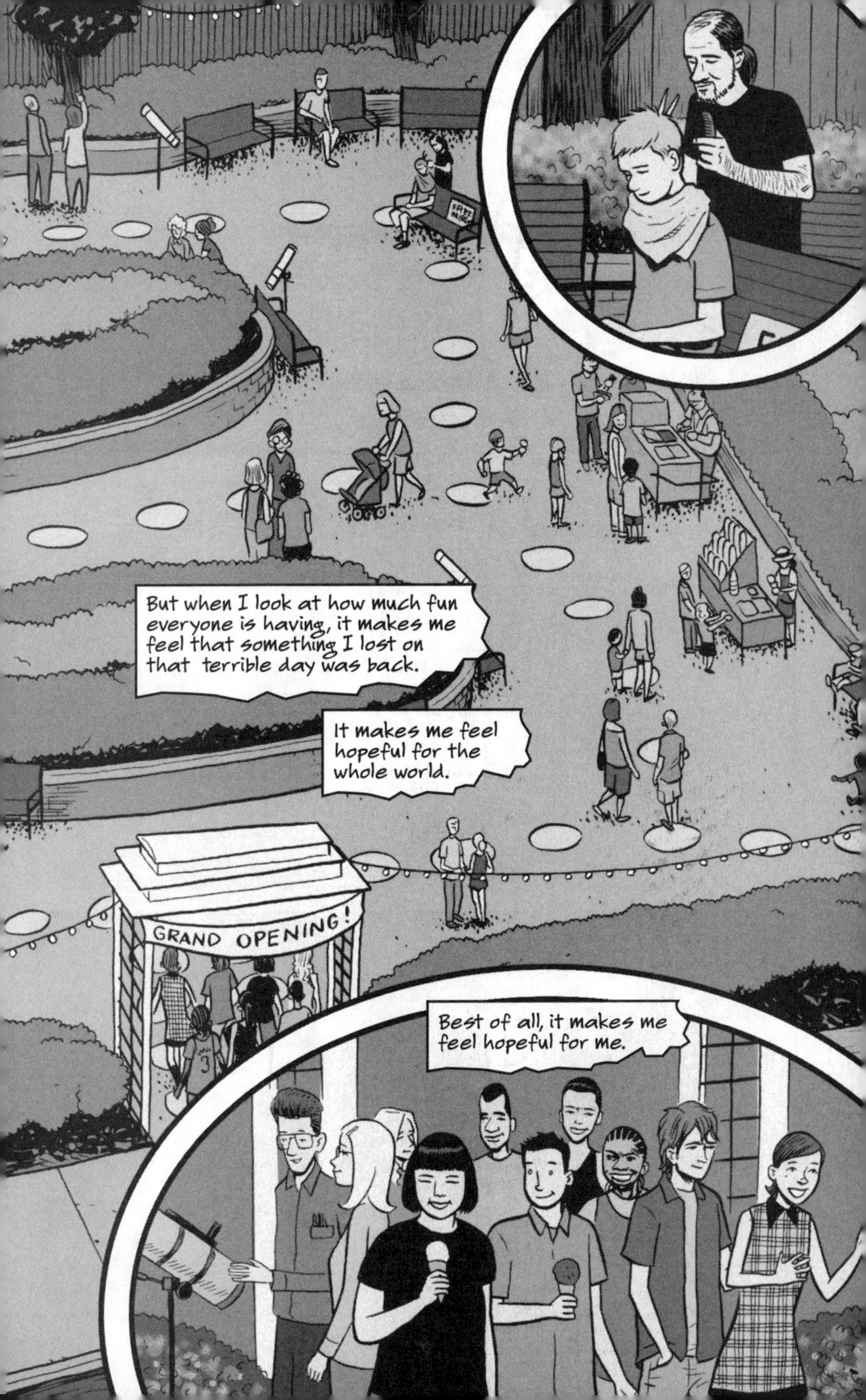
But when I look at how much fun everyone is having, it makes me feel that something I lost on that terrible day was back.
It makes me feel hopeful for the whole world.
GRAND OPENING!
Best of all, it makes me feel hopeful for me.

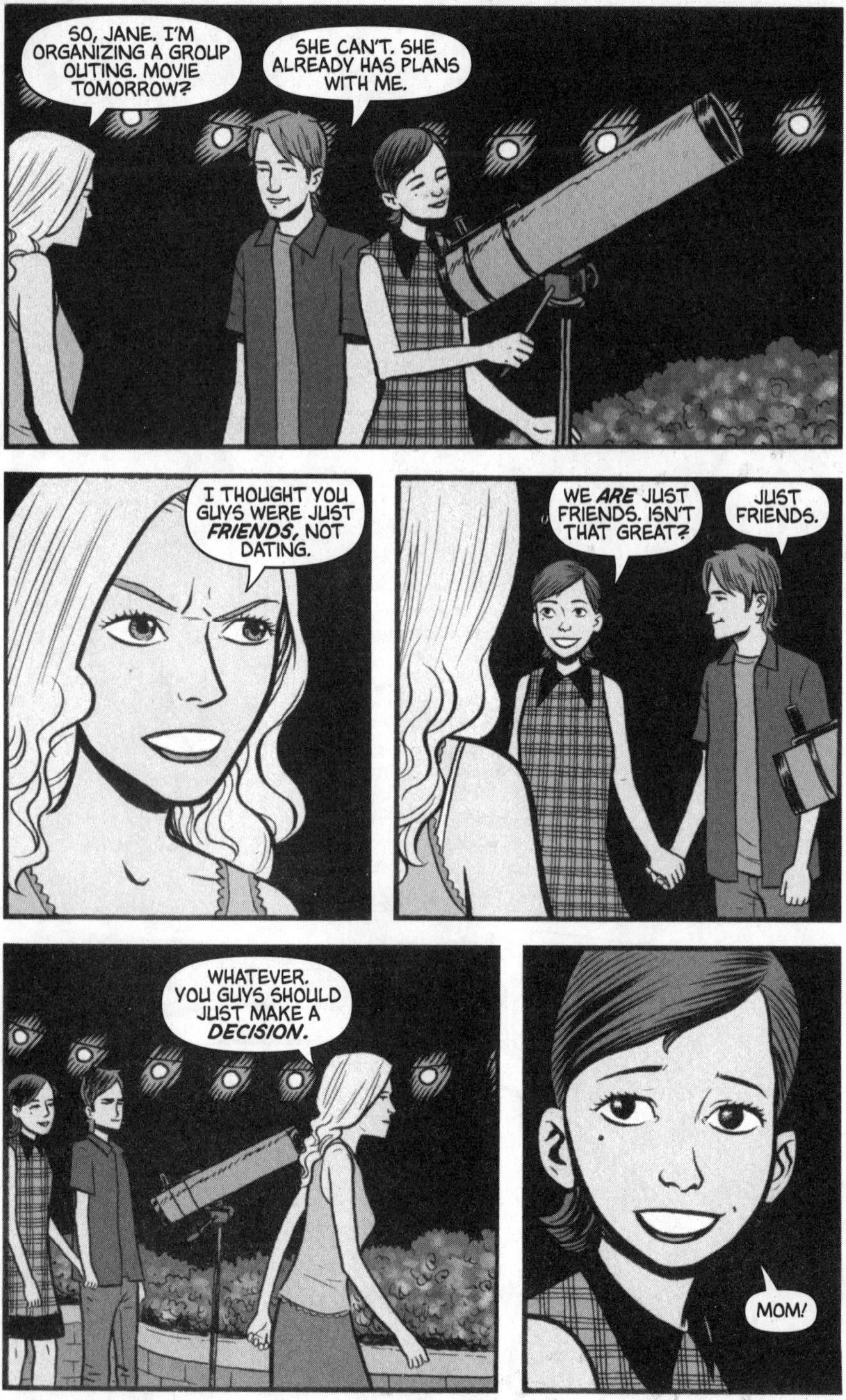
SO, JANE. I'M ORGANIZING A GROUP OUTING. MOVIE TOMORROW?
SHE CAN'T. SHE ALREADY HAS PLANS WITH ME.
I THOUGHT YOU GUYS WERE JUST FRIENDS, NOT DATING.
WE ARE JUST FRIENDS. ISN'T THAT GREAT?
JUST FRIENDS.
WHATEVER. YOU GUYS SHOULD JUST MAKE A DECISION.
MOM!

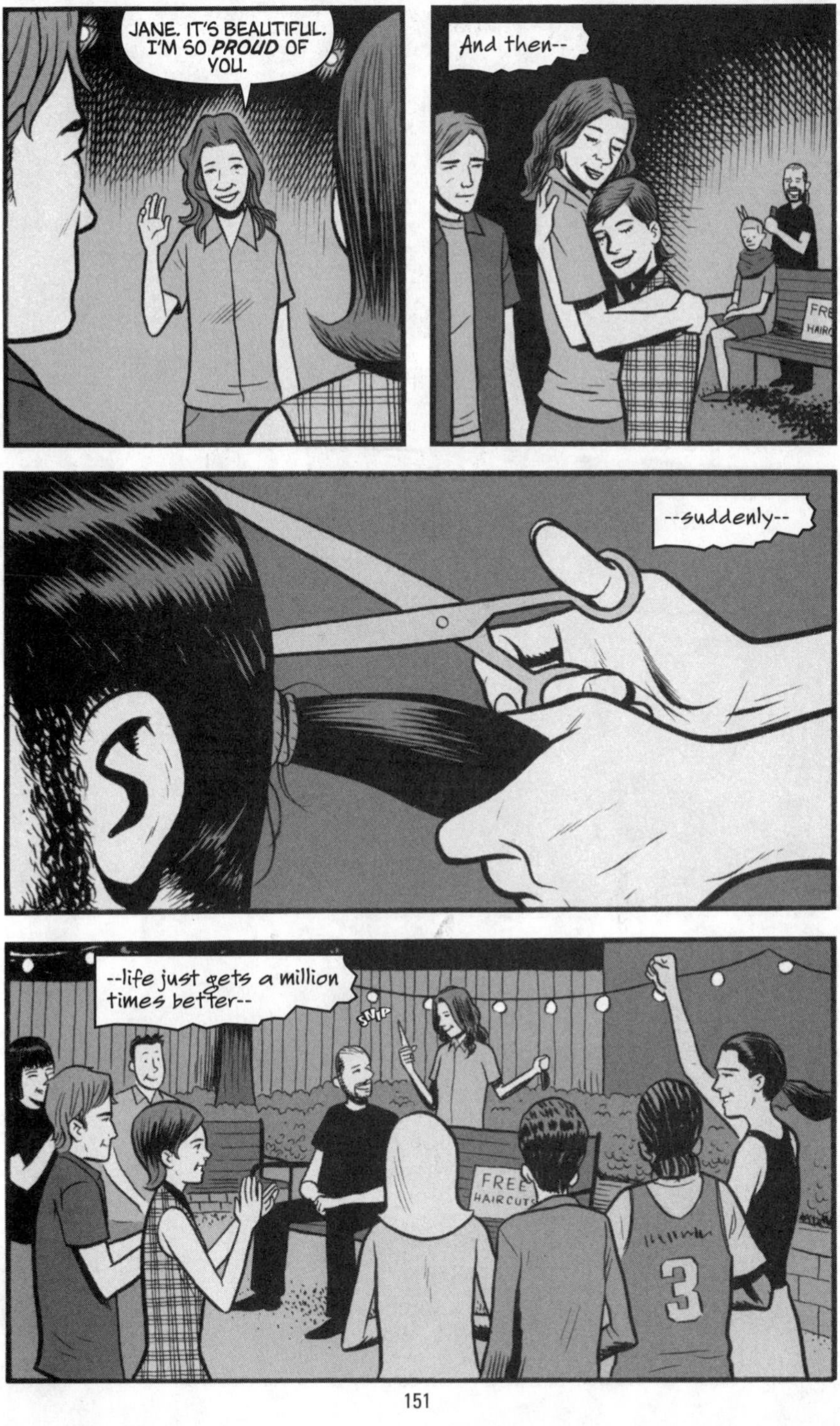
JANE. IT'S BEAUTIFUL. I'M SO *PROUD* OF YOU.
And then--
--suddenly--
--life just gets a million times better--
SNIP
FREE HAIRCUTS

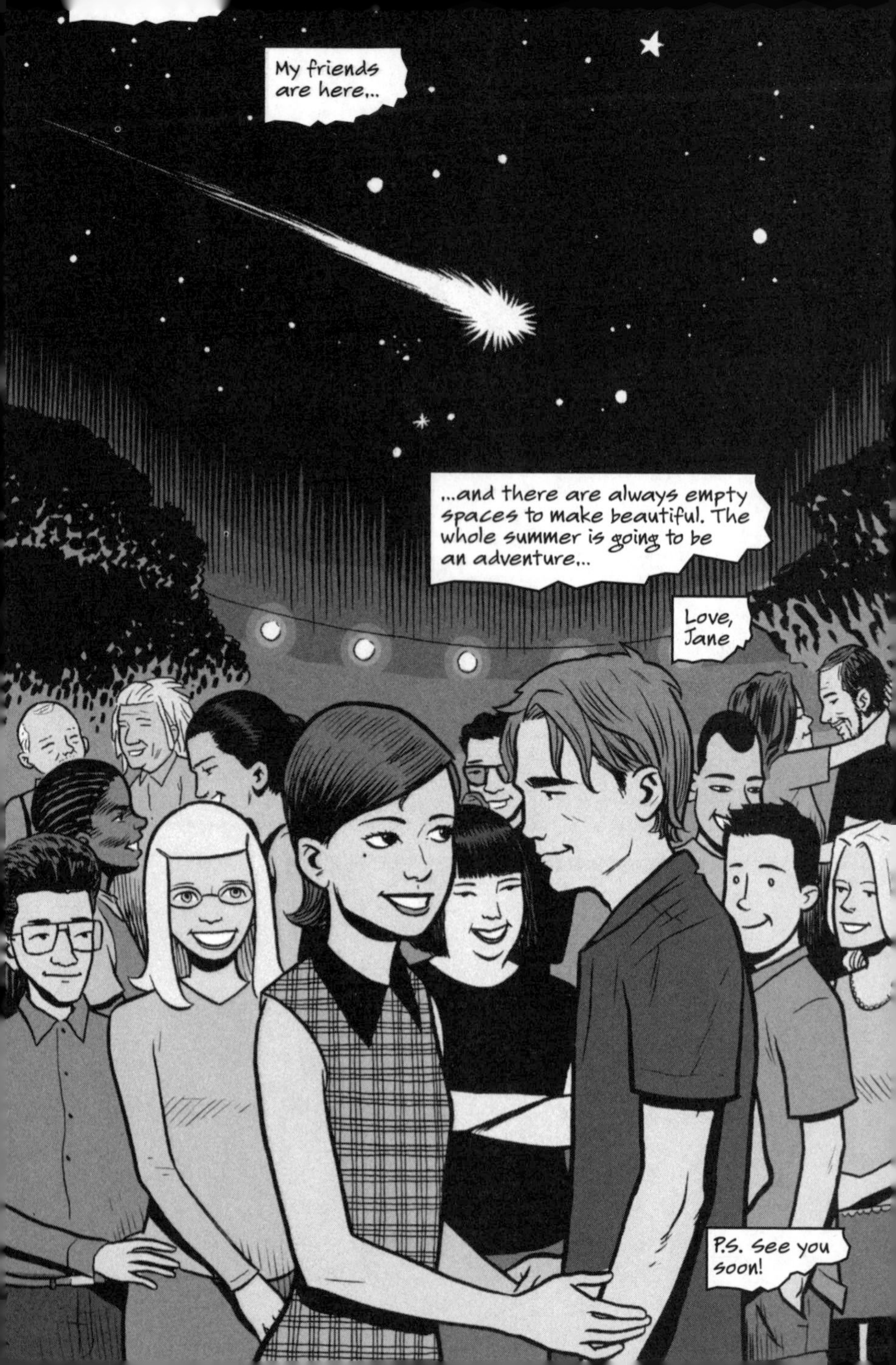
My friends are here...
...and there are always empty spaces to make beautiful. The whole summer is going to be an adventure...
Love, Jane
P.S. See you soon!

Photo by Andrew Takeuchi

CECIL CASTELLUCCI

Cecil grew up in New York City. She's the author of three young adult novels, *Boy Proof*, *The Queen of Cool* and *Beige*. Her books have received starred reviews and been on the American Library Association's Best Books for Young Adults (BBYA), Quick Pick for Reluctant Readers, Great Graphic Novels for Teens and the Amelia Bloomer lists. In 2008, she won the Joe Shuster Award for Outstanding Canadian Comic Book Writer. Cecil is also a playwright, a filmmaker and an erstwhile indie rock musician. She looks for street art whenever she's on a walk. Currently her favorite street artist is Banksy. She splits her time between Los Angeles and the East Coast.

JIM RUGG

Jim grew up and continues to
reside near Pittsburgh with
his wife and three cats.
He's the co-creator of
Street Angel and *Afrodisiac*.
His work has appeared in
Project: Superior, *Project:
Romantic*, *SPX2005*, *Orchid*,
Meathaus, *VH1*, and the
Society of Illustrators
Annual.

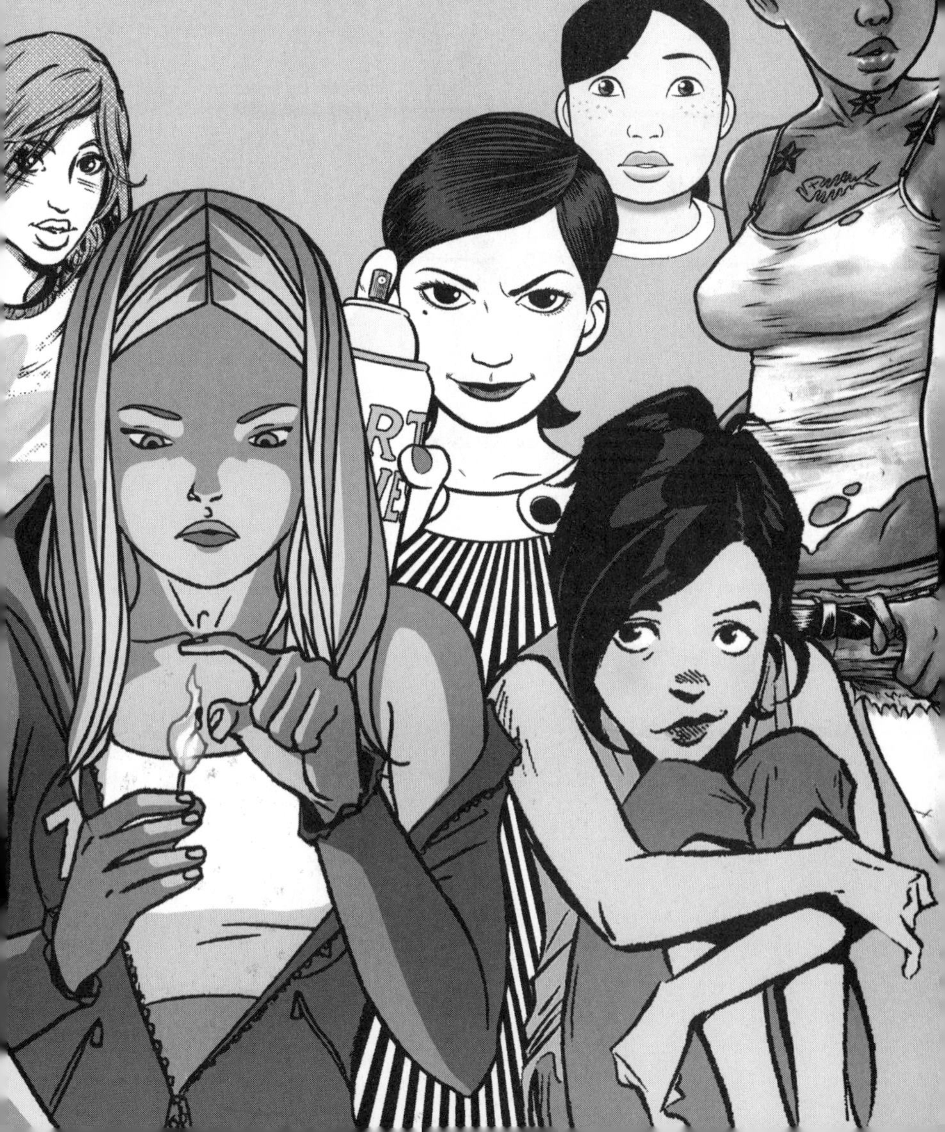
RT

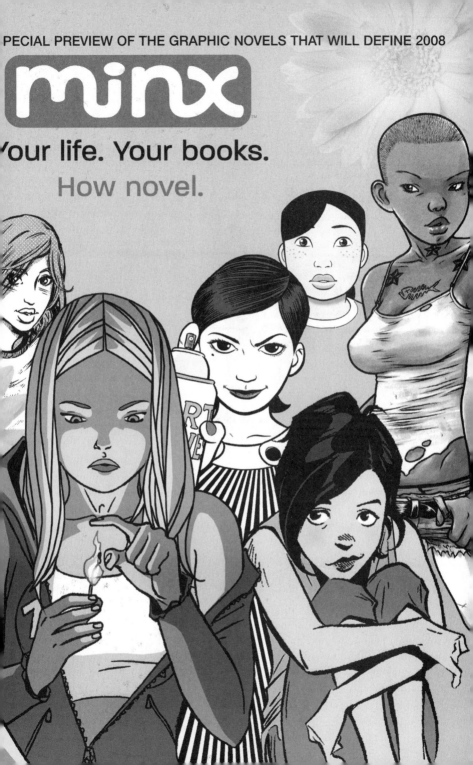

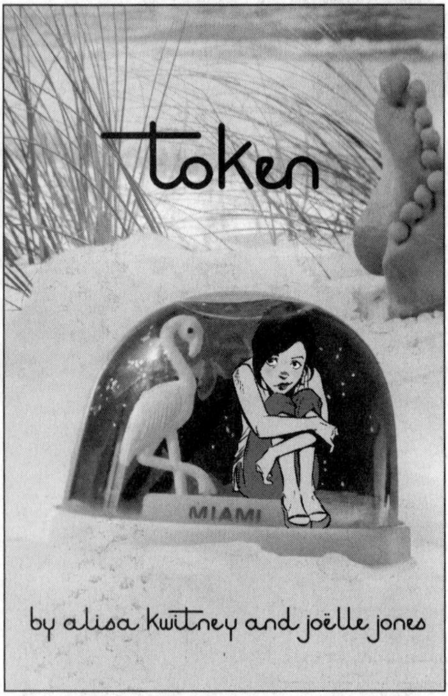
token
MIAMI
by alisa kwitney and joëlle jones

Written by noted comics writer and novelist ALISA KWITNEY

Can a Jewish "girl out of time" and a Spanish old soul survive culture clashes and criminal records to find true love in the sun-drenched, sequined miasma that was South Beach in the Big '80s?

By ALISA KWITNEY & JOËLLE JONES

AVAILABLE IN OCTOBER ■ Read on.

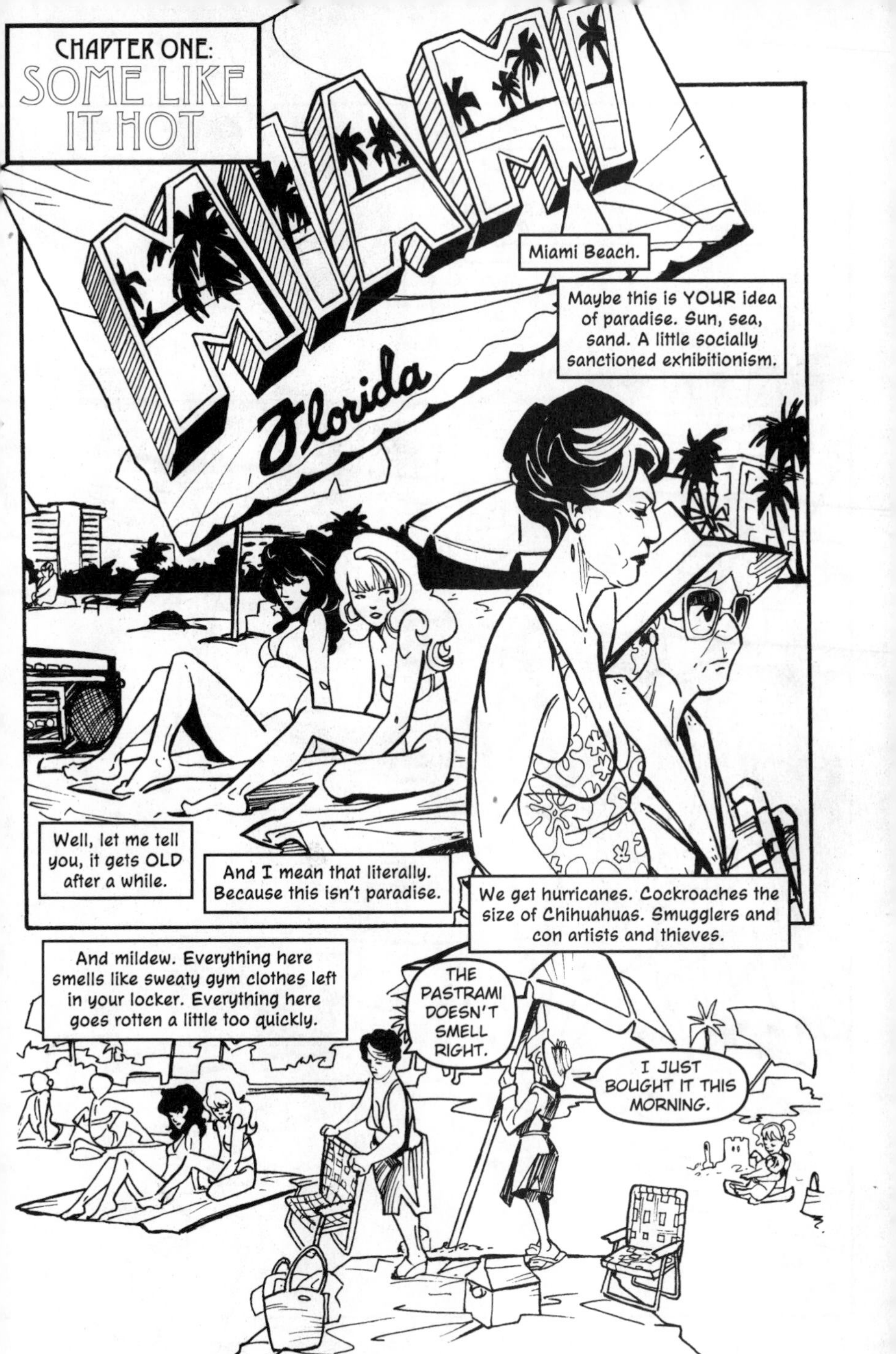
CHAPTER ONE:
SOME LIKE IT HOT
MIAMI
Florida
Miami Beach.
Maybe this is YOUR idea of paradise. Sun, sea, sand. A little socially sanctioned exhibitionism.
Well, let me tell you, it gets OLD after a while.
And I mean that literally. Because this isn't paradise.
We get hurricanes. Cockroaches the size of Chihuahuas. Smugglers and con artists and thieves.
And mildew. Everything here smells like sweaty gym clothes left in your locker. Everything here goes rotten a little too quickly.
THE PASTRAMI DOESN'T SMELL RIGHT.
I JUST BOUGHT IT THIS MORNING.

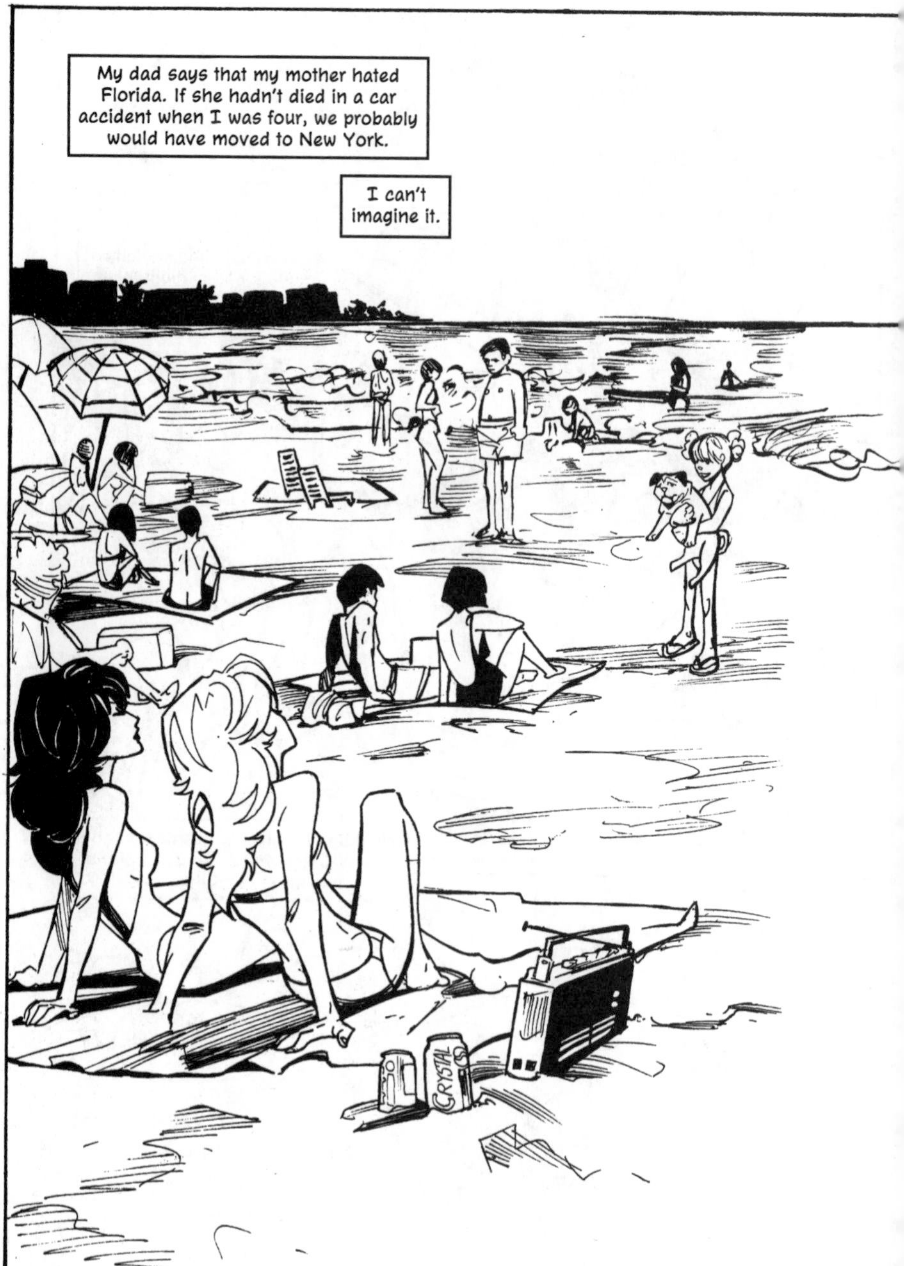
My dad says that my mother hated Florida. If she hadn't died in a car accident when I was four, we probably would have moved to New York.
I can't imagine it.
CRYSTAL

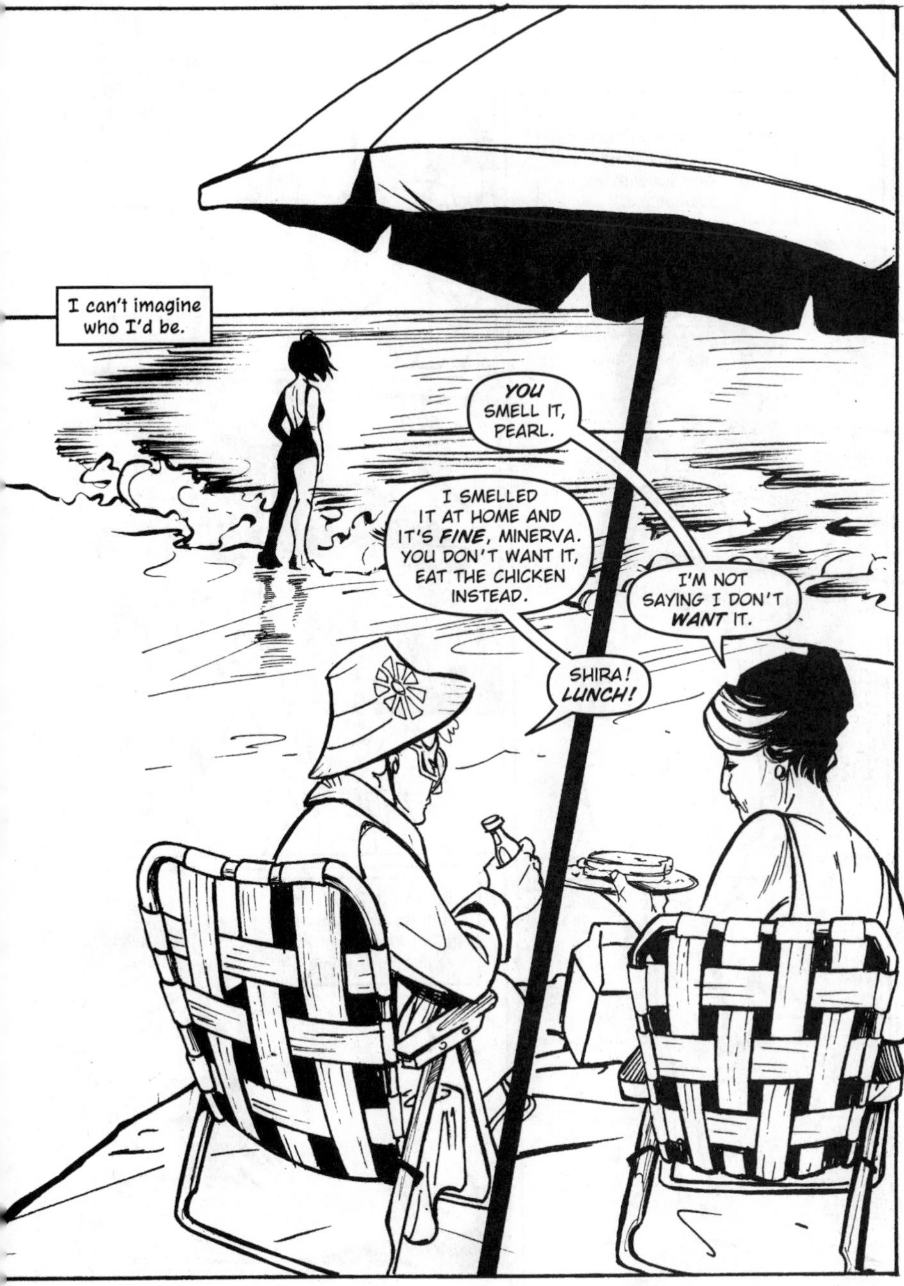
I can't imagine who I'd be.
YOU SMELL IT, PEARL.
I SMELLED IT AT HOME AND IT'S FINE, MINERVA. YOU DON'T WANT IT, EAT THE CHICKEN INSTEAD.
I'M NOT SAYING I DON'T WANT IT.
SHIRA! LUNCH!

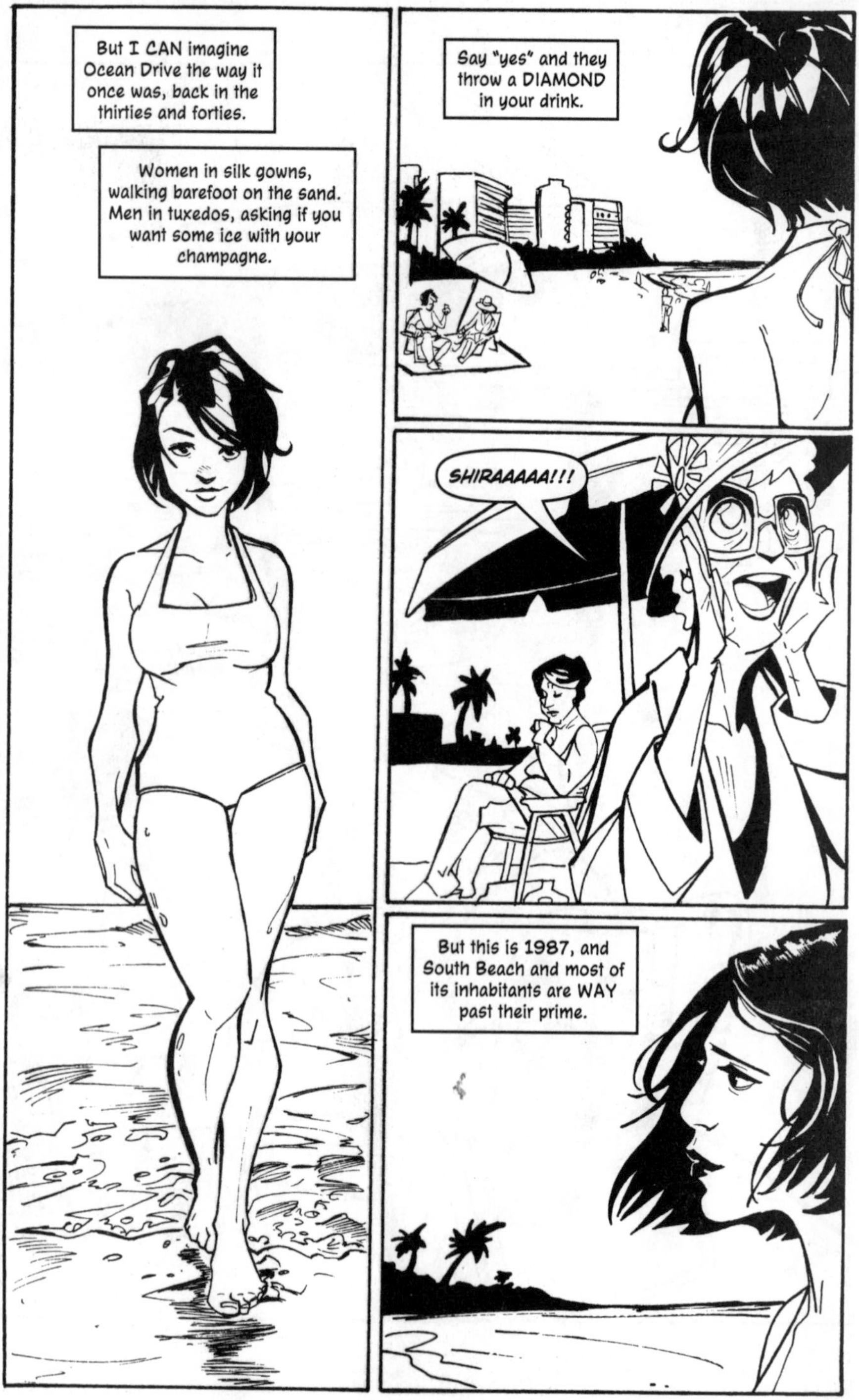
But I CAN imagine Ocean Drive the way it once was, back in the thirties and forties.
Women in silk gowns, walking barefoot on the sand. Men in tuxedos, asking if you want some ice with your champagne.
Say "yes" and they throw a DIAMOND in your drink.
SHIRAAAAA!!!
But this is 1987, and South Beach and most of its inhabitants are WAY past their prime.

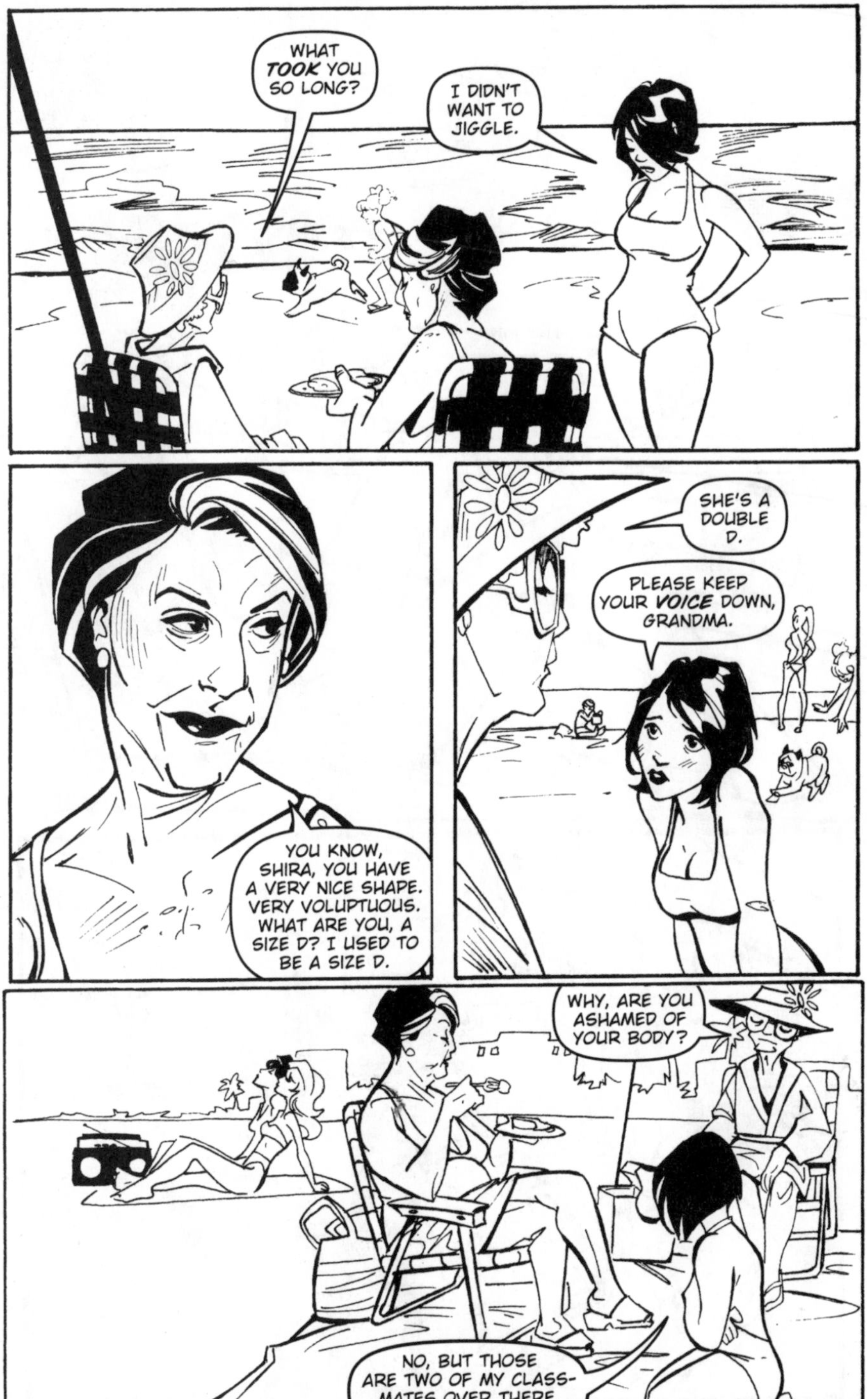
WHAT TOOK YOU SO LONG?
I DIDN'T WANT TO JIGGLE.
YOU KNOW, SHIRA, YOU HAVE A VERY NICE SHAPE. VERY VOLUPTUOUS. WHAT ARE YOU, A SIZE D? I USED TO BE A SIZE D.
SHE'S A DOUBLE D.
PLEASE KEEP YOUR VOICE DOWN, GRANDMA.
WHY, ARE YOU ASHAMED OF YOUR BODY?
NO, BUT THOSE ARE TWO OF MY CLASS-MATES OVER THERE.

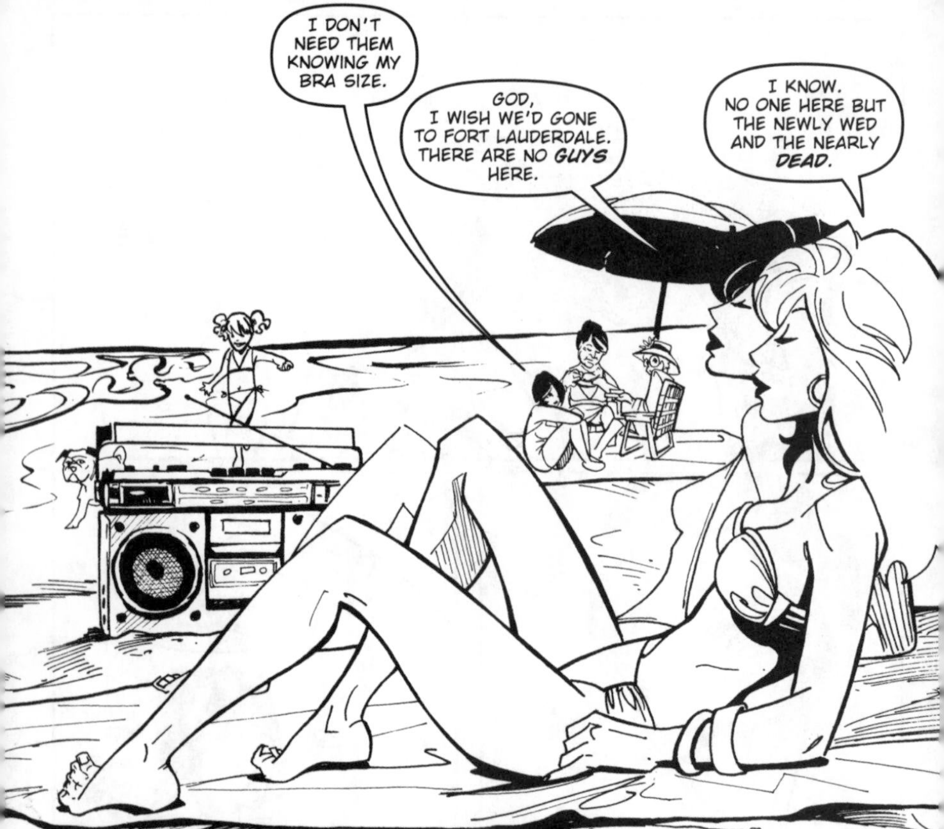
I DON'T NEED THEM KNOWING MY BRA SIZE.
GOD, I WISH WE'D GONE TO FORT LAUDERDALE. THERE ARE NO GUYS HERE.
I KNOW. NO ONE HERE BUT THE NEWLY WED AND THE NEARLY DEAD.

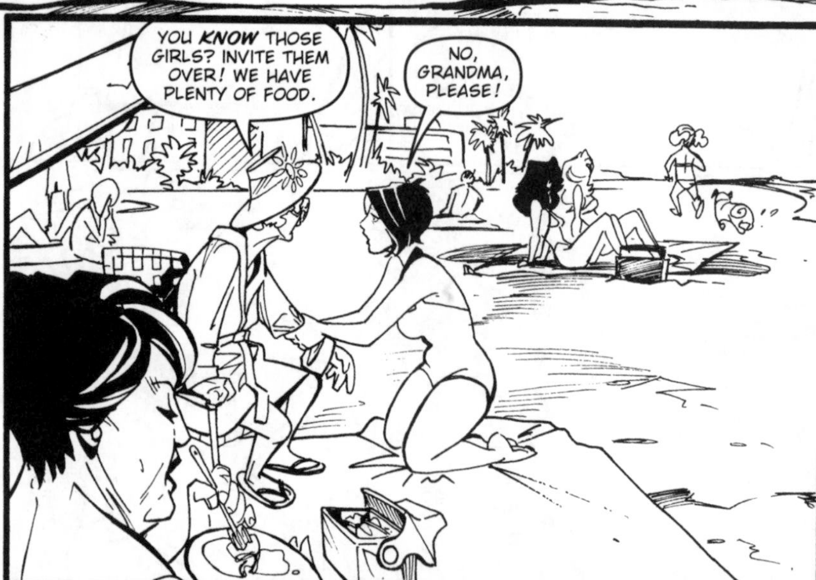
YOU KNOW THOSE GIRLS? INVITE THEM OVER! WE HAVE PLENTY OF FOOD.
NO, GRANDMA, PLEASE!

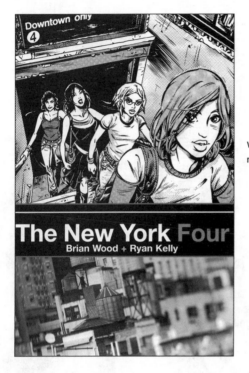

The New York Four
Brian Wood + Ryan Kelly

Written by multiple Eisner Award nominee/indie icon BRIAN WOOD

Experience New York City through the eyes of Riley, a shy, almost reclusive straight-A student who convinces three other NYU freshmen to join a research group to earn extra money.

As the girls become fast friends, two things complicate what should be the greatest time of Riley's life: connecting with her arty, estranged older sister and having a mysterious online crush on a guy known only as "sneakerfreak."

By BRIAN WOOD & RYAN KELLY

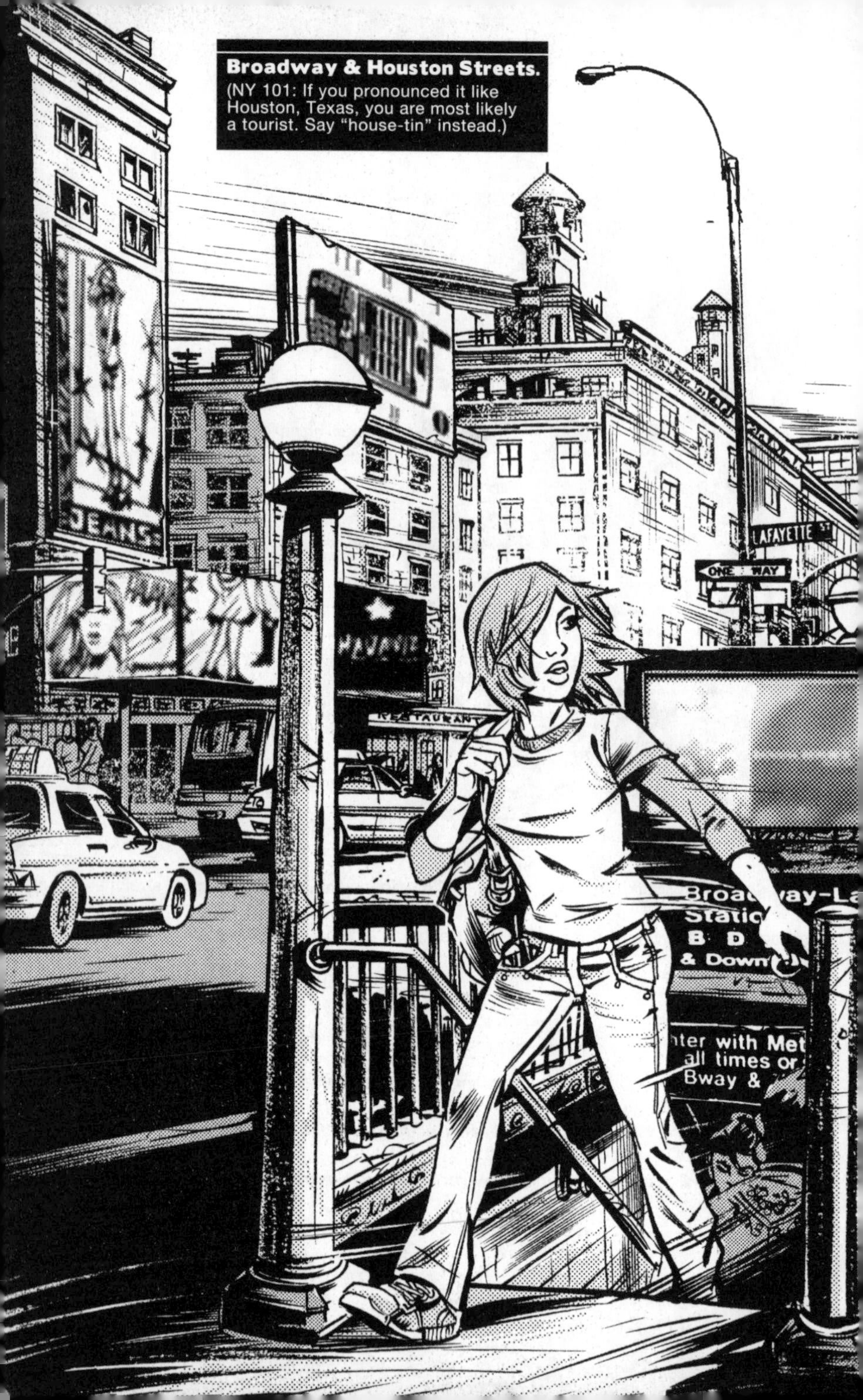

Broadway & Houston Streets.
(NY 101: If you pronounced it like Houston, Texas, you are most likely a tourist. Say "house-tin" instead.)
JEANS
LAFAYETTE ST
ONE WAY
RESTAURANT
Broadway-La
Statio
B D
& Down
nter with Met
all times or
Bway &

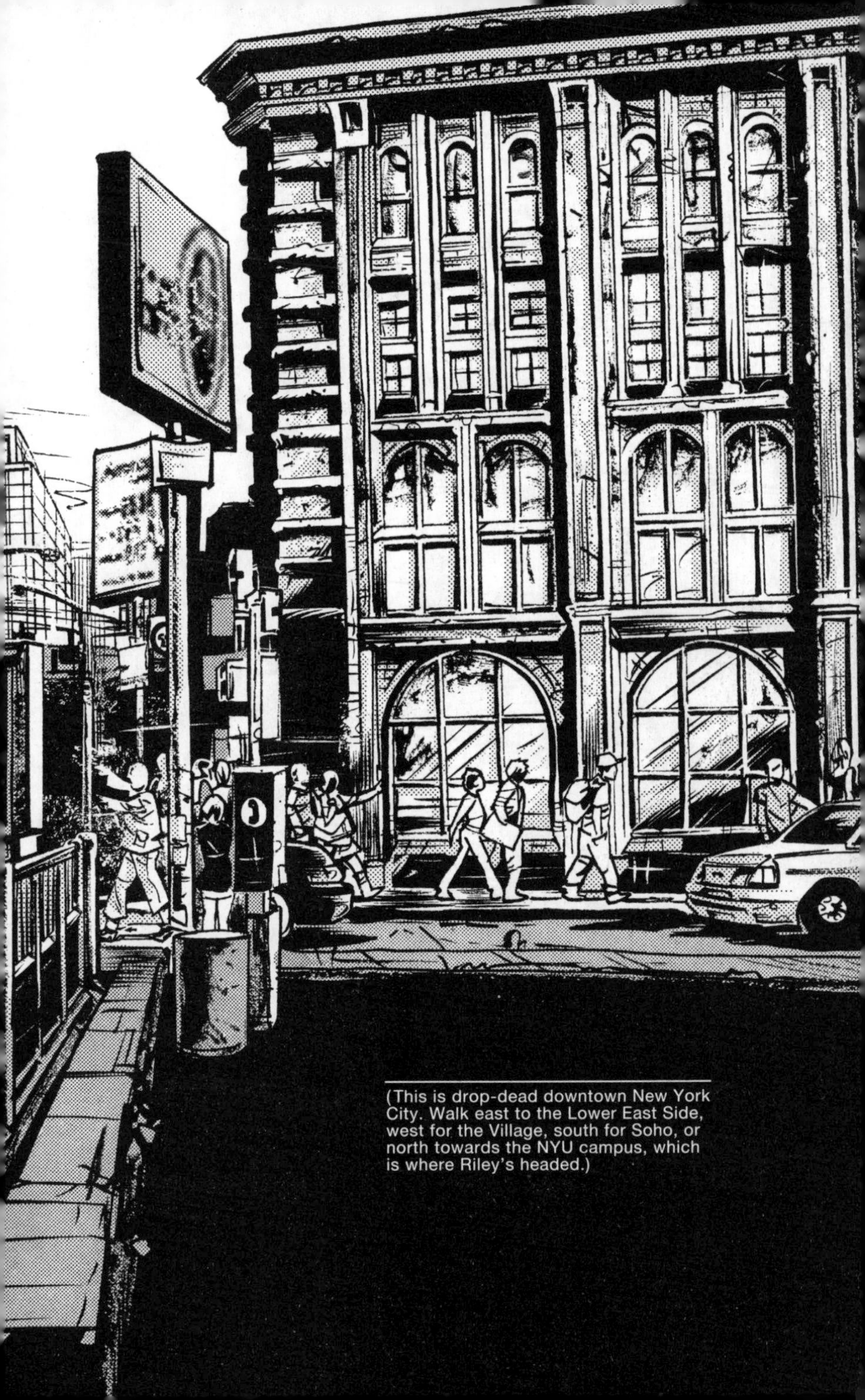
(This is drop-dead downtown New York City. Walk east to the Lower East Side, west for the Village, south for Soho, or north towards the NYU campus, which is where Riley's headed.)

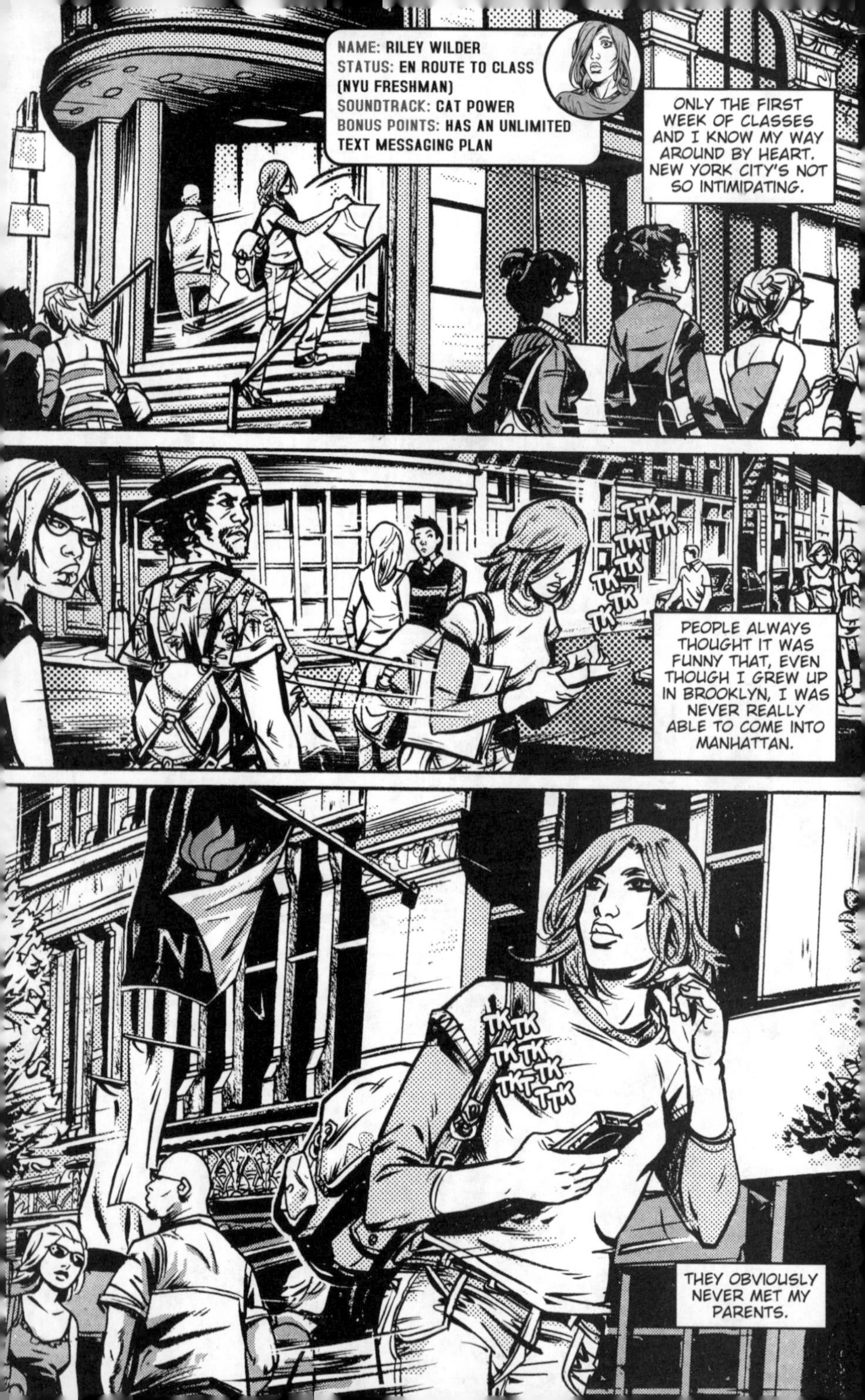
NAME: RILEY WILDER
STATUS: EN ROUTE TO CLASS (NYU FRESHMAN)
SOUNDTRACK: CAT POWER
BONUS POINTS: HAS AN UNLIMITED TEXT MESSAGING PLAN
ONLY THE FIRST WEEK OF CLASSES AND I KNOW MY WAY AROUND BY HEART. NEW YORK CITY'S NOT SO INTIMIDATING.
TK TK TK TK TK TK TK TK TK
PEOPLE ALWAYS THOUGHT IT WAS FUNNY THAT, EVEN THOUGH I GREW UP IN BROOKLYN, I WAS NEVER REALLY ABLE TO COME INTO MANHATTAN.
TK TK TK TK TK TK TK TK
THEY OBVIOUSLY NEVER MET MY PARENTS.

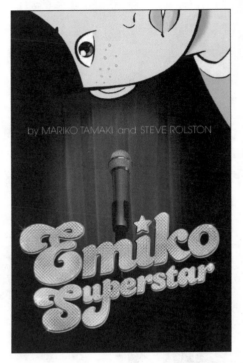

by MARIKO TAMAKI and STEVE ROLSTON

Emiko Superstar

Written by novelist/performance artist
MARIKO TAMAKI

A "borrowed" diary, a double life and identity issues fuel a teenager's quest to find

herself before she cracks and commits social suicide. Watch Emi go from dull

suburban babysitter to eclectic urban performance artist — compliments of one

crazy summer.

By MARIKO TAMAKI & STEVE ROLSTON
AVAILABLE IN SEPTEMBER ■ Read on.

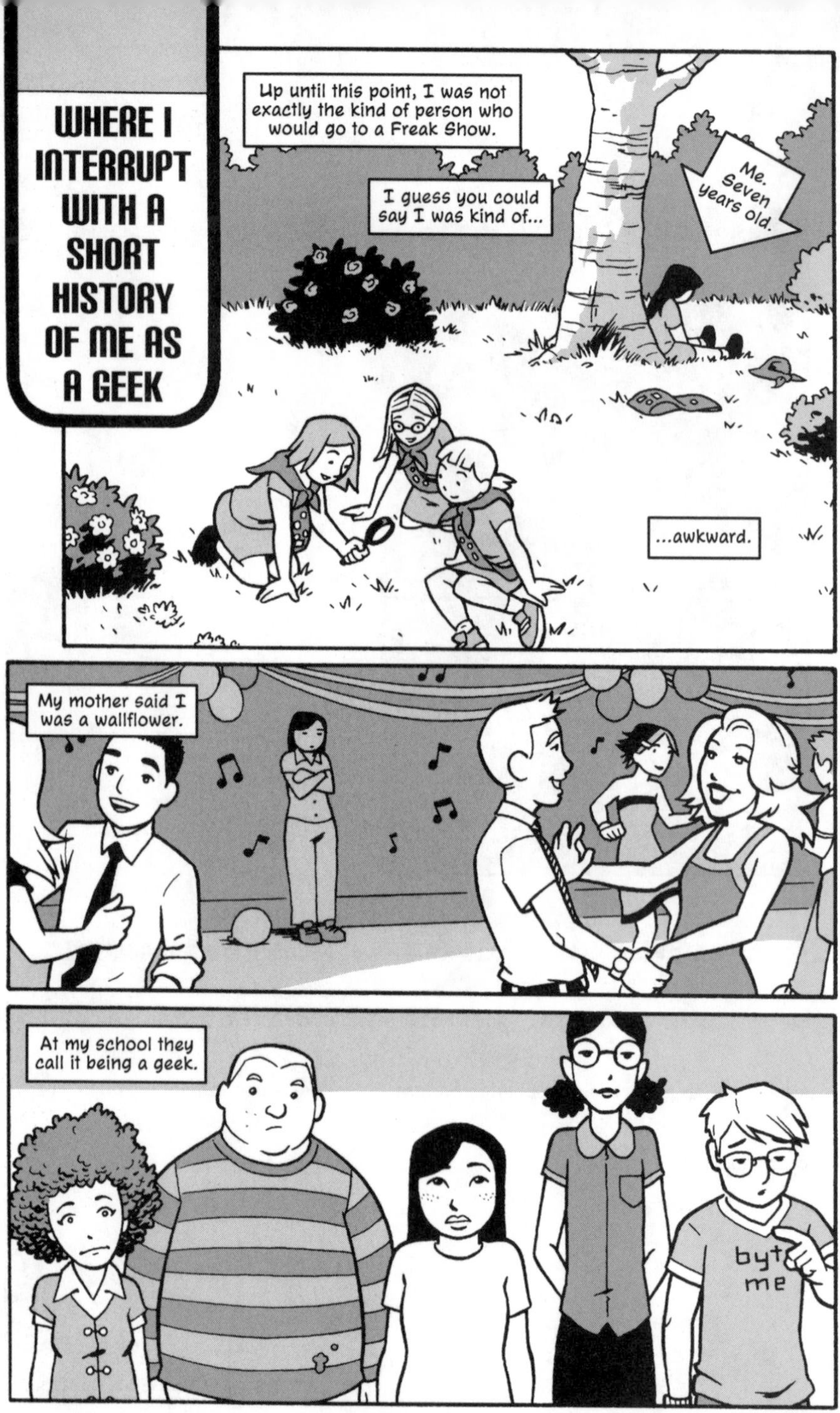
WHERE I INTERRUPT WITH A SHORT HISTORY OF ME AS A GEEK
Up until this point, I was not exactly the kind of person who would go to a Freak Show.
I guess you could say I was kind of...
Me. Seven years old.
...awkward.
My mother said I was a wallflower.
At my school they call it being a geek.
byt me

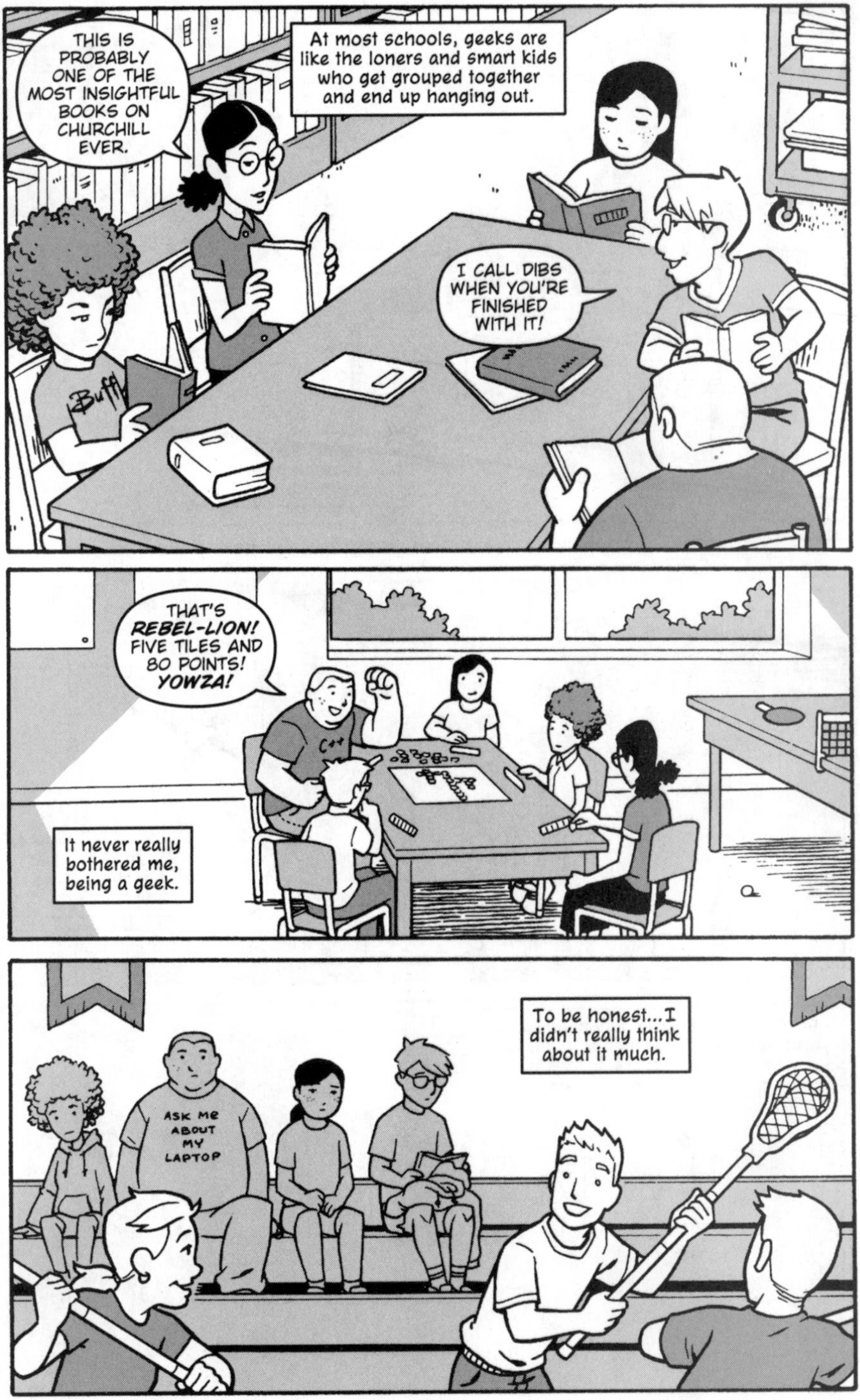
THIS IS PROBABLY ONE OF THE MOST INSIGHTFUL BOOKS ON CHURCHILL EVER.
At most schools, geeks are like the loners and smart kids who get grouped together and end up hanging out.
I CALL DIBS WHEN YOU'RE FINISHED WITH IT!
THAT'S **REBEL-LION!** FIVE TILES AND 80 POINTS! ***YOWZA!***
It never really bothered me, being a geek.
To be honest...I didn't really think about it much.
ASK ME ABOUT MY LAPTOP

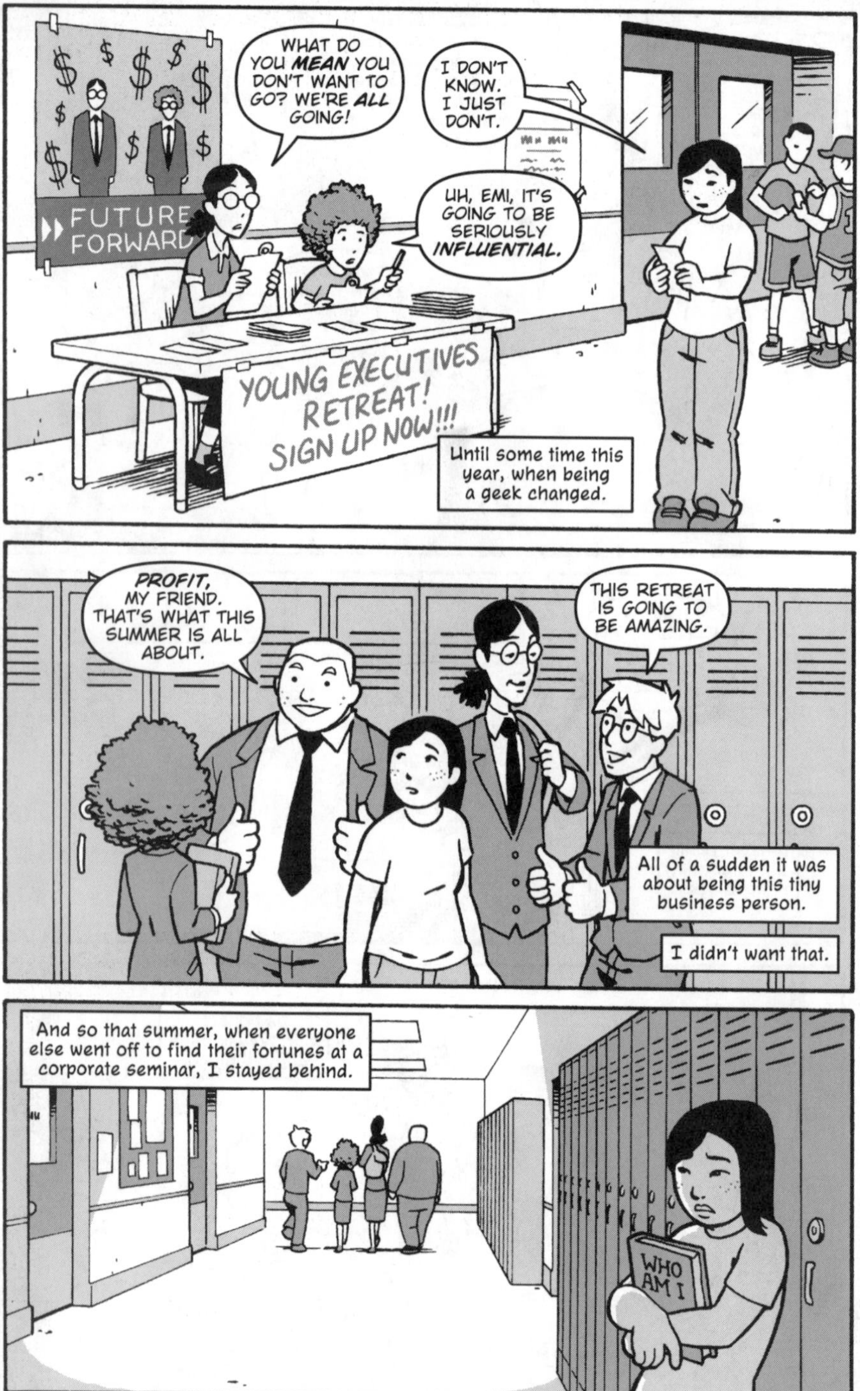

FUTURE FORWARD
WHAT DO YOU MEAN YOU DON'T WANT TO GO? WE'RE ALL GOING!
I DON'T KNOW. I JUST DON'T.
UH, EMI, IT'S GOING TO BE SERIOUSLY INFLUENTIAL.
YOUNG EXECUTIVES RETREAT! SIGN UP NOW!!!
Until some time this year, when being a geek changed.
PROFIT, MY FRIEND. THAT'S WHAT THIS SUMMER IS ALL ABOUT.
THIS RETREAT IS GOING TO BE AMAZING.
All of a sudden it was about being this tiny business person.
I didn't want that.
And so that summer, when everyone else went off to find their fortunes at a corporate seminar, I stayed behind.
WHO AM I

I was at what this book I found described as a "classic crossroads."

Where one thing gets left behind...

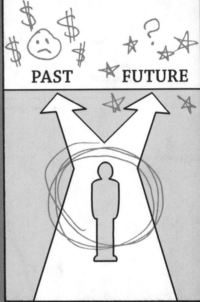

PAST   FUTURE

...and something else gets spotted in the distance.

Your life in pictures starts here!
~A DO-IT YOURSELF MINI COMIC~

Write your story ideas here:

Draw your main character sketches here:

Use the following 3 pages to bring it all together.

TITLE: BY:

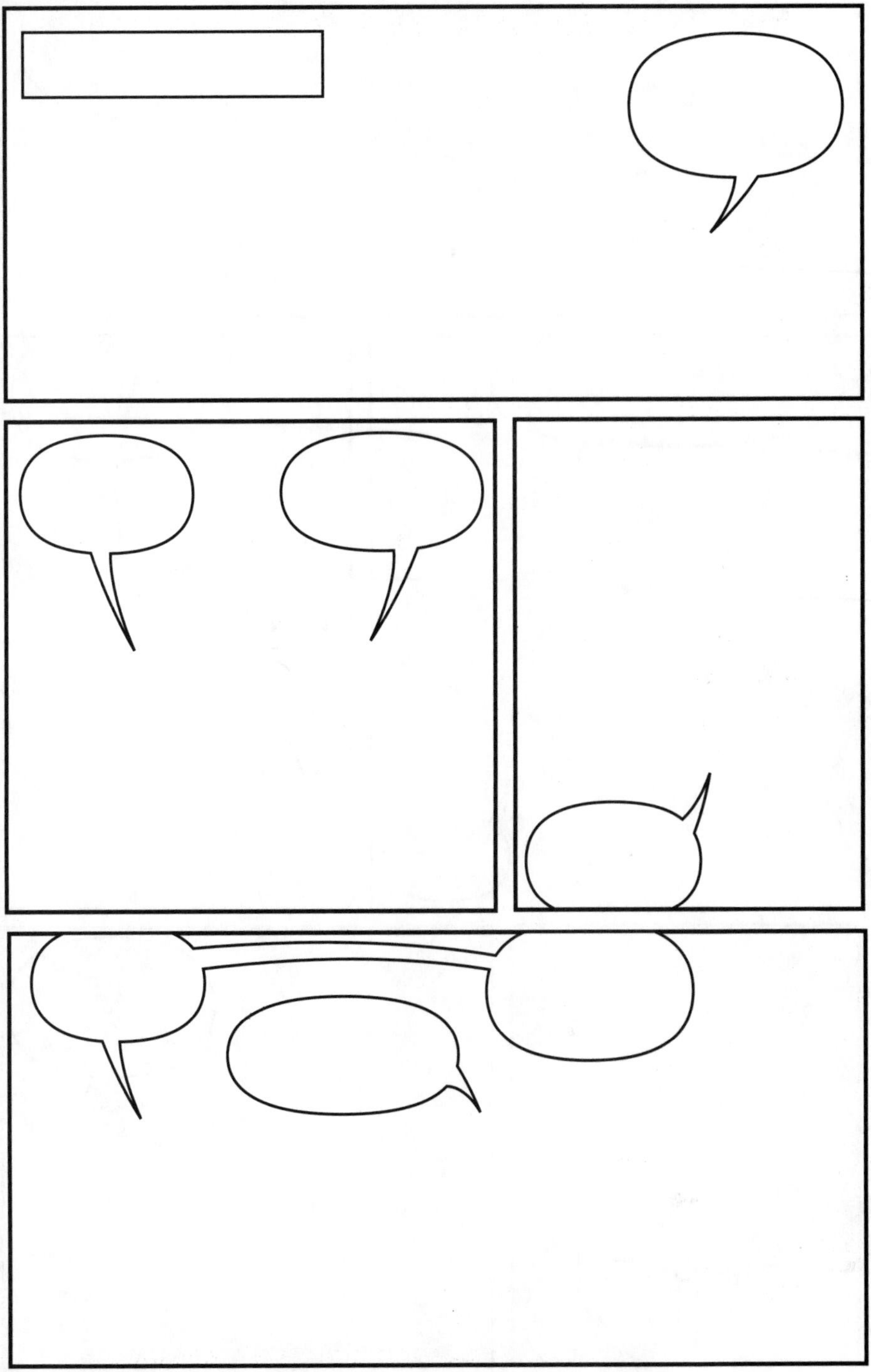

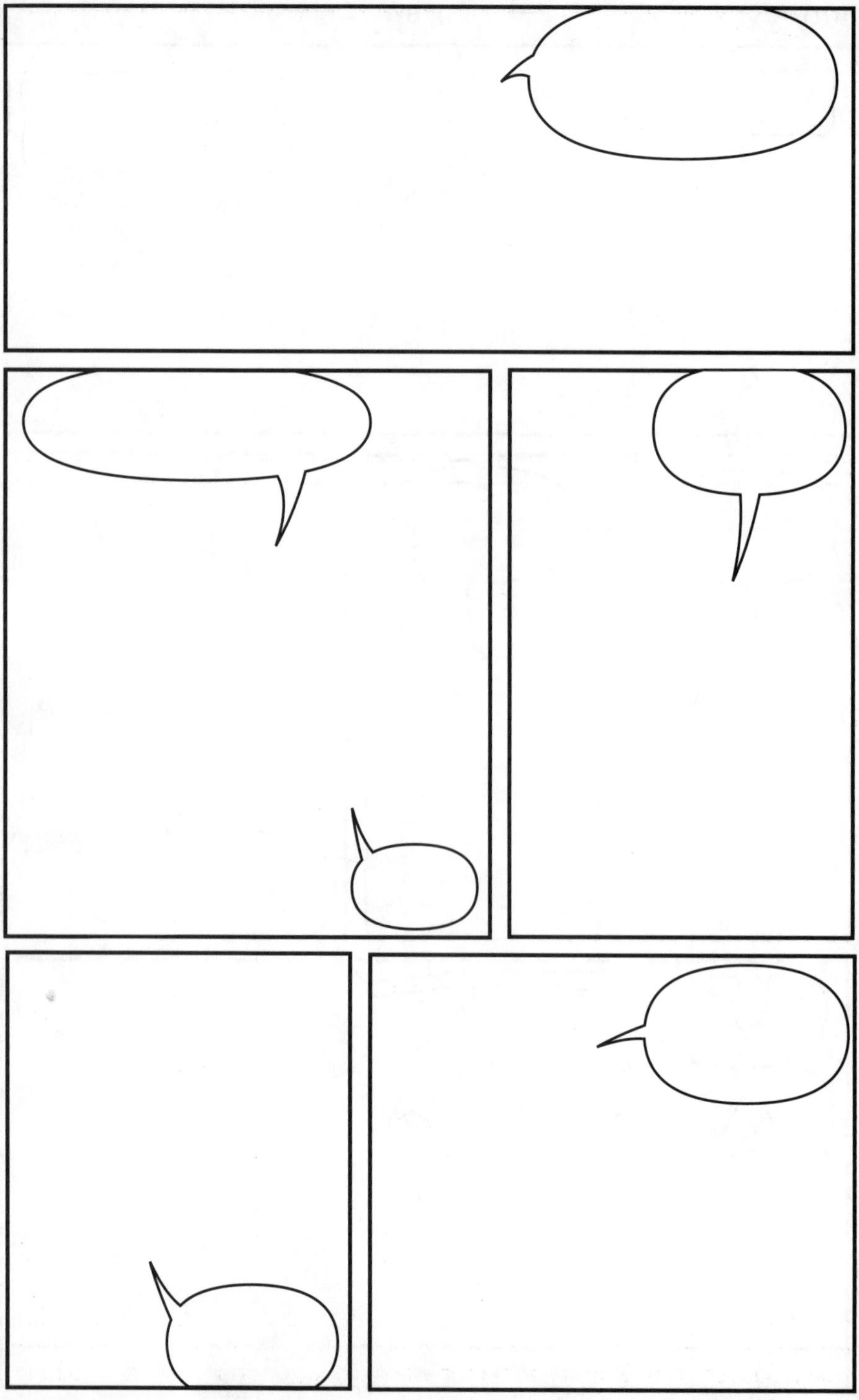

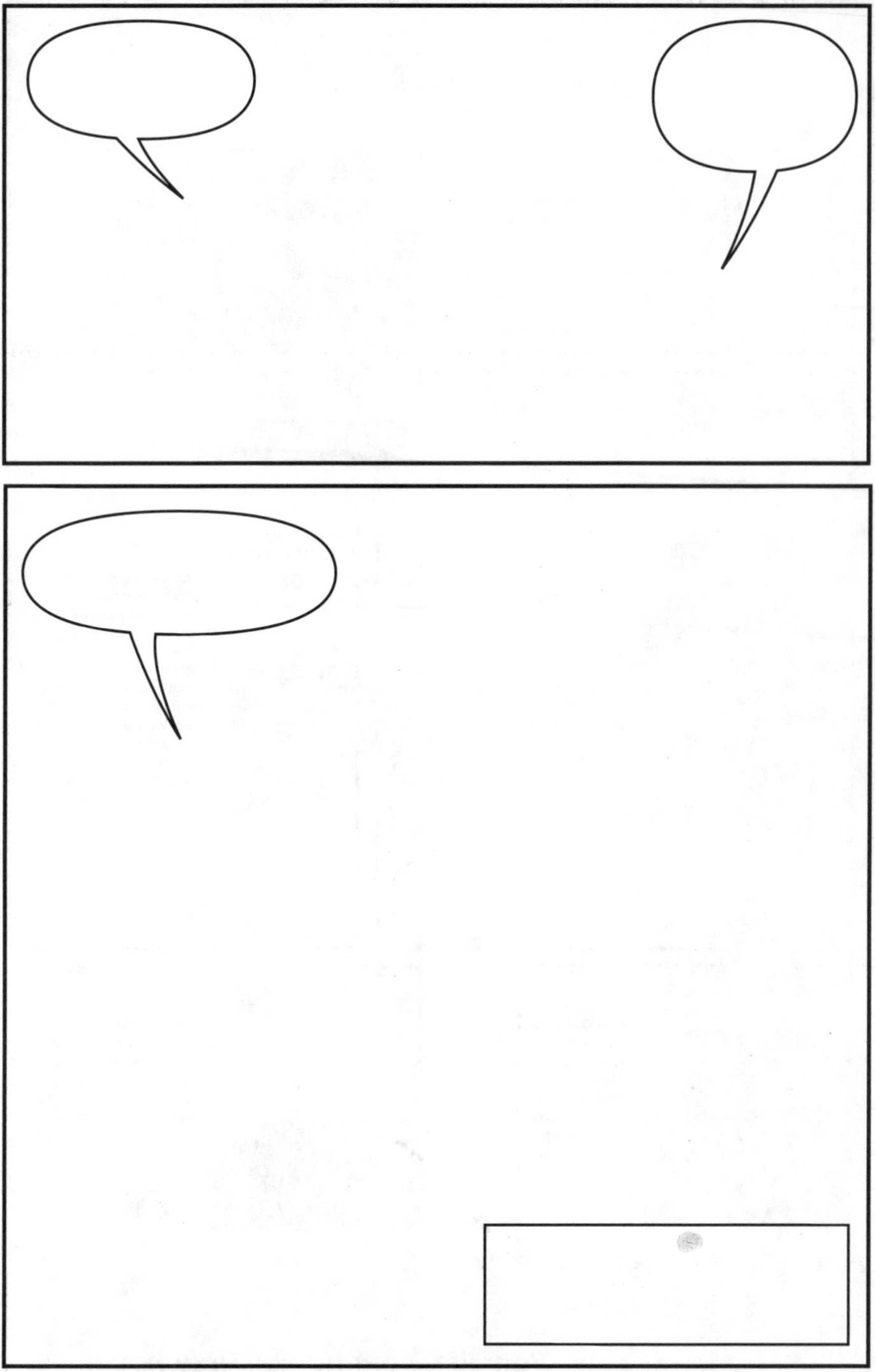

CHECK OUT STORYTELLING TIPS FROM TOP WRITERS AND ARTISTS AT MINXBOOKS.NET

Don't miss any of the minx books:

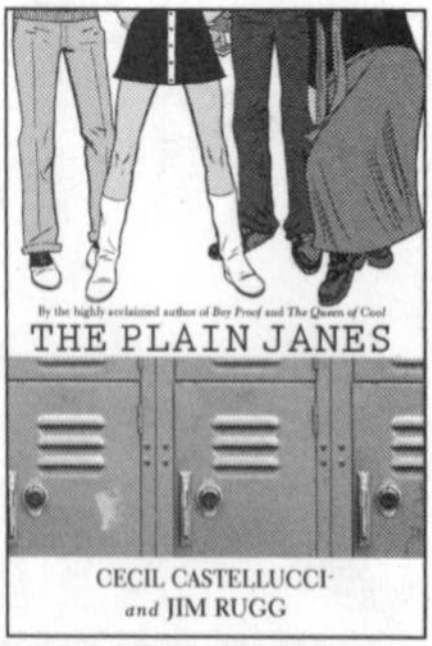
By the highly acclaimed author of Boy Proof and The Queen of Cool
THE PLAIN JANES
CECIL CASTELLUCCI
and JIM RUGG

THE PLAIN JANES
By Cecil Castellucci
and Jim Rugg

Four girls named Jane are anything but ordinary once they form a secret art gang called P.L.A.I.N. — People Loving Art In Neighborhoods. But can art attacks really save the hell that is high school?

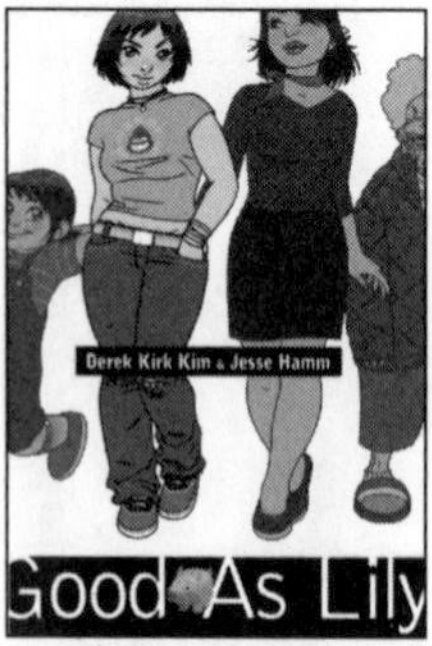
Derek Kirk Kim & Jesse Hamm
Good As Lily

GOOD AS LILY
By Derek Kirk Kim
and Jesse Hamm

What would you do if versions of yourself at 6, 29 and 70 suddenly appear and wreak havoc on your already awkward existence?

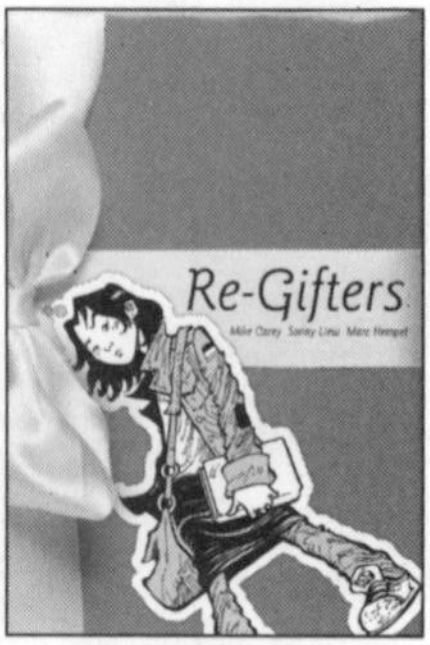
Re-Gifters

RE-GIFTERS
By Mike Carey,
Sonny Liew and
Marc Hempel

It's love, Korean-American style when a tenacious martial artist falls for a California surfer boy and learns that in romance and recycled gifts, what goes around comes around.

YALSA Winner

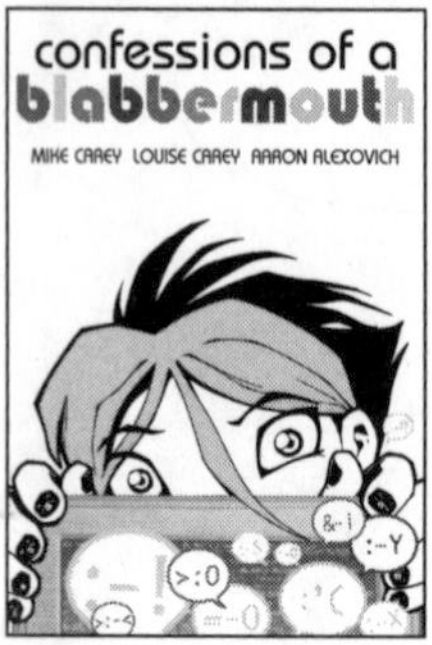
confessions of a
blabbermouth
MIKE CAREY LOUISE CAREY AARON ALEXOVICH

CONFESSIONS OF A
BLABBERMOUTH
By Mike and Louise Carey
and Aaron Alexovich

When Tasha's mom brings home a creepy boyfriend and his deadpan daughter, a dysfunctional family is headed for a complete meltdown. By the father-daughter writing team.

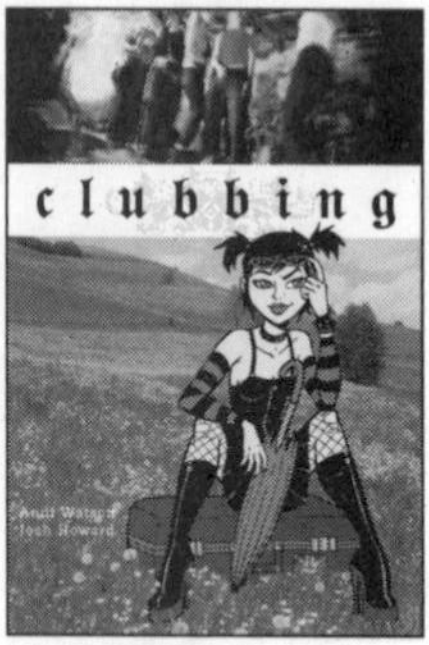
clubbing

CLUBBING
By Andi Watson
and Josh Howard

A spoiled, rebellious Londoner takes on the stuffy English countryside when she solves a murder mystery on the 19th hole of her grandparents' golf course.

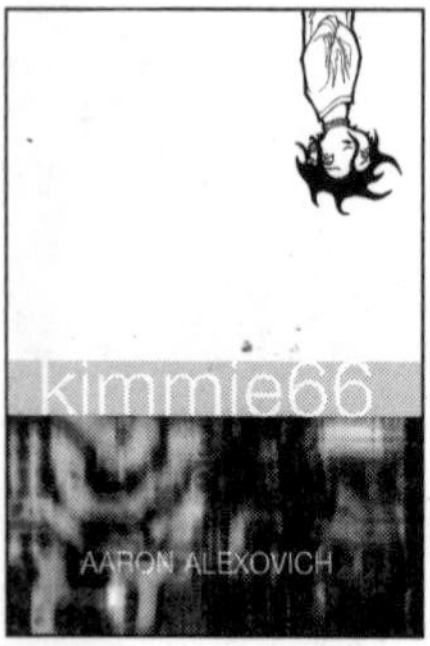
kimmie66
AARON ALEXOVICH

KIMMIE66
By Aaron Alexovich

This high-velocity, virtual reality ghost story follows a tech-savvy teenager on a dangerous quest to save her best friend, the world's first all-digital girl.

Your life. Your books. ***How novel.***

minxbooks.net